CHANCES *are*

CLAIRE HIGHTON-STEVENSON

Copyright © 2025 by Claire Highton-Stevenson

All rights reserved.

No portion of this book may be reproduced in any form without written permission from the publisher or author, except as permitted by U.K. copyright law.

Anti- AI information.

Editing – Linda Slate

Proofing – Crystal Wren

Cover Design – Claire Highton-Stevenson via Canva Design

Contents

Prologue	1
1. Chapter 1	4
2. Chapter 2	9
3. Chapter 3	12
4. Chapter 4	15
5. Chapter 5	18
6. Chapter 6	20
7. Chapter 7	23
8. Chapter 8	26
9. Chapter 9	29
10. Chapter 10	32
11. Chapter 11	36
12. Chapter 12	40
13. Chapter 13	43

14.	Chapter 14	46
15.	Chapter 15	49
16.	Chapter 16	52
17.	Chapter 17	55
18.	Chapter 18	58
19.	Chapter 19	61
20.	Chapter 20	63
21.	Chapter 21	65
22.	Chapter 22	68
23.	Chapter 23	71
24.	Chapter 24	76
25.	Chapter 25	79
26.	Chapter 26	84
27.	Chapter 27	88
28.	Chapter 28	91
29.	Chapter 29	94
30.	Chapter 30	98
31.	Chapter 31	102
32.	Chapter 32	106
33.	Chapter 33	111
34.	Chapter 34	118
35.	Chapter 35	121

36.	Chapter 36	124
37.	Chapter 37	127
38.	Chapter 38	134
39.	Chapter 39	138
40.	Chapter 40	141
41.	Chapter 41	144
42.	Chapter 42	152
43.	Chapter 43	155
44.	Chapter 44	158
45.	Chapter 45	162
46.	Chapter 46	165
47.	Chapter 47	168
48.	Chapter 48	171
49.	Chapter 49	174
50.	Chapter 50	177
51.	Chapter 51	179
52.	Chapter 52	183
53.	Chapter 53	190
54.	Chapter 54	193
55.	Chapter 55	197
56.	Chapter 56	200
57.	Chapter 57	204

58. Chapter 58 — 207
59. Chapter 59 — 212
60. Chapter 60 — 217
61. Chapter 61 — 220
62. Chapter 62 — 224
63. Chapter 63 — 227
64. Chapter 64 — 231
65. Chapter 65 — 234
66. Chapter 66 — 240
67. Chapter 67 — 243
68. Chapter 68 — 248
69. Chapter 69 — 252
70. Chapter 70 — 256
71. Chapter 71 — 259
72. Chapter 72 — 262
73. Chapter 73 — 266
74. Chapter 74 — 270
75. Chapter 75 — 275
76. Chapter 76 — 277
77. Chapter 77 — 281
78. Chapter 78 — 285
79. Chapter 79 — 289

80.	Chapter 80	293
81.	Chapter 81	298
82.	Chapter 82	302
83.	Chapter 83	305
84.	Chapter 84	309
85.	Chapter 85	312
86.	Chapter 86	316
87.	Chapter 87	319
88.	Chapter 88	324
89.	Chapter 89	328
	About the Author	333

Prologue

FIVE MONTHS AGO.

The door swung open, and John bounced through like he'd just won the lottery. He smiled from ear to ear, every tooth visible and gleaming.

"You need to sit down," he said, actually jumping on the spot.

Allegra stared at him, her own face breaking into a grin. How could it not? He was that excited.

"What's going on? Did you book that holiday?"

"No, better than that."

"Not sure there's anything better than that." Allegra grinned. The season had finished for them both. They had three months to do something relaxing and fun before John would be back in pre-season training, and then so would Allegra.

She sat down on the couch, and John joined her. "I've been offered a move to Bayern Munich."

"Oh my God, that's amazing!" Allegra said, understanding now why he was so excited. It was huge. A German superteam, Champions League football, a massive pay rise, and the chance to win medals.

John's grin widened even more, eyes shining with possibility.

"This is it, Allegra. Things are finally looking up for us. We can get a proper place. A house with a garden and maybe even think about kids. A real future."

Allegra nodded, trying to match his enthusiasm. She wanted to share it, to believe it, but deep down, a knot tightened in her stomach.

He meant both of them moving to Munich.

She wasn't ready for that.

There was the language barrier, the distance from home, and the idea of leaving everything she knew behind?

She had her own career, playing here, in Bath Street. She wasn't giving that up.

She forced a smile, hoping he wouldn't see the hesitation flickering in her eyes.

"It sounds incredible, John. I'm happy for you."

He reached for her hand, squeezing it.

"We'll make it work. Together."

Allegra pulled her hand back slowly, her mind already turning over the inevitable.

"John, I belong here. In Bath Street, with the Harriers. I'm contracted for two more years, and if I'm honest, I don't want to leave."

His face fell.

"But this is the big time. This is a hundred grand a week. It's...you'd be—"

"Your W.A.G.?" she interrupted with a small, bitter smile. "I'm happy for you, I really am. But if we're going to continue this—continue us—then it'll have to be long distance."

"Right. I mean, I guess we could make that work."

He was gone the following week. With so much to organise, they barely spoke. When they did, it was short, clipped. Not enough time to do anything meaningful together. He'd begged her to come out, to visit, to see what it was like, convinced that if she just saw it all, she'd want to stay.

And she'd gone.

It had been amazing, but she hadn't wanted to stay. If anything, it had shown her how different life would be *and* how much she would miss.

They broke things off, promising to stay friends and keep in touch.

But as Allegra flew home, she knew that wouldn't be the case. He was on the road to stardom. And she genuinely wished him all the best.

She got home, called the girls, and drank herself stupid at Art. She got so blathered she threw up in the cab on the way home.

But the bender had done what she needed. She'd let John go.

And now, she had her own life to live.

ONE

The hoodie was a mistake.

It was too warm, she now realised, with the summer sunshine that beat down on this side of the stadium.

Allegra Mann shifted sideways, trying to make the bulk of it feel less suffocating without taking it off and drawing unwanted attention to herself.

Sunglasses on. Head down. Knee braced, leg stretched out cautiously into the aisle. Long dark blonde hair tucked neatly beneath a baseball cap, hood pulled up—she hated going incognito but right now, she just wanted to watch the game like a fan, without being pestered.

She'd picked the end seat of the row for several reasons: minimal disruption, space to stretch out, and an easy escape just before the final whistle. But someone was coming up the steps, looking at the numbers and searching for a seat. There were two empty ones beside her.

"Sorry, sorry... Hi... Do you mind?" The woman smiled beneath her Bath Street Harriers baseball cap.

Allegra stood, awkwardly tucking her leg out of the way. The woman slipped past, giving off the kind of energy that apologised even when it wasn't required. She had a bobbed haircut under the hat, her hair sticking out around her ears, a Bath Street scarf that was definitely this season's, and a backpack she nearly caught Allegra with as she turned.

"Sorry, again. Thank you!" She smiled.

Allegra nodded, managed a polite, "No problem," and sat back down.

For all of six seconds.

Another figure appeared, taking the steps up two at a time, holding a takeaway coffee cup in one hand. Her eyes searched and found the woman who'd just arrived.

Sunglasses, long coat, and lipstick that made her lips look plump, kissable. Older, but good for it. She didn't wear a hat. Her hair was perfect, blonde, bobbed to the shoulder.

She looked at Allegra, offered a brief smile—not apologetic, just polite—and waited.

Allegra stood again.

This woman didn't say thank you until she was seated. And then, only as an afterthought.

"Thanks," she murmured, sliding her coat off and glancing towards the pitch. She took a tentative sip from the coffee cup and immediately made a face. "Jesus, Ros. This coffee is truly awful. Genuinely think my tongue has gone into mourning."

Ros laughed beside her. "It's not that bad."

"It's a war crime. Someone should take legal action."

Allegra sat again, quietly trying not to laugh, because she wasn't wrong.

"You alright down there?" the first woman asked, tone dry. "You've had to get up twice in under a minute. Could've charged us."

Allegra shrugged. "I'll send an invoice."

That earned her a second glance from the woman sitting beside her—brief, assessing, and then gone as she turned away.

"I'm Ros," the first woman said. Ros leant forward to look past her friend and continue speaking to Allegra. "This is Blythe," she said cheerfully. "She's new to Woodington."

"Temporarily," Blythe said. "They'll drag me back to London the moment I do something useful, I'm sure."

Her voice was warm without trying to be.

Allegra gave her a nod, even though she had no idea who they were. She smiled and said, "Welcome to the thrilling world of women's football."

Blythe gave her a look. "I'm here under duress, but needs must apparently."

Allegra didn't respond to that. She couldn't. Not with the roar that rolled across the stadium as the players emerged from the tunnel.

Her teammates.

The navy shirts with the red diagonal stripe were crisp and familiar as they jogged into position, ponytails swinging, socks pulled high. Boots hit the turf with a steady rhythm she could almost feel under her own feet, muscle memory still twitching like it hadn't got the memo.

She shifted in her seat, her knee protesting at the awkward position.

She should've been out there. She was *supposed* to be out there. And she would have been, except for that late tackle. Three weeks and it still felt like yesterday.

One second chasing down a ball, the next—impact. Grass. A flash of pain so white-hot it nearly knocked her out.

Now: The brace. The hoodie. The ache.

She swallowed and forced her gaze back to the pitch.

"Is someone hurt?" Blythe asked casually beside her, still squinting towards the players.

Allegra glanced over, surprised. "No, why?" Now she squinted, checking off teammates one by one. Had she missed something?

"You flinched," Blythe said. "Or winced. I don't know, I've only had one cup of tragedy-bean today. But your face definitely did something."

Allegra hesitated. She realised Blythe had been watching her, not the game. She shrugged. "Old injury."

Blythe didn't push, just nodded like she'd made a note for later.

Ros, oblivious, was already clapping along to some chant that had started behind them. She looked like she was enjoying herself. Everyone did, except Blythe.

Blythe leant back in her seat, sunglasses still on.

"So, who are we rooting for?" she asked Allegra, not Ros.

Allegra leant in slightly, offering a small smile. "Bath Street Harriers."

Bath Street had gone ahead.

A long corner from Ladonya Sinclair whipped into the box. Nora Brady knocked it down, and Jas Khan tapped it in from close range—the first goal of the season for the young left back.

Allegra couldn't help it. She fist pumped and cheered with the crowd, the familiar rush flooding through her veins.

But Blythe noticed—again—the brief wince that flickered across Allegra's face.

"That knee giving you trouble?" she asked.

Allegra glanced at her, surprised. "Something like that."

Blythe nodded once, as if filing the answer away again. She didn't pry, just sat back, arms folded now the coffee had been abandoned.

Ros was still clapping enthusiastically, shouting something about Jas being overdue a goal. Allegra let herself exhale, watching her teammates huddle at the corner flag.

She tried to settle back into her seat, but the ache had crept higher—dull and insistent, just under the skin.

When the second goal went in—a free kick from Brady, the ball hitting the post and bouncing back out, straight into the path of Satty Basra, who tucked it away for her fifth of the season—even Blythe jumped up with everyone else.

"What a shot," she said, almost like she knew what she was talking about.

Allegra grinned. "Starting to get it yet?"

"I'm not going to be buying a season ticket anytime soon," Blythe replied, settling back into her seat, "but it has its moments."

"There are worse things you could do on a Sunday afternoon," Allegra offered.

Blythe turned to her with a sly smile.

"Hm. I think I can come up with a few good ideas."

"Oh, like what?" Allegra couldn't help but ask. Was she flirting with a stranger? Maybe.

Blythe caught on, a twinkle appearing in her eye as she turned slightly towards Allegra.

"Would you like to find out?"

With one long finger, Allegra tugged her glasses down her nose—a clear indication she was checking Blythe out. Her weekends were free for a while, weren't they?

"Yes," she said softly, "I'd like to find out."

Blythe raised an eyebrow, amused.

"What's your name?"

For the first time in her life, Allegra cursed her parents' choice. How many Allegra's were there, anyway? Blythe might not notice, but her superfan friend might.

She thought quickly and chose a name that was familiar—her sister's.

"Petra," she said, feeling decidedly awkward and nothing like the namesake.

"Petra, huh? I like it."

Allegra smiled softly, letting the moment hang between them.

Blythe chuckled.

"Well, Petra, it's nice to meet you." She dug into her pocket and pulled out a pristine business card. "Give me a call when you're free."

Allegra barely looked at it. "Got a pen?"

Brow arched, Blythe reached into her pocket and pulled a pen free—an expensive pen. She handed it to Allegra and watched as Allegra turned the card over and scribbled something on the back of it.

"Now you have my number." Allegra smiled and handed back the pen and the card. "Don't lose it."

Two

She pulled the crutches free from under the seat and got herself upright, waiting while the crowd thinned before attempting the stairs. Jubilant fans, still singing, filed past.

It was a good win, and she'd enjoyed being a fan, but now Allegra had to make her way back around the ground.

"I didn't realise you were actually injured. Do you need a hand?" Blythe asked, her hand resting lightly on Allegra's shoulder.

Allegra smiled. "Oh, I'm a dab hand at these now. It's been three weeks—couple more to go." As she spoke, she caught Ros watching her more closely, eyes narrowing as Allegra turned away.

A gap opened and she hopped forward, inching carefully down each step until she reached the bottom. The warmth of Blythe's palm, which had moved down and rested against the small of her back, was both comforting and something else—intimate. She liked it.

At the foot of the stairs, they shuffled along with the steady swell of the crowd. As they neared the corner where most people were filing out, Allegra slowed. She planned to go the other way.

"Well, it was lovely to meet you both," she said, glancing at Ros, who was still watching her closely. The scrutiny was starting to feel ridiculous. With a quiet sigh, Allegra pulled off her sunglasses and smiled as Ros's eyes went wide.

"Bloody hell! Allegra Mann!"

Blythe looked confused, her gaze shifting between them. Then her eyes landed fully on Allegra's and she pulled her own sunglasses off. "Okay...someone want to let me in on this?"

Allegra exhaled and slid her glasses back into place. "I'm sorry. My name's not Petra—that's my sister. I'm Allegra."

Ros nudged Blythe, barely containing her excitement. "She plays...for the team."

It took a moment before Blythe said, "Why didn't you just say that?"

As the last word left her lips, a group of teenagers passed by and instantly broke into a chant.

"Oh, Al-leg-ra Ma-nn, oh, Al-leg-ra Ma-nn..."

The familiar *Seven Nation Army* tune rippled through the crowd. Allegra gave a wave and leant into a quick selfie with one of them, her smile easy but her eyes drifting quickly back to Blythe.

"That'd be why," Ros said with a grin.

"Quite," Blythe murmured, watching the scene unfold. "Is this normal? Is she...safe?"

"Totally. Players always come over and talk to fans," Ros replied. She nodded towards the far side of the pitch where other players were beginning to gather, clapping and signing shirts. "It's part of the whole thing."

"I have to admit," Blythe said slowly, still observing, "this isn't anything like I expected it would be."

More fans wandered past them, offering quick greetings and smiles. Allegra responded politely, but her attention kept sliding back, until the space around them cleared again, and she turned fully towards Blythe.

Their eyes met.

"You good?" Allegra asked, quieter now, more personal.

"I think so," Blythe replied, searching her face. "Still getting my head around the fact that I spent an entire match sitting next to someone who's apparently famous."

Allegra smiled, the corners of her mouth pulling soft and slow. "Only famous on the pitch. Off it...not so much."

Blythe tilted her head. "I don't know. Off it, you're kind of hard to ignore."

That earned her a laugh—low, a little surprised—and a flash of something behind Allegra's eyes that Blythe hadn't seen before—something unguarded.

"Coming to the next one?" Ros asked, her voice cutting in, full of hope and mischief.

Blythe didn't break eye contact. "That rather depends."

Allegra arched a brow. "On?"

Blythe gave a small, teasing smile. "Whether you'll actually text me back."

Ros groaned, throwing up her hands. "You got her number?! Of course you did."

THREE

The noise from the dressing room could be heard halfway down the corridor as Allegra made her way towards it.

Hop, tap. Hop, tap.

The door opened and Taylor Price stepped out.

"Hey, Leggy—how's the knee?" Taylor grinned at her own little play on words.

Allegra smiled. She liked Taylor. They were friends, as well as her being the team physio.

"Feels better, actually. And yes," she said, cutting Taylor off before she could ask, "I am doing what I'm supposed to do." She exhaled and rested against the wall. "I'm just grateful it's not an ACL."

"Great. Well, we'll check things out this week, and if it all looks good, maybe we can ditch the brace."

"That would be nice. I'm getting bored of wearing sweatpants all the time."

Taylor grinned. "Don't worry. You'll be back in all that high-end fashion you like soon enough. An MCL's still painful, though, and it's going to take time. So I'm glad you're listening—doing the right thing."

She checked her watch.

"I've got to go. Carrie's meeting me and I said I wouldn't be long."

"I'm sure she'll wait," Allegra said, pushing herself off the wall.

Taylor turned, walking backwards as she grinned. "Of course she will." She winked, then spun back around and jogged off down the corridor.

Allegra pushed the door open with her hip and twisted her way into the room.

Jas Khan was up on the bench, dancing like they'd just won the FA Cup.

Excited faces turned towards her the second she stepped inside. The room buzzed with noise—laughter, the slap of high fives, the sound of studs clattering against the floor.

They'd beaten Leicester. Three valuable points.

"Oi, oi!" Jas called from the bench, still mid-dance. "Look who's hobbling her way in!"

"Pipe down." Allegra grinned, easing the door closed behind her.

Nora Brady spotted her next and cut through the chaos. The captain's short hair was plastered to her forehead with sweat and her jersey clung to her shoulders, but her focus was steady as ever.

"You alright?" she asked, her hand brushing Allegra's arm in a quiet, grounding gesture.

"Yeah." Allegra nodded. "Getting there."

"Good. We need you back. It's not the same without you."

Before Allegra could respond, Sammy-Jo Costa appeared at her side and threw an arm around her shoulder.

"Please," SJ said loudly, "we've just taken three points off Leicester without her. Maybe we don't need her at all!"

Allegra rolled her eyes. "Rude."

SJ grinned, clearly pleased with herself. "Just saying. You might want to stay benched a bit longer. We're thriving."

Allegra bumped her with her hip. "I'll remember that when you're the one limping through the corridor."

SJ dramatically clutched her chest. "Cold."

Laughter rippled around them, and for a moment, Allegra let herself just be in it—be part of the celebration, even from the sidelines.

When everyone was showered, changed, and heading out, Allegra waited around a bit longer. Sammy-Jo was always the last one to shower and the last one to leave.

The room slowly emptied until it was just the two of them left.

Allegra cleared her throat, her voice barely above a whisper.

"I need a favour."

SJ turned, towel slung over her shoulder, eyes softening with concern.

"What's up?"

Allegra exhaled slowly, her fingers nervously twisting the hem of her jumper.

"I realised, since John left, that I don't like being on my own right now."

"Okay." SJ's tone was gentle, waiting patiently.

"I want to get a flatmate, to share the bills and stuff, but—" She took a shaky breath, eyes flicking away for a moment. "Could I stay at yours until I find someone?"

SJ slid down onto the bench beside her, her presence steady and reassuring.

"You want to move back into my spare room?"

Allegra nodded, a small hopeful smile tugging at the corner of her mouth.

"Just for a bit. Like I said…I'm going to put some feelers out about renting a room."

"It's not like you to be lonely." SJ's voice was quiet but filled with understanding.

"I'm not. I'm not lonely… That's not it." Allegra's eyes shimmered slightly, her voice catching. "It's… I dunno…the silence, I suppose. I've never lived with that before and it kind of freaks me out."

SJ reached out, lightly squeezing Allegra's hand. "I'll have to speak to Daisy, but I don't see it being a problem."

Allegra relaxed, her shoulders dropping. "Thanks, you're the best."

"Well, I am your best mate, so…"

Four

It was Daisy who opened the door, holding out her old key, still on the chain with the gonk keyring.

"Welcome back." Her blonde hair was pulled back into a ponytail, blue eyes sparkling as her face lit up into a smile.

"Thanks, Dais," Allegra said, stepping inside the house that used to be home, back when she was SJ's flatmate, long before Daisy had appeared on the scene and sorted SJ into a half-decent girlfriend.

It was only then Daisy noticed the bags and cases piled on the floor behind Allegra.

"Cabbie left them there… I can't…" She grimaced, lifting one of the crutches.

"Of course you can't."

Allegra shook her head, wincing slightly at the embarrassment of not being able to do the simplest of things.

"Come on, get indoors. I'll bring them in, and then we can make SJ carry them up the stairs later."

Allegra stepped over the threshold, the familiar scent of the place hitting her like a memory—warm, lived-in, and just a little chaotic. Still home, in its own way.

Daisy closed the door behind her and leaned back against it, her smile softening.

"So...how are you doing? I mean *really* doing. It's been a rough few months."

Allegra gave a small shrug, eyes darting around the hallway like it might save her from answering.

"I'm okay. It's just...everything's changed, you know?"

Daisy nodded, arms folding gently across her chest. "Things ended with John. You got injured. That's a lot."

Allegra gave a tired smile that didn't quite reach her eyes. "Yeah. I think I was holding it all together, and then the quiet hit. The stillness. And it turns out, I'm not very good at being still."

Daisy's expression softened even further, her voice warm. "Well, you don't have to be still here. You're not alone, Allegra. Whatever you need, even if it's just background noise and someone stealing your crisps, we've got you."

Allegra blinked fast and nodded, swallowing back the lump that threatened to rise.

"Thanks, Dais. Really."

Daisy rubbed her arm gently, her gaze lingering for a moment longer than usual.

"Go sit down. I'll make us a brew. Then I can tell you how worried SJ's been about you, and how you could probably wrap her around your little finger right now." She winked, trying to keep things light.

Allegra let out a small laugh, grateful for the humour. Grateful for Daisy, for the normalcy, for the way this house still felt like a place she could land without warning.

It was funny, really. When Daisy had first met SJ, Allegra had been all big-sister energy—suspicious, protective, warning her off with narrowed eyes and half-joking threats.

Now? Now they were a proper team. Daisy and Allegra, always ganging up on SJ. And for the first time in weeks, Allegra felt something like herself again.

About an hour later, the living room was filled with the sound of laughter and the rustle of biscuit wrappers. Allegra was curled into the corner of the sofa, a throw blanket draped across her legs, her crutches leaning nearby. Daisy was stretched out at the other end, nursing her second mug of tea.

Some ridiculous dating show was on the telly, all awkward flirting and dramatic voiceovers, and they were both howling at the sheer absurdity of it.

"Oh my God, did he just say he sees her as 'wife material' because she can make lasagne?" Allegra wheezed through her laughter.

Daisy shook her head, grinning. "I swear, these men are just stray thoughts in tracksuits."

The front door opened.

Sammy-Jo stepped inside and paused, taking in the sight of them, Allegra laughing, relaxed, settled beside Daisy. SJ's eyes flicked to the crutches, then back to Allegra's face, softening as she closed the door behind her.

"Well," she said, dropping her bag with a thud, "looks like I missed the party."

Without looking up, Daisy casually said, "Oh, hey, hun. Can you be a darling and run Allegra's things up to her room for her?"

SJ paused, looking back down the hall at the heavy bags she'd passed on the way in.

"Uh...I guess I could...for a fee."

Daisy smirked. "In kind, as usual?"

"That'll do," SJ said, already turning on her heel and marching towards the luggage. "I'll be right back to collect."

As the door clicked shut behind her, Daisy grinned at Allegra.

"And that is how you train yourself an SJ."

FIVE

Blythe stood by the window and stared out over the city. *Was* it a city? It didn't have a cathedral—she'd Googled. It was big enough to count as one, maybe. More likely, it was a town. But city sounded better. Bigger. More important. And Blythe Daniels liked things bigger.

Bigger titles. Bigger risks. Bigger rewards. She liked to win.

Maybe that was why she'd enjoyed the game in the end, despite the sun, the crowd, the coffee, and everything else she'd rolled her eyes at. Or maybe it had more to do with the captivating woman in the seat beside her.

Allegra.

There was something about her—the quiet self-possession, the way she didn't rise to Blythe's sarcasm, didn't try to impress her—she just, was.

And that smile. Yes, that definitely helped.

Blythe's gaze drifted to her phone, sitting silent and black on the side table next to the sofa.

Not her sofa.

Nothing in this apartment was hers—not really. Just a temporary life stuffed into a one-bed apartment. Two suitcases of clothes and a box of essentials—her favourite mug, a book she kept starting and never quite finishing, her laptop. That was all she needed.

The office was paying for it: a six-month secondment to Woodington.

Middle of nowhere. Exiled.

A polite relocation out of sight. And everyone knew why.

Amanda Sanchez. CEO. Polished. Brilliant. Hazardous. And easily the hottest woman inside a Chanel suit to ever take a breath.

Amanda had made it clear what she wanted, and she'd gotten it.

But it hadn't been what Blythe had wanted—not really.

Blythe wanted more.

Not just the thrill. Not just the late nights in Amanda's office with the skyline lit behind them and the taste of power and lipstick on her mouth. That part had been good—unforgettable, even.

But Amanda already had everything she needed, and she'd made no apologies for the fact she didn't need anyone else, and yet, she couldn't stay away. Always drawing Blythe back in until finally, it was Blythe who'd said no.

So here she was.

Reassigned.

Repackaged.

Removed.

She stared out at the streetlights blinking on in a place that didn't know her name. A place that didn't expect anything from her, which, for now, might be its only saving grace.

And still, somehow, her thoughts wandered back to Allegra. That smile. That voice. That heat in her eyes when she'd pulled down her sunglasses.

Maybe, just maybe, Blythe wouldn't mind being seen again.

Even if it wasn't by Amanda.

Especially if it wasn't.

Right now, though, she needed to find a way to make Woodington feel like home.

SIX

Allegra shifted in the bed, wincing as the knee brace pressed against the corner of the sheet. She nudged the duvet back with her leg, trying to find a position that didn't ache. The pillow was just as she remembered it, the mattress familiar beneath her, but her body didn't settle the way it used to.

She stared up at the ceiling. It was the same room in the same flat she'd shared with SJ all those months ago when they were flatmates and best mates, before she'd moved in with John. The walls hadn't changed nor the scuff mark near the wardrobe door. Neither had the slightly wonky blind that always let a sliver of light through.

The space was familiar. Comfortable. But she wasn't.

She sighed, reaching for her phone without thinking, just to check the time, and maybe distract herself with some mindless scrolling and remind herself life wasn't always about crutches and knee braces.

There was a message waiting—unknown number, but not a surprise.

Blythe: Hey, good to meet you earlier. Let's get a drink sometime.

Allegra stared at it a moment, then smiled softly.

A drink sounded…nice.

Despite the lack of interest in football and her slightly brusque manner, Blythe was undeniably hot. There was something very sexy about the confident way she moved, talked, and dressed—like she already knew she owned the place, even if she might hate it.

Allegra: I'd like that. Name the time.

She placed the phone down beside her and lied back with a quiet sigh. Still awkward, still sore, still uncertain. But for the first time in a while, something felt lighter. She smiled as she recalled the evening with Daisy and SJ—how easy it had been.

She needed to remind herself not to intrude too much, though. They were used to their own space, and despite it being almost a year together, they were definitely still in the honeymoon phase.

Her phone buzzed—not a message this time, but an incoming call. Same number as the text.

Allegra sat up, heart giving a little jolt. She hesitated for just a second before answering.

"Hello," she said, cautious but curious.

"Hey," came the reply—that warm, unmistakable voice. "It's Blythe."

Allegra smiled, settling back against the pillows.

"I figured."

"I know I just texted," Blythe went on, "but I don't know… I wanted to hear your voice."

Allegra's smile deepened. "Bold move, Blythe."

"You'll learn that about me," Blythe said, easy and unbothered. "I'm not the kind of woman who sits back and lets the world move on around her."

"No, you didn't strike me as that kind of woman," Allegra said with a hint of flirtation in her voice.

"Really? What kind of woman did I strike you as?"

Allegra considered that for a moment. "Confident. Gets what she wants."

"Maybe." Blythe chuckled. "You didn't strike me as the kind of woman who gives in easily."

Allegra upped her flirting just a little. "I like to think I'm a woman worth working for."

Blythe's voice dipped, just a little. "That's good. I like a challenge."

Allegra smiled, the flirtation curling somewhere low in her chest. It hadn't been that long since someone had looked at her like that—spoken to her like this—but it felt different. Not as a player, not as part of a couple, just…her. And maybe that was what she'd missed most, without even realising it.

"I'm not sure if that's a compliment or a warning," she murmured.

"Both," Blythe said, with just enough playfulness to make it clear she meant it. "But mostly a compliment."

There was a small pause—comfortable, not awkward. Allegra let her fingers rest near the phone, the buzz of the conversation still humming in her skin.

"So," Blythe continued, "how's this weekend looking? If I told you I knew a café that doesn't serve war-crime coffee, would that lure you out?"

Allegra chuckled. "Tempting."

"Is that a yes?"

"It's a maybe. But a hopeful one." Allegra knew it would be a yes, but it didn't hurt to play a little coy, did it?

"Hopeful is good. Let me know. I'll be free…and curious."

Allegra bit her lip, grinning into the dark. "I'll text you."

"Looking forwards to it, Allegra Mann."

The line went quiet a second after she hung up. Allegra lowered the phone to her chest and let her eyes drift closed, her smile still there, soft and real. For the first time in a while, something about the unknown didn't feel so scary.

It felt…interesting.

SEVEN

Blythe looked up at the office block she'd be working in for at least the next six months.

A tower. Ten stories tall. All glass and shine.

Franklyn Financials, Come Again HQ, and on the top floor, the new offices for the Olsen Hotels Group.

She used her pass to get through security and took the elevator to the top floor, where Ros was already waiting as the doors opened.

"Good morning, Ms Daniels," Ros said with a grin, falling into step beside her. "I've organised a staff meeting for ten."

"Good. Let's get the introductions over with," Blythe replied, acknowledging someone as they passed in the corridor. "Then we can get on with setting up the meeting with Gabby Dean."

Ros nodded. "So…you liked what you saw, then? I admit, I was a little hesitant when tasked with taking you."

Blythe ignored the comment. She was used to people in the workplace being a little intimidated by her presence. She liked it that way, if she were honest, which she usually was.

"I think there's a deal to be made that would benefit everyone."

They reached a corner office and Ros opened the door. The name on the frosted glass now read:

Blythe Daniels—Head of Expansion Strategy

There'd been a complete restructure of the Woodington office, shifting more focus to the European hotels within the group. It wasn't as glamorous as London, or the American division, but it mattered.

And at least she had Ros.

They'd been office friends for years. Poaching her as her PA hadn't been difficult, given she already worked in the building. Greg Thorndyke hadn't been happy to lose her, but then again, Greg hadn't been happy about a lot of things lately.

"Coffee?" Ros asked.

"That would be good, yes. Thanks."

At ten, on the dot, Ros opened the doors to the conference room and everyone filed in and took their seats.

All eyes went straight to the woman at the head of the table, already seated, watching them calmly.

Once the last chair scraped into place and the room settled, Blythe stood.

"Good morning, everybody. Thank you for being so prompt—something I hope we'll maintain going forwards."

She brought her palms together, fingers loosely laced, and paused just long enough to command the room's attention.

"As you're all aware, there's been a major restructure within the Olsen Group. The European division is now entirely here in Woodington—which, frankly, makes a lot more sense."

She took a moment to let that sink in, her gaze moving across the table. She clocked every expression—the interested, the uncertain, the ones still deciding what this meant for them.

"We're no longer an outpost. We're the hub. That means new systems, new expectations, and yes, new opportunities. I'm not here to tear things down—I'm here to build. So if you've got ideas, bring them. If you've got problems, bring those too. Just don't sit on your hands."

A few nods. One or two faint smiles. The room was listening.

"Right. Introductions. Let's go around the table."

She listened as several people stood, waffled out their names, and sat back down again. Nothing stuck out. It was polite, rehearsed, corporate.

Then the older blonde woman stood, and Blythe's attention sharpened.

"Good morning. Claudia Maddox. I'm the new Head of Operations. I'll be working closely with you to ensure the Olsen Group expansion across the European market is on brand. I've spent the past two years gaining experience within the group. I'm looking forward to meeting with you one-to-one."

Her delivery was calm, crisp, and confident. No hesitation. No bluffing.

Blythe nodded her acknowledgement, a flicker of interest in her expression.

Then, with the smallest glance to her right, she met Ros's eyes.

An unspoken instruction: *Set that meeting. Sooner rather than later.*

Ros gave the slightest nod in return.

She also caught the eye roll from Greg.

Claudia Maddox, according to her report, had also worked directly under him. In the reshuffle, it was she who'd been promoted—and clearly, that still rankled with him.

Just another reason to like her, Blythe thought, as she listened to the rest of the table stand, one by one, and introduce themselves. Most overembellished their importance, layering on buzzwords and job titles like it might shield them from scrutiny.

But Blythe had already read all their files.

She knew exactly who they were—and more importantly—who they weren't, and who they might be trying to be.

Eight

"Holy shit balls," Sammy-Jo said as she came through the door, practically breathless. "Didn't you see your messages?"

Allegra looked up from where she was lying on the sofa, leg propped on a cushion. "No, my phone's charging upstairs. What's happened?"

Sammy-Jo dropped into the armchair like she'd just sprinted the last stretch. "The boss has resigned."

"What?" Allegra sat up straighter, blinking. "Why? The season's barely started."

"Apparently she's got some personal stuff going on with her mum. Wants to step away with immediate effect."

"But...what about us?"

Sammy-Jo laughed. "Uh huh, all about you." Allegra rolled her eyes at her. "Nora is taking over for this week's game."

"Nora?"

"I know. It's just the one game, though, and she'll have George to help. Gabby's adamant she wants a new manager in place ASAP."

"Bloody hell," Allegra muttered, sinking back against the cushions.

The news sat heavy in her chest. A new manager. That could change everything.

It wasn't that she didn't like George—she respected her, and the team would listen—but it wasn't a long-term solution, although Nora had been doing her coach's badges, and she was married to the owner, but Allegra couldn't see it. Not yet. Nora still had a point to prove on the pitch.

Whoever came in next would need to be a step up. They'd bring new systems, new preferences, maybe even a completely different style of play. They'd want their own players, and Gabby would probably make financial assurances for that.

And she was injured. Not training. Not match-fit. Not even visible.

Her heart dully thudded as the thought took root.

What if they didn't want her?

What if she got left behind?

"I hate this," she said softly, not even sure Sammy-Jo could hear her. "Sitting out. Watching everything change around me."

SJ shifted forwards in the armchair, elbows on her knees. "Hey… You've got nothing to worry about."

Allegra looked at her. "Don't I? What if the new manager doesn't rate me? What if they think I'm too much of a risk, or too slow to bounce back?"

Sammy-Jo shook her head. "You're Allegra Mann. You're one of the best defenders in the league. Anyone with a brain will see that."

"Maybe," Allegra said, but her tone was far from convinced.

She stared at the ceiling, jaw tight. This wasn't how she'd pictured the season going. And now, with the future unclear, she felt more benched than ever.

"Can you grab my phone for me?" Allegra asked.

"Sure." Sammy-Jo stood up and stretched. "Seriously, though, Leg, don't stress. It's gonna be fine. And you know what? Maybe some fresh ideas are what we need."

"Yeah," Allegra muttered, "without us."

"Oi, pack it in." SJ shot her a look as she headed for the stairs. "I know you're feeling down in the dumps with this injury, but it's not like you to get this defeated."

Allegra didn't respond, just stared at the muted TV. It wasn't only the injury. Something else was weighing her down. She just didn't know what it was.

"We have to stay positive," SJ went on. "You have to believe in yourself—your talent, your place in this squad. One change doesn't erase everything you've done."

"I know. You're right," Allegra said quietly.

Sammy-Jo gave her a firm nod. "So—we're all meeting at Blanca's later. You coming?"

Allegra gave her a look. "Of course I am."

SJ grinned. "Good. Just checking you hadn't turned into a total hermit."

NINE

Blanca's was surprisingly busy for a Monday afternoon, but the usual back table was already taken by a handful of players when Allegra and SJ arrived.

Ladonya spotted them first and waved enthusiastically. "Hey! Look who's here—Miss VIP!"

Allegra smiled as the group turned to greet her. Jas made room, patting the seat beside her. "Come on then, injured reserve. Front row."

Kayla leant forwards, eyes wide. "Can you believe it? The boss just resigned out of nowhere."

Jess nodded. "Yeah, family stuff apparently. No one knows much."

"She loved this team," Allegra said softly, meaning every word.

"She built this team," Ladonya added. "Hope whoever comes in next doesn't mess it up."

Allegra glanced around the table—familiar faces, steady friendships—and felt a flicker of calm. This was home.

The door opened and Nora Brady stepped in, pulling up a chair. "Looks like I'm captain of the chaos this week," she joked, earning a few tired laughs.

But beneath the easy banter was a shared understanding—things were about to change.

Nora leant forwards, meeting each of their eyes with steady calm. "Look, I get that things feel a bit up in the air right now. But let me remind you all—we're a team. Nothing's changing that. No matter who's in charge, no matter what comes next, we've got each other."

She gave a small, confident smile. "We win as one, we lose as one, and we keep pushing forwards. That's what makes us Bath Street Harriers."

There was a quiet nodding around the table, the tension easing just a little.

Allegra felt it too—the quiet strength in Nora's words. Whatever the future held, this was home. This was where she belonged.

She'd given up her relationship with John because of this team, because she didn't want things to change. Yet now, with her injury sidelining her, there was nothing she could do but watch from the stands and hope her teammates could hold it all together without her.

Sammy-Jo could sense the tension in Allegra.

"You're not that important, you know," she said lightly, nudging her with her elbow.

Allegra turned to her, eyes narrowing with mock offence. "Shut your trap." But she grinned, the edge of worry softening for a moment. "And get me a drink. A girl could die of thirst waiting for you."

"My round then." SJ sighed, pushing to her feet just as a chorus of cheers went up and drinks orders flew at her from all directions.

"Good luck," Allegra called after her, laughing.

"Don't worry. Soon as that leg's better, it's all on you," Sammy-Jo called back without turning around.

"How is the knee?" Ladonya asked, sliding smoothly into the seat SJ had vacated.

Allegra leaned into her with a soft smile. "Oh, you know...painful, awkward, and healing."

Ladonya gave her an understanding look, but before she could say anything more, Allegra turned the tables.

"How about you? How'd the date go?"

Ladonya rolled her eyes, her Texas drawl then coming out as thick and amused as ever, "Y'all need to learn how to date over here," she said, shaking her head. "Everyone takes you out once and acts like you're married. And God forbid you go out with more than one person—you're suddenly a player."

Allegra laughed. "Well, technically…"

"Oh, don't start," Ladonya cut in. "I'm not looking for a label. I'm just lookin' for a good time and someone who can hold a conversation without getting clingy by dessert."

Allegra raised her glass. "To high standards and good knees."

"I'll drink to that." Ladonya held up a pretend glass, clinking it lightly against Allegra's invisible one. "So, how about you? Since John left…anyone new?"

Allegra felt heat creep into her cheeks, and Ladonya didn't miss it.

"Oh, there is… Come on, dish it."

She laughed, trying to play it cool. "Well, I don't know if there's anything to tell. I met someone at the game yesterday."

"A fan?"

"God, no. I mean, I love them and all, but that might be a bit of a step too far, don't you think?"

Ladonya grinned. "Depends on the fan."

Allegra rolled her eyes. "No, she… I got the impression she'd been dragged to the game against her will, but we got talking and…swapped numbers."

Ladonya leant in with a gleam in her eye. "And?"

"And nothing. Yet." Allegra smiled, lips tugging at the memory. "But maybe something."

"To maybe-somethings," Ladonya said, raising her pretend glass again.

"To maybe-somethings," Allegra echoed, the warmth on her cheeks spreading to her chest.

TEN

Claudia Maddox had been summoned to Blythe's office directly after lunch. Now, she sat in one of the comfortable chairs opposite Blythe, legs crossed, back straight.

Cool and composed, Blythe thought, as she took a moment to study her more closely.

"I understand it was your input that led to this new development idea."

The corners of Claudia's lips curved slightly—just enough to register confidence, not arrogance. She looked proud, and rightly so. More than that, she seemed encouraged her voice had been heard.

"If you mean the Bath Street Project, then yes. I saw potential there and made the case that it was worth exploring."

"I read your file," Blythe said. "It was impressive—especially considering you've only been with us a few years."

There it was again—that smile. A little wider this time. Controlled, confident—and, Blythe had to admit—undeniably sexy. There was something magnetic about her. A quick glance at Claudia's left hand, though, and that train of thought was promptly derailed. *Wedding band. Lucky guy.*

"Thank you," Claudia said. "I'm dedicated when I feel the passion and commitment from the top. For me, this isn't just a job—it's a chance to leave a mark."

Blythe nodded slowly, still assessing.

"Well then, I'm putting you on the project with me. You'll lead the team when I'm not in the room. We've got a meeting with Gabriella Dean tomorrow morning at ten."

Claudia gave a small, measured smile. "That's—I'm very appreciative, thank you. Though I should probably confess now... I'm friends with Gabby. We've already had some muted conversations about the potential of what we're proposing."

"I see." Blythe steepled her fingers. "Then I imagine this will be a very interesting conversation."

Claudia's smile widened, just a fraction. "Gabby's a sharp operator. She won't be walked over—but she's not the type to look a gift horse in the mouth either."

Blythe studied her, unable to hide a flicker of surprise. She hadn't expected Claudia to be quite so connected—or so capable.

Blythe allowed herself a smile. "Then let's make sure what we're offering looks like a thoroughbred."

Claudia laughed softly, and Blythe leaned back, her mind already ticking through the possibilities. If Gabby was already half on board, this negotiation could move quickly—weeks, not months. The kind of turnaround that made people take notice. The kind that would get her name mentioned in the right rooms again—maybe even London.

"Get prepped," she said, her voice lighter now. "Tomorrow might be bigger than either of us thought."

Claudia nodded and stood to leave. Blythe watched her go, a sliver of hope rising beneath the professional calm.

Once the door clicked shut, Blythe turned to her laptop and pulled up the Bath Street file. She'd skimmed it before, but now she needed the full picture: location, capacity, current usage, potential for expansion. The numbers were solid—better than solid—they were exactly what the Olsen Group needed to justify the European restructure.

She leant back in her chair, fingers steepled against her mouth as she thought through the angles. Gabby Dean owned the football club. A hotel development adjacent to the stadium would be a natural fit—hospitality, events, match-day packages. Everything happening was the kind of synergy that made investors salivate.

And if she pulled this project off, if she made this deal happen in weeks instead of months, it would be the kind of win that got noticed—the kind that reminded London she was still valuable. Still hungry. Still worth bringing back.

She'd been exiled to Woodington as a way to cool off the Amanda situation. A polite removal from sight. But this project could change that narrative. This could be her redemption arc.

Blythe pulled up Gabby Dean's file next—owner of Bath Street Harriers. Married to Nora Brady, the team captain. Smart woman, strategic thinker, known for backing bold ideas if the numbers worked. She'd built the club, growing it from near-bankruptcy to a thriving operation in less than five years.

Exactly the kind of person Blythe could work with.

She made notes, cross-referenced timelines, and began mapping out the presentation for tomorrow. By the time she finished, the afternoon light had shifted across her desk and her coffee had gone cold.

A knock at the door pulled her back to the present.

"Come in," Blythe called.

Ros poked her head in, already holding two fresh cups of coffee. "Thought you might need this. You've been in here for hours."

Blythe accepted the cup gratefully. "How did you know?"

"Because you get that look when you're planning something big, and that always requires coffee," Ros said, settling into the chair Claudia had vacated. "So…what's happening tomorrow?"

Blythe took a sip of the coffee—proper coffee, not the war crime they'd had at the stadium—and felt some of the tension ease from her shoulders.

"Tomorrow, we pitch the Bath Street Project to Gabriella Dean. If it goes well, we could have approval by the end of the week."

"And if it goes well," Ros asked carefully, "what does that mean for you?"

Blythe was quiet for a moment. She appreciated that Ros knew her well enough to ask the real question.

"It means I'm not just marking time here," Blythe said finally. "It means I'm building something. It means London notices."

Ros nodded, understanding the subtext. This wasn't just about the hotel. This was about Blythe proving she was still valuable, still capable, still worth investing in.

"You'll nail it," Ros said simply. "You always do."

After Ros left, Blythe sat alone in her office as the sun began to set over Woodington. For the first time since arriving, the temporary apartment and the temporary assignment didn't feel quite so temporary. There was possibility here.

Maybe this was her way back. Maybe she wasn't done yet.

She checked her phone, almost without thinking. Still no message from Allegra.

The thought surprised her. She'd been so focused on the project, she'd almost forgotten about the woman from the stadium. Almost.

Blythe smiled to herself. Tomorrow, she'd close a deal. But tonight, maybe she'd take a walk. Get to know this town a little better. Clear her head.

She had no idea where that walk would lead.

Eleven

Her apartment felt claustrophobic, much smaller than the flat she had in London that overlooked the park.

Blythe missed the high ceilings and the huge windows that allowed the light to flood in and brighten even a miserable day. She missed the hum of the city at night—the distant sirens, the rumble of the Underground, the sense that millions of people were living their lives just beyond her walls. It made her feel less alone, somehow.

Woodington was quiet. Too quiet. The kind of silence that made you aware of every small sound—the hum of the fridge, the tick of the radiator, your own breathing.

She grabbed her keys and headed out. There were two bars, Ros had explained: Art for music and loud escapism, Blanca's for a quieter night.

"Which one are you thinking?" Ros had asked, already knowing the answer.

"Blanca's," Blythe had replied without hesitation. "I'm not in the mood for loud."

Blythe tapped in the postcode to the inbuilt sat-nav in her car and pulled out, grateful for the excuse to leave the suffocating walls behind, even if just for an evening.

She eased her car into a parking spot near the Riverside Development, the steady flow of the water shimmering softly in the fading light. Taking a moment, fingers lightly resting on the steering wheel, she looked around.

The place was alive with activity—cafés spilling warm light onto newly paved streets, small shops lining narrow lanes, and a cluster of people laughing over drinks on outdoor terraces. It wasn't the bustling city life she was used to, but it had its own charm—a quiet energy that suggested there was always something happening if you knew where to look.

She was quietly impressed. For a town this size, there was more going on than she'd expected. Maybe this stint in Woodington wouldn't be so bad after all.

With a soft sigh, she unbuckled her seatbelt and stepped out, the cool river breeze brushing against her face as she ventured towards the evening ahead.

Blanca's was quaint, like an old-fashioned pub, but more chic, more lively, and one hundred percent more gay.

As she walked in, she noticed the already busy crowd that had commandeered most of the seating in the far corner. That was fine, as she was content with sitting at the bar and nursing an Old Fashioned.

Drink in hand, she wasn't expecting the gentle tap on her shoulder and then soft voice that asked, "Are you stalking me?"

Twisting in her seat, Blythe came face to face with Allegra, holding herself up on her crutches while grinning at her.

"Do I look like I need to stalk?" Blythe smiled back. "What are you having?"

"Oh, I already have a drink." She nudged her head back towards the far corner and the tight-knit group. "I just saw you and thought…"

Blythe glanced quickly at the crutches before her line of sight raised back up and she held her gaze. "A lot of effort just to say hello."

Allegra blushed. Blythe considered her for a moment. She was pretty sure the beautiful younger woman got a lot of attention because people were attracted to her, but maybe she wasn't quite so used to enjoying that attention.

"We're just discussing the big drama," Allegra divulged.

"Oh, a big drama." Blythe smiled.

A moment of silence held them still.

"Well, I should probably get back to—"

"The big drama?" Blythe teased.

Allegra lingered. Blythe watched her.

"Do you want to get dinner?" Blythe asked. "Now? I mean…when the big drama has finished being discussed, of course."

"Sure, why not…" Allegra shrugged, a small smile playing at her lips. "I *am* quite…famished."

As Allegra hopped back to the group, she found several pairs of eyes watching her. Grins tugged at lips. Eyebrows lifted in unspoken questions. The air practically buzzed with curiosity, every mouth twitching to ask the same thing: *Who was the woman at the bar?*

It was SJ, of course, who asked first.

"Oh, yeah, and who's the hottie at the bar?"

Allegra rolled her eyes at her friend. She pulled her arms free from the crutches and sat herself down, glancing over at Blythe, who was watching the scene over the rim of her glass.

"Just someone."

A low collective "Oooh" went around the table.

"A someone, huh?" SJ continued, refusing to give up yet. "I'd say she's a someone of interest… Interested in you, anyway, from the way she keeps looking over."

"She's new in town and looking to make…a friend," Allegra said, realising almost instantly that trying to explain—or defend—was only going to fuel SJ's fire, and possibly rile up a few of the others too.

"Yeah, she's definitely looking at you like a *friend*," Ladonya quipped, nudging SJ as the pair exchanged a grin Allegra knew all too well.

"Fine. She's taking me to dinner."

Ladonya and SJ high-fived like kids in the playground.

"Called it," SJ gloated.

"When? We need all the details." Ladonya laughed.

"Jeez, can't a girl have any secrets?" Allegra said, though the smile tugging at her lips gave her away. Truth be told, she kind of liked the attention. "If you must know—now—the moment I'm done with you lot."

"So don't let us hold you up. Hop on over there and get yourself a good time." It was Nora who had piped up, encouraging rather than annoying.

Allegra turned to her. "It's just dinner."

"I didn't know you liked older women," SJ said, casting another glance towards the bar. "Not that she looks old, obviously—she's kind of...hot, if you like that all-business, masc-femme look."

"Clearly...I do," Allegra said, pushing herself up and sliding her arms into the crutches. "So, I'll catch you all later..." She turned to SJ. "Let me know if there's any more news." Then she twisted to face Nora. "Good luck. I'll be in the stands to watch and cheer you on."

As she walked away, a chorus of whoops went up, and she stopped in her tracks, grimacing just as Blythe turned to see what all the noise was about.

"Perfect," Allegra murmured. "I'm going to kill them all...slowly."

TWELVE

The late-night café was busy, but Blythe and Allegra managed to nab a table for two in the corner. The aroma of garlic and onions wafted through the air as they both perused the menus they'd been given.

Allegra used the moment to surreptitiously sneak glances. SJ was right—Blythe wasn't her usual type—but there was something about her that was captivating. Her eyes, maybe, she thought to herself. Steely grey. Allegra could imagine that stare being quite terrifying if you got on her bad side, but when she looked at Allegra, as she'd just done, there was warmth in them.

"What? Have I got something on my face?" Blythe asked, rubbing at her chin.

Allegra smiled. "No, I was…" She looked at her again. "I guess, if I'm honest, you're not my usual type, and so I was just…looking."

"Oh? And what is your usual type?"

Allegra placed the menu down, already decided on what she was having. "I guess, sporty. I've rarely dated outside of football."

Blythe raised an eyebrow. "So I'm a wild deviation from the norm?"

"A little," Allegra admitted. "You don't scream 'team warmup at 6 a.m.'"

Blythe chuckled. "God, no. I scream, 'room service at nine'."

Allegra laughed, the sound slipping easily between them. "See? Not my type. But here we are."

Blythe leant in slightly, her eyes locking on Allegra's. "Here we are." She paused before adding, "You're really quite attractive—and very much my type."

"And what's your type?" Allegra shot back.

"Younger, athletic, a little overconfident…eager."

"Eager?"

"Mm." Blythe settled back, a slow smile playing on her lips. "Always wanting to prove yourself."

"Maybe… I can be pretty enthusiastic on the pitch," Allegra admitted.

"And in bed, too, I'd wager."

A flush of heat crept up Allegra's neck at the bold suggestion.

Allegra cleared her throat, attempting nonchalance as she reached for her glass of water. "You're not exactly subtle, are you?"

"I'm direct," Blythe said, unapologetic. "Life's too short for guesswork."

"You don't think some mystery can be…fun?"

"Oh, I love mystery," Blythe said, her gaze lingering. "I just like knowing when it's worth solving."

Allegra smiled, eyes flicking back to the menu she'd already forgotten. "And am I worth solving?"

Blythe tilted her head, a smile curving her lips. "So far, I'd say yes, but I'm a stickler for really getting to know someone before I invite them closer."

"Good to know."

The waitress returned.

"I'll have the lasagne as well," Blythe said confidently after Allegra placed her order. "Seems we already have something in common."

The waitress walked away, and Allegra sipped her water thoughtfully.

"I've never dated an older woman before," Allegra confessed.

"Well, we're just having dinner," Blythe said smoothly.

"It's still a date," Allegra countered.

"Yes, it is," Blythe concurred. "Although, meeting a beautiful woman at a football match was not on my bingo card this year."

Allegra laughed. "I'm not sure it was on mine either." She studied Blythe again. "For the record, you're very attractive also."

"Good to know." Blythe held her glass up. "So, tell me all about you, Allegra."

"You mean you haven't googled me?" Allegra asked in a playful tone.

"Should I?" Blythe countered.

"Sure, see what excitement you can find." Allegra grinned over the rim of her glass.

Pulling her phone from her pocket, Blythe quickly typed 'Allegra Mann' into Google.

"Golden Girl of Bath Street Harriers…" She smiled. "Catchy."

Allegra blushed. "It's so embarrassing. They asked to interview me about signing for the team, next thing there's an entire spread on me as some kind of supermodel."

"I mean…they're not wrong." Blythe grinned as she placed the phone down. "But I think I prefer to find out about you the old-fashioned way."

"And that is?"

"Just like this, so, tell me…who *is* Allegra Mann?"

Allegra put her glass down slowly and considered the question. "Honestly, right now, I don't really know."

Thirteen

Allegra got home just before midnight and found Sammy-Jo sprawled across the lounge chair, eyebrows waggling like she'd been rehearsing.

"So…been snogging?"

"Are you ever going to grow up?" Allegra rolled her eyes, freeing her arms from the crutches before dropping onto the couch. "Tea would be nice." She tacked on an innocent smile.

"It's too late for tea. You'll be up all night," SJ said, swivelling to face her. "And no, I've no plans to grow up. Terrible habit, that."

Allegra stretched her leg out carefully, wincing.

"You okay? Want painkillers?" SJ was already halfway up, then narrowed her eyes at Allegra's pitiful expression. "Thought so. Tea it is."

"That would be lovely, thank you." Allegra grinned. "And no, there was no snogging. Just a very polite, very sweet kiss on the cheek. She even put me into a cab—and paid for it."

SJ leaned against the kitchen doorway, arms folded. "Wow. Chivalry's not dead, then. You seeing her again?"

"Yeah…I think so. She's…different."

"Older," SJ supplied, turning the tap on.

Allegra let her head tip back against the cushions. It wasn't that big of a deal, was it? "She is. But it doesn't really show. She's—"

"Hot?" SJ's head popped back out, her face full of exaggerated wiggles.

Allegra smirked, shaking her head. "Yes, alright, she's very attractive. Happy?"

"Ecstatic." SJ beamed. "You're basically dating a MILF. Dreams do come true."

Allegra snorted. "You're insufferable."

"And *you're* blushing," SJ shot back, ducking into the kitchen before Allegra could lob a cushion at her.

"Anyway…she's not a MILF, peasant," Allegra deadpanned. "No kids. Not even a cat."

Sammy-Jo swept back in with two mugs, both steaming, and set one carefully in front of her.

"What's this?" Allegra eyed it suspiciously.

"Camomile. Nora swears by it. I think it helps."

Allegra lifted the mug, sniffed, and wrinkled her nose. "Smells like boiled weeds."

"Better than you tossing and turning half the night, like a walrus on speed," SJ shot back, plonking herself down beside her.

Allegra took the tiniest sip, grimaced, and muttered, "Grim."

"Just drink it, and tell me about…"

"Blythe."

"Blythe? That's made up, surely."

Allegra laughed. "Nope, that's her name. It's unconventional, but then—who names their kid Allegra? Or Sammy-Jo?"

"I guess." SJ shrugged, pretending to look wounded. "So, when's the next date then?"

"Dunno. She's going to call me. She's got a big meeting tomorrow with Gabby."

"Gabby?"

Allegra nodded. "I know—no idea why. Blythe's company builds hotels."

"Could just be business. Gabby's got her fingers in a lot of pies, I imagine."

"So many pies." Allegra giggled.

"Nope." Sammy-Jo shot up from the couch. "I'm not thinking about Nora and Gabby… I'm going to bed."

Allegra roared with laughter. "Oh, come on, you've been a Gabby pie once upon a time."

"I'm ignoring you," SJ called back, not turning around as she bounded up the stairs.

Allegra was still grinning when her phone beeped.

Blythe: Hope you got home safely. I'm looking forward to seeing you again soon.

Her smile softened as she typed back.

Allegra: Yes, thank you for organising that. I just settled down with a camomile tea on the couch before I drag myself up to bed. Thank you for a lovely dinner. I look forwards to seeing you again soon.

She pressed send, then let the phone rest in her lap. For a moment, the house felt too quiet, too still. Was she really ready for something new—or was she just trying to convince herself she was?

Her phone buzzed again.

Blythe: Well, I won't keep you then. Sleep well, and I'll be in touch soon. Good night, Allegra Mann.

Allegra: Goodnight, Ms Daniels.

She dropped the phone onto the cushion beside her and grinned. Maybe it wasn't going to be such a terrible few weeks after all.

Fourteen

Crisp autumn mornings were Blythe's favourite. The freshness in the air, the leaves shifting through shades of fire, and the excuse to wear her checked jacket always put a bounce in her step.

The apartment block she was staying in was only a short walk from the office. She liked it that way. It gave her time to gather her thoughts, to clear her head. Most mornings she stopped at one of the many coffee shops on the route. She grabbed a matcha latte before heading back out to join up with Claudia Maddox for their meeting.

Claudia was intriguing. And there she was, outside the office in conversation with a striking woman—tall, not quite as elegant as Claudia—more on the artsy side, with dark hair and brooding good looks.

"Well, well, well," Blythe murmured to herself as she watched the woman lean in and kiss Claudia in a way that was far from friendly. That explained the vibe—and taught her a quick lesson in assumptions. She'd seen the ring on Claudia's finger and automatically imagined a husband.

"Good morning," Claudia said when she spotted Blythe approaching. Her smile came easily, backed by the kind of confidence that didn't need validation. "This is my wife, Scarlett." No explanation, just the fact laid out as it was.

"Hi," Scarlett said.

Up close, Blythe realised her mistake. Scarlett was much more than brooding good looks.

"Hello," Blythe replied, extending a hand. She liked that—taking someone's hand. You could tell a lot about a person by the way they responded.

Scarlett didn't hesitate. Firm grip, steady eye contact.

"I just need to pop upstairs and organise the rest of the office before we head off," Blythe said to Claudia. "Do you want to grab a coffee or something? I'm sure we can spare you for a few minutes." Then, with a quick smile towards Scarlett, "Unless you're in a hurry, of course."

"I do in fact need to be somewhere. Have a great day, though." She turned to Claudia, "I'll see you tonight," and then she backed away and headed in the direction she needed to go.

"She's—"

"Quite wonderful." Claudia smirked as they both watched Scarlett turn the corner—out of sight, but clearly never out of mind. "And quite the surprise, if I'm honest." She chuckled as they made their way into the building.

"I was going to say 'younger', but I'll take your word for it."

"There is that—though not by design. I don't tend to date younger. Actually, I didn't date at all. But if I had, it wouldn't have been a woman, either…and yet, here we are." Claudia smiled, a softness behind it. "Happier than I've ever been."

Blythe nodded and gestured for Claudia to step through the barrier first. "I've found younger to be much more…my type," she admitted. It wasn't information she often shared at the office, but there was something about Claudia that made it feel easy.

"Anyone special at the moment?" Claudia asked, not missing a step as she took in the information about her new boss.

Blythe reached out and pressed the button to call the lift. "I'm not sure, but there is potential there."

"Oh, well, that's always a good start."

They stood silently, side by side, matching outfits almost—Claudia wore a black pencil skirt, Blythe went with slacks. But the tweed jackets and white shirts were uniform.

The lift arrived, doors sliding open, and once again Blythe gestured for Claudia to go first. They stepped inside, turned, and stood shoulder to shoulder as the doors closed.

"How are you settling into life in Woodington?" Claudia asked, quickly glancing sideways before fixing her gaze ahead.

"It's not as bad as I imagined," Blythe admitted. "I discovered the Riverside complex at least."

"Ah, I do enjoy it down there. Blanca's is a lovely bar." She hesitated, then suddenly blurted, "Are you gay? I only ask because…well, I'm finding myself noticing things lately. My daughter, Zara, says it's my gaydar finally kicking in." Claudia chuckled, a touch sheepish. "Sorry. That was probably an inappropriate question for the workplace."

Blythe smiled. Just then, the lift dinged, doors opening to reveal three men waiting to get in. Neither woman moved until Claudia noticed which floor they were on.

"This is us," Claudia said, stepping out. Blythe followed, the men slipping quickly into the lift before the doors closed on them.

"Yes," Blythe said at last, her voice calm but deliberate. The answer clearly caught Claudia off guard. "I am. I don't shout about it, but I don't hide it either."

"I have no intention of gossiping," Claudia assured her.

"I didn't for a minute think you would." Blythe checked her watch. "I'll just be a moment."

"Of course. I'll hang around in the staff tearoom."

Blythe nodded and headed towards her office. Yes, she thought, *Claudia Maddox is a very intriguing woman.*

Fifteen

Claudia drove them the relatively short distance from Olsen's offices to the Bath Street Harriers training centre. They pulled into the car park and found a space beside a large Range Rover.

"Gabby's here," Claudia said, glancing at the car.

Blythe didn't give it a second look, already heading towards the entrance. She wanted to get this project started—or at least over with, if it were a no-go from the start.

"Have you been here before?" Blythe asked as Claudia caught up. "Where do we go?"

"No, actually…I never had the need. I've been to a few games at the stadium they share with Rovers."

"Yes. Small ground, not many amenities unless you like potent coffee and overcooked chips."

Claudia tried not to sound too much like she was gloating when she said, "I've only ever sat in the director's box."

"Good to have you on board." Blythe laughed as they reached the entrance doors. "Let's do this."

A young woman in a navy polo shirt, hair tied back neatly, smiled at them as they approached. "How can I help?"

"We have an appointment with Ms Dean. Blythe Daniels, Olsen Group. This is my colleague, Claudia Maddox."

"Gabby is expecting us," Claudia added.

"Of course." The smile continued. "If I can get you to just look into the camera." She pointed to a small round plastic eye on a bendy stem attached to something on the other side of the counter.

Blythe frowned but stepped forwards.

"Great, and you," the girl said to Claudia.

"Absolutely." Claudia grinned into the camera. "How's that?"

"Perfect. Give me one second and I'll have your passes arranged and grab someone to show you up." She smiled again, then added, "Take a seat, please."

Her eyes led them towards a small seating area, all plush sofas and a table crammed with high-protein bars and magazines to keep you busy while you waited.

Blythe picked up a protein bar and examined it. "Peanut butter and caramel," she read, "not particularly healthy sounding, is it?"

"One of my daughters, Diana, gets those for her partner, Shannon. She loves them. But then she's in the gym pretty much every day, so…" Claudia shrugged. "I'd rather have a peanut butter sandwich."

"Yes…" Blythe answered slowly, placing it back onto the pile. "I'd probably just go without either."

"Claud!" A booming, excited voice echoed from behind them. They both turned, Claudia standing eagerly as the glamorous figure of Gabriella Dean appeared and pulled her into a hug. "So good to see you."

"You, too," Claudia managed to say when Gabby finally let her go. "I didn't realise you'd be coming down to find us."

"And leave my dear friend in the hands of God only knows who at the moment? We're recruiting," she whispered.

"This is Blythe, my boss," Claudia introduced.

"Blythe Daniels. Great to meet you at last." Her hand shot out and was instantly taken by Gabby.

"Lovely to finally put a face to the voice," Gabby remarked. They'd only had one conversation—a quick, 'Are you interested in listening to our proposal?' "Shall we go up?"

She turned on her heel, linked arms with Claudia, and swept towards the double doors, which slid open as soon as she came within ten feet.

Blythe followed, taking it all in. The long corridor was lined with images of footballers—men on one side, the women's team members on the other. She didn't recognise any of the players until she stopped in front of the one who had recently become familiar.

Tall. Athletic. The camera had caught her mid-air, both feet off the ground, arm raised for balance, ponytail whipping as she met her opponent shoulder to shoulder.

She looked immense. Like a warrior.

Blythe's mouth curved, almost against her will. There was something magnetic about the sheer force in that image—the kind of energy that made you want to look twice. She dragged her gaze away, telling herself it was just good photography. But the image lingered in her head, as though daring her not to forget it.

"Allegra Mann, one of our best defenders," Gabby said, noticing Blythe's interest in the artwork.

Blythe nodded but said nothing more. Any thoughts she had about Allegra Mann were internal ones…for now.

Sixteen

Allegra didn't waste any time. She slipped into the room, kicked off her shoes, leant her crutches against the wall, and hauled herself up onto the treatment table, ready for Taylor to check her knee and run through the strengthening exercises.

"How's it been?" Taylor asked from the foot of the bed, that easy smile on her face as always. Her blonde hair was tied back neatly, her white polo shirt crisp against tanned skin. Spain had clearly agreed with her. One week in the sun with her girlfriend, Carrie, had left her glowing.

"Not bad," Allegra replied, swinging her legs up and lying back, "though, I'm still not over the fact you ran off to Spain, while I was stuck here, and didn't take me with you."

Taylor chuckled. The holiday had been a birthday present, a surprise Carrie had arranged. "Not sure you'd have had as much fun as I did," she teased, her cheeks tinting pink at the implication.

"Sounds amazing." Allegra sighed. "I'd kill for some sunshine right now." She flinched as Taylor adjusted her leg.

"Still painful?" Taylor's voice softened with sympathy.

"Not as much. It's a lot better, but every now and then…" Allegra shrugged. "I was on it a lot last night. That's probably why."

Taylor gave her a look, half stern, half fond. "You're supposed to be resting."

"I know..." Allegra braced for the lecture. "I had a date."

"Oh, well, that changes everything." Taylor wheeled her chair over, settling beside her and pressing into the muscles around the knee joint with practised hands.

Allegra grinned despite herself. "It was just dinner. Totally spontaneous. Blythe was at the bar when I met up with the team yesterday. We ended up talking, and...one thing led to another."

Taylor leant back in her chair, eyes narrowing in mock suspicion. "So, Blythe? Tall, confident, and distracting enough that you'd risk undoing weeks of my hard work?"

"She's not particularly tall," Allegra said, rolling her eyes, but smiling. "And I behaved. Barely any dancing, I swear."

Taylor snorted. "That's what they all say. But you've got that look—the 'I really liked her' look. Don't even try to deny it."

Allegra shut her eyes and hissed as Taylor dug a thumb into a tender spot. "You're supposed to be focusing on my leg, not my love life."

"Uh huh, and you wouldn't have mentioned it if that was really the case." Taylor grinned. "And if I really thought this leg could withstand dancing, you'd be playing at the weekend."

Allegra laughed. "I can't wait to dance again."

"So, seriously, Blythe—what's she like? Where did you meet?"

"She's..." Allegra drew out the word, letting it hang a moment before continuing, "older. Really grown-up, you know? I wouldn't have said she was my type, and yet... there's just something about her. Sexy. Confident. Draws me in."

"Oh, we like those." Taylor chuckled. "Deep breath," she warned before bending Allegra's knee gently, keeping the conversation alive as she worked.

Allegra all but growled as the pain passed.

"Go on," Taylor demanded playfully, continuing to bend and straighten the leg.

"We met at the game at the weekend. She's in town for a few months with work, and her friend dragged her along."

"So, not a football fan as such then?"

"Nope. Doesn't have a clue…which is quite nice."

"And what does she do?"

Allegra pushed up onto her elbows, watching what Taylor was doing. "Business. Something office-y and high-powered. She's all *designer suits* and she has that aura about her, you know…she's in charge of things."

"Oh…I do know." Taylor laughed. "I'd put Carrie in that box."

Allegra grinned. "How's she doing?"

"She's great. Of course, she does as she's told under certain circumstances—mainly when it comes to letting me take care of her."

"Us independent types are a struggle," Allegra muttered, half laughing.

Taylor began to rewrap the strapping around Allegra's knee. "You know, sometimes it's okay to be vulnerable."

"I know."

"But you don't like it?"

"I don't enjoy it. There's a difference. Doesn't mean I can't do it." Allegra swung her legs off the table. "It's just easier to get things done when I only have myself to consider."

"I get that." Taylor stood, passing her the crutches. "Keep resting. But also—enjoy spending time with Blythe. Hopefully we'll get to meet her sometime."

SEVENTEEN

Gabby sat back in her familiar chair, the big leather-backed one that always made her look a little larger than life. Claudia smiled across the desk, and Blythe Daniels looked as composed as anyone had ever dared to in this office—which boded well.

"So," Gabby began, glancing between them before settling on Blythe, "let's get into it. What collaborations are the Olsen Group offering, in real terms?"

Blythe leant forwards with practised ease, calm and controlled. "As you know, the Olsen Group specialises in high-quality, affordable, worldwide hotels."

Gabby nodded, lips quirking. "I'm aware. I believe I've stayed in a few." She threw a wink at Claudia.

"I've taken Gabby on several short breaks," Claudia added smoothly. "Last December we had a wonderful Christmas shopping trip in Oslo."

"What we envisage," Blythe said evenly, "is our next venture bringing a touch of Olsen magic to the Woodington area. But when we looked a little closer, we spotted a potential opportunity that might extend our reach towards Bath Street." She tilted her head, eyes steady on Gabby. "Or more specifically—Bath Street Harriers."

"Intriguing." Gabby's smile widened as she steepled her hands on the desk.

Blythe's gaze flicked towards Claudia, the smallest of signals, handing her the floor to continue the pitch.

"Yes," Claudia said smoothly. "And with your recent announcement about building a dedicated stadium for the Harriers, we saw an excellent opportunity for The Olsen Group and Dean Enterprises to join forces. Together, we could create something bold for the community—something that leaves a lasting legacy."

Gabby arched an eyebrow, folding her hands more tightly beneath her chin. "Legacy is a lovely word, Claudia. But it usually comes with a hefty price tag. Why would I let an outside corporation plant their flag on something as personal as this club?"

Blythe leant forwards slightly, her tone even. "Because, Gabriella, the right partnership doesn't take away ownership—it amplifies it. Olsen has no interest in overshadowing the Harriers. What we want is to elevate what you've already built."

Gabby's lips curved, but her eyes remained sharp. "Convince me that's more than just a polished line."

"We want to build a hotel as part of the new stadium," Blythe said, her voice measured but confident. "Somewhere fans could stay when they come for a game, or even when they need the airport. If we were to come on board, the Olsen Group would be prepared to cover part of the cost of building the stadium—up to sixty percent of its cost."

Gabby's brows lifted, interest flickering across her face. "Sixty percent," she repeated slowly, as though tasting the number. She leant back in her chair, steepling her fingers once again. "That's generous. And intriguing. But what's the catch?"

"I'm not sure there is one." Blythe grinned. Sitting back, she crossed one leg over the other, pausing just long enough to let anticipation build before continuing. "We'd be looking at naming rights, shirt sponsorship, and stadium advertising under a fifteen-year deal, with the option to extend if all parties were in agreement."

Gabby snapped her fingers. "Ah, there it is. Not a catch, perhaps, but certainly a condition." She tapped a finger lightly against her chin. "Fifteen years is a long marriage, Ms Daniels. You're sure the Olsen Group doesn't have wandering eyes?"

Claudia smoothly leant forwards, her tone warm but firm. "The Olsen Group are very committed to this project. They already have a firm base here in town, and they understand how important it is to nurture the women's game—especially now, in the wake of another Euros victory for the nation. This isn't just business for them, it's legacy."

Gabby arched a brow once more, clearly intrigued despite herself, and her gaze slid back to Blythe as if to test the truth of Claudia's words.

Blythe didn't flinch under Gabby's scrutiny. If anything, the corner of her mouth lifted, a quiet confidence settling over her. "Claudia's right. The Olsen Group doesn't make short-term plays—we build for the future. A stadium hotel linked with Bath Street isn't just about rooms and revenue, it's about planting something here that lasts. That kind of commitment takes more than contracts. It takes belief in the community, and belief in the club."

She let the words hang for a beat, then added, softer, "And I wouldn't be sitting here if we didn't have both."

Gabby's eyes narrowed slightly, not in suspicion, but in thought. "Interesting…"

Eighteen

Allegra paused, letting her gaze linger on the massive photo of herself mid-leap, ponytail whipping, muscles taut, eyes blazing with focus. The memory was vivid—last-minute goal, the roar of the crowd, the weight of the season pressing down and then lifting, all at once. Victory had been theirs, safely secured, and that adrenaline-charged moment was frozen forever in that image. She shook her head slightly, smiled, and continued down the hallway, crutches clicking softly against the floor.

It wouldn't be long before she was back on the pitch, creating more moments like that.

As she turned into reception, she spotted Sammy-Jo and Nora laughing together at the desk.

"Oh, watch out—Hopalong Cassidy is coming." Sammy-Jo winked as Nora turned.

"Hey, Leggy, how's the…leg?" Nora asked.

"Getting there. Apparently, I'm still not allowed to go dancing." She grinned.

"Shame…especially when you have a potential partner to dance with." Sammy-Jo laughed.

Allegra narrowed her eyes. "You know, you could always take Daisy dancing, and then you'd be able to focus on your own love life."

"That would be fun, and yet, I'd still find time to mess with you and yours."

"Maybe I'll flirt with Daisy instead… I'm sure she's bored of you by now."

Nora stood between them, grinning at their antics. If a person didn't know better, you'd never guess they were best friends.

"So…date went well then?" Nora asked, bringing the banter down a notch.

Allegra shrugged. "It might have done." She looked back and forth between them. "Why are you still here, anyway?"

"Just chatting. It's what captains do," SJ said.

Nora rolled her eyes. "I'm waiting for Gabby. She's got a big meeting, but then we're going to lunch."

From the corridor, the soft click of heels and purposeful steps announced their arrival. Gabby strode in first, her presence filling the space instantly, followed closely by Blythe and Claudia.

Allegra, mid-sentence with Nora and Sammy-Jo, froze for just a heartbeat. Blythe's eyes met hers across the reception area and something unspoken passed between them. A spark? Recognition? A flicker of amusement, maybe?

Sammy-Jo and Nora immediately noticed Blythe, too. SJ's eyebrows shot up, a mischievous grin spreading across her face. "Well, look who's here," she murmured, elbowing Nora.

Nora's gaze lingered a moment longer than necessary, taking in Blythe's confident stride, tailored jacket, and the air of someone used to commanding a room. She smiled knowingly at Allegra, a silent acknowledgement of the intrigue Blythe brought with her.

"Don't be mean," Nora whispered back at SJ.

Allegra shifted slightly on her crutches, feeling heat creep up her neck. She gave a small, almost imperceptible wave, and Blythe responded with the faintest curve of her lips before continuing towards the desk.

Claudia kept pace beside her, offering a polite smile to everyone in the reception area, while clearly unaware of the subtle tension—or excitement—she'd just witnessed.

"Thanks again for the opportunity to discuss this venture," Blythe said, her hand landing softly on Gabby's bicep. "I hope to hear from you soon."

"Yes, absolutely. You've definitely given me a lot to think about." She smiled, then turned to Claudia. "Drinks this weekend?"

"I'll check with Scarlett. You know what she's like for making plans and surprising me."

"Indeed, I do." Gabby grinned. She glanced over at Nora and the other members of her team hanging out. "Maybe we should organise a team meet and get the official supporters club to come along and discuss your plans?"

Blythe nodded. "I'm open to whatever gets this deal done."

Nineteen

Outside, Allegra spotted Blythe perched against a low wall, head bent as she studied something on her phone.

"Did you get left behind?" Allegra called, hopping towards her with a grin.

"Actually," Blythe said, looking up briefly, a small smile tugging at her lips, as she stepped forward, "I told my colleague I had something important to take care of."

Allegra slowed as she reached her, curious eyes flicking to the phone in Blythe's hand. "Something more important than lunch with me?"

Blythe raised an eyebrow, tucking the device into her bag. "Depends on how you define important."

Allegra grinned. "I'd like to think I rank pretty high."

"Noted," Blythe said. Her gaze held Allegra's, teasing, deliberate. "So, what are you doing now?"

Allegra shrugged, brushing a loose strand of hair from her face. "Trying not to fall over my own crutches while I figure out what to do with my free time." She tilted her head, a mischievous glint in her eyes. "Got any suggestions?"

Blythe smiled, slow and knowing. "Maybe I do…but some things are better discovered in person."

"Pretty sure I am standing here, in person."

Blythe checked her watch. "My Uber will be here in a moment. I'm told Joie is the place to eat around here. I have a table booked."

"Good. I like it there." Allegra grinned. She stared at Blythe for a long moment before making a decision. She moved awkwardly, getting closer. "There's something I've been wondering."

"Oh? And what's that?" Blythe asked, unmoving, curiosity flickering in her eyes as they held each other's gaze.

Allegra bit her bottom lip, then released it slowly. "I'm wondering if you kiss as well as you talk."

Blythe's eyes lit up, a smile tugging at her lips. "Only one way to find out," she murmured, tilting her head slightly closer.

Allegra's heart picked up. She stepped the final few inches, closing the space between them, and the world faded into nothing.

Their lips met, tentative at first, a testing brush that sparked immediately. Blythe's hand found Allegra's waist, steadying her, drawing her closer, and the kiss deepened—confident and deliberate, just like her words had promised.

Allegra melted into it, surprised by how natural it felt, and how right. When they finally broke apart, their breaths mingled.

"Not bad," Allegra whispered, a mischievous twist at the corner of her mouth. "But I have a feeling you can do better."

Blythe laughed softly. "Challenge accepted, but first…" Her phone beeped. The Uber was close. "Lunch, and then we'll see about anything else. But you should know something, Allegra Mann…"

"Hm, what's that?"

"I play to win."

Allegra grinned. "So do I."

TWENTY

Joie was about as sophisticated as you could get in Woodington or Bath Street. Tucked into the Riverside Development, where both districts met the smaller towns of Banbury Hollow and Amberfield, it was a delightful place to explore.

The Uber dropped them off as close to the restaurant as it could, but Allegra still had a few metres to traverse on her crutches.

"How much longer are you going to need those?" Blythe asked, nodding towards the walking aids as they walked side by side at Allegra's speed.

"Depends—could be anything from another couple of weeks, to months if I don't do as I'm told."

Blythe smiled, a glint of amusement in her eyes. "You strike me as someone who definitely does what she wants, not what she's told."

"Is that what you think?" Allegra replied, a playful gleam in her own eyes.

"It's definitely the impression you leave," Blythe said.

"I think you're describing yourself, not me."

"I don't have people running around after me," Blythe said, a touch perturbed.

"But you are in control and pulling all the strings?" Allegra smirked, enjoying the little spark between them.

Blythe stopped, waiting until Allegra noticed and turned to face her. She closed the gap, standing as close as she could without touching, and said, "I think you'd enjoy me being in control…pulling the strings." Her voice was low, teasing, calculated.

When Allegra's gaze flicked away, Blythe's finger slid under her chin, tilting her face back to meet her eyes. "Eyes on me." Her thumb traced a slow, deliberate line along Allegra's jaw, a gentle caress that left a shiver in its wake. The warmth of her touch and the intensity of her gaze made the air between them crackle with unspoken anticipation.

Allegra's pulse thundered in her ears, every nerve alive as Blythe leant slightly closer, the faint scent of her perfume wafting in the air.

"I like that," Blythe murmured, voice low and smooth, almost a purr. "That you don't pull away."

Allegra swallowed, her mouth suddenly dry.

"I—" she started, then cut herself off, realising the words didn't matter right now. All that mattered was Blythe, the heat of her presence, and the undeniable pull she felt.

Blythe's hand slid from her jaw to her shoulder, guiding her subtly closer. "Relax," she said softly, playfully, "I'm just teasing."

Allegra's breath hitched. *Eyes on me*—the command carried authority. And the weirdest, most thrilling thing? She *wanted* to obey.

Blythe's eyes flicked down for a fraction of a second, taking in Allegra's reaction, before meeting her gaze again.

"Yes," Blythe murmured, a small, satisfied smile tugging at her lips, "I can be in control, pull the strings…" She leant closer, lips brushing against Allegra's. "But I'm adaptable—that's what makes me successful."

Blythe's kiss was confident, in control, but careful—each movement measured, teasing, inviting Allegra to match her. Allegra responded instinctively, tilting her head, letting herself melt into the connection, savouring the mix of dominance and gentleness.

When they broke apart, Allegra needed to steady herself, grateful for the crutches for once.

"Shall we?" Blythe indicated the restaurant.

"Yes." Allegra managed to find one word that made sense.

TWENTY-ONE

They settled into window seats, sitting across from each other. Orders taken and menus removed, both had opted for sparkling water.

Allegra stared out the window, watching a paddleboarder making their way downriver towards the bridge.

Blythe sipped her drink, quietly observing the subtle shifts on Allegra's face. Stunning, Blythe realised—not just the blue-eyed, blonde, athlete type who could easily turn heads—but something more. Allegra Mann was a tough cookie, of that Blythe had no doubts, yet she radiated a vulnerability so subtle it was almost imperceptible.

Tilting her head, Blythe let a small, knowing smile curve her lips. "Thinking about the paddleboarder…or something else?" Her tone was teasing, but gentle.

Allegra met her gaze, caught off guard, her cheeks warming. She bit her bottom lip before answering softly, "Maybe a little of both."

Blythe's eyes softened, though the glint of mischief never left them. "I like that," she murmured, swirling her water. "It suits you—focused, but with your mind elsewhere, too."

Allegra felt a flutter in her chest at the intensity of Blythe's gaze, drawn in despite the table between them, feeling seen in a way that startled her.

"I'm an excellent multitasker," she said slowly, sipping her water. Then she set the glass down and looked Blythe squarely in the eye. "I guess I was thinking…you're a surprise."

"Oh? In what way?"

Allegra took a breath, her tone earnest. "My last relationship ended some months ago. I wasn't looking for anyone…and then there you were, sitting beside me at a game I should have been playing in."

"A game I didn't want to be at." Blythe chuckled. "But now I'm glad Ros dragged me along."

Considering that information, Allegra asked, "Why *did she* drag you along? And what were you doing at the club with Claudia?"

"Does everyone know Claudia?" Blythe asked, her curiosity piqued further about the enigmatic woman.

Allegra laughed. "We're a tight bunch. She's good friends with Gabby, and Gabby is married to Nora, the team captain. So, often we're all at the same events. But I wouldn't say that I *know* Claudia."

Blythe nodded, offering nothing more.

Allegra waited for the answer to her second question. When none came, she pressed, "So…you were at the club to just stalk me?"

"That's exactly why, yes," Blythe said, raising her hands in mock surrender. "You caught me."

"A secret, huh?"

"Something like that…for now." Blythe smiled, taking another sip of her water. "But I'm optimistic about being able to share more soon."

"Is it the kind of thing that's going to keep you hanging around Bath Street, or once it's done, you'll be gone?"

That was a good question, Blythe thought. "I think the answer to that lies in many places."

Allegra nodded. "I can do friends with benefits if you're not staying."

"Is that your way of saying you want to sleep with me?"

Allegra laughed, a slow, teasing sound. "Do you want it to be?"

Their food arrived—two plates of steaming pasta. The waiter lingered for a few moments, asking about cheese, pepper, and if there was anything else they needed, before finally leaving them to their own conversation.

Blythe picked up her fork, lazily twirling some pasta. "I wouldn't turn you down…but I don't do casual sex."

"And if I only wanted casual sex?" Allegra asked, arching a brow, her fork poised mid-air.

Blythe smiled and slowly finished chewing. "There is absolutely nothing casual about you, Allegra Mann."

Twenty-Two

It wasn't the torrid, rush-to-get-naked kind of encounter Allegra was used to. For one thing, her knee made the idea of being pushed through the door, slammed against the wall, hoisted up and taken, impossible—the kind of thing she'd grown accustomed to with John. This was different. Slower. Charged in another way.

They'd finished their meal, the plates cleared, and Allegra had insisted on splitting the bill despite Blythe's easy explanation that the company would cover it.

"So," Blythe asked, once their coffees were nearly drained, "am I ordering one Uber, or two?"

The ride to the apartment Olsen was paying for was quiet. The kind of silence that wasn't awkward so much as taut, weighted with awareness. They sat close in the back seat, Allegra's injured leg stretched as far as it could go in the limited space, their shoulders brushing as they made room for each other. Neither complained. Neither wanted to.

The ascent in the lift carried its own kind of tension. With her hands occupied by crutches, Allegra couldn't fling herself against Blythe even if she'd wanted to, and Blythe seemed acutely aware that anything too intense might risk setting back her recovery. So they held back. Side by side, they waited, watching the numbers tick upwards, each floor another small spark of anticipation.

"So, to be clear, this isn't casual for me," Blythe said, her gaze fixed on the blurred reflection in the lift doors.

"I know." Allegra's voice was steady, but her jaw tightened. "But to also be clear, if you leave, I won't be following. So…"

Blythe turned her head then, studying her profile. "So you're telling me to think carefully before I kiss you again?"

Allegra finally looked back at her, eyes glinting. "No. I'm telling you if you kiss me again, you'd better mean it."

"Why would I not mean it?"

Allegra only shrugged, letting the silence do the work.

Blythe exhaled, her thoughts already halfway back to London—not a million miles away, but far enough. "I can't promise I won't leave."

"Then you'd better get your head around casual sex," Allegra said lightly, the teasing in her voice undercut with steel. "Because my life is here while I'm at this club, and anyone I get serious about has to understand that."

The lift slowed and juddered to a stop, the doors sliding open to reveal the hallway beyond. Allegra wasted no time, hopping out and turning back with a grin. "Which way?"

"Left," Blythe said, stepping after her. "Last door on the right." She slipped a hand into her pocket and pulled out her key. Her pulse quickened. Was she really about to do this? Casual sex with a gorgeous woman fifteen years younger than her?

She knew she'd regret it if she didn't, but memories of Amanda flickered in her mind—a reminder of the last time she'd tried to set boundaries and ended up carved into a million pieces.

"Come on, slow coach," Allegra called from outside the door, leaning casually against the wall, all cool, calm, and undeniably sexy.

"Are you always like this?" Blythe asked as she closed the gap.

"Like what? You're going to have to be more explicit." Allegra's gaze drifted slowly from Blythe's eyes to her mouth.

Blythe arched a brow, reaching the door. "Are you always this…sexy?"

"Only when I need to be," Allegra purred, twisting until her back pressed against the wall. "Are you always this slow?" Allegra tilted her head, eyes sparkling with challenge. "I'm not very patient."

Blythe's grin widened. "Good. Neither am I."

They stood there, the space between them charged, both fully aware of the push and pull, the game of control and surrender. Blythe finally turned the key in the lock.

Twenty-Three

Blythe kicked off her shoes and hung her jacket on the hook, letting the weight of the day slide off her shoulders. She glanced at the mirror in the hallway, catching a quick reflection. Her hair was perfect—shoulder length and shaggy—the hairdresser had described it, the undercut at the back invisible when left down, a fringe softening the look. Minimal make-up, just enough to hint at features she didn't need to accentuate. Her appeal wasn't in polish or fuss—it was in the way she moved, the quiet confidence she carried, the energy that seemed to ripple off her. She didn't try to impress. She was just herself, always had been.

She let that thought run through her as she stepped into the lounge, ready to take charge, ready to enjoy the afternoon with Allegra. But the moment she entered, her breath caught.

The crutches lay discarded. Clothes were strewn carelessly aside. All that remained for Blythe to remove was Allegra's underwear—and perhaps, a little of her own sense of control.

"Comfortable?" Blythe asked, voice low.

Allegra grinned and stretched out. "No."

Blythe's hands moved to unbutton the cuff of her shirt, her eyes scanning Allegra's exposed skin—perfect, youthful, and slightly sun-kissed.

Matching underwear suggested careful—or perhaps deliberate—choices, and it made Blythe's pulse quicken.

"No? You look pretty relaxed to me," Blythe teased, popping the buttons of her shirt free as she opened it.

Allegra ran a hand through her hair, sweeping it all to one side. "I'll be more relaxed when your mouth is on me."

"Is that all you want?"

"No." Allegra's eyes followed Blythe as she shrugged the shirt from her shoulders, revealing a lace bra and ample curves.

"What else do you want?"

"Why don't you tell me?" Allegra countered, parting her legs just slightly, a teasing challenge in her gaze.

Blythe's hands moved to her trousers, the button a little stiff. "You want…" she murmured, sliding the zip lower, eyes not leaving Allegra's face, "someone…" She pushed them down her thighs, kicked them off, and smiled before easing forwards into the space on the couch between Allegra's thighs, careful to avoid the damaged knee. "To see you."

"And you think that's you?" Allegra asked, reclining against the cushions as Blythe's weight pressed lightly onto her.

"I think I have a good idea. And if given the time, I'll figure out the rest."

"Confident. I like it." Allegra reached up, brushing Blythe's hair from her face. "So…what are you waiting for?"

Blythe laughed softly. "I'm not waiting because I'm slow… I'm waiting because you're impatient." Her fingers traced a deliberate path from Allegra's neck, down to her chest, settling to cup her breast. Her lips followed, pressing warm, teasing kisses against her skin. "I like to savour every sensation. I want to hear you pleading to be released."

"And what if I don't beg?" Allegra whispered, a hint of challenge in her eyes.

Blythe paused, looking up with a confident, almost predatory smile. "You'll beg, Allegra. I promise you that."

Allegra shivered, a mixture of anticipation and defiance rolling through her. She arched slightly against Blythe's touch, testing, tempting, and Blythe responded immediately, leaning closer, lips brushing along the sensitive line of her collarbone.

"See?" Blythe murmured, voice low and teasing. "I know you can be a good girl, when you're encouraged."

Allegra's breath hitched, and she caught Blythe's gaze. Blythe smiled, sensing the thrill of control, and let her hands wander lower, brushing along the curve of Allegra's hips, feeling the tension coil and pulse beneath her fingertips.

"You are something else," Blythe whispered, her mouth ghosting against Allegra's ear. "From the minute I saw you, I was…interested."

A soft moan slipped from Allegra, surrendering just a fraction, letting herself fall into the slow, deliberate rhythm Blythe commanded. Each touch, each movement built the anticipation higher, until the world outside ceased to exist.

"Really? I didn't notice."

Blythe's lips curved as they trailed down Allegra's shoulder, brushing the hollow of her neck. Every kiss was measured, teasing, her hand cupping and kneading, coaxing soft whimpers from Allegra.

"I think you noticed," Blythe murmured, pulling back just enough to meet her gaze. "You're stunning."

"Alright, I get it." Allegra grinned, sliding a hand around the back of Blythe's neck and tugging her down. "Stop talking."

When Blythe didn't immediately obey, Allegra eased her grip, studying her face, caught between desire and curiosity.

Something unreadable registered in Blythe's eyes—desire, yes, but also restraint, as though she was weighing whether to lean in or pull away. Her lips hovered, the warmth of her breath still skimming Allegra's skin.

"You…" Blythe's voice caught for the first time, softer now. She pressed a kiss to Allegra's jaw, then lingered there, her pulse betraying her. "You make it very hard to think straight."

Allegra's grin faltered, her curiosity sharpening. "Then don't think."

Blythe smiled, but it didn't quite reach her eyes. She trailed her thumb along Allegra's cheek, memorising, holding on as if she were afraid to let herself fall too far. "It's not that simple."

Allegra tilted her head, still playful but gentler now. "It feels pretty simple from where I'm lying."

Blythe kissed her again—slower this time, almost reverent—before breaking away just enough to whisper, "You don't know how much I want this. But *wanting* and *should* are two different things."

"Blythe?" Allegra pushed up on her elbows, brow furrowed. "What's wrong?"

Blythe shook her head, reaching for her discarded shirt, buying herself a moment as she slipped her arms into the sleeves. "Nothing's wrong. I just..." Her voice softened. "We shouldn't. Not like this. Not now."

The sharp turn left Allegra blinking, her pulse still racing. "Wait—what? I thought—" She gestured between them, at the heat that had just filled the room. "I thought we were on the same page."

"We are," Blythe said quickly, then hesitated, her gaze dropping. "At least, I want to be. But I can't...rush into this."

Allegra sat up fully, confusion etched across her features. "Rush? Blythe, it's just sex."

Blythe forced a small smile, though it didn't hide the tension in her shoulders. "I know. And that's why I have to stop. Please...don't take it the wrong way."

But Allegra already felt the distance settling between them, the sting of rejection prickling under her skin.

Allegra watched in silence as Blythe reached for her discarded trousers, sliding them back on. The sound of fabric moving against warm flesh made Allegra suddenly aware of her own bare skin, exposed and unguarded. Heat pricked her cheeks, not from desire now, but from vulnerability.

She pushed herself upright, testing her weight on her injured knee. It wobbled, buckled, and she nearly lost her balance. Blythe's hand shot out instinctively, steadying her.

"I'm not an invalid," Allegra snapped, jerking away. The words came out sharper than she intended, more scolding than defiant, but the confusion mixed with the hurt was too much right now.

Blythe stood back, trousers on but undone, the same as her shirt. "I'm sorry if I've confused you."

"I guess that makes two of us."

Twenty-Four

The door slammed behind Allegra.

From the lounge, Daisy called out, "Sammy-Jo, if that's you, go back out and come back in like a normal person."

Allegra exhaled hard, forcing herself down the hall and into the lounge with a smile that didn't quite reach her eyes.

"Sorry, that was me."

Daisy's gaze flicked to the crutches. "You're allowed to bang the door."

Allegra dropped into the armchair with a huff. "For once, I can't blame these for putting me in a mood."

"Oh?" Daisy tilted her head. "Bad news from the physio?"

Allegra shook her head. "No, nothing like that. I just..." She flopped back in the chair and let out a growl. "I went on a date with Blythe again. She was at the ground today, and afterwards we had this spontaneous lunch, and then she invited me back to hers, and we..." Her cheeks burned.

"You were..." Daisy waggled her eyebrows.

"Yes," Allegra admitted with a laugh. "We were...and then suddenly we *weren't*. And I've no idea why, because she does not seem like the type of woman who doesn't do exactly what she wants."

Daisy smirked. "So, what, did you bore her? Forget your best moves?"

Allegra rolled her eyes. "Thanks for the support."

"I'm serious!" Daisy laughed, throwing up her hands. "What, did you start talking about tactics mid-snog?"

"Ha ha," Allegra said flatly, though the corner of her mouth tugged upwards.

Daisy's grin softened. "Okay, okay. But seriously—why's it bothering you this much?"

"Because…" Allegra glanced up at the ceiling. "I haven't had sex since John left. Haven't wanted to—with anyone—since he left. And now I meet this woman…older, someone I'd never usually date, and she…gets under my skin. Makes me want to do things I wouldn't have done before."

Daisy arched a brow. "What kind of things?"

Allegra felt heat rise to her cheeks as she considered the question. *'You'll beg,'* she heard in her mind again. "Nothing pervy…just…there's more to her than just letting her get me off." She thumped the arm of the chair. "But I really did want to get off."

Daisy laughed. "I mean…yeah, that's frustrating."

Allegra huffed. "It's maddening…because I want her, but she's…different. Makes me think, makes me wait. And I *hate* waiting."

Daisy tilted her head, smirking knowingly. "Sounds like you've met someone who doesn't just satisfy the body, huh?"

Allegra groaned softly, burying her face in her hands. "Exactly. She's careful…slow. Drives me insane. And I can't stop thinking about her."

Daisy laughed softly. "So you're frustrated because she won't just dive in?"

Allegra peeked through her fingers. "Yes! It's like…she's in control, and I like that, but I also hate it. I just want to…go."

Daisy shook her head with a grin. "Ah, so she's making you work for it."

Allegra let out a long sigh. "I hate that I want it. I hate that I like it. And I hate that I don't know if she'll stay."

"Playing a game?"

Allegra paused, thinking, then added quietly, "I don't think she's playing games. There's something more there that she's not sharing yet. Something that will make it all make sense and make me like her even more...and then what? I'm all in again with someone who will put their career first and leave me."

Daisy tilted her head. "I thought it was you putting your career first that made you break up with John?"

"It was," Allegra admitted, her voice low, "but I thought he'd at least fight to make it work."

The front door banged again, this time followed by a familiar sing-song call.

"I'm hoooome!"

Daisy and Allegra exchanged a look before Sammy-Jo burst into the lounge, dropping her gym bag with a thud.

"God, I am knackered," she announced, flopping down onto the sofa like she was claiming it for herself. She stretched out and wiggled her toes with a grin. "But! I brought you a present."

Daisy arched an eyebrow. "A present?"

Sammy-Jo rummaged in her shopping bag and, with a flourish, produced a sleek little package with the logo from Come Again stamped on the front. She tossed it across the room to Daisy, who caught it with wide eyes.

"You didn't." Daisy laughed, holding it up.

"Oh, I very much did," Sammy-Jo said, smug. "Figured training was hard enough—I deserved a treat. And you deserve one too."

Allegra groaned, dragging her hands down her face. "Seriously? Could your timing be any worse?"

Sammy-Jo blinked, finally registering the tension in the room. "What? I thought I was improving the vibe!"

Daisy bit her lip to hold back a grin, the amusement dancing in her eyes. "You've definitely...changed it."

Twenty-Five

Can we talk?

That was what the text had said. Allegra stared at it, tossed her phone onto the bed, then immediately reached for it again. She read it a second time, then a third time, chewing at her lip. Her thumbs hovered over the screen before she finally typed:

Allegra: I'm annoyed with you.

The message sent, she watched as the blue ticks appeared, her chest tightening when *Blythe is typing...* flashed into view.

Allegra put the phone down and glanced at herself. She was already in her pyjamas, stretched out on top of the bed, keeping to her room while Sammy-Jo and Daisy got freaky in the other.

Allegra: I'm already in my pyjamas.

The *Blythe is typing...* dots popped up immediately. Allegra liked that—no games, no pretending to be busy. Blythe wanted to communicate, straight and clear.

Blythe: I could come over. You don't need to get dressed. That isn't a come-on, by the way. I just mean I'm willing to put myself out, and you don't have to.

Allegra: Trust me, after this afternoon, that wouldn't have been an option.

The ticks turned blue, but no reply. Allegra stared at the screen, wincing when *online* flipped to *last seen 20:22*. Then—back to *online*. The dots appeared.

Blythe: I'm not going to play games with you, Allegra. I'd like to meet and talk about this afternoon. If you're happy to do that, I'll make myself available. If not, we can leave things as they are. Whatever works for you.

Allegra pursed her lips, reading it twice before typing back.

Allegra: Is that you giving me an ultimatum?

The dots appeared almost immediately.

Blythe: Not an ultimatum. Just honesty. I want to see you, Allegra. But I won't push if you don't want that.

Allegra: I'm at a friend's. You'll have to be quiet.

She hit send, hesitated, then followed up with the address.

Blythe: Twenty minutes.

With her dressing gown pulled tight around her, Allegra made her way down the hall towards the stairs, rolling her eyes at the muffled giggles spilling from Sammy-Jo and Daisy's room.

She used to fly down these steps. Now it was one at a time—crutches down, hop, crutches down, hop—her breath catching with the effort. Muscles she never noticed before burned every time she had to move.

The doorbell rang just as she reached the bottom. She heard movement upstairs.

"I'll get it!" she called, louder than she meant to.

Allegra paused on the bottom step, her hands gripped tightly on the crutch handles. The nerves hit her first—sharp, fluttering—but excitement curled right behind them, stubborn and insistent. For all the confusion of the afternoon, Blythe hadn't bolted. She was here. That meant something.

Crutches forwards, hop. Crutches forwards, hop. The short stretch of hallway to the door suddenly felt longer than ever. She leant against the wall, freeing one hand from a crutch to twist the handle.

The porch light spilled a warm yellow across the doorway, catching the few silver streaks in Blythe's hair, making them glitter faintly in the darkness.

"Hi," Blythe said, her smile hopeful.

"Hey," Allegra replied, her chest tightening as butterflies danced through her stomach. "Come in."

Allegra stepped back, making space for Blythe to pass.

"Are you always in bed this early?" Blythe asked, a teasing lilt in her voice.

Allegra closed the door behind her, a small smirk tugging at her lips. "Only when the need arises to deal with situations that didn't get handled earlier."

"Touché," Blythe said, shrugging. Her gaze lingered just a fraction too long up the stairs, where giggling leaked from behind a closed door.

"In there," Allegra said, lifting a crutch and pointing it towards the door at the end of the hall. "Do you want tea?"

"I'd prefer something stronger," Blythe admitted, and when Allegra gave her a blank look, she added with a laugh, "But tea will be lovely, thank you."

"I'd have preferred an orgasm earlier..." Allegra muttered as she moved past Blythe towards the kitchen.

"Is that really all you want? Sex?" Blythe's voice followed, quieter, but edged.

Allegra turned, surprised to catch the flicker of hurt in her face.

"Because if that's all it is, then I can just leave now and save us both the trouble."

"I'm still pissed off with you," Allegra shot back, planting the crutches with a little too much force. "So until I'm not, you're getting snarky Allegra. Alright?"

Blythe studied her for a beat, then nodded slowly. "Okay. I guess I can handle that."

Allegra exhaled. "Good. Sit down. I'll get us tea."

Blythe's eyes glanced towards the crutches. "Why don't you tell me where everything is, and I'll make it…carry it through?"

"Because that would require me to admit I might need you for something…and I don't." Her words were as firm as her stare.

"Okay." Blythe raised a hand in surrender and stepped back. She turned into the lounge, taking it all in. Small, cosy, homely, with a couch long enough for three and an armchair.

Unbuttoning her suit jacket, she eased herself into the chair, moving slowly, confidently, relaxing against the soft cushion. Her gaze lifted to Allegra, who was watching her like a hawk. "Let me know if I can do anything to be of help," she said, the hint of amusement in her voice belying the intensity of her presence.

Allegra leant against the counter, using one crutch, balancing herself as she tried to reach for the kettle and mugs. Her movements were careful and deliberate, every shift of weight measured.

Blythe stood back up and waited just inside the lounge, watching quietly. Her hands were casually folded, ready to step in if needed, but she didn't move. She let Allegra have her space, giving her the chance to manage on her own.

"Milk? No sugar," Allegra muttered aloud, realising she couldn't reach the milk and tea without awkward stretching. She grimaced, teetering slightly on her crutch.

Blythe stepped closer, offering her hand. "Here," she said gently, "I've got this. Don't risk a fall."

Allegra hesitated, pride warring with practicality. "I can manage," she said, her voice firm. But the next moment, a precarious lurch made her pause. With a small sigh, she nodded. "Fine. You can help."

Blythe moved smoothly, retrieving the milk and setting it within easy reach. She motioned for Allegra to steady herself against the counter while she poured the water into the mugs and stirred the bags. Her movements were efficient, but there was a quiet intimacy in the care she took, as though she'd done this a hundred times before, in a dozen kitchens not her own.

Allegra picked up the milk and tipped just enough into each cup. When Blythe reached to take it from her, their fingers brushed—warm, fleeting, electric. Their eyes caught, held, neither woman looking away.

"Thanks," Allegra said softly.

"No problem." Blythe's voice was calm, restrained, but there was an edge to it—something that suggested, *'I'll handle this for you, if you'll only let me.'* She twisted the cap back onto the carton and slipped it into the fridge with neat precision before turning, both mugs in hand.

"Shall we?" she asked, tilting her head towards the lounge.

Allegra said nothing more, just turned and hopped back into the lounge. But in her head, the thoughts circled like a crowd on match day, chanting louder with every step. For all her stubbornness, Allegra couldn't deny it—she liked Blythe Daniels.

TWENTY-SIX

Blythe waited while Allegra settled onto the couch, her bad leg stretched out over a cushion propped beneath her knee. She slid a coaster closer before setting Allegra's mug within reach, then returned to the armchair.

They studied each other across the small space, Blythe peering over the rim of her mug as she blew across the hot liquid. She took a cautious sip, winced when it scalded her lip, and set it down to cool.

"Thank you for seeing me," she said at last.

"Well, you did ask so nicely."

Blythe let the silence expand, giving Allegra time to soften, to sink into the cushions. When her shoulders finally dropped, Blythe exhaled too.

"I had a lot of…adrenaline earlier. My meeting went well, and I suppose I was just…happy." She gave a small shrug.

"Okay," Allegra said, careful and non-committal.

"And then seeing you, when I wasn't expecting it—it felt like a moment, you know?" Blythe smiled faintly, raking her fingers through her hair to ruffle it back into place. "Lunch was lovely. And in that moment, I convinced myself I was ready. That I was a grown-up who didn't need a Venn diagram to figure out whether I was allowed to enjoy being intimate with a beautiful woman who clearly wanted to get naked with me."

Allegra remained silent.

"The thing is, that's not me, not really," Blythe continued. "There's a part of me that would like to be more... free, unattached, but I can't do it. I need an emotional connection, and when I feel that, then I want to act on it—which is what happened earlier."

Allegra raised her mug and took a sip, her gaze unwavering, but she stayed silent.

Blythe smiled, acknowledging the space to express her thoughts without interruption.

Allegra's silence wasn't empty; it was charged, threaded with curiosity and something heavier Blythe couldn't quite name. The way Allegra's eyes lingered, steady and unreadable, made her want to keep talking, even if every word felt like peeling back another layer she wasn't used to exposing.

"I don't want to play games," Blythe added, softer now, as though confessing a truth meant only for this room, only for this woman. "I've done the casual thing. I even convinced myself I liked it...for a while. But the truth is, I can't switch off what I feel. I don't want to."

Allegra lowered her mug, resting it on her thigh, fingers drumming lightly against the ceramic. Still silent. Still watching.

The smile wavered on Blythe's lips, but she held Allegra's gaze all the same. "You don't have to say anything. I just wanted you to know where I stand. Where I...am."

Allegra set the mug down on the table, ran her tongue over her lips, and for the first time, looked away from Blythe, gathering her own thoughts.

"I'm not dissimilar, not really, but I suppose I find it easier to remain detached," Allegra admitted. "I've fought my entire life to be where I am, playing for a team in the WSL—a high-profile club. I'm at the peak of my career." She swallowed, glanced at Blythe, and found her focused on every word. "I've maybe five years left before I have to re-evaluate what my life will become. I'm not giving this up because someone else's career meant more to them."

Blythe frowned, as though a question had formed on her lips.

"Go on." Allegra offered the space.

"It's just… I wonder where this idea comes from—that if we were to keep seeing each other, I'd be trying to drag you away like some kind of trophy wife. I get that your career is important. If there's anything I understand, it's women in a man's world."

Allegra nodded.

"We've only just met," Blythe said. "And yes, I feel a connection with you. I like you, I'm attracted to you, and I'd like to get to know you more…"

"Wait—so if you feel a connection, what's the problem?"

"My being here is…a punishment," Blythe admitted. Her voice thinned slightly. "I was involved with someone—someone I thought felt the connection too—but for her it was just sex. I'd fallen in love." She gave a small, helpless shrug. "So, rather than face that, she had me moved to Woodington to oversee—" Blythe cut herself short, shaking her head.

"She sounds like a dream," Allegra said, the faintest edge of sarcasm in her voice.

"I'm over her," Blythe replied with a wry smile. "But it wasn't easy…working alongside her every day, pretending I was fine. And I won't lie, I was angry at being pushed out here, when my home is in London." She hesitated, her gaze lingering on Allegra now. "But I can see Woodington has its charms."

"My last relationship was with a man," Allegra said, the words sharper than she intended, fringed with defensiveness.

"Is that meant to deter my interest?"

"Does it?"

Blythe shook her head slowly as she considered the question. "No. Unless you're still—"

"I'm not. It's over. He's in Germany." As Allegra said it, she saw the flicker of realisation cross Blythe's face.

"He wanted you to go with him?"

Allegra shook her head at the situation, a small, bitter smile on her lips. "Yes...but I never considered going with him. I just thought... I thought he'd fight harder to make it work. But he didn't. I stayed, because this—my career, my life—it's mine. Still, it stung." She glanced down at her mug and picked it back up, her fingers tightening around it. "I guess I expected more."

Twenty-Seven

The noise of someone flying down the stairs made them both jump slightly. The lounge door swung open, and in stepped Sammy-Jo, her trademark dark curls hanging loose.

"Oh, uh…" She paused, looking from Blythe to Allegra, then around at the empty kitchen, before glancing back at Allegra. "Just needed…" She thumbed over her shoulder and backed towards the kitchen. "Water."

Allegra arched a brow. "Hurry up then."

Sammy-Jo hesitated for a moment, as if weighing her options, then made a decision. "Hi, I'm SJ," she said, stepping forwards with her hand held out.

Blythe rose to meet her, taking the handshake. "Blythe."

SJ let go of Blythe's hand and gave a quick, assessing glance as the woman took her seat again. "Nice to actually meet you." She started to chuckle, then caught Allegra's narrowed eyes glaring at her. "I *do* live here," she said, backing into the kitchen. Once out of Blythe's view, she wrapped her arms around herself and mimicked a French kiss.

Allegra gave her the finger, then noticed Blythe smirking at them both.

"She's a child," Allegra muttered, as though that explained her own childish reaction.

Sammy-Jo emerged from the kitchen carrying two glasses and nodded at Blythe. "Nice to meet you. Feel free to pop round anytime—I know Leggy would love the company."

"Sammy-Jo," Allegra said with a firmness that clearly hit home. SJ stopped instantly, toed the door open, and escaped.

"She seems fun," Blythe said.

"We're the same age, me and SJ," Allegra added, as though that explained something Blythe should probably ask.

"Okay."

"You're like a proper grown-up, and I'm... That's my best friend, and her immaturity makes me laugh."

"Okay," Blythe said again, this time the corners of her mouth curling. "Am I supposed to make some declaration about age gaps?"

"No, I'm just saying...she's part of the package."

"Of dating you?"

Allegra nodded slowly, feeling a flicker of self-consciousness. Saying it out loud made it feel...real. Vulnerable. She wasn't just talking about her best friend—she was opening a window into her life, her world, and hoping Blythe would understand.

"I can be childish," Blythe said.

Allegra laughed. "No way...never."

"You don't believe me, huh? Okay..." Blythe grinned. "Maybe not childish, but I can be fun. I'm not some stuffy suit who only thinks about work."

"Sounds like you want to prove something—to me... or to yourself?"

"Maybe both." Blythe held her gaze. "I'd like the opportunity to get to know you better and see where we want to take things."

"I'm open to doing that."

Blythe grinned. "Good, that's—"

"I also want kissing," Allegra interrupted, a hint of boldness in her voice.

"Kissing?" Blythe repeated slowly, rising from her chair and crossing the room. She dropped down onto her haunches, cupping Allegra's cheek. "I can do kissing..." she murmured, leaning in.

Allegra's heart skipped. She felt the warmth of Blythe's hand on her cheek, the weight of her gaze, and the slow, deliberate way she leant closer. Her breath hitched, caught somewhere between anticipation and nerves.

"I—" Allegra started, then let the word fall away. There was no need to speak. The moment said everything.

When Blythe's lips met hers, the sensation was soft at first, a little hesitant, gentle, like a question. Allegra's fingers found their way to Blythe's shoulders, gripping lightly as a shiver ran through her. She closed her eyes, letting herself sink into it all—into the closeness, the warmth, the certainty of the kiss.

It deepened, just enough to make her pulse race, but not so fast as to overwhelm. Every careful movement, every pause, made Allegra's chest tighten in a delicious, unfamiliar way. She met every motion, mirroring Blythe, making sure Blythe understood her need.

Pulling back slightly, Blythe rested her forehead against Allegra's. "You weren't kidding about wanting kissing," she murmured, a teasing smile in her voice.

Allegra swallowed, cheeks warm. "I don't joke about serious matters." She smiled, reaching for Blythe and pulling her back in for more.

The second kiss was more urgent, still deliberate, each movement more confident. Allegra felt herself melt into it further, with the steady pressure of Blythe's hands grounding her. For a moment, the rest of the world fell away—there was only the two of them, the quiet hum of the flat around them, and the shared rhythm of breath and heartbeat.

Blythe pulled back slightly, her thumb brushing across Allegra's cheek, her eyes soft and amused.

"I should go," Blythe said, her voice low, almost reluctant. "I've got an early start tomorrow, and I don't want to overstay my welcome."

Allegra nodded, still catching her breath, her fingers brushing against Blythe's hand. "Right. Yeah...I understand."

Blythe smiled, leaning in for a final, lingering brush of lips to cheek. "We'll pick this up soon." A promise in her tone.

Allegra watched her go, cheeks warm, pulse still racing, already counting the moments until she'd see Blythe Daniels again.

Twenty-Eight

Daisy spooned another mouthful of cornflakes into her mouth, her suit jacket slung carelessly over the back of the chair. She glanced up as Allegra shuffled in, still in her pyjamas, hair mussed from sleep.

"Morning," Daisy said brightly. "There's tea in the pot. Want me to pour you some?"

Allegra yawned, waving her off. "No, I'm fine. Thanks, though." Her eyes swept the kitchen. "Where's SJ?"

"Still sleeping."

Allegra smirked. "Wore her out, huh?"

Daisy set her spoon into the empty bowl and leant back in her chair. "Just keeping her stamina up for the important games." She added a cheeky wink.

"Speaking of which, are you going to Everton this weekend?"

"Yeah." Daisy nodded. "Thinking I'll drive up Saturday, grab a cheap hotel, then Sammy-Jo can ride back with me after the game."

"Cool."

"Did you want to go?"

Allegra shrugged. "I can take the coach."

Daisy studied her. "But you don't want to?"

Allegra's shoulders slumped. "No. It'll be horrible… getting there and not being able to play."

"You could always cheer your colleagues on."

"Maybe."

Carrying her bowl to the sink, Daisy said over her shoulder, "Or you could come with me."

Allegra's face brightened. "Thanks, Dais."

"You two are such babies, you know that?" Daisy chuckled, slinging her bag over her shoulder. "Right, I'm off. Try not to get into trouble."

"Have a good day," Allegra called after her, then grinned to herself and shouted down the hall, "I'll organise road trip snacks!"

She hopped into the kitchen and pulled the fridge door open, ruminating over something Daisy had said: *"You two are such babies."*

It was how she felt, wasn't it—immature?

A woman like Blythe Daniels would surely get fed up with her, wouldn't she?

The creak of the stairs broke through her thoughts. Sammy-Jo padded down, hair a mess, wrapped in her dressing gown and rubbing her stomach like a kid fresh out of bed. She yawned loudly, then let out a burp that echoed in the quiet kitchen. Normally it would've had them both in stitches.

This time, Allegra fixed her with a look. "Grow up, SJ."

Sammy-Jo blinked, caught off guard. "Alright, someone got out of bed on the wrong side."

"No. I just think...we're almost thirty. Shouldn't we have grown out of that by now?" She tried to turn, holding the carton of orange juice in the crook of her arm.

"Who cares? We're us. We laugh at stupid stuff." Sammy-Jo reached for the carton, lifting it from Allegra's grasp and plonking it onto the small table.

"Can you get me a glass?" Allegra asked.

Sammy-Jo stared. "Who are you?"

Allegra rolled her eyes and sat down.

"No, seriously. Where's Leggy gone? The woman who laughs at burps and drinks straight from the carton?"

"Maybe...she's growing up."

Sammy-Jo found a glass and handed it over. "Why?"

"What do you mean, why? Because I'm almost thirty and—"

"And you want to impress this Blythe woman," Sammy-Jo finished, arching a brow.

"No," Allegra said too quickly. "Not at all... She's already impressed, actually."

"Uh-huhhhh." Sammy-Jo narrowed her gaze. "If you have to change who you are to fit with people, they're not your people."

"I'm not doing that. I just think there are things we do that maybe...might be...probably are...childish."

Sammy-Jo crossed the small room and perched on the edge of the table, one knee tucked up, foot resting on the chair, the other dangling. "Childish, huh? So burping like a champ and stealing the last bit of chocolate isn't part of the plan anymore?"

Allegra huffed, a reluctant smile tugging at her lips. "It's not exactly...classy."

"Classy? You don't think you're classy already?" Sammy-Jo asked, tapping the glass she'd handed over. "You can like Blythe, want to impress her, and still be the same Leggy who makes me laugh until I snort."

Allegra looked down at the glass, tracing a finger along the rim. "I know, I just... Someone like her...she's a grown-up, you know?"

Sammy-Jo leant closer, her voice softening. "Leggy, anyone worth it isn't going to want perfect. They'll want you—the real you. All the messy, loud, burpy bits included."

Allegra let out a small laugh, shaking her head. "I know. You're right... Maybe she's just not for me."

"Or maybe she is. Maybe she doesn't care, and this is a *you* problem."

Allegra feigned shock. "Me? That can't possibly be true."

Sammy-Jo laughed, ruffling Allegra's hair before hopping down. "There we go—the old Leggy has returned."

Twenty-Nine

Ros poked her head around the door the moment Blythe had stepped into her office.

"Don't forget—you've got that luncheon this afternoon with the local Gay Women's Business Group."

"Yes, it's in the diary," Blythe replied.

"Looks like fun. And you'll get to schmooze Gabby Dean."

"I'm aware of that."

Ros grinned. "Great. So…who's your guest?"

Blythe turned abruptly. "What?"

"Your guest," Ros said more quietly as she stepped fully into the room. "The invitation says that invitees are encouraged to bring someone—either a partner or a friend. I assumed you had that covered. Do you need me to rustle someone up—"

"No, it's fine," Blythe interrupted. "I don't need a date with someone I've never met before. I'm sure there will be others without a guest."

Ros nodded, then smiled as an idea hit her. "What about Allegra Mann? You have her number, don't you? I bet she'd say yes to a free posh meal and an opportunity to dress up."

She'd been about to rebuke the suggestion, but actually…it was the perfect opportunity, wasn't it? It had already been a week since they'd seen each other. A pleasant afternoon with like-minded women, a good meal, and Allegra Mann on her arm? There were worse things, weren't there?

"I'll think of something," she said, smiling at Ros. "Any chance of a coffee? The queue this morning at the shop was ridiculous."

"Of course, coming right up." Ros grinned before exiting and closing the door behind her.

Blythe picked up her phone from the desk and scrolled for Allegra's number.

The phone in Allegra's pocket beeped just as SJ was finishing making their tea. She took one look at Allegra's face and laughed. "That's her, isn't it?" She paused, a sudden thought striking her. "Or have you got another one on the hook making you smile like that?"

"Rude," Allegra grinned, "and yes, it *is* Blythe, if you must know."

"Alright." SJ set the mugs down on the table. "So, what's she after? As if I couldn't guess... Does it involve your underwear and diving deep?"

"Stop it." Allegra laughed.

"Come on, what does it say? Is it filth?"

Allegra looked at her pointedly. "She's asked if I'm free this afternoon to go to lunch with her again."

"Oh, well, that is nice."

"Yes." Allegra nodded, re-reading the text before tapping out a response.

"You don't look too sure," SJ observed.

Allegra frowned and realised she'd told Daisy and forgotten to update SJ on her love life's dramas. "We had lunch last week and then..." She looked up at SJ, grimacing. "We went back to hers and—nothing happened. I mean, we kissed, and I was in my underwear but—"

Sammy-Jo raised both eyebrows. "And you call that 'nothing happened'?"

"What I mean is…I was expecting it to happen, but then…I dunno. Like I said, she's a grown-up."

"So, what was she round here that night for?"

"To explain why she wasn't letting me throw myself at her."

"Gosh, she sounds proper dull."

Allegra made a face. "She is anything but dull. She's hot, kisses like a dream…and no stubble rash."

"Eww." SJ swigged some tea to wash that thought away. "So…are you going to go?"

"Probably. Just waiting for her to give me more details."

"Like…should you wear your good undies?"

"Shut up." Allegra laughed, raising her crutch to gently poke SJ. "I need to know what to wear. I mean, are we just popping into town, or…Joie again?"

The phone beeped.

"Bloody hell," Allegra muttered.

"What?"

"Bloxley Manor… I'll have to go home and dig out a dress or something."

"That is posh. Do you even own anything that posh?"

"I told you—she's a grown-up. If this is her usual lunch date offering, I can't keep up with that."

"Yes, you can. You're no slouch. Attractive, a top athlete, and you can string a sentence together." SJ smirked. "You're the perfect arm candy for a rich older woman."

Allegra flushed, a mix of embarrassment and irritation rising in her chest. "Arm candy? Really, SJ?" she said, half laughing, half scowling. "I'm not just some accessory."

She hated admitting it, but the thought of Blythe showing her off made a flicker of heat rush through her. Not just for the attention—though that was tempting enough—but for the idea that Blythe Daniels might *want* to show her off.

"It's a posh lunch. How often do you get invited to these?" SJ cut into her thoughts. "At least enjoy the food while you're not training."

"Can you drop me at my place so I can find an outfit?"

SJ checked her watch. She had to be at training in an hour anyway. "Sure. You should wear that suit—the fancy black one. And a tie. You femmes always look so hot when you go a touch masc."

Thirty

Blythe leant back in her chair, sifting through a stack of reports, her eyes scanning figures and notes with the practised efficiency that had earned her the reputation she now carried. The quiet of the office was interrupted by the telecom buzzing on her desk.

"Ms Daniels, Amanda Sanchez is on the line," her secretary said, her tone almost conspiratorial.

Blythe paused, a flicker of something she hadn't felt in months—a mix of irritation and…anticipation passing through her. Amanda was not who she wanted to deal with right now.

She picked up the receiver, voice even but edged with cool curiosity. "Amanda."

"Blythe," Amanda purred, and just like that, the months of restrained longing and professional caution resurfaced. Her voice was velvety, teasing, dangerous. Blythe could remember the way Amanda had used those tones in bed—all seduction, like a spell was cast with every word.

"I've been meaning to touch base," Amanda said, though Blythe could hear the unspoken layers behind the words, the way she always did when Amanda wanted something.

Blythe adjusted her posture, steeling herself. "I'm listening."

"The thing is…I'm missing you."

Blythe felt a flash of anger rise, hot and sharp, but she held it down, a master of restraint now. Years of practice had taught her exactly how to keep her emotions in check—especially around Amanda Sanchez.

"I have no doubt of that," she said, her voice steady, confident, calm.

They'd been good together—so good that Blythe had briefly entertained the thought of taking things further, letting herself care more deeply, more permanently. But Amanda didn't play for keeps—not in bed, not in anything that mattered. Accepting that truth had nearly broken her, and Blythe had promised herself she wouldn't allow it to happen again.

"I can't stop thinking about it," Amanda continued, her tone low and deliberate, each word dripping with that effortless, intoxicating charm Blythe had once fallen for so easily. "About us. About what we had."

Blythe gritted her teeth just slightly, forcing herself to keep her posture rigid, her voice steady. "Amanda...you know how this works. You don't do...permanence."

Amanda laughed softly, a sound that had always made Blythe's pulse quicken, like a warning she used to ignore at her own peril. "I never promised permanence. Just...moments worth remembering."

The words brushed against something deep inside Blythe—a memory of heat, laughter, reckless abandon. She could feel the old pull, that familiar ache of wanting what she knew she shouldn't, yet she held the line, her restraint a thin but unbreakable barrier.

"I'm not that person anymore," Blythe said, her voice firmer now, though the slight catch betrayed her. "I've moved on...in my own way."

Amanda's pause was almost imperceptible, but Blythe felt it; the subtle, electric tension of someone who knew exactly how much she could press without shattering the wall entirely.

Amanda's voice dropped a notch, slower, more deliberate. "Do you remember that night in my office?" she murmured, the words curling around Blythe like smoke. "The one where you... Well, let's just say you were very...persuasive."

Blythe's chest tightened, a heat she thought she'd buried, flaring unexpectedly. She had remembered that night—how easy it had been to lose herself in the intensity, and in the way Amanda had oscillated around Blythe until every hesitation vanished.

"I don't think I need reminding," Blythe said, voice measured, though a faint catch betrayed her. "Some memories…are better left…where they are."

Amanda chuckled softly. "Maybe," she said, "but some memories…are too good not to want to repeat."

Blythe leant back in her chair, letting the wall of professionalism and control surround her, but inside, her pulse betrayed her. That memory, that night—it was alive again, and Amanda knew exactly the right buttons to push.

Blythe opened her mouth to respond, to keep Amanda's teasing in check, when her phone beeped sharply on the desk. She glanced down. A message. From Allegra. She opened it instantly.

Her breath caught. The image preview alone made her pause: Allegra—impossibly fit, half dressed, the taut lines of her body on full display. She wore a bra and smart trousers, one hand gripping a tie, a single question mark hovering in the message.

Blythe felt a jolt—part surprise, part something darker, more insistent. The image wasn't just tantalising, it was a reminder of possibility. Of a future she might allow herself to explore. A connection that felt unforced and real. A spark of desire flared, sharp and immediate, contrasting with Amanda's calculated seduction.

She stared at the screen, pulse quickening, mind racing. Allegra was young, bold, dangerous in a wholly different way. A way that didn't come with games or emotional minefields—just heat, honesty, and potential.

Amanda's teasing voice faded to a distant hum in Blythe's ears. Her fingers hovered over the phone, torn between the memory of Amanda and the alluring promise of Allegra.

"So…what do you think? Shall I head down?" Amanda's voice came back, sharper this time.

"I'm afraid I'm going to be busy," Blythe said evenly. "After all, I was sent here so you could avoid me."

"Blythe, don't be like that." Amanda sighed, the familiar lilt in her tone pulling at something deep inside. "We had fun—that was all it ever was. But it could be again. I could bring you back...if that's what you want."

Back to London. The offer was tempting—of course it was. Her life, her work, her world, all centred there. But her eyes flicked to her phone again. Allegra.

"I have to go," Blythe said finally, firm and controlled. "I'm running late for a lunch meeting." She set the phone down. Amanda Sanchez could go whistle if she thought Blythe was still at her beck and call.

Blythe picked up her mobile again, the image filling the screen. Allegra stood with effortless poise, one hip tilted, shoulders relaxed but commanding, the faint curve of a smile tugging at her lips. Even in a simple bra and smart trousers, there was something magnetic in the way she held herself—a confidence that seemed to dare Blythe to look away, a hint of mischief that promised unpredictability.

She couldn't quite describe the question implied in the single question mark, but the answer was already forming in her mind. A slow, deliberate smile curved her lips.

"I'm not sure what the question was," she murmured to herself, voice low and amused, "but the answer is definitely yes."

Her fingers hovered over the keyboard, typing and deleting, until finally she hit send. The thrill of anticipation surged, sharper and more intoxicating than any memory of Amanda could ever be.

Thirty-One

The new address had flummoxed her, but Blythe pulled up and waited outside the electric gates, just as she'd been asked. Looking through, she could see Range Rovers and a Porsche. The flats were luxurious, that was for sure.

Moments later, Allegra emerged, looking every bit as stunning as she'd hoped. Even on crutches, she radiated confidence and elegance—what anyone would call a million-dollar look.

Her long blonde hair was loose, falling effortlessly over her shoulders. The tailored suit cinched at the waist, flattering her figure without shouting for attention. And then there was the tie... Perfection. Even without the heels that would have completed the ensemble, likely abandoned because of the knee injury, Allegra looked commanding and alluring all at once.

Blythe opened the car door and stepped out to greet her. "You look unbelievable," she said, leaning in to brush a quick kiss across Allegra's cheek. When she pulled back, she allowed herself one lingering look, taking in every detail all over again.

"Well, Bloxley Manor is...Michelin-star, five-star, possibly the most impressive place to eat or stay in the area," Allegra said, a subtle mix of pride and challenge in her tone.

Blythe smiled at the effort. Was Allegra trying to impress everyone else, or just her? Either way, it was working. Allegra Mann *was* impressive.

"Let me get the door for you," Blythe offered, moving to open it fully, her gaze unwilling to leave Allegra for even a second.

Allegra manoeuvred carefully towards the car, crutches in hand. Blythe stepped close, offering a steadying touch as Allegra lowered herself onto the seat. The contact was brief, but it sent a tiny spark up Blythe's arm.

"All set?" Blythe asked, voice low, her eyes flicking over Allegra one last time before she pulled the door closed.

Allegra gave a small, appreciative smile. "All set," she confirmed, adjusting her crutches so they rested comfortably beside her.

Blythe settled into the driver's seat, glancing at Allegra as she buckled her seatbelt. "Have you been to Bloxley Manor before?" she asked, her tone casual, though she kept her eyes on Allegra's expression.

Allegra shook her head, a mix of excitement and nerves in her smile. "No, it's all new to me," she admitted. "It's…impressive. Exciting, but also a little intimidating, if I'm honest."

Blythe's smile softened. "I can imagine," she said. "It's not every day you find yourself going somewhere like that. But don't worry, you won't be alone. I'll make sure you're looked after."

Allegra's cheeks coloured faintly, a flicker of gratitude in her eyes. "Thanks. I appreciate that."

Blythe started the engine, letting the hum of the car fill the brief silence. She stole another glance at Allegra—confidence mingled with caution, vulnerability threaded with poise. The mix was magnetic.

"You ready for whatever this place has in store for us?" Blythe asked, a hint of amusement in her voice.

Allegra laughed softly, the sound carrying a little nervous energy. "No promises," she said, leaning back in her seat, though her eyes never left Blythe's.

Blythe gave her a small, conspiratorial smile. "This will be a first for me too. So…we'll be discovering it together."

Allegra turned to her, a playful glint in her eyes. "I like that."

Blythe's smile widened. "Me too."

Blythe pulled away from the kerb and headed onto the main road. She stole more quick glances at Allegra, though she tried to act casual. Each look was charged with something she couldn't quite hide—memories of the photo Allegra had sent earlier, the way it had made her pulse quicken, and the undeniable desire it had sparked.

Allegra caught her eye in the corner of her vision. "You keep looking at me like that…" she said softly, a teasing edge to her voice.

Blythe blinked, caught off guard. "Like…what?" she asked, trying to keep her voice steady.

Allegra's lips curved into a playful smile. "Like you're noticing…all of me," she said, nodding slightly towards her figure. "And maybe thinking I look…irresistible."

Blythe's breath hitched slightly. "Ah." She let a slow, deliberate smile spread across her face. "A little of both, perhaps. And I haven't seen you since last week."

The tension hung between them, crackling in the small space of the car. Each glance, each subtle smile, drew them closer before they'd even reached the manor.

"Is that a bad thing?" Blythe asked, her tone light, though her eyes flicked briefly towards Allegra.

"Depends… Am I going to be disappointed again later?"

The question landed with more weight than Allegra perhaps intended, but Blythe felt it all the same. Her thoughts flew back, unbidden, to Amanda's voice earlier and the way it had stirred something she didn't want to carry into this moment. Allegra's photo had ignited a sharper desire still, but Blythe knew one thing for certain—if she ever took Allegra to bed, it wouldn't be out of spite. Amanda had no place in that picture.

She drew in a quiet breath, letting a smile play across her lips. "I suppose that depends on your definition of disappointed," she said, her tone deliberately measured. "My plan is to have an enjoyable afternoon in a very expensive, very *bougie* place. And then…if I'm lucky, maybe I'll be invited in for coffee. From there…we'll see what happens."

Allegra arched a brow, lips curving into a teasing smile. "Coffee, huh? Sounds suspiciously like code for something else."

Blythe chuckled under her breath, keeping her eyes on the road. "Well, that depends on who's doing the translating."

Allegra laughed softly, but then the sound faded, her fingers absently tracing the seam of her trousers. "Just…don't make it sound better than it is," she said, quieter now, her playful edge giving way to something more vulnerable. "I don't want to be strung along."

Blythe glanced at her, the sincerity in Allegra's voice tugging at her chest. She tightened her grip on the wheel, forcing herself not to reach out when the urge to reassure was so strong. "I wouldn't do that to you," she said simply.

The air in the car thickened, charged but softer, the earlier teasing now underpinned by a note of trust—fragile, but real.

"Just… Let's always be honest, yes?"

Blythe nodded. "That's my philosophy."

Thirty-Two

Arriving at Bloxley Manor, they found the gravel drive lined with sleek cars, the grand entrance buzzing with chatter and movement. Inside, the foyer was crowded, the air warm with the hum of conversation and the faint clink of glasses. A sign on an easel directed guests towards the Women's Business Luncheon.

With a steadying hand at the small of Allegra's back, Blythe guided her in the direction of the arrow. Allegra felt the light pressure of her touch—steady, sure, intimate in a way that made her pulse flicker.

"I thought we were having lunch?" she asked, brow furrowing as she glanced at the sign again.

"We are," Blythe replied, a smile tugging at her lips as her eyes swept across the room.

Allegra followed her gaze, taking in the sea of women in tailored suits, crisp dresses, and polished heels. Realisation dawned, and she stopped short, turning to Blythe with narrowed eyes and a half-smile. "Oh. You didn't just invite me to lunch. You needed a date for an event."

Blythe's answering smile was calm, but there was a flash of something else there—challenge...maybe even admiration. "Is that such a terrible thing?" she asked smoothly.

Allegra huffed out a laugh, shaking her head, though she felt the knot of nerves twist tighter in her stomach. "Do I get hazard pay for being paraded around a room full of power women I've never met?"

Blythe's hand lingered lightly at her back, her smile softening. "You'll be just fine. Trust me."

Inside the dining room, Allegra froze for half a second. The space was vast and gleaming, the low hum of conversation underscored by bursts of laughter and the clink of glassware continued more loudly. Everywhere she looked, women carried themselves with practised poise—wearing sleek suits, elegant dresses, radiating confidence that filled the air as tangibly as the perfume.

It wasn't just Blythe she wanted to impress. This was a room full of older, successful, powerful women. Women who looked like they belonged at Blythe's side far more naturally than she did. She suddenly felt every inch of how much younger she was, not just in years, but experience.

Then recognition struck. Near the centre table sat her boss, Gabby Dean, speaking animatedly with Claudia Maddox. Allegra's stomach dropped.

Her eyes darted across the table. Nora Brady, her teammate, friend, and Gabby's wife, was chatting easily with Claudia's wife, Scarlett. Allegra had met Scarlett before, at bars, after matches, and at the odd event. Their presence steadied her nerves a little, but still, the weight of the room pressed in. Everywhere she looked, she saw confident, formidable, powerful women.

She tugged lightly at the sleeve of her suit, wishing it gave her the kind of authority the others carried so effortlessly.

"Are you alright?" Blythe leaned close, her voice low enough for only Allegra to hear.

"Yes." Allegra smiled nervously, though it didn't quite reach her eyes. "I just... I didn't expect this. I guess I feel a little out of my depth."

Blythe looked a little confused. "In what way?"

"In a 'these women are all so...adult' way."

"And...you're not?"

"I don't feel it, no… I don't really understand why you'd want to bring me to something like this when there are so many more qualified women here."

"More qualified?" Blythe chuckled. "I didn't realise I was auditioning people for the job…" She stared into Allegra's eyes. "You fascinate me."

"Really? Why?"

Blythe didn't look away. If anything, her gaze grew steadier, more intent, as though she wanted Allegra to really hear her. "Because you don't hide what you feel. Because you're not playing a part, even when you think you should be. You walk into a room like this, and you don't try to mask your nerves—and that's rare. Refreshing. Honest."

Allegra blinked, surprised by the warmth in Blythe's tone. She let out a shaky laugh, trying to cover how much the words hit her. "So…I'm fascinating because I'm bad at faking it?"

"Because you don't *need* to fake it," Blythe corrected softly. "And because I'm already more interested in what's going on behind those eyes than in a hundred polished conversations I could have in here."

Allegra felt her breath catch, her heart lurching in her chest. For a moment, the bustle of the room dimmed. She swallowed, trying to steady herself, but the nervous flutter in her stomach was changing shape—no longer just anxiety, but something warmer, deeper, threaded with desire.

"Come with me," Blythe said firmly. She instinctively reached out for Allegra's hand, then hesitated, remembering the crutches. "Please…just follow me."

They moved through the crowd, side by side, Blythe guiding her with a sure but unhurried pace. Away from the buzz of conversation, the air felt easier to breathe.

"Where are we going?" Allegra asked in a whisper.

"You'll see."

Reaching the door to the ladies', Blythe held it open as someone stepped out, offering a polite smile in return for the thanks. She kept it open for Allegra, her eyes lingering on her as she passed.

Inside, the space was hushed. Three cubicles stood empty, the faint hum of music drifting from a hidden speaker. The air carried a subtle scent of peaches.

Allegra tilted her head, brows knitting. "What are we doing?"

Blythe stepped behind her, gently turning her until they both faced the mirror. Sliding her arms around Allegra's waist, she leaned in close, her chin settling against the firm line of Allegra's shoulder.

Her voice was low, intimate. "What do you see?"

Allegra blinked at the reflection, momentarily thrown. "I see...us," she said slowly. "Two women staring at each other in the mirror." Her tone carried a trace of confusion, as if unsure what answer Blythe was searching for.

Blythe's eyes held hers in the glass. "And what do you see when you look at yourself?"

Allegra hesitated. The longer she met Blythe's gaze, the more the question pressed on her. "I don't know... I see someone who's immature. Inexperienced. Someone who doesn't have the skills or the style to be dating a woman like you." The admission slipped out in a rush, her voice softer than she meant it to be.

Blythe tightened her arms around Allegra's waist, leaning a little closer until her breath brushed Allegra's ear. "That's not what I see," she shared, her gaze never leaving the mirror. "I see a woman who's full of life. Eager. Curious. Honest. Fun. Someone who makes me feel more awake just by standing next to her."

Allegra's breath caught again. The reflection blurred for a moment as her eyes prickled, her defences faltering under the warmth of Blythe's words.

Slowly, Blythe loosened her hold, giving Allegra the space to move if she wanted to. Instead, Allegra turned in her arms, crutches shifting awkwardly against the tiled floor until she steadied herself. She lifted her chin, all nerves and wanting, eyes searching Blythe's face.

"Blythe..." she whispered, unsure if it was a question or a warning.

But Blythe didn't move away. Her hands hovered, then settled gently back at Allegra's waist, and Allegra leaned into her, closing the space between them. Their lips met softly at first, tentatively, as if testing the reality of the connection. Then Allegra deepened the kiss, her fingers curling in the fabric of Blythe's jacket, pulling her closer.

The world outside the bathroom dissolved—no voices, no chatter, no powerful women to impress—just them.

When they finally parted, their foreheads resting against each other, Allegra let out a shaky laugh, sounding breathless. "You really know how to catch a girl off guard." Eyes sparkling with mischief and desire.

Blythe's lips curved into a slow, satisfied smile. "That's part of the fun," she replied, brushing a strand of hair from Allegra's face. "And you... You make it hard for me to resist." She leant forwards again, pressing a tender kiss to Allegra's lips, soft and reassuring this time. "So, I'd really love to go and eat some fancy food and spend an hour or so with you. But if you don't feel up to it, we can head straight back to the car and go somewhere else."

"No..." Allegra flattened her palms against Blythe's lapels, steadying herself. "I want to... I want to grow."

"My darling, you are already more grown than you realise," Blythe said, her smile warm and steady. "I don't want you to change to fit in. Just be you, and let them change to fit *you* in."

Thirty-Three

Allegra drew in a quiet breath, letting her nerves settle as Blythe guided her through the bathroom door. The faint clatter of cutlery and the soft chatter of conversation washed over them as they stepped back into the room.

Blythe's hand rested lightly at the small of her back, grounding her with a warmth that made her shoulders feel a little less tense. Every so often, she'd catch Blythe looking at her, and it sent a thrill up Allegra's spine.

As they moved back through the crowd, familiar faces came into view again. Gabby Dean offered a polite nod, her presence commanding as always. Nora's smile was warm and reassuring, while Scarlett's glance held curiosity and quiet approval. Claudia Maddox's raised eyebrow and sly smirk gave Allegra a thrill.

The space was alive with movement and low laughter, polished voices carrying over the occasional scrape of heels on the marble floor. Allegra felt the weight of the room pressing in again, but Blythe's calm, sure presence beside her made it feel manageable, even exhilarating.

They found a spot near the buffet and Blythe leant close, her voice just above a murmur. "See? You belong here."

Allegra let herself grin, a little breathless, part disbelief, part delight. "Maybe…"

Blythe glanced over her shoulder. "I need to speak with Gabby at some point."

"I'll be fine. I'm friends with Nora. And Scarlett." Allegra tilted her chin towards them.

"And I work with Claudia, as you know," Blythe added.

Allegra nodded. "I mean, I assumed so when you were both at the club together."

"So, they're both married to younger women?"

Allegra's smile turned serious. "Do not even think about proposing. I'm bisexual, not a U-Haul lesbian."

Blythe laughed loudly, drawing a few curious looks from those nearby. She leant closer again, voice teasing, "But...you *are* marriage material."

"True. I *am* a total catch," Allegra countered, smirking.

Before she could respond further, a familiar perfume reached her, and she turned just in time to see Gabby Dean over Blythe's shoulder.

"I'd absolutely vouch for the ham. Divine," Gabby said, smiling. "Allegra, how is my star defender doing?"

"Hi, Gabby. I'm on the mend—back before you know it," Allegra replied. "Brace is coming off soon."

"That's what I like to hear." Gabby turned towards Blythe. "And you came together?"

"Yes, Allegra was gracious enough to be my date for the occasion," Blythe said smoothly. "It's quite the event, isn't it? Who knew so many gay women lived in the area, let alone were in business?"

Gabby spun around, smiling at the familiar faces. "Yes, it's taken a little while to grow, and obviously we include all the queer labels, which is why you'll find the odd husband lingering." She laughed, adding, "I've just been speaking with Claudia..." She turned back to Allegra. "You don't mind if I steal her away for a moment, do you, Leggy?"

"No, of course..." Allegra said with a warm smile.

"I'll be right back," Blythe reassured her.

"It's fine. Take your time. I'll go and annoy Nora," Allegra said with a grin, heading across the room.

Nora waved her over, and by the time Allegra reached them, Scarlett had already pulled out a chair.

"Well, what did you do to get yourself dragged here?" Nora teased.

"A lunch at Bloxley Manor, and you're complaining?" Allegra shot back with a laugh.

Scarlett stretched, a small yawn escaping. "There is that."

Nora grinned and nodded towards Blythe. "So...still seeing..."

"Blythe," Allegra answered quickly. "Though I don't know what we are yet. Dating feels...a little further down the line."

"Who's Blythe?" Scarlett asked.

Nora leaned in, pointing discreetly. "The woman talking to Gabby and Claudia."

"Oh. I met her last week." Scarlett's eyes widened slightly. "She's attractive."

"Well, duh," Allegra replied. Her gaze swept the room, found Blythe, then flicked back to Nora. "Can I ask you both something?"

"Absolutely," Scarlett said, shuffling closer.

"Spill it," Nora added.

Allegra hesitated, then blurted, "It's just... How did you feel about it? Dating someone older?"

Scarlett shrugged, matter-of-factly. "It was the norm for me. I prefer it."

Nora nodded. "I didn't think about it much. I wasn't looking for it, but when someone like Gabby comes along...who am I to say no?" She laughed.

"But..." Allegra trailed off.

Scarlett touched her arm gently. "What's really bothering you?"

Allegra followed their eyes towards the trio across the room—Blythe, Gabby, Claudia—elegant, composed, laughing together as though they belonged on some higher plane. "Look at them," she said softly.

"You don't think you fit with that?" Scarlett asked.

Allegra exhaled slowly. "I mean... Okay, without sounding big-headed, I know I'm attractive, I dress well... I can hold my own there. But sometimes...I just feel like such a child."

Scarlett tilted her head, studying Allegra with a faint smile. "You don't strike me as a child. You strike me as someone who knows what she wants."

Nora leant forwards, lowering her voice. "Besides, do you really think Gabby or Claudia were born poised? Please. You should've seen Gabby trying to flirt the first time we met—awkward as hell. We all grow into it."

Allegra managed a laugh, though it came out tight. "You're just saying that."

"No, I'm really not," Nora said firmly. "And Blythe? If she's with you, it's because she wants to be. Trust me, they're all past the point of caring about what anyone else thinks of them."

Scarlett squeezed Allegra's arm. "If anything, the fact you even care enough to ask these questions? That's the opposite of childish."

Allegra let their words settle, a little warmth blooming in her chest, even as doubt whispered at the edges. She glanced back towards the crowd, and her breath caught when she realised Blythe was no longer with Gabby and Claudia.

Nora gave a quick nod, alerting Allegra to the incoming presence.

"She's looking at you like you're the breath of air she needs," Scarlett whispered quickly. "Just enjoy it."

Allegra nodded before turning in her seat and finding Blythe standing beside her. "You're back."

"Did you think I'd leave you?" Blythe asked, a small teasing smile tugging at the corners of her mouth.

"No, I—I'm just…glad," Allegra admitted, heat creeping into her cheeks.

Without a thought, Blythe slid an arm around Allegra's waist, drawing her up until their bodies brushed. "You missed me?"

"Maybe…" Allegra replied, her tone coy, mischief sparking in her eyes, buoyed by a newfound confidence following Nora and Scarlett's pep talk. "Want to escort me to the bathroom again?"

Blythe caught the unspoken invitation beneath the words. "Of course. Wouldn't want to leave a lady in distress—not when she's waited so patiently."

"Oh, I can be as patient as you like..." Allegra leant in, lips curving into a genuine smile, "but be warned—I'm not short of other offers."

"Noted." Blythe's voice had dropped, soft and low.

They'd barely taken two steps towards the corridor when a voice cut across their path.

"I don't think we've met..."

An older woman, poised in a manner that spoke of generational wealth and confidence, stood blocking their way. Her dress was understated but immaculate, her jewellery catching the light with quiet authority. She extended a perfectly manicured hand towards Blythe. "Lorelai Standforth."

Blythe shifted smoothly into a charming facade, taking the offered hand. "Blythe Daniels. And this is Allegra Mann."

Lorelai's gaze flicked briefly to Allegra, her polite smile not quite reaching her eyes, before sliding back to Blythe as though Allegra was little more than an afterthought.

Allegra straightened on her crutches, heat prickling at the back of her neck. She'd half expected this—Blythe drawing the kind of attention that seemed reserved for women who looked like they belonged in this room. Women who carried the same polished power as Lorelai Standforth.

"You're new," Lorelai observed, her voice smooth, assessing. "I noticed you...talking with Gabriella and Claudia."

"Yes. We have some business to discuss, and Gabby was kind enough to invite me—us," Blythe corrected, tightening the arm around Allegra's waist with deliberate emphasis.

Lorelai's eyes dropped to the gesture. "And you, dear? Just tagging along with your...mother?"

Allegra stiffened, humiliation crashing hotly through her. Blythe felt it instantly, her own expression cooling.

"Actually," Blythe said, her tone velvety but edged, "Allegra is my date."

"Oh..." Lorelai's lips twisted into something that was almost a smile, mostly a sneer. "You're one of *those*."

Allegra's brows knit together. "One of what?" she demanded, irritation flaring sharper than her nerves.

Lorelai brushed a hand against Blythe's arm in a gesture far too familiar. "Don't worry, darling. We've all been there. New town, new faces…needing someone on our arm until we find our feet. There are cheaper options, however." She winked, letting her know she was one option.

Allegra's stomach lurched. "Is she calling me a hooker?" she whispered, her voice cracking with disbelief.

Blythe turned on Lorelai, her glare sharp enough to cut glass. "I wouldn't have thought anyone in this room would have the audacity to suggest such a thing."

Lorelai's face flushed, but she didn't retreat. Her eyes slid past Allegra, in an act that made it very clear how little Lorelai thought of her.

Heat rushed to Allegra's cheeks, burning with embarrassment. Her grip on the crutches tightened and her breath caught. The confidence she'd carried only moments before slipped like sand through her fingers. Around them, the chatter of conversation seemed louder, sharper, as though every woman in the room had overheard.

She shifted her weight, trying to stand taller, but the ache in her knee and the sting of Lorelai's dismissal only made her feel smaller and exposed.

"Lorelai, was it?" Blythe spoke quietly, almost dismissively, leaning in with an edge of steel to her voice, "How dare you insinuate that this remarkable woman might be on my arm for reasons other than she chooses to be."

Lorelai's mouth opened, words faltering. "I didn't—"

Blythe raised a hand, silencing her. "No, not 'I didn't.' The next words out of your mouth need to be, 'I apologise.'"

Lorelai exhaled sharply, shoulders stiffening. "I'm sorry."

"Not to me." Blythe's glare sharpened. "To Allegra."

At last, Lorelai turned, forced to really look at her. "My apologies, Allegra. I made an…unfortunate assumption."

"Damn right you did," Allegra said, her voice thick as tears pricked hotly at the corners of her eyes. She turned to Blythe, blinking them back. "I'd like to go."

"Of course. I'll get the car."

Thirty-Four

Allegra settled into her seat and let out a shaky sigh as Blythe pulled away, tyres crunching over the gravel.

"I am so sorry," Blythe said, voice tight, glancing at her as she reached for Allegra's hand. "She had no right to—"

"It's what people think, though, isn't it?" Allegra snapped, turning sharply towards her. "I'm either a hooker...or your daughter." Her mouth twisted bitterly. "And I don't even know which one's worse."

Blythe's jaw tightened, and for a brief moment, the calm mask cracked. "And if she thinks that, it's her problem, not yours! Don't let her, or anyone else, make you feel small."

Allegra's eyes flashed. "Yeah, well, you're not the one being mistaken for a prostitute or a child. Easy for you not to care."

Blythe's hand tightened on hers. "I care—about you."

"You don't know me," Allegra shot back. "Maybe she's right. Maybe I *am* a child."

"That's not how I see you," Blythe said firmly, her gaze steady.

"That's because you want in my pants," Allegra blurted, sharper than she meant, pulling her hand free from Blythe's grasp. Regret hit immediately. "I'm sorry—that was uncalled for." She looked away, shame filling every crevice of her being.

"It was," Blythe replied, calm but pointed, letting the words land. "And maybe, if you don't want people thinking of you as a child...you might want to stop behaving like one when you feel threatened."

Allegra's eyes cut back towards her, but she stayed silent, accepting the telling-off for what it was: deserved.

Blythe's gaze lingered on her for a second, steady and questioning. "Why does what she said bother you so much?"

Allegra hesitated. "I...I don't know," she admitted, her voice quieter than she'd expected.

"I think you do," Blythe said softly. "I think as much as I've been hesitant, so have you—but for a very different reason."

"I guess..." Allegra exhaled, eyes flicking towards the dashboard. "When she insinuated I was your kid... It hit home. You being older, wiser, just...a grown-up. And I'm—"

Blythe noticed an open stretch up ahead and gently steered the car to the side of the road, stopping and letting it idle.

"Go on," Blythe prompted, her voice low, patient, encouraging.

"I just... The more we get into this, the more I feel...immature, out of place," Allegra admitted.

"Do you want to stop seeing each other?" Blythe asked softly. "I can take you home. We can pretend this never happened if that's what you want." She took Allegra's hand again, holding it until Allegra's eyes met her own. "I'm attracted to you, not your age, but if it's too much of an issue for you, I don't want to be the woman who pushes for something that isn't being given freely."

Allegra shook her head. "Before that...*woman*," she said, a faint edge of venom in her voice, "I was taking you to the bathroom to kiss you again. And then she said what she said and now it's all spoiled. I feel like a child for even being upset about it, because if something like that had happened with John, I wouldn't have cared. I'd have given her a mouthful and—"

"So why didn't you?" Blythe asked, her gaze steady.

"I didn't want to embarrass you," Allegra admitted, letting her head fall back against the headrest. "Bloxley Manor, a room full of all the influential business owners..."

Rain lashed down out of nowhere, a huge black cloud gathering above and dumping down on what was already a miserable afternoon.

Allegra's breath shuddered. "I just… I don't think I'm ready for someone like you."

Thirty-Five

The door softly clicked shut, the quiet finality of it far too neat for the storm raging inside her. She'd wanted to slam it to make the whole block hear how gutted she felt, but all that came was a soft, pathetic snap of the latch.

Her flat greeted her with its usual silence, suddenly colder, emptier than it had ever been. She hovered in the hallway, clutching the crutches a little tighter, and wondered why she hadn't just asked Blythe to leave her at Sammy-Jo's. At least there she wouldn't be alone with her thoughts.

But the thought had barely formed before her throat tightened and her vision blurred. Tears came hot and sudden, breaking through her defences until she was shaking, chest heaving, with no one there to see her unravel.

Blythe had been kind about it—gentle, understanding—and somehow that only made it worse. Kindness cut deeper than cruelty ever could. She dragged herself into the lounge, tossed the crutches to the floor with a hollow clatter, and collapsed onto the couch. Curling around a cushion as though it could shield her from the ache inside, she sobbed, every breath shuddering, every thought another blow as she berated herself for falling apart.

She hadn't cried like this in years—unstoppable. She pressed her face into the fabric, trying to smother the sound, but the questions kept pressing in: Why couldn't she just shake this off? Why did it matter so much that Blythe was older, more confident, more certain? Why did every glance, every comment, remind her of the gaps between them—ones that Blythe herself didn't even seem to notice?

She hated that she cared, hated that she couldn't just enjoy what was happening without overthinking it—without feeling like the girl in the wrong shoes at the wrong party.

The ache in her chest deepened, and she held tighter to the cushion, as though it might answer the questions she couldn't bear to ask herself.

Blythe sat in the car outside, not having driven away after dropping Allegra off, and stared through the window, not really seeing anything as it was misted inside and damp on the outside. She couldn't get her head around it.

Here she was, in a new town, meeting new people, clawing her way through the wreckage of the last six months of her life—and then she met Allegra: stunning, sharp, with a laugh that had already carved its way under her skin. A woman she absolutely knew was attracted to her, and yet…

Her gaze drifted back to the building, and to the rows of windows catching the pale afternoon light. Which one was Allegra hiding behind? Which one held the answers Blythe didn't yet have?

She exhaled, fogging the glass further, her hands tightening on the steering wheel. For all her certainty in business, she suddenly felt unmoored here. Allegra had looked at her like she was everything she wanted, and then in the next breath, like she wasn't sure if she wanted her at all.

Blythe leant back in the seat, closing her eyes for a moment. She'd told herself she was ready—ready to move forward, ready to want again. But if Allegra wasn't, what then?

Her phone rang in her pocket, the sudden buzz making her start. She pulled it out and glanced at the screen. Amanda.

Blythe let it ring. The name flashed, faded, and vanished into silence. Her chest tightened in a way that had nothing to do with fear, and she felt a warmth stir lower, a reminder that some things didn't fade as easily as she told herself they should. She shoved the phone back into her pocket, letting the heaters clear the misted glass.

She didn't look back at the building again.

The one thing she had learned, with absolute clarity, was: stop chasing women who don't want you.

And maybe…maybe she wasn't entirely ready for Allegra either.

Fingers tightening on the wheel, she pulled away from the kerb and felt the vibration of her phone ringing again.

THIRTY-SIX

"Where are you?" Sammy-Jo's voice asked in the voice message she'd just played.

Noticing the time and that the room had grown dark, Allegra wiped her face and sat up.

Allegra: Sorry, came back to mine. X

It didn't take long for a flurry of texts to follow.

SJ: Got it...next time let me know you'd rather be shagging, I was worried.

SJ: Also...well done.

SJ: Daisy says whoop whoop!

The warmth, the teasing, the familiar ease—it was a balm against the storm still thrumming inside her chest. For a moment, she let herself forget the sting of Lorelai, the tension with Blythe, even the ache of missing what she'd lost with John.

And yet, her thoughts drifted back to Blythe—to the pull she couldn't deny, the way Blythe's eyes had lingered, the way her touch had made her heart race. She shook her head softly, trying to push it down, but the flicker of longing remained, stubborn and insistent.

Life was messy, complicated, and exhausting, but somehow, it was still hers to navigate. And she wasn't entirely alone.

Allegra: Nothing happened. I'll be back tomorrow.

The tick turned blue and the call came immediately. She hesitated, fingers hovering over the screen. But this was Sammy-Jo. If she didn't answer, SJ would be halfway here in Daisy's car before Allegra could blink.

"Hey," Allegra said into the phone, forcing a brighter tone than she felt.

"What's going on?"

"Why would you think something was going on?"

"Because you're there, and not here…and she's not with you. Or is she? Wait! Have I interrupted a 'nothing happened because it hasn't happened yet, but it's about to' situation?"

Allegra couldn't help the small smile tugging at her lips. "No, you haven't interrupted. She dropped me off…and she's gone home."

"Coming back later then?" Sammy-Jo's voice held that familiar, teasing note, the one that always made Allegra laugh.

"No. Not coming back later. Actually…she's just not coming back." The words tightened her throat as she spoke them aloud.

"Oh… Something happen? Did she upset you?"

Allegra could picture Sammy-Jo now: upright, tense, ready to go to battle for her, acting the way she'd wished John had—maybe even Blythe, too. Why did nobody seem to want to fight for her?

"I'm just not ready to date someone like Blythe," Allegra admitted, letting the narrative she'd been telling herself spill out.

"Someone like Blythe? Hot, successful, well-off…and you're attracted to her?" Sammy-Jo's voice still carried that teasing lilt, but she had a point—one Allegra was absolutely not ready to deal with.

"I just think we're not on the same page right now. She wants something serious and I'm…not there yet. I don't want to waste her time…or mine."

"Right," Sammy-Jo said slowly. "Makes sense, I guess…" A pause stretched, then her voice softened, "So why are you hiding out over there?"

"I'm not hiding," Allegra replied, too fast to sound convincing.

"Okay, whatever you say. But I know you, and you're not fooling me. When you're ready to come home, I'll be here to talk."

Allegra smiled faintly. *Home.* Just a word. Only four letters, and yet it meant everything to know that was what SJ thought of her presence and position there.

"I know…and I love you for it," she said softly, the admission slipping out before she could second-guess it. "I'm just going to head to bed. Tomorrow will be a better day, I'm sure."

"Alright," SJ replied, her tone warm but tinged with quiet concern. "We'll talk tomorrow. Night, Leggy."

"Night." Allegra ended the call, staring at the darkened ceiling, the word *home* still echoing through her chest.

THIRTY-SEVEN

The coach cruised to a stop outside the West Ham ground, the air inside it buzzing with pre-match nerves and chatter. Allegra hobbled down last. Her knee was feeling better, but she didn't want to think too much about it yet in case there was a setback. Her hoodie was pulled low. She was being more supporter than player these days. Nora had insisted she come anyway. "Team presence," she'd called it, and Allegra hadn't argued. She needed to be busy, and with Daisy visiting her parents and SJ playing, being at home would be lonely.

Inside the stadium, the Harriers spilled into the changing rooms while Nora started giving out orders with a steadiness that made Allegra proud. The new gaffer's voice carried authority, her instructions clipped but calm, even if she was only in charge for today. Allegra lingered near the door, soaking in the atmosphere and the smell of it all. It should have been enough just being here, part of it, but she couldn't wait to get back to playing again.

With forty-five minutes to go, the team walked out onto the pitch to warm up. The small group of travelling fans cheered and tried to make more noise than their numbers suggested they could. Allegra grinned. Wasn't this what they'd all dreamed of as kids?

The whispers started quickly, moving like static through the staff, the subs, even the kit girl.

"Is that..." she overheard someone say as they strolled past her.

"With Gabby, yeah."

"Katrine Gustafsson."

Allegra followed the glances until her gaze landed on the glass-fronted box above. Gabby was easy to spot, poised and self-assured as ever. But it was the woman beside her who drew every eye—tall, blonde, unmistakably Scandinavian. Katrine Gustafsson, the retired Swedish international-turned-coach, linked to half a dozen managerial jobs this season, and now sitting right there with Gabby.

Allegra caught SJ's attention and jerked her chin upwards. It took a moment before Sammy-Jo found the box, then her jaw dropped. She elbowed Jas Khan and tipped her head, the three of them suddenly buzzing with the same thought.

Down on the pitch, Nora's voice cut through the chatter. "Alright, focus. Forget about everything else. The only thing that matters is this pitch, today, right now."

"Won't be long," Taylor said, nudging Allegra's arm, "till you're back out there."

"I know." Allegra smiled and nudged her back. "So, what do you know?"

"About?" Taylor asked, turning slightly towards her. They stood side by side, arms folded, watching the squad get put through its paces.

"Katrine Gustafsson?"

Taylor shrugged. "If she doesn't play for the Harriers, I really have no clue."

Allegra laughed. "She's a big name in management. Rumour is she's sitting with Gabby."

"Oh, well then, maybe she's the new manager."

"Duh." Allegra nudged her again. "I'm going to wander up there and see what I can find out."

Allegra slipped away from the touchline and made her way up through the stands, crutches clicking against the concrete. She caught the lift just as the doors were closing, and a few minutes later found herself stepping into the corridor that led to the executive seats.

Gabby spotted her through the glass and lit up instantly, pushing the door wide. "Allegra! Just the woman I wanted to see."

Inside, the air was warm, filled with the low murmur of conversations and the faint clink of glasses. But Gabby only had eyes for her. "Come in, come in. I want you to meet someone."

Katrine Gustafsson rose from her seat with effortless grace, tall and composed, her handshake firm and professional. "Allegra Mann," she said, her accent curling around the syllables. "I've heard a lot about you."

"Hopefully good things," Allegra managed with a smile, suddenly aware of how underdressed she felt in trainers and her club hoodie.

"The very best," Gabby assured, practically glowing. "Our star defender. Even sidelined, she's invaluable. Leads from the stands as much as on the pitch."

Katrine's cool blue eyes lingered on her, not unkind, just...assessing. "And how is the knee?"

"Getting there," Allegra replied, tightening her grip on the crutch handles. "Hopefully getting the brace off this week and losing the crutches. Harder watching than playing, if I'm honest."

"That is always the way," Katrine said, a flicker of empathy in her expression. "But patience now will make the return stronger."

Gabby beamed between them, delighted. "You see? Exactly what I keep telling her."

Allegra nodded, but there was a strange flutter in her chest—part pride, part unease. Whatever this was, it felt bigger than her, and she wasn't sure if that thrilled or terrified her.

"So, does this mean..." Allegra asked, feeling bold.

Katrine smiled. "We'll see."

Blythe arrived at the office early. It was predictably empty for a Saturday morning. Only the cleaners had been through overnight, and they'd done their job well enough.

She powered up her laptop, pulling figures and data files together, noting the kinds of details her team had been busy compiling. A ping announced a new email. She ignored it—just one more in a sea she didn't want to drown in yet.

Her coffee steamed at her elbow. She lifted it absently, gaze drifting to the rain streaking the window. Droplets slid against each other in crooked races. She picked one to follow.

It lost.

With a sigh, she set the cup down and reached for her phone. Reflex. Habit. Hope. Maybe Allegra had changed her mind and sent some kind of message to soften the silence.

She hadn't.

For a fleeting moment she'd considered flowers, or some grand gesture to sweep Allegra back. But that was the old Blythe. The one who gave too much, too fast, who carved out space for someone else at the cost of her own. That woman was supposed to be retired.

Her fingers struck the keyboard harder than intended, waking the screen. Spreadsheets and graphs filled it in cold precision. She closed her eyes, let the numbers blur, then forced herself to focus.

This was her Saturday activity now. Her life for the foreseeable future. The sooner she made peace with it, the better.

Engrossed in her work, Blythe didn't hear the lift doors open, or the sharp rhythm of heels striking marble before they softened on carpet. She barely registered the sweep of her office door until movement flickered in her peripheral vision.

She looked up.

There in the doorway stood a figure poised like she owned the space—dark hair falling loose around a striking face, a crisp white blouse tucked neatly into a navy pencil skirt that hugged in all the right places. Confident. Unapologetic. Sexy in a way that felt intentional.

Blythe's hand froze on the keyboard. For a moment, she simply stared.

"Amanda..." The name left Blythe's lips before she could stop it, tasting unfamiliar now. The devotion that used to lace it was gone, replaced with a tension she couldn't quite name. Excitement still thrummed in her veins, though whether it was anticipation or fear, she couldn't tell. With Amanda, it was usually both.

"Blythe." Amanda's smile slid into place, slow and devastating, her voice purring with an intimacy that wrapped around the room. She stepped inside, closing the door behind her with casual ease. "I messaged you...but you didn't answer. And you know how much I hate being ignored."

Her blouse shifted as she leant against the edge of the desk, the faint scent of her perfume cutting through the air. Blythe forced herself to look back at the screen, at the safe, impersonal numbers that couldn't hurt her. But her chest tightened, her pulse betraying her calm facade.

Amanda tilted her head. "Don't tell me spreadsheets are more fun than me."

Blythe felt the words—or more, the demand beneath them. *'Look at me. Give me your attention.'* They curled around her, tugging at something she wasn't sure she could resist.

"Just doing the job you pay me to do," she said, her tone as even as she could make it.

Amanda's smile widened, slow and knowing. She reached out, the tip of one finger tracing a delicate line along Blythe's forearm, her touch feather-light but electric. "I don't pay you to work Saturdays."

Blythe exhaled through her nose, steady but sharp. "Don't you?"

They both knew the truth. Executives like Blythe weren't bound by office hours. They were paid to bleed for the company, to chase openings and deadlines until the next hotel stood gleaming. Saturdays, Sundays, evenings—it was all fair game.

Amanda's eyes glittered. "Maybe…but today's different."

Blythe sat back in her chair, pulling her arms out of reach from those tantalising fingers that had traced her skin, fingers that still burned like a phantom touch.

"Why's that?"

"I thought we could catch up…hang out," Amanda said, mischief threading through her voice. "Like old times."

"Old times?" Blythe repeated, wary, though her voice betrayed the hitch of memory.

"Mmm-hm." Amanda leant further across the desk, twisting until she was perched fully on it. With a casual push, she slid the laptop aside, clearing her stage. Then, with deliberate slowness, she inched up her skirt until she had room to swing her left thigh over Blythe's lap, the invitation blatant, impossible to ignore.

"You know…" Amanda's lips curved into a smile, equal parts promise and provocation. "The best times."

Blythe's pulse betrayed her, quickening even as she leant back, creating space where Amanda was determined to take it away.

"This isn't—"

Amanda angled her head, the faintest pout tugging at her lips. "Isn't what? Professional?" Her fingers skimmed the edge of Blythe's desk, trailing lightly as though claiming her—owning her. "We were never very professional, were we?"

Blythe swallowed hard. The scent of Amanda's perfume—something floral with an edge of spice—wrapped around her like memory. Old nights. Bad decisions. Long mornings pretending it had meant more than it did.

She should stand. Step back. Reclaim the distance Amanda so effortlessly erased. But Amanda's thigh hovered inches from hers, the warmth of her body bleeding across the space, tempting and taunting her.

"You shouldn't be here," Blythe said, though the protest came out thinner than she'd intended, betraying her own nerves.

Amanda's voice lowered. "And yet...here I am." She shifted, sliding down until she was straddling Blythe's lap, close enough that every subtle movement sent heat spiralling through Blythe.

"Tell me to leave," Amanda whispered, her voice a tease as her mouth hovered mere inches from Blythe's. "I'll go. Do you...want me to go?"

Blythe's chest tightened, the words she wanted to say caught somewhere between caution and craving. Her hands hovered near Amanda, unsure whether to push her away or pull her closer.

Amanda's lips brushed against hers in the faintest, ghosting touch, a whisper of contact that made the air between them tremble. Her voice dropped, intimate and low. "I've missed this... Missed you," she murmured, each syllable threading into Blythe's pulse.

Blythe's breath faltered. Desire and restraint collided, a sharp, delicious tension she couldn't ignore. She wanted to pull Amanda closer, to feel more, but a part of her held back, fierce and wary, knowing exactly what giving in might cost.

For a heartbeat, they simply stayed there, lips almost touching, the world around them dissolving into a charged silence, each waiting to see who would surrender first.

THIRTY-EIGHT

The final whistle blew and Allegra threw her hands in the air, cheering. It had been scrappy, feisty, but one goal from the back of Satty Basra's head had been enough to secure the valuable points.

"Was a good game," Katrine said, sidling up beside Allegra and joining in the clapping as the team slowly made their way towards the travelling fans.

"Yes. I mean…could have been better, but under the circumstances…"

Katrine nodded. "I think we have a good place to start." She patted Allegra's shoulder as she turned to leave.

"Does that mean…" Allegra asked, her eyes wide with excitement.

Katrine looked to Gabby. "I'll see you Monday morning, yes?"

"Absolutely. Welcome to Bath Street Harriers." Gabby beamed and shook Katrine's hand. "Good to have you on board."

"I think we are going to do great things together." Katrine smiled at Allegra. "And you're going to be pivotal, so I'll expect a treatment update this week."

"I'll deliver it personally." Allegra grinned.

"Do that." Katrine turned back to Gabby. "So, shall we get the paperwork over with?"

"I think we should. And then…a little champagne?"

"Make mine an apple juice and you have another deal." Katrine laughed. She looked back at the team, still lingering with fans, taking selfies, signing shirts, enjoying the celebrations together. "I like what I see here—a real club, with integrity and ambition."

"That's the Harriers," Gabby agreed.

"I'll just visit the ladies' room and meet you back here?" Katrine asked.

"I'll be here," Gabby said, her cheeks flushed from the smile stretching across her face.

Allegra moved closer, standing beside Gabby as they both watched Katrine leave the room. Once she was out of sight, the two of them turned to one another and let out a shared scream of excitement.

"Did Nora know?" Allegra asked once their voices had settled.

Gabby pressed her lips together and shook her head. "No, we don't really talk about work at home. And even though I was bursting to say something, I couldn't...not until I had her signed up."

"She's going to be over the moon. All of them will be. Katrine Gustafsson?" Allegra shook her head in disbelief. "Maybe that fourth spot is something we can really aim for."

"The plan is to win the WSL," Gabby said adamantly, "but we'll take fourth this season."

"I'm going to go down and see the players... I'll try to keep it to myself."

Gabby laughed. "Send Nora up, and then you can tell everyone."

"Yes." Allegra fist-pumped. She grabbed her crutches and began hopping her way out of the room. "You're awesome," she said to Gabby before disappearing into the corridor.

She was still beaming as she reached the dressing room, the air thick with the buzz of post-match celebration. At the centre of it all was

Sammy-Jo, dancing in her shorts and bra, boots kicked off, socked feet sliding over the floor.

Nora sat quietly on the bench, and Allegra called out, "Nora. Your wife wants you."

Nora nodded but didn't move.

Edging closer, Allegra leaned in and whispered, "She said 'now'. You really do want to go right now."

Nora's cheeks warmed.

"Not for that, you pervert…although when you hear what she's got to say…" Allegra winked.

Nora's eyes narrowed. "What's she want to say that she's shared with you?"

Allegra giggled. "Oh, trust me…when you find out… Go!"

Nora finally stood, making her way out of the room, and Allegra spun back to face the rest of the team. "Oi! Listen up!" she shouted. A few heads turned, but many others were lost in the music, dancing and laughing.

Allegra shot Jess, who was manning the stereo, a sharp look and drew a finger across her neck. "Shut it off."

Bemused, Jess shrugged and hit stop. The room fell into sudden quiet, the only remaining sounds Sammy-Jo and a few others singing, until everyone realised Allegra was standing there.

"Thank you," Allegra said, letting her gaze sweep over the team. "I've got some news…exciting news. News that's going to make you—"

"Spit it out, Leggy," Sammy-Jo interjected.

Allegra smirked. "Or I could just leave you all in suspense."

"Leggy!" several voices groaned in protest.

"Fine. We have a new manager."

The room erupted into chatter and excitement.

"Is it…you know?" Jas asked, eyes wide.

Allegra's grin broadened. "If you mean Katrine Gustafsson," she paused, letting the suspense build, "then yes. KG is our new manager."

"Holy fuck balls!" Sammy-Jo exclaimed. "That's—"

"Yes, it is!" Allegra laughed, letting herself be swept up in the energy. For the first time in a long while, she felt fully part of the group again.

Thirty-Nine

The kiss was slow, deliberate, yet carried the confidence Amanda always seemed to wield with ease. She'd never lacked that skill, that uncanny ability to slip past any barricade Blythe erected, to scale walls that were meant to keep Blythe safe. How could Blythe resist? Why should she?

Her lips parted, welcoming the offered tongue, and in an instant her brain turned to mush. All sensible thought scattered, drowned beneath the rush of heat that surged through her. Blood pulsed downward, filling her clit with a throbbing ache that demanded relief. Amanda's soft, knowing moans only fanned the hunger, urging her towards that familiar, dangerous desire to touch her old lover again.

Amanda deepened the kiss, her tongue teasing, retreating, coaxing until Blythe was chasing it without even realising. A low chuckle vibrated against her lips, a sound that reminded Blythe this was a game Amanda knew how to win.

"Still the same," Amanda whispered between ghosted kisses, her breath hot against Blythe's mouth. "One taste and you melt for me."

Blythe's fingers curled into the armrests of her chair, holding herself back, as if the grip could anchor her against the tide of need threatening to pull her under. She wanted to say something sharp, some denial of how she wasn't that easy, that she'd grown past Amanda's spell—but

Amanda's hand slid to the back of her neck, and the words died unspoken.

"Don't fight it." Amanda brushed her lips over Blythe's once more. "You know how good we are together."

Blythe tore her mouth away, chest heaving, lips tingling with the aftershock of Amanda's kiss. "I can't do this again."

Amanda cocked her head, eyes glittering with amusement. "Do what?" she purred, her fingers sliding down the front of Blythe's shirt, teasing open the first button with practised ease. "Have some fun?"

"I'm serious, Amanda." Blythe caught her hands firmly, holding them still against her chest. The tremor in her voice betrayed the warring parts of her—wanting, resisting, aching. "I'm not looking for fun. I want commitment."

For the first time, Amanda's smile faltered, just a fraction. Her eyes narrowed, curiosity laced with challenge, as though Blythe had just changed the rules of their game.

For a heartbeat, Amanda stilled beneath Blythe's grip. Her gaze softened, the playful spark dimming just a little as she searched Blythe's face. Then, with a small smile, she let out a quiet breath.

"Okay," she murmured, almost as if testing the word. "Let's try that."

There was no teasing lilt this time, no calculated edge, just a low, sincere promise that made Blythe's chest tighten. Amanda's hands relaxed under Blythe's, her touch lighter now, tentative in a way Blythe had rarely seen.

It was enough to make Blythe's heart stumble, to make her wonder if maybe…just maybe…

"Do you really mean that?" Blythe asked, voice low, cautious, despite the heat coursing through her.

"I said so, didn't I?" Amanda's fingers returned to the buttons of Blythe's shirt, deliberate and teasing. "When have you ever known me not to mean what I say?" She leant closer, voice a whisper that scraped along Blythe's nerve endings. "I want you."

The space between them dissipated, the kiss harder this time—a point to prove. Blythe stopped fighting it. Her hands moved, coming to rest lightly on Amanda's thighs as Amanda's fingers tangled in Blythe's hair, pulling her closer.

Fingertips traced the edge of the lace stockings, inching higher, reverent and deliberate.

Before she knew it, Amanda was perched back on the desk, shifting slightly as Blythe eased the fabric of her skirt higher, sliding her underwear in the other direction. Blythe sank to her knees, taking in the scene—the familiarity of Amanda's body, the small mole high on her inner thigh, the scent that always drove her wild. Every detail drew her in, leaving her senses on fire and her restraint dissolving.

She would worship her in the only way she knew how. Her face pressed between Amanda's thighs, mouth and tongue working in perfect rhythm, lapping at the sweet, heated flesh. She drew out Amanda's moans, sinking her teeth just slightly as she worked her clit, watching her lover buckle and writhe, all traces of the composed CEO gone.

Heels dug sharply into her sides, fingers tangling in her hair as Amanda guided her even closer. A satisfied grin flickered across Blythe's face as she felt just how close Amanda was.

"Yes, just like that, baby," Amanda groaned, tugging and squeezing with abandon. "You know exactly what I like, don't you?"

Blythe heard her, but speaking would only break her focus.

"Inside," Amanda commanded. "Make me… I want to lose…"

Blythe understood. *Control*—that was the word unspoken. Always so taut, so in charge, so put together. And yet, there was nothing Amanda craved more than being consumed and fucked out of her senses, losing herself completely in someone else for a few moments—just a glimpse of surrender, letting her body take over her mind.

And when that happened, she would become feral—a woman utterly undone by desire, a woman Blythe could abandon herself in for hours, locked away in her empty office, Amanda Sanchez attending to her every need.

FORTY

Two weeks had passed, and Allegra felt the anticipation building as she closed the physio's office door behind her. A little yelp of excitement escaped her lips as she bounced lightly on her now strong, brace-free knee, crutches abandoned and forgotten beside the door.

The freedom felt electric, almost surreal, and a wide grin spread across her face. She tested her weight again, rocking from heel to toe, feeling the knee respond exactly as it should.

"Yes!" she whispered to herself, laughter bubbling up before she even realised it. Light training was back on the cards—cautious, careful, but exhilarating. For the first time in weeks, she felt like herself again.

Stepping further into the hallway, she did a small hop, then a jog on the spot, savouring the newfound strength. Every step was a victory, every movement a reminder she was back in control, ready to chase the pitch and the game she loved.

Her first port of call was down the corridor to the plush, newly refurbished office of Bath Street Harriers' freshly installed manager, Katrine Gustafsson. Allegra knocked, paused a second, then pushed the door open and peeked inside. Katrine sat at her desk, glasses perched on her nose, a training session looping on her laptop screen.

"Hey," Allegra greeted as Katrine looked up.

"Allegra, come in." Katrine beckoned her in with her fingers. "Take a seat." She smiled, then added, "Good news, I hope—I don't see crutches."

Allegra grinned. "I'm back in light training. Mostly muscle strengthening and gym work, but yes, I'm almost there."

"This is excellent news." Katrine returned the smile. "I assume Taylor and the team are working out a plan?"

"Yep. I've got the weekend to rest a little more, then Monday I'll be in the gym and pool."

Katrine glanced at the calendar. They were midway through October already. "Hopefully we'll see you back with the team after the winter break…if you do what you're told, work hard, and stay focused."

"Don't worry," Allegra said, forcing a confident edge to her voice, "I'm completely focused. Absolutely nothing else going on in my life that would get in the way." She added the last part with a mental shrug, trying to push down the twinge of disappointment that still lingered around Blythe. But this was proof, wasn't it? She didn't need any distraction like that—not right now.

"Well, I suggest you get home and do what you've been told, and we'll see you bright and early on Monday."

Allegra nodded, springing up with a touch of extra bounce. "I'm going to take my place back in the team," she said with certainty.

"I think Kunkel might have something to say about that," Katrine replied cheerfully. But they both knew the truth: A fit Allegra Mann was a first-name-on-the-team-sheet situation.

"I'll be at the game on Sunday."

"Good. I'll see you there."

Allegra closed the office door behind her and walked slowly down the corridor, her eyes catching on the framed photographs lining the walls—moments from the club's history, players who had moved on, legends from its early days before Gabby Dean had taken charge. She lingered on the small captions beneath each image, absorbed enough she didn't notice the nearby door opening until the sound of voices spilled out.

"...I look forward to hearing more from you, Leila. And Gabby, shall we do lunch this week to discuss—" Blythe's voice faltered mid-sentence.

Allegra froze. She had a choice: pretend to keep reading the captions or turn and face the woman who had been haunting her quieter moments—immature avoidance or grown-up confrontation.

She closed her eyes, counted to three, then turned with a bright smile.

"Allegra..." Gabby spoke first. "Were you waiting to see me? I didn't know we had an—"

"No," Allegra cut in lightly. "I just came from Katrine's office and was..." Her gaze slipped to Blythe, who quickly looked away, though the darker woman standing beside her seemed curious, her eyes holding on Allegra a moment longer. "Heading home, actually. Just gave the boss the news that I'll be back in light training on Monday."

Gabby grinned. "Fabulous. We can't wait to have you back."

"Yes...me too." Allegra forced a smile, but her eyes betrayed the hesitation. She risked one last glance at Blythe—searching, hoping for something—but was met with silence and a studious avoidance that cut sharper than words ever could.

Swallowing down the lump in her throat, Allegra turned and made for the stairs, each step carrying her farther away from whatever that had been, whatever it still was. Blythe couldn't even look at her, and that hurt more than Allegra wanted to admit.

FORTY-ONE

Friday night arrived and Sammy-Jo was restless, pacing by the sofa. "Let's just go out," she said, glancing at Daisy.

Daisy was already curled up in her slippers, blanket over her knees, the TV glowing in front of her. "I'm tired, baby. The office was chaos today with the new range coming out." She reached for SJ's hand and tugged her down onto the couch beside her. "Why don't you see if any of the team are out? Where's Allegra? She could do with blowing off some steam."

"Upstairs. She's been quiet. I thought she'd be buzzing now she's got rid of the brace and the crutches." SJ paused, chewing her lip. "Maybe you're right…" Her eyes flicked towards the hall and the stairs. "I'll go ask her. You sure you don't want to come?"

As if to underline the point, Daisy let out a wide yawn. "Nope. I'm going to finish this, have a bath, and fall into bed."

"Okay. I'll see if Leggy wants to do something."

SJ sprang up and all but bounded up the stairs, rapping on Allegra's door in less than thirty seconds. "Leggy, wanna go out?"

"Out where?" Allegra asked, tugging the door open.

Sammy-Jo grinned. "Was thinking Blanca's, but if you fancy a boogie—" She did a playful shimmy in the doorway. "I'm up for Art."

Allegra hesitated. "I can't. I need to focus on getting fit again."

"That's Monday," SJ shot back. "You've got until then to skive off and have some fun."

"And be a gooseberry to you two?"

SJ laughed. "Nope. Daisy's not coming. You'll be my date for the night. That way, if anyone tries it on, I'll just point at you and say, 'Uh-uh—taken.'"

"You could just say that anyway, without pointing at me."

SJ shrugged with mock innocence. "Sure, but the visual always works best." She pulled a pitiful face. "So, will you please come out with me?"

Allegra sighed, fighting a smile. "Fine. But only Blanca's. I want to sit down, not be dragged onto a dance floor."

"Yes!" SJ fist pumped. "Meet you downstairs in..." She glanced at her watch, then back at Allegra, still in a tracksuit, hair scraped up, no make-up. "Thirty minutes."

"I'll never be ready in thirty minutes."

"You will if you stop blathering and get on with it."

Sammy-Jo pushed the door open and the hum of the bar spilled around them. "I'm just saying—if this is what you throw together in thirty minutes, I finally get why you're the club's hottie."

"I am not the club's hottie." Allegra laughed, rolling her eyes.

"Yes, you are. Everyone knows it." SJ kept at it, grinning like a cat with cream. "We even voted for you in that online poll last month."

"You did not." Allegra's cheeks warmed and she ducked her head.

Nodding, Sammy-Jo smirked. "Oh, we did. Got the academy girls in on it too. Even the lads over at Rovers." She gave Allegra a once-over and shrugged. "Face it—you're the glamour at Harriers."

"I would argue Astrid is far more glamorous than me," Allegra countered. The tall Scandinavian was basically a Viking warrior as far as anyone was concerned.

They reached the bar.

"She came second in the vote," Sammy-Jo shot back smugly.

"What can I get ya?" Sadie, the owner, leaned on the pump with a knowing smile. "The usual?"

"You know me too well." Sammy-Jo watched as Sadie poured the perfect lager shandy. "And what's my girl here having on her last chance before giving up the booze?"

"White wine spritzer, please," Allegra said, returning Sadie's smile.

"Coming right up."

Sammy-Jo raised a brow. "I thought you'd be celebrating. No crutches, brace off, back to training Monday."

"I am—just without the need to get drunk, fall over, and bust my leg again."

Sammy-Jo laughed. "Fair point." She leaned against the bar, eyes scanning the room. Then she stilled. "Uh...so, Art's probably buzzing tonight. Bet most people are there."

Allegra shrugged, tapping her card on the machine before taking her glass. "Maybe."

"Wanna head over instead?"

"Not really." Allegra took a sip and turned to survey the crowd herself, only for Sammy-Jo to step in front of her, blocking her line of sight.

"Look—don't freak out, alright?"

Allegra narrowed her eyes. "You know saying that is exactly *how* to make me freak out. What is it?"

"That woman you were seeing? She's here." Sammy-Jo tilted her head towards the corner.

Since that afternoon in her office when Amanda had come to her, things had shifted. She'd been unusually attentive ever since—late-night phone calls, an invitation to dinner in London the previous weekend, and then not leaving her bed for almost two days. Blythe had come back to Woodington aching in all the best ways.

This weekend, Amanda had arrived an hour ago, right on time, sweeping in with her usual confidence and insisting they go out.

"I want to see somewhere other than between your thighs…at least for a few hours," Amanda had teased, laughing as she swapped her office armour—pencil skirt and silk blouse—for a shorter skirt, cropped top, and a bolero jacket. She looked stunning, and Blythe couldn't deny it.

But seeing Allegra in the corridor a few days earlier had rattled her. Chalk and cheese, those two—one dark, one blonde, one tall, one compact. Amanda had a decade on Allegra, and Blythe had six on Amanda.

It shouldn't have mattered. And yet…

It had shaken her. Made her admit, at least to herself, that even with Amanda back in her bed, there was still a space she hadn't managed to fill. A space that stubbornly belonged to someone else, someone who clearly wasn't interested.

But Blythe had pushed it to the back of her mind. She had what she'd always wanted—Amanda Sanchez—and this time they were taking each other seriously.

"We'll start at Aston's, grab something light to eat, then move on to the bar. You'll love it. The whole complex is built around the river. If the Harriers deal goes south, it's a great fallback. Something smaller, of course—more boutique."

Amanda's brow lifted, just enough to show she was listening.

"How's the deal going?"

"Slowly. Gabby Dean is no slouch. I met with her financial adviser this week—Leila Ortez, from Franklyn Financials."

"And?"

"It went well. We're meeting again next week. I'll present the plan in more detail now that the drawings are finished."

Amanda's lips curved into a wicked smile. "You know I get so turned on when you talk business." She tugged Blythe off to the side of the footpath, her hand brushing lightly against Blythe's lower back, fingertips sending a shiver up her spine. The night air was cool against their flushed skin, the hum of the street and distant music from the bars fading into the background.

"Yeah?" Blythe breathed, caught off guard by the sudden closeness.

"Mm, find a quiet corner and I'll show you." Amanda's gaze lingered on her, a playful glint in her eyes as she leaned closer—jasmine and something warmer—filling Blythe's senses.

Blythe laughed, the sound nervous and excited. "Maybe I should just take you back to my pokey little flat now."

Amanda tilted her head, brushing a strand of hair from Blythe's face, her fingers ghosting over her cheek. "And spoil all my fun getting you worked up all night? Uh-uh." She stepped back just enough to nudge Blythe gently with her shoulder, their bodies still humming from the touch.

She glanced towards the bar ahead. "Is that the bar?"

"The rainbow flag give it away?" Blythe asked, feeling the warmth of Amanda's hand where it had brushed her waist.

Amanda pressed up against her, rising onto her toes slightly, lips ghosting against hers, a whisper of a kiss that made Blythe's knees weak. "Get me drunk, then fuck me till Sunday," she murmured with a look that spoke only of sin.

Blythe's breath caught, the combination of the fresh night air and the heat of desire coiling in her stomach. Her fingers brushed Amanda's hand, holding it briefly, savouring the intimacy in that simple contact before the world fell away to just the two of them.

"Only if you tell me how you want me to fuck you?"

Amanda groaned softly, the sound vibrating against Blythe's chest.

"Fingers first...then your mouth and when I'm..." She laughed, a shiver running down her spine at the memory of the last time.

"Feral?" Blythe offered with a teasing smirk, her fingers now brushing a stray lock of hair from Amanda's face.

"Hm hm...the strap, from behind, hard." Amanda's eyes shone, and her fingers grazed Blythe's wrist, a light, lingering touch that made her pulse quicken.

Blythe closed what little space was between them, her lips brushing against Amanda's ear as she whispered, "You're driving me crazy."

A soft laugh escaped Amanda in response, her hand lingering at Blythe's side, tracing the curve of her hip with delicate, teasing pressure.

"That's the plan." Amanda laughed, tugging her hand and moving them forwards. "Get me drunk."

I Made the Right Decision

Allegra's eyes swept the room, scanning the crowd, and then she saw her. Blythe was standing near the DJ booth, a glass of wine in hand, catching the light just so. Their gazes met across the room, and for a long, suspended moment, everything else seemed to blur. No music, no chatter, no clinking glasses—just the quiet electricity of recognition and memory.

Blythe's eyes widened slightly, surprise and something softer—something like longing—flickering across her face. She didn't look away. Allegra felt the familiar pull—a mix of curiosity, tension, and a pang of something she wasn't ready to name.

"Why don't you go and talk to her?" SJ leaned in and said quietly. "You know you like her."

"It's not that simple. I do like her, but..."

Allegra's attention sharpened as she noticed the attractive woman laughing lightly at something someone had said. The woman's gaze swept the room, caught Allegra for a second, then returned to Blythe.

In a fluid motion, she leaned in and pressed her lips to Blythe's, soft and insistent. Blythe's eyes closed, her hands moving up instinctively, caught in the warmth and familiarity, while Allegra froze, the sight hitting her sharper than she'd expected.

"Oh, well, maybe not then," Sammy-Jo said, quickly turning away and back to her friend. "You alright?"

"Sure," Allegra said, but her eyes told another story as she continued to stare at Blythe and the woman French kissing. "You know, maybe I should get drunk."

"No, I don't think that's a good idea at all." Sammy-Jo pulled her phone from her pocket. "In fact, I'm going to call us a cab and—"

"The fuck you are," Allegra snapped. "I'm not leaving with my tail between my legs like a child." She turned to Sadie, "Vodka and coke, please…double." Then back to SJ, "If I'm going to be immature, it's going to be carnage."

"That's what I'm afraid of… We can go to Art—get drunk there."

Amanda pulled back from the kiss, a satisfied smile tugging at her lips. She glanced around the bar and spotted Allegra staring at them from across the room. Amanda's brow arched. "Who is that girl?" The word *girl* landed heavier than she intended, a subtle edge in the way she spoke it.

Blythe felt a moment of unease, the pang of something she hadn't acknowledged before. For the first time, she wondered if Allegra had been right—that the gap between them was too big, too much to bridge.

"She's a footballer…for the team," Blythe said, her voice steady, though her mind screamed at her for honesty. *Why hadn't she added, 'That's someone I dated a few times when I arrived'? Why hadn't she warned Amanda, prepped her?*

Amanda tilted her head, studying Allegra for a beat, curiosity and something unreadable in her gaze. Blythe shifted slightly, caught in the pull of both fascination and guilt, realising how much she'd left unsaid—and how complicated things were potentially about to get.

"You know…I think right now would be a good time to, what was it you said, 'Fuck you till Sunday.'?"

Amanda grinned, a wicked glint in her eye. "I must admit, I do feel like your hand inside my knickers right now would be something I'd very much enjoy."

Blythe drained her wine in one swift gulp. "Then let's go."

"Give me two minutes—ladies' room—and then...I am all yours."

Blythe watched her saunter off, hips swaying, then glance back over her shoulder with a teasing wink. Blythe tugged her jacket on, patted her pockets for keys, and let out a small, eager breath. The sooner they were out of here, the better.

"I guess I made the right decision," Allegra said from behind her.

Blythe's shoulders stiffened. She gritted her teeth before turning slowly. "I'm sorry it looks that way, but I can assure you this was as unexpected for me as—"

Allegra scoffed. "I really don't care. I'm just glad I found out who you are now, before I made a bigger fool of myself."

"Allegra, it's not like that—"

"Isn't it?" Allegra turned on her heel, walking away without a backwards glance.

Blythe stood frozen, torn between running after her and holding her ground. Her chest ached with the words she hadn't said.

"Ready to go?" Amanda reappeared at her side, all glossy smiles and confidence, a living reminder that Blythe already had everything she thought she wanted.

Forty-Two

"Okay...just stand right there. Don't move." Sammy-Jo braced one palm against Allegra's chest while digging around in her pocket for the key. The pair of them were getting drenched from the sudden downpour.

"I just dunno...why..." Allegra slurred, swaying like a metronome gone rogue.

"Nope, I dunno either. Let's get you inside and then we can work it out," SJ muttered, having no clue where Allegra's rambling brain was headed.

She'd watched her down four more double vodka and cokes before Sadie leaned over and quietly admitted she'd called a taxi. Allegra had tried to argue she was fine, then promptly staggered three feet sideways into the bar's coat rack.

"Right, in we go." SJ shoved the door open, slid her arm under Allegra, and wrestled her inside.

Any chance of sneaking in quietly evaporated when the brolly stand toppled with a crash. A photo frame slid off the wall, which SJ managed to catch mid-fall, only to knock the stand over again in the process.

"What in the hell is going on?" Daisy's sleepy voice carried down from the banister.

"Nothing, babe, just a...well, just—"

Daisy was already stomping down the stairs. One glance at Allegra clinging to SJ's shoulder and swaying like a drunk pirate, and her lips pressed into a thin line.

But before Daisy could scold, Allegra's face crumpled. Tears spilled fast, surprising even her.

"I'm such an idiot," she blurted, words tripping over one another. "I didn't go for what I wanted, and now I've ruined everything, because I'm scared and stupid and—God, isn't that childish?"

Her voice cracked on the last word, her body shaking with sobs.

Daisy's tiredness melted away instantly. She crossed the hall in two strides, brushed Allegra's damp hair back from her face, and gently guided her to sit on the bottom step.

"Hey, shh…" Daisy said softly, crouching in front of her. "You're not stupid. You're just hurting. We'll figure it out in the morning, alright?"

Allegra sniffed, still hiccupping through her tears. "I just… I let John…and now Blythe…" She blinked through blurred, alcohol-softened vision and focused on Daisy. "Why does nobody fight…for me?"

Sammy-Jo opened her mouth to say something comical, but Daisy shot her a sharp, warning look: *Not now.*

"I don't know the answer to that, sweetie," Daisy said, voice gentle, "but what I do know is a good night's sleep will help clear your head. Come on, let's get you up to bed, and in the morning, we'll work it out."

Allegra let herself be pulled to her feet. "Just want…someone…to see…" she murmured, wobbling, lurching towards the wall as Daisy held on tight, "me."

"I know," Daisy whispered, pressing a reassuring hand to her back. "And we do. Lots of people see you."

Allegra shook her head. "No… I'm just… All I… Just a pretty face."

"Well, there's no denying that," Daisy smiled, "but we know you're more than just that." She kept encouraging upwards movement. Five steps done, several more still to go. "And we need to get you out of these wet clothes."

Allegra stopped suddenly and fell back against the wall, reaching up and cupping Daisy's face as she tried to focus. "I just want my, you." She smiled.

"Well, you can't have her." Sammy-Jo laughed, coming up the stairs to help Daisy get Allegra to bed.

"No." Allegra laughed. "Not Daisy… She's all… But she's lovely, and…" she dragged the words out, "a grown-up."

"You don't see her when I put my cold feet on her—nothing grown-up about that reaction." Sammy-Jo chuckled, taking the playful punch to the arm that came her way.

"Nobody likes cold feet on them." Daisy grinned. "Are you going to help or hinder?" Turning her attention back to the task at hand.

"Help, obviously." Sammy-Jo laughed, grabbing Allegra around the waist and lifting her off her feet, carrying her up the remaining steps. "See? Always helpful."

Forty-Three

Her head thumped—loud, insistent, and angry with every subtle movement. It took a full three minutes to roll onto her side and focus on the clock. The bright numbers swam into view: 10:14.

Beside it sat a glass of water and two painkillers. She smiled faintly—that would be Daisy, she thought. But then another thought struck, unbidden and sharp: Blythe...and that woman.

Allegra groaned, burying her face in the pillow. "Why did you let that get to you?" she muttered to herself, reaching for the painkillers and swallowing them down with the water.

A gentle tap at the door, twenty minutes later, still sounded like a battalion breaking it down. Allegra mumbled a weak, "Yes?"

The door opened and Daisy poked her head in. "Can I come in?" she asked softly, before entering anyway, carrying two mugs of tea.

Bracing herself, Allegra shifted upright against the pillows. She closed her eyes as the pain settled, the edges of it dulling now that the painkillers had begun to kick in. Still, her head felt like it had a pinball in it, ricocheting around.

Daisy set the mugs down carefully on the bedside table, the warm steam curling between them. "Tea. How are we feeling?" she asked softly, perching on the edge of the bed.

Allegra blinked slowly, trying to focus. "Like someone's been pounding my head with a sledgehammer...and my brain's doing somersaults." Her hand drifted to the pillow, gripping it lightly.

"Yep, pretty much what I expected you'd say. SJ filled me in. I'm sorry you had such a shitty night."

"It's been a shitty year, if I'm honest." Allegra picked up the closest mug, cradling it as if it could steady her. "First John, then the injury, and then... I don't even know why I'm this upset. We only went on a few dates. It's not like we were in a relationship."

"You liked her, and time has no bearing on that. Look at me and Sammy-Jo."

"True. But still...I can't help feeling like I messed up."

"My mum would say, 'Daisy, what are you going to do?' and that's the only question you need an answer to."

Allegra sighed. "I know... I guess I just need to keep focusing on me, get back to full fitness, and start playing again."

Daisy patted her knee. "That sounds like a plan." She stood, brushing her hands on her jeans. "Let those tablets kick in some more, have a shower, and then we're going out for lunch."

"We?"

"You and me. Sammy-Jo's off helping my dad fix a car." Daisy shook her head with a smile. "I've no idea how much use she'll actually be, but he loves having her around, so who am I to complain?" She shrugged. "I was thinking Aston's. They do a nice lunch, and the sun's out... Might be warm enough to sit outside."

"Thanks, Dais."

"SJ said you can get ready in thirty minutes. I'll give you the hour." Daisy winked and slipped out before Allegra could argue.

Allegra finished the tea, the warmth helping to push back the last fog of her hangover. She swung her legs out of bed and bent to look for her phone, finally spotting it on the floor under the frame. The screen lit up when she picked it up.

One message.

Blythe: We need to talk.

It wasn't until they'd settled at a table in Aston's, inside, thanks to the ominous grey cloud rolling overhead, that Allegra finally pulled out her phone and slid it across to Daisy.

"What am I supposed to say to that?"

Daisy read the message, eyebrows lifting before she handed the phone back. "Well, what was your first reaction?"

"Fuck off." Allegra said it louder than intended. Several heads turned. She raised her hands in apology. "Sorry."

Daisy chuckled. "How do you feel about it now?"

"Like…it's an opportunity to fight my corner, maybe. It can't be serious with this woman, surely? It's been like three weeks…"

"Maybe it was just someone she met last night and it isn't serious?" Daisy suggested. "That would make more sense, right?"

"I guess so." Allegra picked up the menu. "I guess I won't know unless I find out."

"What are you going to say?"

Allegra put the menu down and picked up her phone. "I could go with sarcasm, but I figure I'll be a grown-up and try something real."

"Good."

FORTY-FOUR

Allegra: I'm not sure what you mean by that to be honest. I'm not going to lie and say it isn't good to hear from you.

Blythe read the message while Amanda soaked in the bath, where she'd been for the past hour. In the kitchen, the smell of the casserole drifted through the flat as it bubbled away in the oven.

She still wasn't sure why she'd felt the urge to text Allegra that morning—only that it had seemed like the decent thing to do. She'd lain awake half the night, turning it over, imagining how she would have felt if the tables were turned. Allegra didn't know about Amanda. She hadn't known there was an Amanda.

From Allegra's perspective, it must have looked as though Blythe had moved on without a second thought, as though their connection had been a casual distraction, a fleeting game. *A while-the-cat's-away* scenario.

She felt like she owed it to Allegra to explain. And, deep down, there was a small, stubborn spark of wanting to see her. Blythe closed her eyes and shoved the thought aside. Amanda was everything she'd wanted—here, present, committed to them.

A part of her had assumed Allegra would simply delete the message, and that would be the end of it. Blythe would have attempted to try and explain herself and could have walked away, guilt-free.

So why did she feel it anyway? Guilt. She'd been honest. She'd wanted more, and if Allegra had said yes, she'd have told Amanda she was seeing someone.

Or would she have? Would she always be tempted by Amanda? Always ready to surrender completely, to give herself over in ways only Amanda could draw out of her?

She swirled her wine glass, watching the liquid form a tiny whirlpool, and tried to ignore the tug in her chest that wouldn't be quieted.

Blythe: Thank you for replying. I wasn't sure if you would or not. I'd really like the chance to talk, if that's available.

She'd barely put the phone in her pocket before it vibrated against her leg again, forcing her to fish it out.

Allegra: I'm free now.

Blythe's thoughts raced. Could she just go and meet Allegra now? Amanda was in the bath, they had a night planned together, but maybe it was better to get it over with—put a gentle, final nail in the coffin, rather than let the tension stretch for days.

Her gaze drifted to the bottle of wine they'd opened earlier. She hadn't finished her glass yet, but Amanda had, and Blythe had topped her up a few minutes ago. She grabbed her wallet and keys.

Blythe: Where?

"I'm just popping to the offy for another bottle of that wine—it's almost gone."

"Oh, good idea. Get something sweet too. Chocolate," Amanda called from the bath.

"Anything in particular?"

"No...just chocolate. Nothing in it."

"Got it. Won't be too long."

The first thing Blythe did was stop off for the wine and chocolate. She absolutely wouldn't be a liar, no matter how much this felt like sneaking around.

She arrived at the same house as before. The same one she'd come to the last time they'd needed to talk. Maybe that should have told her something.

The door opened before she could even press the bell. Dark curls, lots of them—Sammy-Jo. Blythe remembered her. This time, though, the friendliness was gone.

"Do not mess her around," Sammy-Jo said flatly, stepping aside to let Blythe in. Then she was gone, thumping up the stairs, leaving Blythe to find her own way into the lounge again.

But Allegra wasn't sprawled on the sofa this time. She was glammed up, polished, ready to step out. Sensational. For a moment, Blythe wondered if it was for her. Allegra caught the look instantly.

"Don't worry. I'm heading out." Her tone was cool, distant.

"You look amazing," Blythe said anyway, because it was true.

"Hm. So...what's to talk about?"

Of course there'd be no small talk. Allegra was always straight to the point.

"I just thought it was necessary to put the record straight about...last night. And about...Amanda."

The name landed like a slap. Allegra visibly recoiled, heat flooding her face. "Go on."

"Amanda and I have been—"

"I knew it," Allegra's voice sharpened. "You had a girlfriend the entire time. That's why you were so hesitant." Anger flared in her expression, the kind that came with feeling used.

"No. That's not it. But I can see how it looks."

Blythe exhaled slowly, forcing herself to meet her eyes. "The reason I'm here in Woodington, overseeing this expansion, is because of Amanda. We weren't... We weren't in a relationship. Not to her anyway. I wanted more, and she didn't. So she moved me out—away from temptation, I suppose."

Allegra ran a hand across the back of her neck, her palm settling on her shoulder as though she were holding herself together.

"I was free. Perfectly within my right to start seeing you—or anyone I wanted to. And I wanted to see you." Blythe paused, giving her a beat to process. "But you made it very clear it wasn't something you wanted."

Allegra's throat bobbed, her eyes tightening, but she stayed silent.

"And then Amanda turned up. Out of the blue. She's...changed her mind. She's willing to give me the commitment I wanted. And so—"

"So...what?" Allegra snapped, her voice low, cutting. "You needed to come here and rub it in my face? Is that it?"

"No." Blythe shook her head, her voice softer now. "I just thought you deserved an explanation."

"Maybe what I deserve," Allegra said, voice trembling but steadying as she went, "is someone who doesn't give up on me the first time I panic. Someone who really sees me, who understands me. And maybe that's on me—for not being capable of explaining myself properly." She nodded faintly, the words landing more for her than for Blythe. "But what I don't deserve is carrying the weight of your guilt, or...whatever this is. I won't do that, just so you can feel better about your choices."

Her gaze sharpened, though her mouth curved into something closer to grace than anger. "I hope Amanda is everything you wanted, and that you live the longest, happiest life together."

She crossed the room, opened the lounge door, and held it—a quiet, firm invitation to leave.

As Blythe passed her, Allegra's voice dropped, softer, raw. "I really liked you. I'm sorry I couldn't be who you needed me to be."

FORTY-FIVE

Blythe sat in the car outside, her hands slack on the wheel, eyes fixed on the wine and chocolate on the passenger seat—the tokens meant for a lover waiting at home. In that moment, she knew with a clarity that scared her: she had never been more drawn to another person than she was to Allegra Mann.

Every word Allegra had spoken echoed inside her, not just flat words but sharp, precise strikes that left her hollowed out. She'd come here seeking absolution, but what Allegra had given her was truth.

With a shaky breath, she turned the key, the engine flaring to life. She pulled out of the space too fast, foot pressing harder than necessary, as though speed could drown the echo of Allegra's voice.

Allegra was right. She hadn't come to be honest—she'd come to soothe her own guilt, to be forgiven.

Amanda was curled up on the sofa when Blythe walked back in, hair damp from the bath, a blanket tucked around her shoulders. She glanced at the bag in Blythe's hand, then at the clock on the wall.

"That took a while," she said lightly, though there was an edge of curiosity beneath it.

Blythe surprised herself with how smoothly the lie rolled off her tongue. "The first off-licence didn't have it, so I thought I'd try a different shop before giving up and getting something else."

The words *giving up* ricocheted inside her skull, an echo of Allegra. She forced a smile as she pulled out the bottle and the chocolate.

Amanda's attention returned to the television, satisfied, but Blythe felt the ground shift beneath her. If lying came this easily, what else might?

The smell of the casserole rose up and wrapped around her, warm and grounding, tugging her mind away from everything else.

"I'll dish up. Table or laps?"

Amanda gave a tired smile, stretching under the blanket. "Let's do laps. I'm exhausted." Then, with a sly smirk, she added, "But don't worry, I'll be fully charged to go again soon enough."

Blythe grinned despite herself. The seduction was just too easy—effortless, natural. Everything Amanda said, every flicker of that confidence, seemed to take hold of her clit, winding her tight before she even had a chance to resist.

They sat side by side, bowls in their laps, the TV flickering unnoticed in front of them. Blythe ate mechanically, chewing without tasting, nodding along to Amanda's little comments but not really hearing them. Her mind was elsewhere, replaying words she didn't want to keep replaying.

Amanda was the first to finish, setting her bowl aside with a little clink. She turned towards Blythe, stretching lazily, then in one fluid motion, slipped her camisole off one shoulder and then the other, baring her breasts.

"You look tense," Amanda murmured, her eyes narrowing with a teasing smile. "Have I not relaxed you enough?"

"Just...a lot on my mind," Blythe murmured, setting her bowl aside, though her eyes didn't waver from Amanda's body—soft curves, taut skin, dusky nipples that had already learned the shape of her mouth.

Amanda shifted, smooth and feline, until she was kneeling at Blythe's side. She leaned closer, her hand braced on the back of the sofa, and coaxed her nipple nearer, hovering just close enough that Blythe's lips parted on instinct.

"There..." Amanda's voice dripped silk, self-assured, certain of her effect. "I know you like that."

Blythe's tongue flicked out before she even thought about it, the taste already familiar, the reaction immediate. Her pulse throbbed in her throat, in her belly. It was so easy—too easy—to lose herself in this, to drown out the echo of another woman's voice with the press of Amanda's body.

Amanda shifted with practised ease, sliding one toned leg across Blythe's lap until she straddled her fully, her weight pressing Blythe into the sofa. Her palms found Blythe's shoulders, pinning her back, and her chest hovered just close enough to brush against Blythe's lips.

"Touch me," she whispered, not a request, but a command.

Blythe's mouth opened, warm and eager, tongue first circling one nipple, then the other. Amanda gasped and arched into it, her head falling back, the camisole twisted uselessly around her waist.

"Finger me..." Amanda's voice came lower, breathier, each word thick with promise. She rocked her hips forwards, her heat pressing against Blythe's stomach. "...the way I like it. Slowly."

Blythe's hand slid up the bare skin of Amanda's thigh, the muscle flexing beneath her touch. She hesitated for just a heartbeat, mind echoing with Allegra's voice, with those words—*giving up*—but Amanda's grip tightened in her hair, pulling her back to the now.

And then Blythe gave in, her fingers easing between Amanda's thighs, stroking, teasing, feeling the heat through the thin lace. Amanda shifted against her hand with a small, needy sound, hips tilting forwards to press closer.

Blythe's thumb traced the damp outline, teasing the barrier that separated her from slick skin. Amanda gasped and leaned in, her lips grazing Blythe's ear. "Don't make me beg."

The words rolled through Blythe's body, tightening low in her stomach. She slid her hand beneath the edge of the lace, before her fingers found wet heat waiting for her, hot and ready as though it had always been there.

Amanda exhaled sharply, her breath catching. "Yes...just like that. Slow..."

Forty-Six

Daisy gave Allegra a round of applause the moment the door closed and Blythe left, and she and SJ came down the stairs.

"If ever a performance deserved an award, Allegra Mann…"

Allegra closed her eyes and tried not to let the tears slide, willing her perfectly applied make-up to not smear and leave her looking any more like the clown she felt she was. Her chest still throbbed with the leftover ache of words spoken, truths laid bare, and regret that tasted a little like shame.

"She sat in her car for ages before she drove off," Sammy-Jo said, shaking her head. "I watched out the window. She looked like she was either contemplating life, or trying to remember if she locked her steering wheel."

Allegra gave her a wobbly glare. "SJ, you're impossible."

"Impossible? Me? I am the epitome of helpful observation," SJ replied with a mock bow. "We should check the doorbell video. Maybe she was practising her dramatic exit for a Netflix series and we missed the slow-motion hair flip."

Daisy chuckled, shaking her head. "If that's the case, I'd nominate her for Best Supporting Ex in a Romantic Tragedy."

Allegra groaned, but a small laugh escaped despite herself. "I can't believe you're making this funny."

"Hey," SJ said, hands on her hips, "laugh it off now—you're going to need all the energy for round two of crying later."

Allegra rolled her eyes but couldn't hide the corners of her mouth twitching upwards. Maybe it wasn't *all* catastrophic. Maybe a little humour could sit beside the heartbreak, at least for tonight.

"Ugh, let me get out of all of this and then…pizza?" Allegra said, her hand already on the banister, ready to run upstairs and change into her pyjamas. A lazy Saturday evening in front of the TV with her besties awaited.

"I'll order," Sammy-Jo said.

"I'll open the lemonade and make us mocktails," Daisy offered.

"You two are officially the best people anyone could need."

"Back at ya," Sammy-Jo saluted. "Although there's only one of you."

"You only need one." Allegra grinned as she turned and legged it up the stairs.

But once she reached her room and closed the door the facade crumbled. The smile dissolved, the lightness drained. The hope she'd been clutching onto slipped through her fingers. Blythe hadn't come to fight for her, hadn't come to talk about them. She'd come only to soothe her own conscience.

She moved to sit in front of the mirror, staring at her own reflection. The lashes, the lipstick, the carefully sculpted lines—all armour she'd rushed into place before Blythe arrived. Slowly, she began to remove it. One swipe, then another, until the woman beneath stared back at her—flushed, tired, vulnerable.

Sammy-Jo was right. She was pretty. She could be glamorous when she wanted to be. But more than that, she was a good person. One day, she told herself, pressing the damp wipe against her cheek, someone would see it all. And maybe, just maybe, they'd stay.

But right now, she would allow herself to feel the hurt. Not wallow in it, but not squash it down the way she had with John and everyone who'd come before him. This time, she'd let it sting, acknowledge it for what it was. Maybe that was the only way she could finally grow out of whoever she was right now—scared, small, convinced she was somehow less than. Because she wasn't. She wasn't inferior, and she wasn't going to falter now.

She pressed her palms flat against the dressing table, staring into her eyes in the mirror. The woman looking back was hurting, yes, but she was also strong.

"You are a warrior, Allegra Persephone Mann—even if your parents did saddle you with a ridiculous name."

She smiled at herself, a real smile this time. The sadness still lingered, and that was okay.

Forty-Seven

Gabby's office had never been busier. If she wasn't in meetings with staff—most often Katrine, her new manager, who insisted on keeping her fully briefed—then she was fielding Leila Ortez dropping in to untangle the financial knots of the stadium build, or Blythe Daniels pressing to move their agreement forwards. And then, of course, there was Nora. Her wife's visits were designed to lift her spirits, though the methods were hardly professional. Not that she'd ever complain about those stopovers.

With the door swinging open more often than it stayed shut, Gabby had begun to wonder why she bothered closing it at all.

At last, she leant back in her chair and savoured five uninterrupted minutes with a cup of coffee before her next conversation with Blythe. So far, nothing had been settled—just an agreement to keep talking.

The confident knock on the door made her pause. She glanced at the clock and sighed. Credit where it was due: Blythe Daniels was never late—a definite point in the Olsen Group's favour, along with the frankly ridiculous amount of money they were prepared to pour into the project. And if Gabby were honest, that money would be the difference between a good stadium and an outstanding one.

The door opened and in stepped Blythe, as polished as ever. Tailored suit. Immaculate hair. Always business. Gabby wondered briefly if she herself could pull off a shorter, shaggy bob, but Nora's withering stare when she'd floated the idea still lingered in her mind.

"Blythe. Good morning. Coffee?" Gabby rose, offering her hand.

"I won't, thank you—I've already had several."

"Good weekend?"

"Uh..." Blythe's hesitation was small, but Gabby noticed. Of course she did. "It was...fulfilling," she said at last, with a smile that didn't quite reach her eyes.

"Well, that's good."

They settled into their usual seats, opposite sides of the desk.

"I hear the team won again?" Blythe offered.

"They did. Katrine's had a brilliant start—long may it continue. We've got a short break now."

"Lovely. Maybe that means we'll have more time to finally thrash this out." Blythe smiled as she leant forwards. "In fact, we're aware of a prime piece of real estate about to hit the market."

"Oh? I've not heard of anything in Bath Street other than the land we're already considering."

Blythe eased back in her chair, unbothered. "There've been discussions back in London. The group feels Woodington would be the stronger option—and the most beneficial—for both the hotel and the stadium."

Gabby barked a laugh. "You want me to uproot the club, lock, stock, and barrel, into our neighbour's backyard? Not going to happen."

Blythe didn't flinch. "It's not about neighbours, it's about growth. Woodington offers better transport links, a larger footprint, and a community eager for investment. Bath Street is...limited."

"Limited?" Gabby's voice sharpened. "Bath Street is this club's heart. People here built it brick by brick, stood in the rain when no one else cared, raised the money when sponsors wouldn't. You can't measure that in transport links."

Blythe's smile softened, as if she'd expected resistance. "I admire your loyalty, Gabby, I really do. But loyalty doesn't pay for steel and concrete. Progress means making hard choices."

"And progress," Gabby shot back, "doesn't mean selling your soul. This isn't just a business deal. This is our identity. And if Olsen Group wants in, they need to understand that from the start."

Blythe held her ground. "I'm not suggesting you abandon history, Gabby. I'm suggesting you build a future that honours it in the right location."

Gabby folded her arms. "The right location is here. Where our fans live, where the community breathes us in and out every day. You could offer me a palace in Woodington, and I'd still choose a home here, even if it's smaller, even if it takes longer."

Something in Blythe's jaw tightened. "You make it sound so simple," she murmured.

"It is," Gabby said firmly. "You don't rip up roots just because the grass looks greener next door."

"I'll pass the message on, but I expect they will want me to push this."

"Then let me save you the trouble." Gabby smiled, though her eyes carried the weight of steel. "The deal's off."

Blythe blinked, stunned at the bluntness. Few people ever dared to cut her off like that. Fewer still did it with a smile. For a split second, her composure almost faltered, the image of Allegra's eyes in the lounge doorway flashing across her mind, the echo of *giving up* still rattling around her skull.

She straightened in her chair, mask snapping back into place. "Noted."

Gabby leant forwards, softer now. "Look, Blythe, I know how these groups work. They dangle money, they whisper about greener pastures, but this club is about more than the pound signs. You'll get further with us if you understand that."

Blythe offered a professional smile, one that never reached her eyes. "I'll make sure they're aware."

FORTY-EIGHT

"Not acceptable," Amanda said into the phone. "We're pushing hard on this, Blythe. The land in Woodington would give us a much better access point to pick up airport visitors."

"I know that, but unfortunately that's not a selling point for Gabby Dean. She's adamant the deal is off if we persist with the Woodington site."

"Then you're going to have to change her mind. We're not ploughing millions into Bath Street when there is now a more viable site." Amanda sighed. "Do I need to be more clear?"

"No, I'm just relaying the meeting."

"I'm disappointed, Blythe. I really thought you'd have this signed and sealed by now. Is your mind elsewhere? Is our fucking keeping you from getting the job done?"

Blythe's fingers tightened around the phone. She didn't speak immediately, just inhaled and let the tension roll down her shoulders.

"I—no," she said finally, voice measured, professional. "It's nothing like that. Gabby's not budging, and I'm ensuring I respect the club's legacy whilst pushing our side as far as I can."

Amanda's sigh was audible. "Blythe, I don't need excuses. I need results. You know what this could mean if you don't deliver. Are you even trying?"

Blythe closed her eyes for a second. "I'm trying. I'm pushing. I just…have to navigate Gabby's stance carefully. You know I don't do reckless."

Amanda's pause was long enough to make Blythe swallow hard. "Fine. But I expect you to keep me updated every step. No surprises, no delays."

"I will," Blythe replied, gripping the phone like a lifeline. "Every step."

She hung up and let out a breath, but a flicker of anger slid in—*"Is our fucking keeping you from getting the job done?"*

What had that sounded like? Firstly, insulting, suggesting she couldn't do her job because Amanda Sanchez enjoyed sitting on her face too much. It hadn't been phrased as, "Are we getting in the way?" or "our relationship?" No. It had been reduced, stripped bare, and boiled into one word: *fucking*. Just sex.

Blythe stared at the empty mug on her desk, the words echoing louder than they should have. She picked up the phone again and dialled.

"Yes, Blythe?" Amanda said, sounding utterly unbothered.

"What did you mean by that?" Blythe asked.

"By what? Get the job done?"

"No, the part about…" she lowered her voice, "us fucking."

"What about it? I meant what I said. If us fucking is a distraction for you…"

"Our relationship isn't distracting me from my job."

Amanda remained silent. Blythe could hear the faint clatter of someone moving in the background, the subtle strain in Amanda's voice making her chest tighten as Amanda placed a hand over the phone to address whoever it was, a muffled string of words before she was back.

"Blythe, whatever you want to call it doesn't detract from the question—is it distracting you?"

"Whatever I want to call it?"

"Yes."

Blythe felt it hit—hard and centre—like someone had pressed a hot hand against her chest. Her heart thudded against her ribs, each beat echoing in her ears. Her stomach knotted, and a prickling heat rose to her face.

"Blythe…you asked me to be more…present, and I have, haven't I? But we both know I'm never going to be the moving-in kind of woman. Why can't we just enjoy what we have?"

"I'm an idiot," Blythe muttered, her voice tight, almost swallowed by the sudden rush of adrenaline. Then louder. "An absolute idiot."

"Blythe, can we have this discussion at the weekend?" Amanda asked. "I've got a huge amount on, and a meeting I'm already late for."

"Right… I guess you'd better get on. And Amanda, I won't be available at the weekend."

"Oh, for goodness' sake, Blythe, it's just a word."

"It's not just a word," Blythe said, her throat dry, the words scratching as they left her mouth. "It's commitment. It's loyalty."

"I am loyal. I'm not fucking anyone else," Amanda argued, the sharpness in her tone sending a shiver down Blythe's spine. "I only want to fuck you."

She put the phone down.

FORTY-NINE

She'd left the office after her conversation with Amanda, her chest still tight, the words repeating in her head. Ros had strict instructions to hold all her calls—especially Ms Sanchez's—but Blythe hadn't added why.

A quick stop at the flat let her shed her work clothes. Jeans and a soft sweater replaced the sharp lines of business attire, comfortable trainers and a rain jacket rounding out her armour.

And then she was out again, needing air, needing space.

A long walk along the embankment had taken her from the complex, past the quiet hum of streetlights reflecting off the river, all the way to Banbury Hollow. She might have gone further had the path not been so muddy, sucking at her trainers with every step.

Turning back, she used the torch on her phone to light the way as darkness settled in around her, the cool night wrapping tightly, almost like it wanted to hold her still.

She didn't want to go back to the flat yet, a place where Amanda still lingered. Her perfume clung faintly to the air, sharp and intoxicating, her lace knickers still in the laundry basket as a small, knowing reminder. Images of them together played across Blythe's mind—on the bed, on the couch, in the shower—each memory warm, heated, feral.

And then another image flickered—different, unexpected: a woman, half-naked on the same couch. Alluring, yes, but in a quiet, vulnerable way rather than with Amanda's deliberate seduction. It pricked at something inside Blythe, a tug of longing mixed with guilt, leaving her chest tight and her pulse uneven.

Blanca's on a Wednesday evening was quieter than the weekend, but the rowdy students on a happy hour budget kept the staff busy enough. Blythe nursed a rum and coke, filtered over ice, condensation beading and running down the glass, soaking the warm palm that wrapped around it.

"Can I get you another?" a voice asked, breaking Blythe from her thoughts. She looked up and found kind eyes smiling at her across the bar. "You look like you're in a world far away from here."

Blythe chuckled, a small, self-aware sound. "Yes, something like that." She tilted the glass, melted ice sloshing lazily against the sides. "Sure, one more won't hurt."

"Long day?"

"No, nothing like that," Blythe answered, offering a sad smile as she dug her wallet from her bag.

"That stool has seen many with a face like yours," the woman grinned, pouring a shot of rum into a measure.

"I'm Sadie."

"Blythe." She placed her debit card on the bar. "A face like mine?"

Sadie nodded as she pressed the button that shot cola into the glass, the fizz rising like tiny fireworks. "Yes—wistful, like there's a decision to be made, or has been made, and you're not quite sure if it was—or is—the right one."

"Astute," Blythe said. "But I guess you get a lot of people sitting in bars, contemplating."

Sadie nodded and slid the glass across the bar, condensation trailing against the wood. "Yes, that's true. And most want to talk about it."

Blythe laughed, a low, wry sound. "Not this one."

"Fair enough. Offer stands if you change your mind." Sadie tapped the screen on the till and held the device out for payment.

Blythe pressed her card against it, her gaze lingering on the bartender a moment longer than necessary. "Maybe when I've finished this and my tongue's loosened."

She lifted the glass and took a sip—cold, sweet, fizzy—the bite of rum warming her throat as the cola fizzed across her tongue, grounding her in the moment. It wasn't as if she had anyone else to talk to, and hardly the kind of thing she could share with Ros.

"I've been on that side of the bar, many times," Sadie said softly, polishing a glass. "We're like vicars, sworn to keep the secrets offered whilst intoxicated."

Blythe shook her head and smiled. "You certainly have a way about you that's disarming, I'll give you that."

Sadie dropped the towel. "Why don't I grab a glass and come around that side to join you? You want to talk, you can. Or I can tell you about the history of the bar and how I met the love of my life in here."

"Won't you get in trouble for slacking off?"

"The boss is pretty cool… That's me, by the way. I'm the boss."

"Ah, well in that case…" Blythe tugged a stool out with her foot, the scrape loud against the floorboards, and patted it. "Why the heck not?"

Fifty

Katrine Gustafsson had a lot of ideas about fitness and training—most of them very different from their previous manager. Ninety-minute blocks, twice a day. One session in the gym, one on the pitch. Relentless, structured, efficient.

But Allegra had her own schedule, one that felt just as gruelling. Thirty minutes grinding out miles on the stationary bike, sweat dripping into her collar. Thirty minutes in the pool, arms slicing through the water in steady rhythm. Thirty minutes on managed weights, muscles burning as she counted each controlled rep to strengthen the area around her knee and get her entire body back to its fittest.

Right now, she was absolutely done in.

"Coming down the Riverside?" Sammy-Jo asked as she wandered into the lounge. One look at Allegra and she raised a brow. "I'm gonna guess that's a no then."

Allegra yawned, stretching her arms. "I want to... I'm just so tired. Gunnar is a tyrant."

"We're only grabbing something to eat. And it's only me, Jess, Jas, and Ladonya. Nora said she might pop in, and Astrid is a maybe. I'm driving."

"I guess it's better than laying around doing nothing and then just going to bed."

"There ya go. Up and at 'em."

"Ugh," Allegra groaned, pulling herself up. "Do I need to get changed?" She looked down at her hoodie and yoga pants, then up at SJ's expression.

Sammy-Jo made a face. "Nah, it's just food with friends."

"Yeah, but Astrid might turn up, and she's going to be—"

"I thought we weren't bothered about the labels?" Sammy-Jo interrupted with a raised brow.

"I mean…maybe a little bit." Allegra grinned, rubbing the sleep from her eyes. "Gimme ten minutes."

"I'll give you fifteen, but then I am going…so move it, Mann."

"Don't boss me, Costa," Allegra shot back, but she was already on the stairs and heading towards her room.

"Someone has to," SJ called after her, a small smile tugging at her lips. She grabbed her phone and called Daisy. "Hey."

"You persuade her?" Daisy asked, her voice warm, a faint clatter of dishes audible behind her.

"Course I did." Sammy-Jo grinned.

"Told you, she just needs encouraging."

SJ checked the hallway and up the stairs before lowering her voice. "Well, I've got some of the girls on board to keep dragging her out. That way it won't look like it's just us being too—"

"We care—that's allowed. She's our friend," Daisy said firmly.

"She'd do the same for me, so…" SJ's eyes flicked to the noise from upstairs. "Right, I'm going to go and let you enjoy your evening. See you later?"

"Yep, I'll be home."

"Good…'cos I was thinking—"

"Uh huh…I was thinking the same."

SJ exhaled happily. "I really love having a girlfriend."

"I really love sex, so I guess it's a match made in heaven." Daisy laughed, warm and easy over the line. "Later, baby."

Fifty-One

"Do you always sit around talking to strangers about their woes?" Blythe asked. They'd settled comfortably into a booth, drinks in hand, trading small talk and people-watching, catching the glances of those clearly more interested in them than in their own company.

"Sometimes," Sadie said with a smile, propping an elbow on the table. "Feels like a rite of passage, I suppose. And obviously, it helps when said strangers actually want to talk…which, I think you do."

Blythe exhaled, easing back against the seat. Her eyes met Sadie's and lingered there, steady but uncertain. "What confuses me most is that I'm not this person. In any other aspect of my life, I've got it together. But women…" She gave a rueful laugh, shaking her head. "That's a whole different ballgame."

"I get that a lot," Sadie said gently, nodding as though she'd seen this play out many times. "You'd be surprised how many competent women are unravelled by unavailable ones."

Blythe turned her glass slowly in her hands, watching the condensation trail down her fingers. "It's not even that she's…wrong. Amanda is—" She broke off, searching for words. "She's magnetic. Clever. Fun. I never feel bored with her. But sometimes it feels like I'm just…part of her entertainment package."

Sadie nodded slowly, letting the silence stretch before answering. "The thing is," she said at last, "there's a difference between someone who makes you feel alive, and someone who makes you feel seen. It took me a long time to learn that."

Blythe's jaw worked side to side, the words sinking deeper than she wanted to admit. "Seen," she repeated quietly.

Sadie gave a half-smile. "Magnetism is easy. Lust is easy. But the person you build a life with? That's someone who knows when you're putting on a show and loves you anyway. Not because you keep them entertained, but because you're you."

For a moment, Blythe said nothing, the clink of glasses and bursts of student laughter filling the gap between them. She lifted her drink again, but it wasn't thirst she was trying to soothe—it was that hollow ache at the centre of her chest.

"I guess so."

"So, what is it about this...Amanda, that's causing so much confusion? Is it just sexual?"

"Maybe..." Blythe rolled the rim of the glass against her lip, her voice low. "I thought it was more. And maybe on my part it is..."

"But?"

"I don't feel like she's ever going to be on the same page as me."

"And what's your page read like?"

Blythe let out a low laugh, but it sounded tired even to her own ears. "That's the thing, isn't it? I don't even know. Stability? Someone who wants...something real. Commitment."

Sadie nodded, her gaze steady, unflinching. "That sounds less like confusion, and more like clarity."

Blythe huffed, running a hand through her hair. "Yeah, well...clarity doesn't always stop you wanting someone you know you shouldn't."

"True," Sadie said softly, "but it does give you a choice. Wanting is instinct. Choosing is where the power is."

Blythe swallowed hard, staring into the fizz of her drink. She wasn't used to being laid so bare, especially not by a woman she'd only just met. And yet, it felt like Sadie had pulled the knot in her chest into the open, where at least she could see it.

Blythe forced a small smile, tilting the glass so the ice knocked against the side. "You make it sound so simple."

"It's not simple," Sadie said, sitting back. "But it is straightforward. People complicate things because they're scared of what happens if they stop making excuses."

"And if the excuse is…she makes me feel alive?"

"Then maybe ask yourself if it's her, or if it's the chaos she brings."

Blythe laughed, louder than intended, but it eased something in her. "God, you should be charging by the hour."

"Don't worry, your rum and coke covers the session," Sadie teased lightly.

For the first time that evening, Blythe felt the edge of a real smile tug at her mouth.

"But…that's not all, is it?" Sadie said, her grin easy, almost teasing. "Allegra Mann?"

Blythe's eyes narrowed. "How would you know about—"

"Well, I admit, I saw you two in here once. And then again at Joie, when I was having lunch with Natalie."

Blythe blinked. "Natalie?"

"My partner." Sadie's smile softened at the mention, a fondness flickering in her eyes. "She likes to drag me out of here once in a while and remind me there's life outside these four walls. I enjoy letting her." She gave a small shrug, the kind that spoke of contentment more than duty. "So, where does Allegra come into this?"

"We went on a few dates, got to know one another a little…before Amanda dropped back into my life. I was interested in seeing where things might go…but she ended things with me."

"Still pining for John?" Sadie asked, her tone gentle, nonjudgmental.

Blythe shook her head and murmured a small, "I don't think so." She exhaled slowly. "She struggled with the idea that I'm older than her."

"And that's not something you can change."

"Exactly. So I respected it, but now…"

"Now?"

"I'm not sure what's going on with Allegra."

"But you still want to find out?" Sadie asked, her voice calm, steady, offering a kind of anchor.

Blythe nodded, letting the tension ease slightly from her shoulders. "Maybe… When everything with Amanda is settled."

Sadie held her glass up, the amber liquid catching the low bar lights. "That's a good plan." She clinked glasses with Blythe, the small sound grounding them both in the moment.

.

Fifty-Two

Franklyn Financials' offices were two floors below the Olsen Group's. In a bright, glass-walled meeting room, Gabby Dean sat at the head of the long table, her posture straight and commanding. Beside her, Leila Ortez had files neatly arranged, ready for reference. Claudia occupied the opposite side, her own meticulously organised papers spread out, and Blythe took the seat beside her.

"I take it, by the fact we're having this meeting, that the Olsen Group has rethought their idea to move the Harriers out of Bath Street," Gabby said, a hint of triumph tugging at her lips.

"I wouldn't say that," Blythe replied evenly. "We still believe the best plan would be to move—"

Gabby shook her head and laughed, standing abruptly. "Are we done here?"

Blythe let out a slow breath, leaning slightly forwards. "I'm hoping we can continue the discussion whilst I try to persuade the powers that be why it matters so much for the Harriers to remain in Bath Street."

"It's been a week, Blythe. I made it clear—nothing anyone says will change my mind."

"I understand that, but I have people I need to convince," Blythe replied evenly, keeping her tone measured.

"Then do that," Gabby said firmly, her eyes unyielding. "Otherwise, this is just wasting everybody's time."

Claudia raised a hand. "I think what we're hoping is to reach an agreement—something Blythe can take back to Olsen that they won't be able to refuse."

Gabby turned to her friend, her expression sharpening. "Then convince me."

Leila leant forwards, her melodic French accent precise as she slid a file across the table towards Blythe. "Let's start with some basics." She began distributing pages. "As you can see, the initial build costs of a stadium specifically for the women's team are substantial, but fully manageable through private investment."

Blythe's eyes flicked over the spreadsheets, noting the detailed projections, sponsorship deals, and community programmes. Every figure reinforced what she'd suspected: Gabby could do this entirely on her own.

Gabby's voice cut through the hum of discussion. "If Olsen wants to be involved, it will be on my terms, not theirs. This is our club, our history, and our decision."

Leila nodded, her gaze steady. "Exactly. The Harriers stay in Bath Street. The club retains full control. Anyone wanting a seat at this table must respect that."

Blythe felt the weight of it. Gabby wasn't just firm—she was immovable.

"Obviously, having a hotel on site increases earning potential for both parties," Leila continued, her voice even and precise. "But it's not essential for what the Harriers need."

Gabby tapped a finger on the table. "We could go with naming rights, advertising, sponsorships—the usual. But if that can be packaged into a deal that helps build the stadium whilst letting me retain more of my investment, I'm happy to listen. Otherwise, I'm building this on my terms."

Blythe nodded, silently acknowledging the challenge: If Olsen wanted in, it would be on Gabby's rules and no one else's.

"Then let's thrash out that agreement, and I'll go back and fight for the outcome we all want. But you have to remember, Gabby, I'm employed by Olsen—it's my job to pursue what they want."

Gabby's smile was cool, assured. "And you've done so admirably. But right now, there's a deal to be made. It can include Olsen...or not. I'm not short of offers for those naming rights."

"Okay, so shall we get down to business before I'm fired?" Leila teased, sliding another file closer with a playful wink.

"Camille would rather lose her own arm than let you go." Claudia laughed.

Leila's lips curved knowingly. "Camille at home isn't Camille at work. And I like it that way."

Blythe sat back, studying them—friends, colleagues, women who had each other's backs. It was rare in her world and oddly refreshing.

For a fleeting second, she wondered what it might be like to be part of something that solid, something where loyalty wasn't conditional or bartered. With Amanda, it had always felt like standing on shifting ground—one wrong word and the balance tilted. Here, in this room, it felt different. Secure. Grounded.

She pushed the thought aside, reaching for her pen as Leila spread out the next set of figures.

Blythe closed her eyes and leant back in her chair as Amanda stared across the desk at her.

"So, change her mind," Amanda said, palms pressed flat against the wood.

"Not going to happen, Amanda. I don't know how many ways you need to hear it, but there is only one way we get to build this hotel, and it's Gabby Dean's way."

Amanda pushed off from the desk and sat back, one leg crossing over the other as her chair inched away, making more space between them. "Not what I want to hear, Blythe."

Blythe shrugged, leant forwards, and with one forefinger, nudged the file back towards her. "We have a great deal in place."

Amanda's suit was immaculate, navy wool cut to flatter every line, her lipstick still perfect despite the long day. Usually, that image alone sent something sparking beneath Blythe's skin. Tonight, though, nothing. Just the cool weight of reality settling in her chest.

Finally, Amanda reached for the file, flipped it open, and began scanning the pages. Her jaw tightened, lips pursing as she read.

"We get the naming rights for ten years," Blythe said crisply. "We also get access to every visiting team, every concert provider…and I'm networking with several local business owners to create diverse and unique experiences our guests can expect by staying at the Olsen Stadium Hotel."

Amanda closed the file and looked up at Blythe. "I'll have the board take a look at it."

Blythe smiled. "Good." She stood, smoothing down her own suit. "Let me know the decision. I'll have the paperwork drawn up and ready."

Amanda nodded. But when Blythe turned to leave, she said, "I'm sorry."

The words caught Blythe on the hop. She turned back to face her. "For what?"

Standing, Amanda considered her words as she edged around the desk and perched on the corner. "I wanted us to work. I guess I'm just not cut out for it—being who you need me to be."

Now it was Blythe's turn to nod, surprised by Amanda's candour.

"I like my life the way it is," Amanda continued. "I want you in it, but I understand that you need something—someone—else…and I can't give you that."

Blythe's lips curved into a small, rueful smile. "We had fun though, didn't we?"

Amanda's shoulders eased, the tension in her jaw softening. "Yeah. We did."

It wasn't love, not the kind that lasted. But hearing Amanda admit it, and parting on that note, felt like the best ending Blythe could have hoped for.

"I'll wait to hear back from you regarding the proposal."

Amanda nodded, lifting the file into her hands. "Yes. Good work. I'm sure there'll be an agreement and then you can get back to your office here."

"Right, yes…that would be…" Blythe hesitated. A couple of months ago, the thoughts had consumed her—getting back to London, back to Amanda, back to her old life. But now, she found she liked Woodington more than she'd expected. "Well, have a good night."

"You too."

By the time Blythe got back to Woodington, it was almost ten. The bars and nightlife were in full swing down by the river, though it was only a Thursday, so the streets weren't packed. The faint tang of beer and fried food drifted from open doorways, mingling with the crisp night air.

She wandered into Blanca's for a nightcap, not expecting it to be bustling, but quiz night was wrapping up and almost every table was filled with people huddled over papers, whispering, then scribbling answers. The low murmur of conversation and the occasional burst of laughter made the bar feel alive and intimate all at once.

Blythe found an empty seat at the bar and claimed it, the worn leather cool under her fingers, and smiled as Sadie spotted her and sauntered over.

"Late night at the office?"

"Something like that," Blythe said, shrugging off her jacket and hanging it on one of the hooks beneath the bar. The faint smell of her day—coffee, paper, and city air—clung to her coat. "I'll take a rum and—"

"Coke. I remember." Sadie winked and reached for a glass, the clink of ice dropping into it filling the brief pause between them.

Sadie set the drink in front of Blythe. She leaned against the bar, nodding towards a corner table where a small group of friends were gathered, laughter drifting from their cluster.

Sadie leaned in slightly, a small smile tugging at her lips. "Just a heads up… That table in the corner—Allegra Mann."

Blythe's eyes followed her gaze. Allegra was there, tucked into a booth, laughing with her friends. Nothing dramatic, just…her. Blythe felt that familiar tug in her chest, a mixture of curiosity and something sharper she couldn't name. She took a slow sip of her cocktail, letting it settle her nerves.

"Yeah, I see her," Blythe said quietly, turning her attention back to the drink in front of her. "Don't make a big deal out of it."

Sadie shrugged, a smile tugging at her lips. "Not my style. Just thought you'd want the heads up."

Blythe nodded, fingers curling around the glass. The fizz from the cola tickled her nose as she took a slow sip, forcing herself to focus on the sweetness and burn of the rum instead of the quiet tension that suddenly settled over her.

"Thanks." Blythe stared ahead at the bottles lining the back of the bar.

"So, good day?"

"Yeah, I think so, actually." Blythe nodded, returning her attention to Sadie. "I had to go to London for an important meeting and was expecting a harder battle than I got, and then…Amanda apologised, which threw me for a loop."

"She didn't sound the kind to apologise. You okay about it?"

"I am. I mean, I think I already was. She's a lot of fun, and yeah, in another life, maybe it would've worked between us."

"Equally, *you* can't be forced into being someone you're not either."

"Exactly. So, I'm just…moving forward, I guess. Focusing on what's in front of me rather than what could've been." She let out a small sigh, swirling the ice in her glass. "It's strange, but it feels…liberating, in a way."

Sadie nodded, eyes steady. "Sometimes the hardest part is accepting that enjoying someone doesn't always mean being meant for them. You're handling it well, Blythe."

Blythe smiled faintly, letting herself settle into the warm hum of the bar, the soft buzz of other patrons around her, and the faint clink of glass as Sadie topped up her drink. "Thanks, Sadie."

Fifty-Three

Sammy-Jo nudged Allegra. "Eleven o'clock."

"What?" Allegra said, eyes still on the page, studying the answer they'd just written down.

"At the bar. Your woman just walked in."

Allegra felt a flutter low in her stomach as she looked up and spotted a familiar figure. "She's not my woman," she said defensively.

Nora turned in her seat to look. "Gabby likes her."

"You want her to be your woman," Sammy-Jo teased with a grin. "What did she say?" she asked Nora before Allegra could respond.

"Not much. I just overheard her and Claudia chatting about some deal they're doing, and Gabby said she liked Blythe—said she had integrity."

"Cool… What deal are they doing?" Sammy-Jo asked, glancing at Allegra, who was still staring across the bar.

Nora shrugged. "No idea."

"What do you mean, no idea? You live together."

"I know, but we don't really talk work at home," Nora said. She pointed to the paper in front of Allegra. "I still say number four is pufferfish."

Allegra rolled her eyes but crossed out shark and wrote pufferfish instead.

"Why don't you go and talk to her?" Sammy-Jo said.

"Who are we talking about?" Jas asked, looking up from her phone, completely oblivious to the conversation.

"Are you cheating?" Sammy-Jo asked.

"No," Jas said quickly, placing her phone face down on the table.

"Why not? We could win if you did." SJ winked. "Anyway, we're talking about the woman at the bar."

Jas glanced across. "The older woman in the suit?"

"Uh huh."

Allegra huffed.

"Why are you huffing?" Sammy-Jo asked, switching her attention back to Allegra.

"I'm not."

"You definitely did," Jas piped up.

"Yeah, that was absolutely a huff," Nora agreed.

"Okay, if you'd all like to hand your paper to the table next to you for the final marking..." the compère announced over the microphone.

Allegra slid theirs across to a woman on her left and took the next table's sheet in return. "I wasn't huffing."

"You were," Sammy-Jo continued to poke.

"Fine, I was," Allegra admitted with another huff. "It's just...every time anyone mentions Blythe, it's always with the precursor of the older woman."

"So?" Nora said, reaching for her pint of shandy.

"So...I don't understand why everyone always needs to point that out."

"It's just a description," Jas said. "Of the three people at the bar, she's the older one. That's all. Like you'd all say I was the dark-skinned one."

Allegra frowned. "I would not."

"Oh, well I would." Jas tilted her head. "What would you say then?"

"If I was describing you out of us?" Allegra asked. Jas nodded. "I'd say you were the... " She hesitated, then huffed again. "I'd say you were the youngest."

"Ha! So you've proved my point."

"Oooh, how would you describe me?" Sammy-Jo asked, bouncing in her chair.

"Annoying."

Nora and Jas burst out laughing.

"Fair," Sammy-Jo said with a grin. "Go and talk to her."

"No," Allegra said firmly. "She's with someone else."

"Did someone put a ring on it?" Jas asked, grinning. "Because if there's no ring…"

Sammy-Jo nodded. "Yep. No ring means—"

Allegra cut her off. "I can ask Daisy on a date?"

"Er—no. That's different." Sammy-Jo suddenly looked a little unwell.

"Did you put a ring on it?" Allegra teased. "See how stupid that sounds?"

"Yes, fine. Fair enough," Sammy-Jo muttered. "But I still think you should talk to her."

"And I still think you should stop talking."

"And the answer to question one is…mince pies!" the compère announced with the enthusiasm of someone who clearly believed they were destined for greater things.

"We need more drinks," Sammy-Jo said, snatching the paper from Allegra. "Off you go…it's your round."

There was no argument. It was true—it was her round, and she could do with getting up and stretching her leg for a bit.

"Same again?" she asked, trying to sound casual, though the thought of walking up to the bar and standing within feet of Blythe filled her with a rush of something that might have been excitement—or fear.

"Yes. Three shandies and a J20," Nora said with a knowing smile.

Allegra pushed her chair back and stood, checked her pockets for her purse, then lifted her chin and turned towards the bar. Towards Blythe.

Fifty-Four

"Incoming," Sadie said, glancing over Blythe's shoulder.

"Really?" Blythe asked, keeping her tone light, though her fingers tightened a little around her glass. She took a quiet, steadying breath.

"You've got this," Sadie murmured before turning her focus to the approaching figure of Allegra Mann—goddess of the football pitch, if half of her regulars were to be believed. Honestly, Sadie couldn't argue. All long legs and that blonde ponytail swishing like it had its own fan club.

"Hey, same again?" Sadie asked as Allegra reached the bar.

"Please," Allegra said, sliding into the space beside Blythe. She glanced right and offered a small smile. "Hi, Blythe."

"Allegra." Blythe lifted her glass slightly in greeting, her lips curving just enough. "How are you?"

"Oh, you know…getting there."

"Great to hear." Blythe smiled, turning a little in her seat until she was facing Allegra and able to study her, to enjoy a moment of just looking. "You look amazing."

"Uh huh," Allegra managed before pressing her lips together.

"So…enjoying the quiz?"

Allegra leant on the bar but turned her head, smirking. "If we knew the answers, I'd enjoy it more, but we're stuck with Sammy-Jo, so…"

Blythe laughed. "Understood."

A brief silence settled between them as they both watched Sadie farther down the bar pulling the last of the three shandies.

"I was thinking..." Blythe began, not actually thinking at all but winging it and hoping, "do you think we could start over?"

Crystal blue eyes lifted to meet hers—curious, cautious. "What do you mean?"

"I mean..." Blythe shrugged, trying to appear casual. "Go out with me. On a date. Dinner."

Allegra laughed, the sound soft but incredulous. "We've been there, Blythe. And anyway...you're seeing someone else, remember?"

"I'm not," Blythe said quickly. "I was...but I decided that wasn't a relationship I wanted."

Allegra's brow lifted, suspicion flickering behind her eyes. "Really?"

"Really." Blythe held her gaze—steady, but soft.

"And now you want me again?"

Blythe ran a fingertip around the rim of her glass. "I always wanted you."

Allegra shook her head, a small, disbelieving smile tugging at her lips. She took a step back, then met Blythe's gaze again. "I'm not that easy."

"Okay..." Blythe said slowly as her smile grew wider. "Can I take that as a challenge?"

Sadie appeared with three pints and set them on a tray, then reached behind her for a J20 from the fridge. "On the tab?"

Allegra smiled. "Yes, thank you." She reached for the tray, then paused and turned back to Blythe as she considered something. "Yes. You can take it as a challenge."

Sadie placed a clean glass on the shelf before she turned back and leant lightly against the bar. "She's given you something to think about," she said, a knowing glint in her eyes.

Blythe smiled, still watching Allegra as she moved away. "Something like that."

"She seems good for you," Sadie added. "You look...lighter already."

Blythe laughed softly, finishing the last of her drink. "Do I?"

"Yes." Sadie nodded. "Maybe you've found something worth chasing."

Blythe set her glass down, the smile still hovering. "Maybe I have."

Sadie straightened and gave her a warm smile. "I look forwards to the next instalment."

Blythe slid into her jacket, glanced once more towards the table in the corner, and then headed for the door, a quiet determination in her step.

Allegra walked away from the bar and felt a small smile curve her lips—right up until she looked up and found three sets of eyes fixed on her, all wearing the same shit-eating grin.

Still, she could feel the weight of Blythe's gaze on her back and the lingering awareness of being watched. It sent a tiny thrill through her. There was no denying it now—she found Blythe Daniels overwhelmingly attractive.

The way Blythe's eyes didn't just look at her—they *saw* her. Allegra remembered how it had felt to sit near her, to have her full attention, the heat of her touch. She wanted all of that again.

"So, I'm not asking how that went. I can tell by the way she didn't take her eyes off you and left," Sammy-Jo said.

Allegra snapped around. "She's left?"

"Literally just a second ago," Jas chimed in. "She was smiling, though. Whatever you two talked about…it had an effect."

Allegra slid the tray onto the table, and hands immediately reached for drinks.

"So, what did you say?" Nora asked, voicing what they were all thinking.

"It was more what she said," Allegra began. "Firstly, she isn't seeing that woman anymore. And secondly, she said she'd always wanted to see me—and asked me on a date."

"And you said yes?" Sammy-Jo filled in eagerly.

"I said I wasn't that easy." Allegra took a sip of her shandy. "She asked if that was a challenge...so I said she could take it that way."

Sammy-Jo grinned. "Well, this is going to get interesting. Let's wish Blythe all the best."

She raised her glass, and the others clinked theirs against it in unison. "All the best, Blythe."

Fifty-Five

There was a brightness in Blythe's step the following morning, drawn from the kind of quiet confidence that made everything feel a little sharper, the air a touch lighter. Her coffee tasted better, her reflection looked a fraction less tired, and even the walk from the car park had felt purposeful. She wouldn't have admitted it to anyone—not even Ros—but the salacious thoughts of Allegra lingered, tucked behind every rational task and sensible thought.

"Ros, just the woman," Blythe said as she rounded the corner and found her assistant typing away at her desk in the outer office.

Ros glanced up, eyebrows lifting. "Morning."

"Can you find out if there are tickets available for the game this Sunday?"

"The game?" Ros looked genuinely puzzled.

"Yes, the game, the match, whatever it's called. Bath Street Harriers." Blythe waved a dismissive hand, trying for casual, though there was an undeniable flash of mischief in her eyes. She turned as if to leave, then hesitated. "They are playing at home, right?"

Ros nodded slowly. "Yes, Sunday. Midday kick-off against London City."

"Right, so…tickets?"

"I'll have a look. I'd imagine you can still get some. How many?" Ros got up and followed Blythe into her office.

"Just the one," Blythe said quickly—maybe too quickly. "Oh, and I need a shirt."

Ros frowned. "A Bath Street Harriers shirt?"

"Yes, with Allegra Mann's name and number on it." She smiled as though that were an obvious conclusion and sat down.

Ros blew out her cheeks, amusement playing across her face. "I'll have to go and actually get it because it's too late to order and have it delivered." She checked her watch. "The club shop should be open."

"Perfect. Off you pop then. Have an extended lunch break. I'll see you back here at one."

As Ros disappeared, Blythe sank further into her chair, unable to stop the small smile that formed. Her heart gave a quiet, hopeful flutter.

Allegra had given the go-ahead to attempt a wooing, and that was something Blythe fully intended to do.

She picked up her phone and opened her contacts. It amused her slightly that Allegra's name sat right above Amanda's. Three times already that morning, she'd gone to write a text and changed her mind. Slipping into a simple 'good morning' felt lazy, she decided. Every message now needed to matter—concise, intentional, meaningful.

Blythe: I'm unsure what your day looks like now that, I assume, you're back in training…but I've booked a table at Banjo, 7pm. I'd love to spend some time with you. Bx

"Busy?"

Blythe looked up from her desk to find Claudia standing in the doorway.

"Not really," she said with a small chuckle. "Until we get the go-ahead from corporate, I'm in a bit of no-man's-land."

"It is a tad frustrating," Claudia agreed, stepping further into the office. "But it is what it is, I guess."

Blythe gestured towards the chair opposite with an easy sweep of her hand. "So, what can I help you with?"

Claudia blushed faintly as she sat, crossing one leg over the other. "Well, it's more what I can help you with—if you're interested."

"Oh, do tell," Blythe said, her tone light as she mirrored the smile.

"I'm wondering what your long-term intentions are here." Claudia gave a soft laugh. "That didn't quite sound how I meant it to. What I mean is—will you be moving back to London, or can we perhaps persuade you to linger a little longer?"

Blythe smiled, leaning back in her chair. "That depends on whether there's something worth lingering for."

Claudia's lips curved, amusement sparking in her eyes. "Oh, I'm sure we could find you a reason or two."

Blythe's mouth twitched, just enough to suggest a secret: A long-legged, blonde reason mostly, she considered. "I haven't decided. The offer to return is on the table, but I don't know—Woodington has its charm."

Claudia nodded, thoughtful. "It does. People underestimate that. The pace, the community—it gets under your skin."

"It does," Blythe agreed, eyes drifting briefly to the window, where sunlight streaked across the glass. "More than I expected."

Claudia smiled softly. "Well, that sounds like the beginning of something, not the end."

"So, what was the reason you asked?"

"Ah, well..." Claudia sat forward, her tone brightening. "The Women in Business group has its tri-annual meeting next month, and it's an opportunity to put forwards potential new members. Gabby and I both thought you might be that potential."

Blythe nodded. It was a solid network to be part of, she knew that. But the sour taste left after her guest appearance—the delightful Lorelai incident that had sent Allegra running—didn't exactly fill her with enthusiasm.

"Can I think about it?"

"Of course."

When Claudia left, Blythe exhaled, glancing at her phone again. Still no reply. But for the first time in a long while, she didn't mind the waiting.

Fifty-Six

Allegra stepped out of the pool, water streaming down her legs, and grabbed a towel, wrapping it tight around herself before yanking off her swim cap. Her ponytail tumbled free, damp strands clinging to her neck. Her lungs burned from the effort, but her knee—blessedly—didn't ache at all. She grinned across at Taylor.

"All good?"

"Yes." Allegra reached for a second towel, draping it over her shoulders. "Didn't feel a twinge. I just need to build my fitness levels back up."

"That'll come," Taylor said, falling into step beside her as they headed for the changing room. "We'll up the gym work for a bit and see how that goes. I think we're definitely on track."

Allegra nodded.

At the lockers, Taylor gave her arm a quick pat. "Just remember, don't overdo it. Stick to the plan, and we'll have you back on that pitch in no time."

"I know," Allegra said, smiling as she reached for her bag. "Thanks, Tay."

"Go shower, I'll log the session." Taylor gave her a quick nod and disappeared towards the office, leaving the changing room quiet except for the distant hum of the pool filters.

Allegra sat down on the bench, towel still tight around her shoulders. The ache in her muscles felt good—earned. She rubbed a few stray droplets from her leg, half-expecting to feel that familiar pain in her knee, but there was nothing. For the first time in months, it felt like hers again.

She reached into her bag for her phone, intending to check the time, and froze when she saw the message waiting on the screen.

Blythe: I'm unsure what your day looks like now that, I assume, you're back in training…but I've booked a table at Banjo, 7pm. I would love to spend some time with you. Bx

Her heart gave an unhelpful flutter. Banjo. Seven o'clock. Blythe.

Allegra smiled to herself, thumb hovering over the screen, unsure whether to reply or just let the anticipation sit there a little longer. But that wasn't her style—she didn't play games. Her hesitation, in truth, wasn't about whether she liked Blythe. It wasn't even about the age thing.

It was how quickly Blythe had moved on.

She had questions—about it all—about them, about what this actually meant to Blythe. What if Amanda clicked her fingers again?

Allegra exhaled slowly, then tapped out a reply, her towel slipping a little as she leant against the cool tiles. If Blythe wanted to see her, then fine, she'd see her. But this time, she wasn't walking in blind.

Allegra: Banjo sounds good. 7 works. There are some things I think we should talk about—if you're willing.

She stared at the message for a few seconds, debating whether to add a smiley or sign it off, but decided against it. Simple was better. Clearer.

She hit send, tossed her phone into her bag, and let the smallest traitorous smile tug at the corner of her mouth.

Sammy-Jo honked the horn and waved demonically at her from across the street. Laughing, Allegra checked for traffic and then jogged over.

"What are you doing?" she asked as SJ brought the window down.

"Thought you might fancy a lift?"

"Home?"

"Yes, though I need to stop at the shop first. Daisy's left a list of things she wants for dinner tonight."

Allegra opened the door and got settled in the passenger seat. "What's she cooking?"

"No idea," SJ said, waiting for the seatbelt to click into place. "Whatever requires a red pepper, garlic, chicken legs, paprika, and onions."

"Sounds nice. I'm going to be out, though."

"Out, or out-out?" Sammy-Jo waggled her brows.

"For dinner," Allegra said, before adding, "With Blythe."

SJ laughed. "Fuck me, she doesn't waste any time, does she?"

Allegra stared out the window. "I guess not. But it's probably prudent that we talk."

"Prudent? Did you have a dictionary for lunch?"

The punch to SJ's thigh didn't hurt as much as her dramatic "Ow!" suggested.

"I'm just improving my vocabulary, that's all," Allegra said with a smirk.

SJ snorted. "Well, *prudent* or not, I think it's a good idea. You've got questions, she's got answers. Might as well get them out in the open."

Allegra nodded slowly, the town sliding by outside the window. "Yeah. I just need to know what I'm walking into, you know? She says she's done with that woman, but…it's all a bit quick."

"Maybe she realised she was wasting her time with the wrong person," SJ said. "And you, my friend, are the right one."

Allegra rolled her eyes, though a faint smile tugged at her lips. "You've been reading too many romance novels."

"Excuse me, I live with Daisy. Everything in our house has a happy ending."

"Except your DIY projects."

"Oi!" SJ shot back, grinning. "You're just jealous of my shelf."

Allegra laughed, shaking her head. "Sure. Let's go with that."

But as the laughter faded and the radio filled the quiet, Allegra found herself gazing out the window again. The thought of seeing Blythe tonight made her pulse quicken—not just from excitement, but nerves, too.

It wasn't lost on her things could go either way. Dinner could be the start of something—or the closure they both needed. And for the first time in a while, she wasn't sure which she was hoping for more.

Fifty-Seven

The sun had already set, and the early winter chill had begun to settle in as Blythe switched on the light and opened her wardrobe. She rummaged through hangers, her fingers brushing over fabrics until she found a pair of navy cords. She grabbed a light blue shirt, weighing her options, before finally pulling out exactly what she wanted: a navy-blue knitted tank top.

Smart, yet casual. Comfortable, but put together. She held it up for a moment against the shirt, and over the trousers, letting her thoughts drift to Allegra and the evening ahead, the small thrill of anticipation warming her against the cold creeping in through the window.

A hot shower had already set her blood racing, and now, as she dressed and checked her watch, excitement began to bubble beneath the surface.

This was her moment. Her chance to step into the evening with purpose, to put forward a proposal so compelling, Allegra wouldn't be able to say no. She imagined the conversation, the laughter, the shared glances—moments that could seal the deal and set the stage for happier times ahead.

Allegra stared at herself in the mirror. The dress, the heels, the hair, the make-up—all of it was perfect for a date. She was sure of that.

"Why are you pulling that face?" Daisy asked from where she sat on the edge of the bed. "You look stunning."

Turning, Allegra smiled briefly. "Is that the image I want to give?"

"I think so." Daisy laughed. "Knock her socks off—and anyone else who happens to look your way. It won't do her any harm to see just how many people want Allegra Mann."

Looking up at the ceiling for a moment, Allegra then turned back to the mirror. "I like the way she looks at me. As if she actually likes *me*, not just the idea of sleeping with me."

"Then she's a winner already," Daisy said, grinning. "You can still knock her socks off."

Allegra stayed quiet.

"You are who you are, Leggy. Benefitting from great genes is just luck of the draw. Anyone who meets you knows you're more than a pretty face."

"I know, I just… Is it even a date? I mean, I know she thinks so, but do I? I'm basically there to talk."

"Pretty sure that's what a date is for." Daisy smiled and stood. "I don't know where this self-doubt in you keeps coming from lately, but it's going to have to leave." She took hold of Allegra's shoulders and turned her to face her. "Now, SJ's downstairs waiting to drive you, and she'll come pick you up at any time, but…if you decide not to come home…" She laughed. "Just have fun."

Allegra took a deep breath and smiled. "Okay, you're right."

She grabbed her coat and bag, still feeling the echo of Daisy's laughter behind her as she headed downstairs. The sound of a car horn blaring twice made her smile—Sammy-Jo, impatient as ever.

When she opened the front door, the cold hit first, then SJ's voice.

"Bloody hell, Leggy!" she called, leaning across the passenger seat to stare at her through the open window. "You're not going for dinner—you're going to ruin someone's life dressed like that."

Allegra laughed, pulling the door open. "It's just dinner."

"With Blythe," SJ said pointedly, eyes raking her outfit with exaggerated appreciation. "That's not 'just dinner' attire. That's 'hope she's wearing clean undies' attire."

Allegra rolled her eyes as she slid into the seat. "You're disgusting."

"Honest," SJ corrected, grinning. "And impressed. You look incredible. She won't know what's hit her."

As they pulled away from the house, Allegra smoothed her dress over her knees and exhaled quietly. "It's not like that. We're just going to talk."

"Yeah, sure," Sammy-Jo said, flicking on her indicator. "And I only go to the gym for the vending machine."

Allegra laughed despite herself, shaking her head. "You're impossible."

Fifty-Eight

Of all the eateries she'd been in so far, Blythe was pretty sure Banjo might be her favourite. Claudia had told her about it—fancy enough without being pretentious—and said she often came here with her daughter and her friends.

"You'll love it," Claudia had said.

And so far, she was right.

Arriving early, Blythe sat at the bar and ordered a cocktail—Love on the Brain—a lot of rum. The name felt apt. She perched on the stool facing the door, crossing her legs and pretending to scroll through her phone while she waited.

The door opened three times, and each time, disappointment trickled through her. But then she saw the car pull up outside, headlights slicing through the dark, and the door open. One long leg slid out, followed by the rest of her—Allegra Mann—statuesque, confident, utterly impossible to look away from.

Blythe's breath caught. The faint golden light from the restaurant spilled across Allegra's hair. She straightened fully, gave the street a brief glance, and started towards the entrance. She didn't rush. She didn't need to. Every movement was measured, effortless—like she owned the night without even trying.

When Allegra stepped inside, she took a moment to scan the room, and when her gaze landed on Blythe, her lips curved into the kind of smile that made the wait worthwhile.

Blythe felt her pulse quicken. She lifted her glass slightly in greeting, trying to look calm—businesslike even—but the flutter beneath her ribs betrayed her as Allegra closed the space between them.

"Hey," Allegra said, stopping in front of her, eyes noting the glass. "What are you drinking?"

"Love on the Brain," Blythe replied with a smirk, warmth curling through her tone. "And a lot of rum." She took a sip through the straw. "Kind of apt, don't you think?"

Allegra reached for the drinks menu, glancing at the bartender as he came closer. "I'll have a Flirtini," she said.

The bartender nodded, before slipping away to create it, and Allegra settled onto the stool beside Blythe. She stole a quick glance at her, noting the ease with which Blythe held herself, the faint smirk that hinted at amusement—and maybe something more.

"You look…amazing," Blythe said, letting her eyes linger just a moment longer than necessary.

Allegra laughed softly, a little breathless, cheeks warming. "So I've been told. You look nice too."

"Well, one thing I am very good at is presentation." Blythe smiled. She caught the waiter's eye. "Would our table be free?"

"Of course, come this way. You can leave your drinks. We'll bring them over." He smiled at them both.

Blythe stood, waited for Allegra to follow suit, and then walked behind her.

"I'm not that easy, remember," Allegra said quietly over her shoulder, before following the waiter.

"No, you are not," Blythe murmured to herself, a grin tugging at her lips. "And I wouldn't want you any other way."

They took their seats at a table by the window, tucked into a quiet corner and away from prying eyes and listening ears.

"Thank you," Blythe said to Allegra, adding, "for accepting my invitation."

"Well, we should probably talk, shouldn't we? And that's not going to happen if we don't sit down together."

"That's true." Blythe smiled and paused as the waiter returned with their drinks. "Thank you," she said, taking the menu he offered. "This is on me, by the way," she added quietly once he'd stepped back.

"No arguments from me." Allegra opened the menu, scanning the steak options. "The Wagyu looks good."

"Worth every penny," Blythe replied with a grin.

When it came to ordering, Allegra chose the salmon, her fingers lingering on the napkin as she tightened her resolve, finally looking up at Blythe.

"What do you want from me?"

Blythe sat back, studying Allegra. "Starting easy, huh?"

"I told you, I'm—"

"Not easy." Blythe's smile widened. "Okay, cards on the table. What I want has never changed. I like you. I'm attracted to you. You're beautiful—stunning—but I need more than surface level. I think you're smart, funny, and you have integrity. And I want to find out where this can go." She leant forward, brushing her fingers over Allegra's hand that still lingered on the napkin. "I want to go on dates, get to know you…romantically."

"What's different from last time?" Allegra asked, holding her stare, curiosity and caution shimmering in her eyes.

Blythe pulled her hand back and lifted her glass, taking a measured sip through the straw as she considered her words. "I think when we first met, we were both in very different places. Now…I feel like maybe we're edging towards being on the same page."

Allegra picked up her glass, tilting it slightly as she took a sip.

"Let me ask you the same question," Blythe said, eyes locking with Allegra. "What do you want from me?"

"Sex," Allegra said, straightforward, her tone serious.

Blythe blinked, then nodded slowly. "Just sex?"

"No," Allegra added quickly, pressing her lips together for a moment. "But I want to be clear—I want sex. Lots of it, actually." She let the honesty hang between them. "If I get involved with anyone again, it needs to be sincere, and intimate. And I need you to not let me run away the next time I panic."

Blythe considered her. "And what does that look like in practice?"

Allegra's eyes narrowed just slightly, a spark of challenge in them. "It looks like giving me some space. Not just taking me at my word and walking away…into someone else's bed."

Blythe let the words settle, then reached back across the table, her fingers brushing lightly against Allegra's. "I can do that. But for the record, I didn't just jump into someone else's bed. Things with Amanda were—"

"She's pretty," Allegra interrupted.

"Yes," Blythe acknowledged, "she is…but like I said, I need more than surface level." Their fingers intertwined. "Amanda isn't who I want. You are."

"Prove it," Allegra challenged

"If you let me, I will," Blythe responded, quiet confidence settling in her tone. The waiter reappeared with their meals, and Blythe released her grip on Allegra's fingers to make space as she picked up her cutlery.

They ate in a comfortable silence at first, broken only by the occasional sip or clink of glassware. Blythe's eyes drifted over Allegra, noting the way the low light played across her cheekbones and the subtle tilt of her head. She allowed herself a small, wry smile, the kind that carried both amusement and affection.

Allegra caught the look, causing her cheeks to faintly blush. "What?"

"Nothing," Blythe said, her voice warm, a small smile playing at her lips. "Just appreciating my company."

Allegra's grin was slow, deliberate. "I missed you."

Blythe's eyes sparkled. "I missed you too."

"I'm scared," Allegra admitted, her voice dropping just slightly, "that I'll let you in, fall in love with you, and you'll leave." The words surprised even her, but they were the truth. "I wanted to keep things casual because then, when you left, it would just be what was expected. But the truth is… I'm scared of being hurt again."

"I'm not planning on hurting you." Blythe's voice was low, steady, the warmth in it threading through the quiet of the corner they occupied.

"Nobody plans to... I know that, but..."

Blythe remained still, letting her speak the words she needed to say.

"You already did. Seeing you with Amanda..." Allegra's words were tight, her fingers brushing the edge of the table as her eyes narrowed.

"I'm sorry," Blythe said earnestly. "I respected your decision. And honestly, I was hurt by it too. I didn't understand it, but I respected it—I respected you."

"I know, and I love that about you, I do." Allegra shifted, the leather of her chair creaking, a small smile appearing before she pressed her lips together and paused for a moment. "And I know it must seem quite childish, having a fully grown adult sit here and tell you she might panic and run."

"I don't think it's childish. I think...you've been hurt, and trauma can show itself in different ways." Blythe regarded her, conveying security and warmth. The noise of the restaurant fading into the background as their world narrowed to just the two of them.

Fifty-Nine

Blythe paid the bill as Allegra finished the last of her second drink. She felt the warmth of it settle through her chest, a gentle buzz that made the edges of the evening feel softer. She watched Blythe with a quiet attentiveness, noticing the easy way she smiled at the waiter, the polite confidence in every gesture. They were small things, but they made Blythe even more magnetic.

Sexier somehow.

Maybe she'd had too much alcohol. She didn't drink much usually. Not at all when she was fit and playing, but she was weeks off from that, so she figured SJ was right—enjoy it while she could.

"Are you in a rush to get home?" Blythe's voice brought her back from her thoughts.

"No, I just have to call SJ to pick me up when I'm ready."

Blythe glanced out of the window. "How would you fancy a walk down to the Riverside?"

"Hm. That's a long walk." Allegra chuckled, tugging slightly at the edge of her sleeve. "I'm not sure I'm supposed to be doing that."

"Oh, of course," Blythe said, cheeks warming. "I didn't think."

"We could get a cab and then walk along the riverbank for a bit," Allegra suggested, a small grin appearing.

"I would like that," Blythe said, pulling her phone free and bringing up the Uber app. It wasn't even 9 p.m. yet, and the evening was still young. "The car will be here in three minutes."

Blythe stood and reached for Allegra's coat, holding it up for her to slip her arms into.

"Thank you."

Blythe's fingers lingered just a moment as Allegra slipped into her coat, the soft wool settling around her shoulders. "My pleasure," she said, voice low against Allegra's ear.

Allegra felt a little breath catch in her chest. "Shall we?"

Blythe nodded, stepping aside as they saw the Uber pull up to the kerb. She opened the door to the taxi. "After you."

The ride was smooth and quiet, and Blythe was perfectly fine with that. They sat on opposite sides of the back seat, not touching, but each resting a hand in the space between them, just inches apart.

Blythe thought about reaching out, but hesitated—not because she feared being rebuffed, but because she wasn't sure she'd be able to let go once she did.

She smiled to herself as she looked out of the window. Her nervous system felt calm. She felt calm. Settled in a way she hadn't been for a long time.

When the car stopped, Blythe was out and around the back before Allegra had even reached for the door handle. She pulled it open, smiling as surprise crossed Allegra's face.

"Chivalrous."

"If you'll let me, yes," Blythe replied.

Allegra stepped out, standing just inches from her. Her eyes studied Blythe's face. "I think I could get used to it."

They stood there for a long moment, engrossed in one another and in their thoughts.

"Close the door, love, I've got another passenger to get to." The driver leant through the gap between the seats, his tone friendly enough as he made his point.

"Oh—yes. Sorry." Blythe shut the door, and they both watched as the car pulled away.

"So, how about that walk?"

"Let's do that," Allegra agreed.

They'd taken two, maybe three steps when Blythe felt it—the softness and warmth of fingers sliding against her palm as Allegra silently took her hand.

She was about to comment on it when Allegra said, "Don't make a big deal of it. Just go with me."

"Okay. I prefer that." Blythe glanced at her quickly. The streetlamps and lights from shop windows and neon café signs painted shifting shadows across Allegra's face. She looked like something carefully created—something Blythe could stare at for hours. "But I should point out that I spend my life curating, organising, building, and planning. So as much as I do love a relationship that grows organically, and as much as you require patience from me…that needs to be reciprocal."

"I know." Allegra smiled shyly at her. "Shall we get a hot chocolate?"

Blythe followed Allegra's gaze to their right, towards the small coffee shop still just about open.

"That's a big yes from me."

Allegra's smile turned into a grin as she tugged on Blythe's hand, pulling her towards the door. "My treat," she said when she noticed Blythe's other hand drift towards her jacket's inside pocket.

"I thought you were letting me be chivalrous?" Blythe said playfully.

Allegra stopped and turned back to her, her fingers gliding down the lapels of Blythe's blazer. "I think you're allowed to be the princess occasionally."

Blythe mirrored her movements, her palms rising to cup Allegra's cheek. "I'll happily be your princess," she murmured, "but you'll be my queen."

She didn't wait for a response—didn't care where they were. She leant in and pressed her lips against Allegra's.

"Was that okay?" she asked when she pulled back, noticing the slightly glassy look in Allegra's eyes.

"Which part?" Allegra's voice was soft. "The kiss, or being your queen?"

"Either. I don't want you to feel uncomfortable." Blythe moved to step back, but Allegra gripped her hand more tightly.

"Don't do that," she whispered. "Don't pull away. Just...give me a moment."

"I was giving you space, that's all. Not pulling away."

Allegra nodded slowly. "I'm just... I've never been anyone's queen. I'm not even sure what that really means. I've been a token, an exhibit...something to show off." Her eyes shimmered. "But the kiss—I liked the kiss."

Blythe smiled gently. "Then we'll start there," she said quietly. "No exhibits. No pedestals. Just you, and me...and whatever this turns into."

"We're closing in a moment. Did you want to order something?" a voice called from behind them.

Blythe peeked over at the woman behind the counter, who was smiling knowingly at them. "Two hot chocolates to take away, please."

Standing side by side, fingers linked, they waited in comfortable silence. It didn't take long before the barista brewed two steaming cups, clicking the lids into place as the scent of cocoa curled through the cool night air. Allegra handed over a ten-pound note with a quiet "thanks".

"Thank you," Blythe said, taking both drinks before passing one to Allegra. Their fingers brushed, a spark of warmth cutting through the chill.

"Careful," Blythe added with a grin. "It's hot."

"I can handle hot," Allegra replied, smirking as she blew gently across the lid.

They stepped out onto the pavement, the quiet ripple of the river not far off, streetlights shimmering across its surface. For a while, they walked in easy silence, shoulders occasionally brushing, steam rising between them. Neither said a word—but both knew the night wasn't over yet.

SIXTY

The temperature dropped as they neared the end of the path before it turned into the grassy, now muddy, continuation. Neither of them were wearing appropriate shoes, and Blythe was already worried about how far they had walked.

Conversation had been easy, playful. Hands were still held. It felt like the perfect date. But she knew she was wrong.

As they stopped, Blythe said, "We should turn around and go back, don't you think?"

Allegra glanced around. They were alone—nothing but the gentle current of the water and the stars overhead. "I think you're right, but—"

"But?"

Closing the space between them, putting herself face to face with Blythe, Allegra leant in, her breath warm against Blythe's mouth. "I think you should kiss me again."

"Oh, you do?" Blythe chuckled, her pulse quickening.

"Mm hm." Allegra nodded. "I mean…as your queen, I could just order it."

Blythe laughed, taking the empty cup from Allegra and dropping both cups into the bin. "You seem to have come around to that idea quite quickly."

"Just testing the water…"

Deciding not to question further, Blythe reached for Allegra's coat, her fingers gripping either side of the zip. She pulled her forwards, earning a small yelp as the sudden movement caught Allegra by surprise.

Before either could speak again, Blythe pressed their lips together, firm and insistent, claiming the kiss as if it had always been hers to take. Allegra's hands went to Blythe's shoulders, pulling her closer, while Blythe's fingers travelled up and threaded through the ends of Allegra's hair, tilting her head slightly, deepening the kiss. The heat between them spread immediately, urgent and unrelenting, each movement bold, each breath shared.

Even as the world around them continued—the chill of the night, the distant hum of the city—it felt as if time had set a rhythm that belonged only to them.

Allegra's breath caught, a shiver running through her as Blythe's hand stroked her jaw, gentle but intentional. When they finally parted, their foreheads rested together, chests rising and falling in sync.

"Was that…enough testing the water?" Blythe whispered, voice low, teasing.

Allegra smirked, breathless. "I think we might need more…practice."

"I'm a big fan of that kind of practice." Blythe held her arm out for Allegra to take. "But maybe somewhere warmer—you're shivering."

Allegra looped her arm through the space Blythe's elbow made and pulled herself closer. "I don't think it's the cold causing that reaction."

"Ah, well, that's an even better explanation." They walked on. "Would you like to get a nightcap at Blanca's?"

"No, I think I've had too much alcohol as it is. I might not be fully fit yet, but I'm already way over the limit I'd usually set for myself. And it's getting late."

"Okay, I get it."

"It's not a brush-off," Allegra explained. "I want to stay out all night with you. I'd take you home and let you fuck me all night, but…I need to not lose myself in this. I need to remain focused on my fitness and—"

Blythe stopped walking and pulled her close again. "I get it." She held Allegra's gaze firmly, her voice steady, "I'm a slow burn, remember. I'm not here to rush you, Allegra. I want us to move at a pace that works for both of us."

Allegra exhaled slowly, her fingers tightening slightly around Blythe's biceps. "Thank you. That matters. I don't want to feel like I'm holding something back because I'm playing a game to make you chase me. I'm worried about losing control."

"You won't," Blythe assured her. "And I'm not going anywhere. I also don't want you to feel like you have to run from anything. Not tonight, not ever."

Allegra let a small, relieved smile form. "That…that means a lot."

"Now, let's get you home."

They fell back into a comfortable silence, walking side by side, hands linked, the night around them quiet except for the soft crunch of their shoes on the path. It wasn't fireworks or declarations—it was understanding, trust, and a shared space that felt rare and solid.

SIXTY-ONE

Allegra closed the door to her room and sank back against it, feeling hornier than she had in years. She shut her eyes and replayed the kiss—the way her body had melted as Blythe took control, those hands against her skin again. Even now, she could feel the sensation thrumming through her nerve endings.

She kicked off her heels, dropped her bag and coat, and reached behind to slide the zipper low enough to grab and pull the rest of the way down. The fabric fell away as she walked towards the bed, pooling at her feet.

Her reflection in the mirror stopped her movement. Tanned skin from the summer, with faint lines where her shorts and T-shirt had blocked the sun. Soft white lace still covered her modesty—the same underwear she'd worn the night she'd been this naked with Blythe on her couch.

She smiled to herself, her palm flattening across her chest and smoothing the skin in slow motion. A part of her hungered for that touch again, to feel this raw and vulnerable. But fear kept it at bay.

Her phone buzzed, pulling her out of her head and back into the room. She bent down and picked up her dress, folding it over the chair at the vanity before reaching into her bag for her phone.

Allegra sank onto her bed, pulling the covers up around her legs. Her phone felt warm in her hand, the screen lighting up her face in the darkened room. She couldn't stop the small, breathy smile that had settled on her lips.

Blythe: One day I won't be sending this message. You'll be here, wrapped in my arms, and I'll whisper against your ear that I adore you.

Allegra's thumb hovered over the screen, heart thudding in her chest. She typed back, carefully at first, fingers shaking slightly.

Allegra: You have a lot of faith in my being in your bed.

A few seconds later, Blythe's reply appeared.

Blythe: It's a given…and I like to plan for things.

Allegra bit her lip, cheeks warming. She shifted slightly under the covers, the sensation of the soft sheets against her skin suddenly more noticeable. Her fingers drummed lightly on her phone as she thought about the kiss, the heat of Blythe's hands, the way she'd taken control.

Allegra: I might just let you plan a little…

Blythe: Oh? Do you approve of my plans?

Allegra felt a thrill run through her at the simplicity of the question. She pressed the phone against her chest for a moment, feeling the rapid beat of her heart, the pulsing ache between her legs.

Allegra: I'm…intrigued.

Blythe: Careful, you might be giving me ideas.

Allegra's lips curved into a mischievous grin as she traced idle circles on her skin under the sheets, letting herself imagine the possibilities. Heat pooled low in her body, insistent, demanding attention.

Allegra: I might be testing how exciting you can be.

Blythe: I'd say that's an experiment to be done in person…

Allegra felt the flush spreading across her body, the warmth engulfing her. She lied back, letting the phone light up her face, fingers ghosting over her skin as she typed the next message, the words carrying a confidence she hadn't felt all day.

Allegra: You have no idea the effect you're having on me right now…

The reply came almost instantly.

Blythe: I might have some idea.

Allegra swallowed, a shiver sliding through her at the thought of Blythe's calm, knowing smile hovering over her. Her fingers drifted along the edge of her knickers, teasing herself.

Allegra: Tell me.

Her touch moved unconsciously, slipping beneath the lace, exploring the warm, slick heat Blythe's words inspired.

Blythe: Maybe you're alone…in your room…laying on your bed, the phone in your hand… One hand.

Allegra felt her body react, a sharp contrast to the cool sheets. She tugged the phone closer, fingers trembling slightly as she typed.

Allegra: And the other hand?

Blythe: Why don't you tell me, Allegra? I think you want to…

It felt as though Blythe was there with her, watching her fingers move, teasing her, pacing her desire without ever rushing it.

Allegra: You already know.

Her pulse quickened as she watched the screen, clit throbbing as she slowed her movements in anticipation of what Blythe would say next.

Blythe: I do…and I want you to tell me. All of the details, Allegra.

"Fuck," Allegra murmured, words lost in the sensations building inside her. Her fingers moved faster, the phone abandoned on the bed as need took over. Her mind was awash with thoughts of spelling it out, telling Blythe exactly what she was doing and why—those ideas only deepening the ache between her legs.

The phone buzzed again on the sheets. She ignored it, too close now to let anything get in the way of what she needed.

Every touch, every slick movement, sent shivers through her. She pressed her body into the mattress, letting the warmth and desire consume her. The thought of Blythe watching—even from afar—was so hot.

Curiosity got the better of her. Fingers scrabbled for the phone, pressing buttons and unlocking the screen to reveal the message.

Blythe: The idea of lying beside you, hearing you moan and slip into that delirious state of pleasurable release…turns me on so much.

Allegra's breath hitched, every nerve ending alive with sensation. She couldn't stop the small, shuddering moan that escaped her lips as her fingers moved again, almost of their own accord.

Allegra: I'm already there just thinking about you.

Her cheeks burned. She wanted Blythe watching every movement, every small gasp. The thrill of being seen, even through a screen, made her hips surge upwards. Her fingers teased herself, the sensations sharper knowing Blythe was enjoying it from afar.

Allegra: I want you to know how much...how desperate I am for you right now.

She pressed the phone to her chest for a moment and urged herself over the precipice. When the phone buzzed again, it was all she needed.

Blythe: I want to be that person for you.

SIXTY-TWO

Match day Sunday was hectic. A home game, kick-off at midday, and Sammy-Jo had already gone to the training ground for breakfast with the team and last-minute instructions from Katrine about tactics.

Allegra woke with a spring in her step. After Friday night's very successful date, Blythe had given her space on Saturday, surprising her by not bombarding her with messages or pushing to meet up. That was how most of her relationships had gone before. The moment she'd given the go-ahead to be intimate in any way, they'd been relentless, trying to get her into bed as often as possible.

"You look like you've just discovered the cure for something horrible," Daisy said, sliding onto the sofa beside Allegra. One leg curled underneath her as she cradled her mug, steam wafting into the air.

Allegra smiled. "Maybe I have."

"Gonna elaborate, or leave me guessing?"

Shifting to mirror Daisy, Allegra's face lit up further. "I was just thinking about my previous relationships with people. Well...I think half the reason they failed was because they were set up that way to begin with."

Daisy leant in, curiosity catching her eyes. "How do you mean?"

"Like...I wasn't that into them. Don't get me wrong, at the time I thought I was. I threw myself at some of them—especially John. But now, I'm starting to understand that maybe it was because I wasn't afraid of it ending."

"But you were upset when John left, right?"

Allegra nodded. "Yes. At the time I thought my heart was broken, but now...I think it was more my ego that got dented. I felt rejected."

"Wow. This is enlightenment, Leggy. And how does that make you feel?"

"Strangely...optimistic." She grinned, the warmth in her chest making her shift a little closer to Daisy.

"And does this revelation have anything to do with Blythe?"

The smile widened. "Maybe... I think she's a big part of it. She really listens, and I know now that I got all caught up in my ego again when she respected what I'd said and walked away. She wasn't leaving me...I was the one pushing her."

"So, does this mean you and her are together?"

Allegra shrugged. "I think I still need to work on that, but...I'm hopeful. It's certainly where she wants us to head, and I can't deny that she's making it very difficult not to want it too—"

"But?"

"Maybe my ego still needs a little work."

Daisy placed her mug down and took Allegra's hand, her touch warm and grounding. "Just be honest, at every step. She sounds like someone you can be vulnerable with." She released Allegra's hand and leant back, settling into the sofa. "I think people take your self-confidence and assuredness as a sign you don't need anything else from anyone, and that's maybe a box you've let yourself fall into. We all need someone else from time to time, and it's okay to let them know that."

"I want to be that person. I want to trust someone enough to let them in, and I think I just need someone who actually wants to do that—someone who'll stick around when I get scared. Blythe somehow makes it easier for me to be that honest."

"Because she listens."

Allegra nodded. "And she's not desperate to get me into bed." She chuckled. "I mean, she absolutely wants to sleep with me, but she's… What did she call it? A slow burn?"

"Oh, nice."

"Yeah? I mean…I have needs." Allegra giggled, the warmth of the laughter filling the room.

"Personally, I think there's nothing sexier than someone who wants to know you. And I think you think that too…after everything you just said. She's sexier because she's not pushing for sex. You're being more vulnerable because she's giving space for that to happen."

"Yeah…I guess so."

Daisy glanced up at the clock. "Coming to the game?"

"Yes. Can I cadge a lift with you?"

"Absolutely."

Sixty-Three

Blythe pulled the new football shirt on and paused, reconsidering. The weather was grim—not raining, but the temperature was definitely dropping as October edged towards its end.

She'd need a coat, a big jumper at the very least, which made the shirt almost pointless. Unless... A thought struck her. She peeled the shirt off, grabbed one of her thermal jumpers, pulled it on, and then layered the shirt over the top.

It looked a little ridiculous, the long sleeves bunching awkwardly underneath, but hell—she could be a little ridiculous for Allegra Mann, couldn't she?

Then another thought hit her: was Allegra even going to the game? Pulling out her phone, she tapped out a quick message.

Blythe: Are you busy today?

Barely a minute passed before Allegra responded.

Allegra: Going to the game with Daisy, but I'm free afterwards.

Blythe: Great...Maybe see you there.

Allegra: You're going to the game? I thought you hated football.

Blythe smiled, her thumb hovering over the keyboard for a moment before replying.

Blythe: I have a sudden interest in hot women running around in shorts...a specific hot woman.

Allegra: I'm not sure who you might be referring to. X
Blythe: You'll find out. Where are you planning to sit?
Allegra: Prawn sandwich seats.

The message bamboozled Blythe. She frowned, trying to figure out if that was a typo or a real place.

Blythe: I have no idea what that means.
Allegra: Haha, sorry. It means with the posh lot—the board.
Allegra: Do you want to sit with us? I can probably get you in, and you're friends with Gabby, so she'd say yes. If you want to, of course.
Blythe: Are the benefits of this prawn sandwiches?
Allegra: Not a chance. But you might get a pie at half-time. Meet me outside the main reception on the east side of the stadium.
Blythe: I'll see you there—thirty minutes.

Allegra's last text was a thumbs-up. Grabbing her coat, she pulled it on and filled her pockets with keys, phone, and her wallet.

It would be a bugger to park, she thought at the last minute. She called an Uber.

Allegra spotted Blythe weaving through the crowd, coat pulled tight around her. Her heart skipped a beat. She remembered Friday night, and suddenly Allegra was painfully aware of how much she'd missed seeing her. And then she remembered the texts, and that Blythe knew what she'd been doing.

"Hey," Blythe said, her smile warm and easy as she reached Allegra's side.

"Hi," Allegra replied, trying to sound casual, but knowing she didn't. Her fingers twitched at her side, betraying the flutter in her stomach.

Blythe leant slightly closer, her voice dropping to a low. "I've been thinking about Friday," she murmured, letting the words brush just above Allegra's ear.

Heat shot straight to Allegra's cheeks. She opened her mouth to respond, then closed it again, tongue-tied. "Oh...really?" she managed, her voice betraying more than she'd intended.

Blythe's eyes sparkled with mischief. "Yes. I had a really good time."

Allegra laughed nervously. "Uh...yeah. It was definitely interesting." She turned towards the building. "This way."

They fell into step together, but Allegra couldn't focus on anything except Blythe's nearness. The playful tension between them made her pulse race faster than she liked to admit, and she realised just how much she had been looking forwards to this moment.

"Hey, Carol, can you... I need a pass for..." She faltered, suddenly unsure how to describe Blythe. Partner felt far too serious, girlfriend sounded weird, and it was still too early for any of that.

"Friend. Blythe Daniels," Blythe supplied smoothly, stepping forwards and taking the lead in finding a solution for Allegra.

"Yes," Allegra agreed. "She's sitting with me in the players—"

"No problem," Carol said. "Just sign in here." She placed a book and pen on the counter and twisted it around for Blythe to sign.

"Great," Allegra said, surprised at herself as she reached for Blythe's hand and pulled her towards a short set of stairs.

She led the way until they reached a door that opened out to reveal the stadium. The pitch spread wide before them, the roar of the crowd swelling from a distant hum into pulses of sounds—drums, chanting, the buzz of anticipation that made every match day electric.

Before they stepped out, Blythe caught Allegra's wrist and gently pulled her to one side. There was no one else around as she slid a hand behind Allegra's neck and drew her close, kissing her with sudden, searing intent. The world fell away—the noise, the cold, everything but the press of Blythe's lips and the rush of heat that followed.

"Sorry," Blythe murmured against her mouth, breath warm and uneven. "I just...wanted to do that from the moment I saw you."

"Nothing to be sorry about," Allegra said softly, trying to catch her breath. "I like you kissing me."

"Good."

They stood there, suspended for a heartbeat longer, eyes locked, until the sound of approaching footsteps broke the moment.

"Blythe, what a nice surprise…" Gabby Dean appeared, all smiles and enthusiasm. "I didn't know you were coming to the game."

"No—last-minute thing," Blythe said, her voice slightly unsteady as she tore her gaze from Allegra.

"Allegra. How are you doing? Nora says it won't be long before we have you back."

"Fingers crossed," Allegra replied, looking away and down the hall, avoiding eye contact from both women.

Gabby looked between them, a knowing smile flickering across her face before she squeezed past. "Enjoy the game."

When she was out of sight, Allegra exhaled, still feeling the ghost of Blythe's kiss on her lips. "She knows."

Blythe turned to her, eyes curious. "Knows what?"

Allegra hesitated, then let the truth slip out before she could overthink it. "That we're into each other."

Blythe's smile deepened, slow and certain. "Sweetheart, anyone looking at us and not seeing that has an eyesight problem."

SIXTY-FOUR

Blythe moved along the row of seats Allegra pointed towards.

"This is Daisy," Allegra said as they settled in behind another pretty blonde with a ponytail. "She's Sammy-Jo's girlfriend."

"For my sins," Daisy quipped, turning with a grin. "You must be Blythe."

"For my sins, yes," Blythe replied, matching her tone.

"Lovely to meet you." As the laughter faded, Blythe glanced around. Gabby sat a few rows ahead with a cluster of men in suits.

At that exact moment, Gabby turned, caught Blythe's eye, then looked back at Allegra before winking at Blythe. It wasn't often anyone could make Blythe blush—but Gabby had done just that.

"So, this is a tad nicer than the seats on the other side," Allegra said, amused.

"Hm?" Blythe blinked, then smiled. "Oh—yes, definitely. Comfier with the padding. And warmer."

"Heated in here," Allegra said, nodding. "Do you want a drink? We've still got a few minutes. There's usually something to eat, too." She thumbed over her shoulder towards the door they'd come through.

"I'm okay for now, thank you." Blythe unzipped her jacket. "I might just take this off…" She slipped one arm free, then the other, and let the jacket fall away.

"You bought a shirt?" Allegra's grin spread.

"Not just any shirt." Blythe laughed, turning around so her back was to Allegra.

"Oh my God." Allegra burst out laughing, covering her mouth with her hand as she read the name and number. "Mann—number five? You got my shirt?"

"Of course I did," Blythe said, still smiling as she turned back to face her. "I may know absolutely nothing about football, but I know who I want to watch…and I know who I want."

Allegra's smile faltered, just for a heartbeat, as the weight of Blythe's words sank in. Blythe didn't rush to fill the silence—she gave her room to process it.

When Allegra finally spoke, her voice was quiet but steady. "After the game, can we go back to your place?"

Blythe reached for her hand. "Anything you want to do today is fine by me."

The corner of Allegra's mouth lifted. "Anything?"

Now it was Blythe's turn to pause, to study the mischievous glint in Allegra's eyes. "Yes."

A loud roar swelled around them as the teams walked out onto the pitch. The rumble of the crowd rose into cheers, drums thudding, chants echoing through the stands. Everyone stood to clap—everyone except Allegra and Blythe, still caught in their small, private moment.

"Should we be clapping?" Blythe asked, her fingers still loosely linked with Allegra's.

"Probably." Allegra grinned, pulling her gently to her feet. She released Blythe's hand so they could join in the applause.

"Who are we playing?" Blythe leant closer to be heard over the noise.

"We? You a Bath Street fan now, huh?" Allegra laughed.

"I'm an Allegra Mann fan. Wherever she plays, I'm a fan." Blythe nudged her shoulder lightly.

The crowd slowly settled back into their seats, and Blythe followed when Allegra did the same.

"London City," Allegra said.

"Are we expecting to win?"

Allegra turned slightly, the spark of competitive pride in her eyes. "We *always* expect to win."

The line-ups finished over the loudspeaker, and as the whistle blew, the players dropped to one knee. Blythe leant in close, her voice low enough for only Allegra to hear. "You're beautiful, do you know that?"

Allegra's cheeks flushed. "Does it sound arrogant to say I know?" she said softly. "I've been told it my entire life. Google me—no one ever mentions how good a footballer I am until they've commented on what I look like. So yes..." she sighed, "I know I'm beautiful. But when you look at me that way..." Her eyes flicked to Blythe's, warm and searching. "That's when I actually feel it. And that's the part I don't often know."

"That insight into yourself—that's what truly shows your beauty."

Daisy leant back towards them, grinning. "If you two don't get married, I'm going to bang your heads together."

"Shut up." Allegra laughed, giving Daisy a playful shove back into her own seat.

"I'm just saying..." Daisy twisted around, murmuring, "You're cute together."

"I agree," Blythe said easily, her focus flicking towards the pitch just as a player took a shot on goal. "Ooo, I think we almost scored."

Allegra chuckled, patting Blythe's thigh. "That wasn't us, babe."

SIXTY-FIVE

This time, when Allegra reached the door to Blythe's flat, she didn't step inside first. Instead, she caught Blythe by the wrist and pulled her in close, kissing her—the kind of kiss that left no doubt about what came next. The kind of kiss that said, 'we're not waiting'.

Blythe responded instantly, pushing her gently backwards until Allegra's shoulders met the wall of the corridor. Their breaths mingled, the air between them charged.

"I want you," Allegra murmured against Blythe's skin as her lips brushed the line of her neck.

Blythe's fingers curled into the fabric of Allegra's shirt, her breath hitching. "Are you sure?"

Allegra pulled back just enough to meet her eyes, her hands framing Blythe's face. "I've never been more sure of anything." Her thumb traced the curve of Blythe's cheekbone. "I was scared before—scared I wasn't enough… that I'd mess it up. But I'm not scared now."

Something shifted in Blythe's expression. She kissed Allegra again, slower this time but no less intensely. When she drew back, her voice was rough. "Bedroom."

They barely made it inside. Blythe slamming the front door behind them as they moved, locked half in embrace, half in exploration, towards the bedroom.

Allegra's hands slid under the hem of Blythe's football shirt, fingers brushing against the thermal jumper beneath, lifting them both, as she was urged backwards, their mouths never quite separating.

"God, you're impatient," Blythe said, but there was laughter in her voice.

"You're overdressed." Allegra laughed.

Blythe lifted her arms, letting Allegra strip both the shirt and jumper off in one go.

They stumbled through the bedroom doorway. The late afternoon sun filtered through the windows, casting everything in soft amber, making it feel romantic and sensual.

Allegra's calves hit the edge of the bed and she sat, looking up at Blythe standing before her, hair slightly mussed, eyes dark, wearing only her bra.

"You're beautiful," Allegra breathed, her hands settling on Blythe's hips, pulling her closer until she stood between her knees.

Blythe's fingers threaded through Allegra's hair, tilting her head back. "So are you." She leant down, kissing her deeply again, and Allegra's hands slid further up to warm skin. Blythe shivered, and Allegra felt a surge of confidence—this woman, so controlled in every other aspect of her life, was beginning to unravel under her hands.

Allegra reached for the clasp of Blythe's bra. Her fingers trembled slightly—not from uncertainty, but from the excitement of the moment.

"Hey." Blythe caught her hand. "We don't have to rush."

"I know. I just... I want this. I want *you*."

"You have me," Blythe said simply, removing her hand to allow Allegra to complete the task.

She finished unhooking the bra, sliding it down Blythe's arms, and for a moment she just looked, taking her in. Then she leant forwards, pressing her lips to the soft skin just above Blythe's heart, feeling the rapid thrum of her pulse.

Blythe's hands tightened in her hair, a quiet sound escaping her throat before whispering, "Allegra..."

"Tell me what you want," Allegra murmured against her skin, her hands mapping the curve of Blythe's waist, the dip of her spine.

"You. Just you." Blythe's voice was ragged now. "To touch me."

Allegra's mouth traced a path lower, and Blythe's breath came faster, her fingers gripping Allegra's shoulders. When Allegra's lips closed around her nipple, Blythe gasped, her knees nearly buckling.

"Bed," Allegra said, pulling back with a grin. "Before you fall."

Blythe laughed and pushed her backwards onto the mattress, following her down. "You're bossy when you're horny."

"You love it."

"I do." Blythe settled over her, straddling her hips, and the weight of her made Allegra's head spin.

She made quick work of Allegra's shirt, tossing it aside, then paused, hands resting on Allegra's stomach, just looking at her.

"What?" Allegra asked.

"Nothing. Just... I've thought about this. About you."

Allegra reached up, cupping Blythe's face. "Me too."

Blythe leant down, kissing her slowly, thoroughly, whilst her hands explored—tracing ribs, the curves of her breasts, the athletic lines of her body. Allegra arched into the touch, a soft moan escaping as Blythe's mouth followed the path her hands had taken.

"You're so responsive," Blythe murmured against her skin.

"I haven't had sex for months," Allegra joked, her voice breaking as Blythe's hand slid lower, fingers deftly unfastening her jeans.

"Can I?"

"Yes. God, yes."

Blythe shifted and eased the jeans down. Allegra lifted her hips to help, suddenly desperate to feel skin against skin. When they were both finally bare, Blythe settled beside her, one leg draped over Allegra's, their bodies aligned.

"Hi," Blythe whispered, smiling.

Allegra laughed softly, some of the intensity morphing into something tender. "Hi."

Then Blythe's hand moved between them and all coherent thought fled. Allegra's eyes fluttered closed, her breath coming in short gasps as Blythe touched her with confidence.

"Look at me," Blythe said, and Allegra forced her eyes open. "I want to see you."

It was intimate in a way that went beyond physical. Allegra was being seen—being *known*. Her hand found Blythe's hip, pulling her closer, and then she reached between them, mirroring Blythe's touch.

Blythe's eyes widened, then darkened, a low moan escaping. "Allegra..."

They moved together, finding a rhythm that felt instinctive. The room filled with the sounds of their breathing, whispered names, soft encouragements. Allegra felt the tension building, coiling tighter with every touch, every kiss.

"I'm close," she gasped, her free hand fisting in the sheets.

Blythe stilled her hand and Allegra's eyes flew open, a protest forming on her lips. But then Blythe was moving, kissing a slow path down Allegra's body—between her breasts, across her stomach, lower still.

"Blythe—" Allegra's voice broke as realisation hit.

"Let me," Blythe murmured against her hip, her breath warm. "I want to taste you."

Allegra's hips lifted involuntarily, and Blythe's hands slid beneath her, holding her steady. Then her mouth was there, and Allegra cried out, her head falling back against the mattress.

"Oh, God—"

Blythe moved her tongue with deliberate intent—exploring, learning what made Allegra gasp, what made her thighs tremble. She was thorough, unhurried, as though she had all the time in the world to unravel her.

Allegra's hand found Blythe's hair, fingers tangling in the strands. "Don't stop. Please don't stop."

Blythe hummed against her, the vibration sending a fresh wave of heat through Allegra's body. Her tongue circled, then pressed, and Allegra's back arched off the bed.

"Blythe—I'm—"

"I know. Let go. I've got you."

The tension snapped, and Allegra shattered, Blythe's name torn from her lips as pleasure crashed over her in waves. Her thighs clenched around Blythe's head, entire body trembling, and Blythe didn't let up, drawing out every last tremor until Allegra was boneless and gasping.

When she finally stilled, Blythe pressed a soft kiss to the inside of her thigh, then another, before crawling back up Allegra's body. She settled beside her, one hand stroking damp hair back from Allegra's flushed face.

"You okay?" Blythe asked softly, her lips quirking into a satisfied smile.

Allegra turned her head, still trying to catch her breath. "That was... Christ, Blythe."

Blythe laughed, the sound warm and content. "I'll take that as a compliment."

Allegra reached for her, pulling her into a kiss, tasting herself on Blythe's lips, which somehow made everything feel even more intimate. When they broke apart, she grinned. "Your turn."

"Allegra, you don't have to—"

"I want to." Allegra rolled them over and kissed her way down Blythe's body, taking her time, savouring every gasp and shiver. When she finally settled between her legs, she looked up, meeting Blythe's gaze. "I really, really want to."

Blythe's breath hitched, her fingers gripping the sheets. "Well, when you put it like that..."

"Tell me if I do something you don't like."

"Trust me," Blythe said, voice already rough, "I don't think that's going to be a problem."

Allegra grinned, then lowered her head. The first touch of her tongue made Blythe's hips jerk, a low moan escaping. Allegra took her time, exploring, learning the same things Blythe had just been educated on.

"God, Allegra—" Blythe's hand found her hair, not pushing, just holding on. "Just like that. Don't—don't stop."

Allegra didn't. She focused, intent on giving Blythe everything she'd just been given. She felt Blythe's body tense, heard her breathing quicken, and then Blythe was crying out, her back arching as she came undone.

Allegra stayed with her through it, gentling her touch as Blythe's body slowly relaxed. When the tremors finally subsided, she pressed a soft kiss to Blythe's hip before crawling back up beside her.

They lay there, hearts racing, bodies trembling, neither quite able to speak yet.

When Allegra could finally breathe again, she turned her head to find Blythe watching her, a soft smile on her lips.

"Worth the wait?" Blythe asked, her voice hoarse.

Allegra pulled her close, kissing her softly. "Absolutely. Though I don't plan on waiting that long again."

Blythe laughed breathlessly. "I'm not sure I could now, either."

"Round two then?"

SIXTY-SIX

Round two became rounds three, four, five, and a stay over.

"You can stay as long as you need, but I have to get going," Blythe said from the end of the bed, already dressed in her work attire of a navy fitted suit, and adjusting the cufflinks on the shirt she wore.

Allegra studied her from the pillows—somewhat masculine, but with a very feminine edge. The best of both, Allegra considered.

"I should probably get home. I have more rehab this morning."

Blythe finished with the cuff and looked down at her lover, still under the covers, hair hanging loosely, coffee cup cradled in her hands.

"If I didn't have this meeting..." Blythe said, her voice trailing.

"Oh? What would you do?" Allegra purred. She moved the cup to one hand before pulling back the covers to reveal the nakedness that had kept Blythe entertained for the past fifteen hours.

"Do not tempt me." Blythe smiled, though her gaze lingered. She walked around the edge of the bed and leant down, kissing Allegra slowly. "But soon, yes?"

Her hand rested gently against Allegra's thigh, inching slowly upwards until the side of her finger pressed against Allegra's clit.

"Unfair..." Allegra murmured against her lips, her breath hitching.

"Two can play that game." She stood. "Come over tonight and I'll make good on it." Blythe winked. "I'll get Ros to send over my itinerary for the week. Maybe we can make some plans to do something together."

"More sex?"

"As well as that..." Blythe picked up her keys from the side. "I'm very serious about us. I want to know you, not just fuck you."

"Hm, but you do it so well." Allegra grinned, stretching her arms up.

Blythe laughed. "It's not exactly difficult when you're so responsive."

Allegra moved quickly, crawling to the edge of the bed, right in front of where Blythe stood. On her knees, she reached for Blythe, pulling her closer by the lapels of her jacket.

"I'll be thinking of you inside me all day."

Blythe moaned. "God, that's...going to be my thought all day too." Her hand cupped Allegra's jaw briefly before she stepped back. "I have to go. But later..."

Allegra held on. "Kiss."

Stepping back in and closer to temptation, Blythe cupped her jaw once more, this time holding her still whilst she kissed her with intensity.

"You're making me wet," Allegra teased.

"And you know how to deal with that, don't you?" Blythe grinned, reminded of the night before and Allegra's little performance, culminating in one of them bringing herself to release whilst the other was forbidden to touch. "Torture," Blythe murmured. "Beautiful torture."

"Mm hm..." Allegra fell back against the crumpled duvet, her eyes on Blythe, her hand slipping between her legs. "I do."

Blythe watched for a moment. Then she glanced at her watch. She had thirty-five minutes till she was due at the office.

She pulled her phone free and found a number.

"Ros, make sure I have everything for the meeting on my desk ready. I'll be there in twenty minutes." Ros must have spoken because Blythe stood there listening, eyes intense, darkening as she watched nimble fingers working Allegra's wet, swollen clit. "I just have a last-minute issue that needs my urgent attention."

She ended the call and bent low. Grabbing at Allegra's ankles, she yanked her lover down the bed until her backside was perched on the edge. Allegra gasped at the sudden movement.

"Blythe...you're supposed to be—"

Before Allegra could say another word, Blythe was on her knees, head between Allegra's thighs, her mouth replacing those fingers.

"God...yes, just like that..." Allegra mewled as she twisted and arched and writhed.

SIXTY-SEVEN

"So, we've made the decision to go ahead and accept the plans and move forwards with the new stadium complex," Amanda Sanchez said, displaying so much confidence that anyone listening would have thought this was always the plan.

Blythe had zoned out. The taste of Allegra still lingered on her lips.

Voices hummed in the background as she thought about the previous twenty-four hours and her newly developing relationship with Allegra. A smile tugged at her mouth before she could stop it.

"There's no need to look quite so smug, Blythe."

It was only the gentle nudge on her arm from Ros that brought Blythe's thoughts back into the room. Heat crept up her neck.

"Sorry, what was that?"

Amanda rolled her eyes. "The smug smirk—is that really necessary?"

"Ah, yes… No, that was…" She could hardly say she'd been thinking about the way Allegra had looked sprawled across her bed, the sounds she'd made, and the text that had come through twenty minutes ago: *Still thinking about you.* "You're right. Sorry, that was completely… It's all water under the bridge now. Gabby Dean is looking to move forwards. If the board is agreeable now, then we can start really moving."

"Right... So, I'll leave that in your...capable hands..." Amanda said, her eyes fixed on Blythe.

Ros cleared her throat. "I'll get us all some coffee, shall I?" she said, standing and not waiting for an answer from either of them.

When Ros was gone and the door was firmly closed, Amanda tilted her head a little. "Are you still of the mind that our little arrangement isn't what you want?"

Another time, another place, and that kind of question would have had Blythe like putty in her hands. But now, in this time, this place? Not anymore.

Allegra flashed across her mind again. The difference between the two women was stark.

"I think, as we discussed previously, that's run its course."

Amanda nodded. "Well, that's a shame. I quite fancied a night of being bent double whilst you—"

"I get the picture, but no. Actually, I'm seeing someone."

"Oh." Amanda looked genuinely surprised. "That's... I'm happy for you." She smiled, but the smile didn't reach her eyes. Blythe caught it but said nothing. "Is she local?"

"Yes. And it's very new, so..."

"All fucking and fun?"

Blythe smarted at the sly dig. "I'd like to think that it's more than that, but it is recent, so we're enjoying getting to know one another."

Amanda's jaw tightened briefly, but then she caught herself. "I'm really pleased for you, Blythe, and I hope it works out."

"Me too."

As they stood, Amanda packing her briefcase, she said, "I'll make arrangements for this to be a permanent decision."

Blythe frowned. "How do you mean?"

"I think it best that you remain in Woodington, on hand to deal with any issues we might have." Her tone was carefully neutral, but her eyes held something else entirely.

Blythe paused, letting the word settle: *permanent*. A few months ago, she'd have baulked at the idea. Woodington had been a temporary assignment, a stepping stone back to London. But now, with Allegra, maybe it wasn't such a bad place to be.

"I thought I'd be returning to the London office—wasn't that the deal?"

Amanda locked her briefcase before turning her attention to Blythe. "Things change." She smiled. "It's for the best. I need you..." She faltered. "I need you here."

The door opened and Ros reappeared with a tray laden with mugs and a coffee pot. She paused, noticing the atmosphere could be cut with a knife.

"We can reconvene once the plot has been agreed upon and planning is in place." Amanda walked away from the table, back straight, pencil skirt and jacket fitted to perfection.

"That's going to take time, months at best," Blythe said.

Amanda stopped and turned. "I'm sure you can find ways around those obstacles."

And then she was gone.

Blythe exhaled slowly, tension draining from her shoulders as Amanda's distance from her increased. Ros put the tray down onto the table. "Are you two still—"

"No, we're not," Blythe interjected with a little more anger than she'd thought she'd feel.

Ros raised an eyebrow but said nothing, pouring coffee with her usual deliberate care. The rich aroma filled the room, cutting through the lingering tension. She passed a cup to Blythe, who took her seat again. The leather creaked softly beneath her and Blythe wrapped her hands around the mug, letting the heat seep into her palms.

"When you get a moment, tell Claudia I need to speak with her regarding the stadium complex. We need to push on that now. I want shovels in the ground within six months."

"That's going to be a task."

"It always is, and have I ever failed before?"

Ros grinned. "Not since I've been here."

"Right, so...let's get moving. Claudia first. Then I want Gabby Dean and I to have a frank conversation about land purchasing."

"Okay. And do you need reservations for tonight?"

"No, I'll be at home this evening." She stood and went to leave, cup in one hand while the other set about smoothing down her jacket, still feeling the ghost of Allegra's fingers tugging at the lapels earlier. "Oh, I need my weekly itinerary sent to Allegra Mann."

"Allegra Mann?" Ros smirked. "Now it all makes sense…"

"What does?"

"Why Ms Sanchez is not happy with you. I take it the shirt worked?"

"The football shirt was indeed a hit." Blythe smiled, her voice warming at the memory. "A big hit."

Ros's smile softened. "Good. You deserve that."

Blythe grinned. "I do, don't I? And so does she. She's quite…magnificent."

"I'll take your word for it," Ros said, sipping her coffee. "And I'll have everything organised in a jiffy. Will you be taking off early?"

Looking at her watch, Blythe shook her head. "No, I want to get everything in order. I also want to speak with the estate agents regarding the land options. Ms Dean might not be in a hurry to complete this project, but Olsen are."

Ros nodded. "Like you said, you've never failed yet, so…all is in hand."

"Good. I'll be in my office."

Before she entered the hallway, her phone buzzed in her pocket. She slipped her hand inside and retrieved it, flicking the screen awake to see a new message from Allegra.

Allegra: Swimming pool session today…I guess I'm just going to be wet all day…

Attached: image.

The body, she recognised instantly. Heat flooded through her, sudden and sharp. Allegra was clad in a bikini—one of those with shorts, more sports-style than bathing style. Blythe's mouth went dry.

Another message beeped.

Allegra: Can you handle this, Blythe?

She exhaled slowly, thumb hovering over the keyboard. This woman was going to be the death of her.

Blythe: I can handle it, Allegra. Be prepared...

Allegra: Promises, promises, darling... Do you own any toys?

Blythe entered her office and closed the door. She leant back against it for a moment, composing herself. She placed her coffee cup down onto the desk, her fingers trembling slightly as she typed.

Blythe: What kind of toys do you want to play with?

The three dots appeared immediately, then disappeared. Then appeared again.

Allegra: Surprise me...

Sixty-Eight

Blythe opened the door barely seconds after the bell buzzed and was set upon in an instant by a perfectly made-up Allegra grinning into the kiss.

"Mm, that's…quite the greeting." Blythe chuckled as they broke apart.

Allegra bit her lower lip and looked as though she were primed to pounce once more, when Blythe pressed a palm to her chest, trying to hold her back, but she couldn't stop herself from being drawn closer, nose to nose, breaths mingling.

"Hi," she said, staring into crystal blue sparkling back at her. God, those eyes…

"Hey," Allegra replied in a sensual whisper.

"Maybe we should close the door before you rip my clothes off…"

Allegra laughed and glanced back over her shoulder at the wide-open door. "Maybe… That not your kink?"

Heat crept up Blythe's neck. She stepped back, pulling Allegra inside with her, and kicked the door shut. "Not so far…but I'm open to finding out…one day."

Allegra's grin turned wicked. "I'll hold you to that."

She stepped past, and Blythe paused for just a second to remind herself this was real—it was happening. She was getting involved again, with Allegra. The thought made her smile.

"So, what's the plan for tonight?"

Allegra's voice drew her to turn around. Her breath caught at the sight—black lace, all curves and confidence.

Allegra stood in the doorway to the lounge in just her underwear. The coat she'd been wearing now lay discarded in a puddle on the floor behind her. Allegra leant against the doorframe, one hip cocked, watching Blythe's reaction with obvious satisfaction.

"Christ, Allegra."

"I did tell you… I want lots of sex." She pushed off the doorframe and reached behind to unclasp her bra. "And you did say…" It sprang loose. "You could handle it." She shimmied and let it fall away. Catching the strap in one hand, she held it up in front of her then let go.

They watched it flutter to the floor between them, then Blythe's gaze rose slowly—up the lithe, athletic legs, toned torso, and now bare breasts that were small, perky, and perfect. Blythe swallowed hard. Her fingers flexed at her sides, itching to touch.

"I'm 44, not 84. I can handle anything you need." Blythe smirked as she took a first, confident step towards her. "Take those off." She advanced another two steps.

Her eyes glanced down at the lace knickers, the command in her voice enough to make Allegra's eyes grow wider. A flush crept across Allegra's chest. "Oh, you like that…"

"Like what?" Allegra asked, her voice husky, but her fingers were already gripping the sides of her underwear and pushing downwards. Slowly. Deliberately.

"Being instructed what to do…" Blythe paused, watching the performance. "Don't stop." Blythe's gaze darkened, hungry.

As she stepped out of the material, it joined her bra and coat, redundant on the floor. Standing tall again, her eyes met Blythe's. "Not usually…" She looked almost confused, a small frown as she contemplated it. "I guess I like *you* instructing me." The admission seemed to surprise her as much as it did Blythe.

Blythe moved closer. She felt the heat radiating from Allegra's skin. The scent of her arousal was intoxicating. She kept her eyes on Allegra's as her hand moved between them. "Wider," she said, and Allegra implicitly understood and adjusted her stance—feet shoulder-width apart, vulnerable and exposed.

Her breath hitched when the first touch of Blythe's fingers fluttered across her clit, pressure firming as she delved deeper. "You're already wet." There was satisfaction in Blythe's voice, possessive and pleased.

"I told you that earlier..." Allegra said, her eyes closing at the sensations beginning to take effect.

"Eyes on me," Blythe instructed. Allegra's eyes snapped open, locking onto Blythe's. The intensity there made her knees weak.

Blythe smiled.

"Don't get cocky about it," Allegra warned, but then her mouth twisted slowly into a grin.

"I would never abuse my power," Blythe said before sliding her fingers inside Allegra, curling them slowly to press just where it mattered most. Allegra gasped, her hips involuntarily jerking forwards. A small guttural moan tore from Allegra's throat, raw and unguarded.

"Fuck," Allegra breathed, the word barely audible.

"Uh huh, that's my intention," Blythe teased, her movements slow, deliberate. She pressed in, lips ghosting Allegra's mouth. "You like that?"

"Y-y-yes..." Allegra stuttered as her eyes fluttered closed again. Blythe let it go this time, allowing her the moment to fall into her own headspace. Blythe watched her face soften, pleasure washing over her features.

But she wouldn't allow it for long. She wanted Allegra present for this.

Just as she fell into a rhythm Allegra was comfortable with, Blythe shifted her thumb to press against Allegra's clit—soft and hard, all at the same time— swollen and needy and wet. Blythe could feel her pulse there, rapid and desperate. Allegra's eyes flew open again, and her mouth gaped, a sharp cry escaping her.

"That's it. Eyes on me," Blythe repeated. Her voice was firm but not unkind, commanding Allegra back to her. "I want to see the moment your body gives me what we both want."

Allegra wobbled, reached up quickly to grasp at any part of Blythe she could grab hold of for balance. Her fingers fisted in Blythe's shirt, knuckles white.

"I've never…so…slowly." The words came out fragmented, her ability to form coherent thoughts slipping.

"Uh huh." Blythe ghosted her mouth again. "Not everything needs to be a rush, Allegra." She adjusted the angle of her fingers, found that spot again, and maintained the same maddening, deliberate pace. "Sometimes slow is better. Let me show you."

SIXTY-NINE

Thursday morning, Allegra sauntered into Sammy-Jo and Daisy's home looking like she'd been dragged backwards through a hedge. A baseball cap covered her hair, sunglasses covered her eyes, and the coat she wore was done up tightly. Despite the attempt at coverage, she was practically glowing. She dropped her bag onto the hallway floor and stopped dead in her tracks when SJ stepped out from the lounge, arms folded, eyes firmly on her, taking in every detail with obvious amusement.

"The wanderer returns," she said dryly before breaking into a slight smirk. "Having fun, are we?"

Daisy popped up over SJ's shoulder and grinned. "I would say that's a yes."

"More like a *hell* yes," SJ added.

"I might have bitten off more than I can chew." Allegra grinned. "And I am delighted to be a glutton for it."

SJ and Daisy exchanged a look. "Good for you," Daisy said warmly. "You deserve to be happy."

"Is your phone dead?" SJ quipped. The lack of any messages over the past three days and nights only disgruntled her a little, though her tone suggested it was more than a little.

"You saw me at training." Allegra unbuttoned the coat and slipped it off.

"Only to wave at," SJ complained. "I was worried about you."

Guilt flickered across Allegra's face and she softened her tone. "You're right, I'm sorry." She hung her coat on the banister. "I should have checked in. I was just—"

"Occupied?" SJ supplied with a knowing grin. "Yes, we know what you 'was just'…" SJ laughed before changing it up with, "Cup of tea?"

"Have we got time?" Allegra picked up her bag and slung it over her shoulder, heading up the stairs. "I've got to be in the pool in an hour, and I need to grab a shower and get changed."

"We've got time," SJ said.

"Not me, I'm late already," Daisy said, passing SJ. She leant in quickly and planted a quick kiss on SJ's lips before shoving the last piece of her toast into her mouth and chewing. "Catch you all later," she said, edging out the door and closing it behind her.

Silence settled between them for a beat.

"Right, you get a shower, I'll put the kettle on." SJ paused. "And then you're going to tell me everything."

A plate of toast, a mug of tea, and SJ's grinning face greeted Allegra when she came back down fifteen minutes later. She was dressed in her club tracksuit, but had her hair still wrapped in a towel.

"Thanks," she said, sliding into the chair opposite Sammy-Jo, reaching for a triangle of toast. "I'm starving." She took a large bite, closing her eyes briefly in appreciation.

"She not feeding you?" SJ asked, before her face turned mischievous. "Or too busy eating something else?"

Allegra rolled her eyes but couldn't suppress her grin. "You're terrible."

"Like you'd let me off the hook if the roles were reversed." Sammy-Jo laughed.

"Fair." Allegra swigged her tea. "And yes, she feeds me." She jumped up and grabbed a bottle of water from the fridge. Cracking the lid, she downed half in a long gulp, then wiped her mouth with the back of her hand.

"Dehydrated too." Sammy-Jo winked. "So, I take it things are going well?"

Allegra took her seat again and grinned at her friend. "Yeah, it's definitely an experience I'm enjoying."

"Uh huh, and the 'older' thing? You over that?"

"I mean…I'm not even noticing it. It's just…Blythe. That's all that matters."

Sammy-Jo grabbed a slice of toast. "She doesn't look older."

"I would say she's more refined than us," Allegra answered, holding her next piece of toast in front of her as she considered the thought. "Like, she dresses more grown-up, but then…she's more on the masculine side of style, so maybe that's all it is."

"Maybe."

Allegra looked all dreamy. "Yep, shirts with cufflinks… It's kind of hot, and those trousers and jackets are all made to measure. Yeah, it's hot. And the way she wears them?" Allegra added, her voice dropping slightly. "Confidence looks good on her."

SJ shook her head, still grinning. "You've got it bad, but whatever floats ya boat."

"I'm definitely floating," Allegra muttered, taking another bite of toast, a dopey smile still on her face.

"Well, let's float out the door then, cos we have to get you back on the pitch." SJ puffed out her cheeks. "And Kunkel is great, but she can't keep playing ninety minutes every week."

"Yeah, I know. We got away with it at the weekend." There was guilt in her voice. She hated watching from the sidelines.

SJ nodded. "Should have won, though."

"It'll come." Allegra's jaw set with determination.

"Yep. When Harriers' number 5 is back."

Allegra drained the last of her tea and stood. "Right, let's go then. Can't keep everyone waiting."

"*You* can't," SJ said, standing up and taking the plates to the sink. "I, on the other hand, am infamous for it."

SEVENTY

Blythe yawned.

"Tired?" Claudia asked as they drove in her car across town to meet with Gabby and someone from the local council.

"Sorry, yes. It's been—"

"Allegra is a very captivating young woman," Claudia interjected. When Blythe turned and frowned at her, surprised she would guess that was the issue, Claudia continued, "Oh, you haven't seen?"

"Seen what?"

Claudia blushed slightly. "You might want to google the local gazette…and look at today's front page."

Blythe pulled her phone free and began typing until the screen showed an image, headline, and short bio.

Harriers' Goddess Mann Soft Launches New Love.

The image was of them both, leaning in towards one another, laughing and smiling as Blythe wiped a crumb from Allegra's cheek. She remembered it well—the pie at half-time, along with the flirting.

"Oh, goodness," Blythe said as she continued to read on. Her stomach flipped—not unpleasantly, but with surprise.

Allegra Mann seems to be putting her rehabilitation time to good use, forging a new relationship that she seemed only too happy to flaunt in the stands at the weekend. Mann, who has been out injured in recent months with an MCL injury, was seen cavorting with an as-yet unknown woman. Sources close to the couple are tight-lipped around the new love interest's identity, but if these photos are anything to go by, Allegra Mann's soft launch might very well become the next big news story to come out of BSHWFC.

She stared at the photo for a long moment. They looked...happy. Natural. Like they belonged together.

"So it *is* Allegra Mann keeping you up all night," Claudia said, glancing over with a knowing smile. "Good for you."

"Does Allegra know about this?" Blythe asked, suddenly worried.

Claudia shrugged, lifted the indicator, and turned suddenly to the right. "No idea. I assume not if she didn't mention it to you."

"We've been kind of...busy," Blythe admitted with just a touch of heat rising to her cheeks. Her body's response was ridiculous, really—she was forty-four years old and blushing like a teenager.

"Hm, they do tend to have an exuberance of youth that keeps us on our toes." Claudia laughed. "Personally, I am all for it."

"Well, quite...I agree, and obviously it's very early days and the honeymoon phase, so I'll deal with a few late nights." Blythe grinned, happy to have someone to share her enthusiasm with. "I'm sure I'll hear about it from Allegra the moment she finds out we're the talk of the town."

"There are worse things to be."

"Like what?" Blythe asked. "The woman who couldn't get the stadium built on time?"

Claudia indicated left and took the turn. "You've never been the talk of the town? I can't believe it."

"Surprisingly, I prefer a quieter life when it comes to who I am sleeping with."

"So, the rumours of Amanda Sanchez were unfounded?"

Blythe coughed. "Seriously? That's the talk of the office?"

"Oh, yes. But...not in a mean way...just that people noticed a few things, and you know how they love to talk."

"Well, I will neither confirm nor deny said rumours, because either way, it's a moot conversation."

"Noted." Claudia smiled. "Fair enough. Though, for what it's worth, Allegra seems like a much better fit."

"What makes you say that?" There was genuine curiosity in her voice, not defensiveness.

They drove in comfortable silence for a moment as they searched for the entrance to the land they were here to discuss, before Claudia spoke again. She chanced a glance at Blythe. "For a start, you're smiling."

Blythe touched her face unconsciously, as if checking. "Am I?"

"Happy looks good on everyone, and that's no different for you," Claudia said warmly, pulling up at a large pair of gates beside Gabby's Land Rover and another car. The occupants of both were standing together, talking as they waited. Gabby spotted them and waved.

"Well, enough of my love life. Let's see if we can agree on this land." Blythe opened the car door, stepped out, and said a confident "Good morning" that echoed back at Claudia. Professional Blythe was back in place.

"Oh, it's a good morning alright." Claudia grabbed her briefcase from the back seat and followed, still smiling to herself.

Seventy-One

Allegra and Sammy-Jo arrived at the training ground and were about to part ways when someone called out a wolf whistle at Allegra. It was Jas Khan, grinning from across the car park.

"Someone's in the news," Jas said loudly.

Allegra froze. "What?"

Sammy-Jo pulled out her phone immediately. "Oh, this I've got to see."

Allegra turned, confused, as several teammates emerged from the building, phones in hand and matching grins on their faces.

"Check out the headline maker in The Gazette," Jas said, now almost halfway across the tarmac.

Allegra looked at SJ, whose face had lit up.

"SJ, what is it now?" Her face fell as SJ held up the phone and the headline. There she was, laughing with Blythe, looking completely smitten.

"Oh, no." Allegra's jaw dropped as she read it. "Why do they do this? Literally every journo at the game is there to report on the team. Why do I always end up as some kind of toy for them to play with?"

"Because you're the face of the club," SJ said quietly, her earlier amusement fading.

"Because you're gorgeous," Jas added, shrugging. "It's inevitable."

Allegra shook her head. "That doesn't make it okay. It's shit," Allegra said angrily. "Seriously, I'm a person with feelings, not just something to gawp at."

The grins had faded from her teammates' faces. "You're right," someone said. "That's not cool."

Jess wrapped an arm around Allegra's shoulders. "You look happy, though, mate, and that's all we care about."

Allegra's anger softened slightly. She leant into Jess for a moment.

Allegra looked at the photo again. It was true—they looked good together. She did look happy—stupidly, ridiculously happy. Then she had another thought. "Shit. I need to let Blythe know." Panic crept into her voice. "What if she's upset? What if she didn't want this public yet?"

She pulled out her phone, fingers already moving to Blythe's contact.

SJ pulled her to one side, shooing everyone else away. "Listen, if you're going to chase a professional athlete and turn up to the game wearing their shirt, you're kind of implying you're okay with anyone knowing."

"Do you think so?"

"Yeah." Sammy-Jo nodded emphatically, her curls bouncing. "But give her a call anyway. She needs to know it's happened."

"Ugh, just when everything in my life feels more settled—"

"It *is* settled," SJ said, touching Allegra's arm and calming her friend in an instant. "Blythe likes you. She's not stupid. She knows what it means to date someone like you."

"Someone like me?"

Sammy-Jo nodded. "Yes, you're beautiful, inside. You're fun, smart, talented. That's a whole lot before anyone even starts with how you look. And didn't you say she was the one who didn't want to rush in, wasn't pressuring you, listens to you?"

Allegra nodded. Her eyes were already welling up.

"Right, so if she knows all of that, then she knows she's going to spend her entire life with people looking in your direction, at you both…cos she's not fallen out of the ugly tree and been hit by every branch either, has she?" She chuckled. "You make a striking pair, and look at you…" She held the phone up, pointing to the photo. "That's fucking love right there. So yeah, she knows what she's getting dating someone like you."

Allegra's breath caught. No one had ever put it like that before.

Allegra threw her arms around Sammy-Jo's neck. "You're the bestest friend." Her voice was muffled against SJ's shoulder, helping to disguise her rising emotions.

"Obviously." SJ laughed and hugged her back. "Now call your woman and then get your arse to the pool."

When SJ walked away, Allegra made the call. The phone rang in her ear and wasn't answered. She disconnected. Her heart was still racing.

Allegra: Hey, just a heads up… There's something in the local paper about us.

She was just about to put the phone in her pocket when it buzzed.

Blythe: I know, I saw it. We'll talk later.

Allegra stared at the screen, trying to read between the lines. She wasn't sure how that sounded. Was it "it's okay, we can talk later," or "she saw it and she's not happy about it," talk later? The lack of emojis, the period after "later"—it all felt…ominous.

She shoved the phone into her pocket. There was no point worrying about it now. Whatever Blythe meant, Allegra would find out soon enough. She started to walk across the car park towards the building and Taylor, who would be waiting at the pool.

"Allegra!" a voice she didn't know shouted, and she turned to find a man with a camera trained on her. Her stomach dropped. "Who's the new woman?"

She ignored him and kept walking. But she could hear the rapid click of the camera shutter behind her, capturing every step.

"Just fuck off and leave me alone," she muttered to herself.

Seventy-Two

Blythe was on a high. Gabby had agreed—the land option was perfect for the new stadium build. More meetings were in the pipeline, but things were now going to start moving, she was sure of it. Everything was falling into place.

She'd literally just walked through the door of her flat, kicked off her shoes, and shed her jacket when the doorbell rang.

Grinning, she walked casually down the hallway and opened it to find a very serious-looking Allegra standing there, dressed down in a grey sweatsuit and trainers, hair up as it usually was, bare-faced, not even a hint of lipstick. Her eyes were red-rimmed.

"See, I told you it would be a nightmare trying to date me," she said, walking inside with purpose. "Honestly, I'm just… I'm sorry you've been caught up in it all."

Blythe opened her mouth to respond, but Allegra was already halfway into the lounge.

Blythe closed the door and followed silently down the hall behind her as she continued the tirade.

"Like, this is what I meant. Doesn't matter what I do, it always comes back to what I look like and who I'm sleeping with." She threw her hands up, and Blythe stopped in the doorway and leant against the frame, much like Allegra had done earlier in the week, only Blythe remained fully clothed as she listened.

"And it's not even a story. Like, who cares who I'm sleeping with? Outside of Bath Street, maybe the wider WSL circles, I'm a nobody…literally not important, and yet every headline about the team will always include 'Allegra Mann, Goddess Defender'." She drew her palms out in an imaginary headline maker as she spoke. "Of course, now you're dragged into it, and I get it. I totally get it if you want to split and run." Her voice cracked slightly on the last word.

She finally stopped pacing and looked at Blythe, waiting for the inevitable. Silence hung between them. Allegra's chest was heaving, her eyes bright with unshed tears.

Blythe pushed off the frame, took a step towards her, and took hold of both biceps. Staring intently into watery eyes, she asked, "Would you like a hug and then a cup of tea?"

The gentleness of it broke something in Allegra and she burst into tears, nodding as she fell into Blythe's arms. Her whole body shook with the force of her sobs.

"I'm just so—"

"I know," Blythe soothed, holding her close, warm palms gently rubbing her back. "I know… It's unfair." She pressed a kiss to the side of Allegra's head. "You're allowed to be angry about it," Blythe murmured against her hair.

Blythe didn't rush her, didn't try to fix it. She just held on.

Only when Allegra stopped shaking did Blythe pull back, one palm moving to cup Allegra's cheek. Her thumb brushed away a lingering tear. "Okay?"

Allegra sniffed. "Yeah, sorry." Her voice was small, raw.

"No, don't ever be sorry." Blythe smiled at her and brought her fingers along Allegra's jaw, her thumb tipping her chin up. "You never have to be sorry for being you—ever." Her hand slid down Allegra's neck and gripped lightly as she leant in and kissed her gently. When she pulled back, Blythe's eyes were soft, certain. "It's beautiful—you…are beautiful."

Allegra's breath hitched, fresh tears threatening. But this time they weren't from anger or frustration. Allegra closed her eyes, leaning into the touch.

For a long moment, they stayed like that.

"I'll make some tea," Blythe said, taking a step away. "And then we'll talk about getting some dinner, yes?"

"I'd love that, yes." Allegra smiled and breathed easily for the first time that evening.

"Why don't you get comfortable and I'll organise everything? Then we can snuggle up on the couch and watch a film, maybe?"

"That sounds perfect," Allegra said softly. "Thank you."

"Not at all. I'll be right back."

Kettle on, Blythe pulled mugs from the cupboard and set about adding teabags, when she felt arms wrap around her waist and Allegra press up against her back.

"Okay?" Blythe asked, one palm automatically covering Allegra's forearm. She felt Allegra nod against her and squeeze tighter. Blythe smiled, even though Allegra couldn't see it.

"I just feel a bit…"

Blythe twisted around till they were face to face, Allegra's arms loosening just enough. Blythe's hands settled on Allegra's hips.

"If closeness is what you need right now, then that's okay to ask for."

Allegra sighed. "I guess I feel a bit needy…clingy, and that feels like a very scary place to be." She wouldn't meet Blythe's eyes.

"What's the worst-case scenario if you were to allow yourself to just feel that and ask for it?"

Allegra blinked, caught off guard by the question. "That…you'd think I was too much. That you'd walk away."

"Do I look like I'm walking away?"

Allegra smiled. "No." Relief flickered across her face.

"So, what's the worst case now?" Blythe asked, touching her face. Her thumb traced Allegra's cheekbone gently.

"That you'll say no, ignore me…want something else from me."

Blythe's expression softened even further and she nodded. "I'm hearing you." She turned back to the mugs as the kettle boiled. "I'm going to make some tea and we're going to sit together on the couch and decide on dinner, and if you need to be close, then I am all for that." She poured the hot water, then turned back to Allegra. "In fact, I'd quite like it. Does that sound manageable?" she asked, meeting Allegra's eyes.

Allegra exhaled slowly, nodding. "Yeah. That sounds…really good."

Seventy-Three

Long legs stretched out, her head resting in Blythe's lap, the soft fingers threading through her hair were relaxing. Allegra's eyes were half closed, the tension from earlier finally melting away.

"It doesn't bother you that your face is plastered all over town?" Allegra asked sleepily.

"I wouldn't have chosen it," Blythe responded. "But it is what it is. I'm dating a goddess after all." She said it teasingly, but there was warmth beneath it.

Allegra could hear the smile in her words. Despite everything, her own lips curved upwards.

"Admittedly, I didn't think about it. Maybe I should have, but I just wanted to go to the game and show you that I was serious about us, and I thought the shirt would be a fun way to do that."

Rolling onto her back, Allegra stared up at Blythe. "It was. It was also kind of cute." She paused. "More than kind of," she amended quietly as she turned back onto her side.

"Good, that was the intention." Blythe's fingers resumed their gentle path through Allegra's hair. "I'd do it again," Blythe said softly, "article or no article."

"They'll keep digging." Allegra sighed.

"Let them. I'm not ashamed of who I am, or what we are."

Allegra's chest tightened—in the best way.

The doorbell buzzed, and Allegra pushed herself up into a sitting position. "I'll get it." Her legs were a bit stiff from lying down, but she didn't mind.

"I'll get us some plates," Blythe added as she pushed herself up onto her feet, too. She watched as Allegra shuffled towards the door. "And enjoy the view," she murmured to herself.

"I heard that!" Allegra called from the hallway.

Blythe laughed as she entered the kitchen. She was just through the door when she heard Allegra say, "Uh, excuse me, you can't just come in."

Stepping back into the lounge, Blythe was greeted by two women. One looking furious, and the other icy. Allegra stood by the open door, arms crossed defensively. Amanda had brushed past her without a second glance.

"I'm here for my things," Amanda said. She turned and looked Allegra up and down before completing the one-eighty and marching to the bedroom. Allegra closed the front door with deliberate control, her jaw tight.

"Amanda, what are you doing here?" Blythe chased after her, stopping next to Allegra. "I'm so sorry about this." The situation was mortifying—her boss, also her ex, barging in while they were supposed to be having a quiet evening.

"It's fine, just...she's leaving, right?" Allegra's eyes followed Amanda into the bedroom. There was steel beneath Allegra's calm tone. She'd seen Amanda with Blythe before and knew exactly who she was.

"Yes," Blythe said emphatically. She squeezed Allegra's hand briefly before following Amanda into the bedroom.

She watched as her ex-lover and current boss went from drawer to drawer, searching for things Blythe knew weren't there. Amanda rarely left anything when she stayed over, and anything she did leave was disposable— toothbrush, hairbands, a cheap T-shirt she'd picked up that first night she'd stayed over and not come prepared.

This was not about her things. This was a power play.

"Amanda?" Blythe spoke calmly but firmly.

Amanda didn't answer, just kept rifling through drawers with increasing aggression.

"Amanda," she repeated more firmly.

"What...Blythe?" Amanda spoke sharply, stopping what she was doing and spinning around to face her.

"What are you doing here?"

Amanda's gaze moved past Blythe, over her shoulder. Blythe turned and found Allegra standing in the doorway. Her expression was unreadable, but her posture was protective.

"Your little plaything going to stare at me all day?" Amanda said, still watching Allegra.

Blythe's jaw tightened. "Don't."

"The little plaything was invited," Allegra replied. Her voice was steady, unbothered. She wasn't backing down. "Unlike some people," she added coolly.

The doorbell buzzed for a second time.

"Allegra, would you?"

The stare-off continued for another half a minute, when the doorbell buzzed again. This time Allegra turned away.

"What are you doing here, Amanda?" Blythe asked again.

Amanda turned her attention to Blythe. The fight gone as she accepted the inevitable.

"I thought we could talk, but I see now..."

"I told you I was seeing someone," Blythe said gently.

"I know." Amanda sagged. "I just thought..."

"That you'd come over, find me lonely, and seduce me like old times."

Amanda's eyes looked towards the doorway and watched as Allegra walked past carrying a large white plastic bag, the aromas drifting into the room—a reminder of the evening Amanda had interrupted.

"I should go," Amanda said firmly.

"Yes," Blythe said. "And you can't do this again, okay?" Amanda said nothing but went to walk past. Blythe caught her arm. "I said, you can't do this again...okay?"

Amanda glanced down at the hand and shrugged her off. "You won't have to worry about that." Her voice was cold, final.

And then she was gone. The door slammed just enough to make an impact. The silence that followed felt heavy. Blythe blew out her cheeks before leaving the bedroom and wandering into the kitchen.

Allegra was decanting the food onto plates, her back to Blythe.

"She's gone," Blythe said.

"I heard that too," Allegra said with a smile. She turned to face Blythe. "Seems like everybody wants you."

Blythe's laugh was a little embarrassed.

"I'm only interested in *you* wanting me."

"Good…because I do." Allegra turned, holding two plates. "Can you grab the apple juice?"

SEVENTY-FOUR

The following morning, Blythe stepped into Gabby Dean's office unexpectedly. She hadn't called in advance, she didn't have an appointment, and she wasn't here for business.

"An unexpected pleasure, Blythe," Gabby said from her seat behind the tidy desk.

"Yes, I'm sorry about that. It'll only take a moment."

"Take a seat. Tell me what's got you looking all bothered this morning?"

Blythe sat down, one leg automatically crossing the other as she got comfortable. Comfortable was relative, however, as her jaw was set with determination. "We have a problem," she said calmly.

"We do?" Gabby arched a brow. "And that is?"

"Allegra."

Now Gabby frowned. "What about Allegra?"

Blythe uncrossed her legs and sat forward. "These stories the press print about her, it's not on." Blythe shook her head. "It's upsetting for her."

"I can imagine it is... That's the press for you," Gabby answered. "I'm not sure what I can—"

"Make it stop," Blythe said, as though it were as simple as that.

Gabby laughed lightly. "If I could do that, then I'd do so in a heartbeat. I've had my share of headlines. Is this because of the photos of the pair of you from the weekend?"

"It's about the unfair way in which she's singled out because she's pretty, and how every headline involving her always revolves around that."

"And who she's sleeping with..." Gabby added gently. "Which is you...am I right?"

The heat rising on Blythe's cheeks answered the question for her.

"Look, I don't like it any more than you do, but I don't control the press, nor should I. Anyone getting into the business of entertainment, in any aspect, knows they may become subjected to media issues. We teach everyone at the club how to deal with that. If Allegra is having issues that she isn't sharing..." Gabby leant back in her chair, studying Blythe.

"She's not complaining. She knows the deal, she's accepting of it, but it still affects her, Gabby, and surely you want a fully fit, mentally adjusted Allegra Mann back on the pitch?"

Gabby was quiet for a moment, considering. "What exactly are you asking me to do, Blythe?"

Taylor stood beside the treadmill, smiling as Allegra approached.

"Really?" Allegra said, her own smile beaming as she understood what was happening.

Nodding, Taylor patted the machine. "Walking first, then we'll gradually increase speed and incline to see how the knee handles the stress."

Allegra bounced up and down. "I can't believe it. I thought another week at least."

"No, you've done everything you should. All the scans indicate we're in a good place. Water work has helped build up the supporting muscles, and everything looks good. This is the big test now. Let's see how it goes."

Allegra stepped onto the treadmill, hands gripping the rails. She was ready.

The machine started, and she kept the pace nice and slow. Just walking. Every step felt deliberate, careful. She was hyperaware of every sensation in her knee.

She glanced down at Taylor and asked the one question she'd been holding back from asking, "When do you think I might actually be able to play again?"

"Let's not get ahead of ourselves, but...if all continues as it has been..." She shrugged. "Christmas?"

Allegra ran the maths in her head. The last game before the Christmas break was the middle of the month, so...six weeks away. Six weeks. She could do six weeks.

"It will be managed minutes, though," Taylor jumped in before Allegra got too worked up. "Nobody is rushing you back after all the hard work we've done."

Allegra nodded, forcing herself to stay calm. "Managed minutes. I can work with that."

"Realistically, we're looking at New Year before you're fully back," Taylor said as she watched. Allegra's gait was smooth—no hesitation, no favouring.

"Yeah, I'll take that, but if I can get back on the pitch, in a Harriers shirt, just for a couple of minutes, I'll take that as the best Christmas present."

Taylor smiled. "Then we'll make it happen."

Taylor leant over the machine and pressed buttons that raised the incline and sped up the belt. "Well, then let's go for that." She held her palm up, and Allegra slapped against it with her own. The sound echoed in the gym—a promise sealed.

Allegra grinned, her stride lengthening as the treadmill picked up speed. This was progress.

Several minutes went by, the incline raised, the speed upped. It was still not anything to get a sweat on, but it was feeling tougher. Allegra groaned. "Okay, I'm starting to feel the burn."

"No pain, though?" Taylor checked.

Allegra shook her head. "Nope, all good, just the muscles aching."

"Good, they need it." Taylor laughed. "Although, reading about your love life in The Gazette, I'm sure they're getting a workout."

"Ugh, that bloody paper." Allegra shook her head again. "I honestly don't get it." Her stride faltered slightly as anger crept in. "There must be more interesting things to write about."

"Yeah, but lazy journalism will always be around. People love gossip, and readers lap that stuff up." She reduced the incline. "Anyway…I thought you looked cute together."

Allegra couldn't hold off the smile. "We do, and that is why it's so frustrating. It's really early days and we're trying to enjoy it, getting to know each other, and now the bloody paper has to go and ruin things by printing stuff that shouldn't matter."

"True." Taylor's expression shifted, more serious now.

"I had them waiting at the gate for me this morning. Not, 'Oh, hey, Allegra, how's the injury?', or 'When will you be back?' No, it's, 'Who's the girlfriend?' That's what they wanted to know. Two of them—one shouting questions and one with a camera, snapping away like I'm some kind of freak in a show."

"That's awful," Taylor said quietly. "I'm sorry you're dealing with that." Then Taylor stared, blank-faced, her jaw tightening. "That's harassment. Have you reported it to Gabby?"

"It's the job. I'm 'a celebrity'." She used air quotes and pulled a face and a silly voice along with it. Then she huffed, "Just have to ride it through until they start writing about my looks again." The bitterness in her voice was unmistakable.

Taylor's phone beeped. She glanced at the screen. "Speak of the devil," she quipped. "Gabby wants to see me in her office." Taylor's brow furrowed slightly. It was unusual timing for a summons, but she kept her expression neutral. "You okay on here? Another ten minutes and then we'll get into the weights."

"I'll be fine," Allegra confirmed, her pace steady on the treadmill. She was already eyeing the equipment like a reunion with old friends. "I've missed you," she said to them. A genuine smile broke through the frustration from moments before.

Taylor grabbed her phone and headed for the door. "Be right back."

SEVENTY-FIVE

Taylor entered Gabby's office and found her boss smiling at her.

"Thanks for popping up. I won't keep you long," Gabby said, indicating the empty chair for Taylor to sit in.

"No problem," Taylor said a little warily. She'd never been called to the office like this before and was a little unsure what it was all about.

"So, Allegra Mann, what can you tell me?" Gabby sat back and pulled her glasses off her face, nibbling the end of one arm.

"Oh, right. Uh, yes, she's on track. I've literally just left her on the treadmill, so fingers crossed, we're...yes, all good."

Gabby studied her for a moment, as if weighing whether to ask more. Gabby nodded, taking it all in, then she leant forwards, dropping the glasses onto the desk. "That's good to hear. We could do with her back out there. How is she...in herself?"

"What do you mean?" Taylor edged closer, as though they were both being drawn into a secret conversation.

"Mentally, is she doing okay?"

Taylor hesitated, choosing her words carefully. "Oh, I mean...that's not really my expertise."

"I know, but you spend more time with her than most. Have you noticed anything?"

Taylor shifted in her seat. "Is there a specific concern?"

Gabby considered it. "The story in The Gazette."

"Oh, that."

"Yes, that. It's a little over the top. I'm concerned that it might affect Allegra's mental health and therefore impact her performances on the pitch."

"Well, I wouldn't like to say how it's affecting her mental health, but I think it's okay for me to say that…yes, I think it affects her. She literally just had a small rant about it down in the gym." Taylor bit her lip for a second before adding, "There were journalists at the gate this morning, asking about her love life. That's bordering harassment, isn't it?"

Gabby's jaw tightened. She pressed her lips together and stood up, straightened her jacket, and smoothed her skirt before she moved towards the window and stared out. The training pitch was visible below, where players were running drills—her responsibility.

"I don't know. I'm going to speak with Michael about it."

"The police liaison guy?"

Turning, Gabby nodded. "Yes. I'm not happy about any of our players being treated like this. And I'm angry with myself for needing it to be pointed out to me."

"You can't be everywhere at once," Taylor said gently. "I don't think Allegra would blame you for anything."

"No, of course not, and I'm not taking responsibility for shitty journalism, but I do take it seriously about protecting the players…all staff, from this kind of thing." She walked back to Taylor. "Thank you for telling me. And for looking after her." She paused. "How did she seem otherwise? Beyond the rant?"

"She has a goal. She's focused on that."

"Excellent. Okay…that's all for now." Gabby smiled. "Oh, and Taylor, this is between us, right?"

"Of course. But I do have to get back to her and spend the next hour with her, so I'll keep an eye on her."

SEVENTY-SIX

Claudia held the door open as Blythe entered the room. It was just them. Ros would be joining in a moment with files and coffee.

"You look…" Claudia studied her for a moment. "Still tired, but with added pissed off. Are we in for a fun day?" She smiled and took a seat.

Blythe exhaled and let her shoulders drop. The weight of the morning already pressing down on her.

"You know when it's just been one of those times when…a punching bag might be handy?"

"Hm," Claudia said, legs crossed, hands in lap, staring up at her. "I'm all ears?"

"This is why office romances shouldn't be allowed." Blythe shook her head. "Because I actually want to talk about it, but it would be highly unprofessional to do so."

"Well, there is that." Claudia straightened. "But I like to think we have established a professional working relationship these past couple of months, and I'd hope you would have noticed I am not one for office gossip."

Blythe weighed this, then nodded slowly. "You're the one who told me I was the talk of office gossip."

"Yes, because I thought it was only fair to ask outright rather than accept office gossip to be true."

Rubbing her temple, Blythe sat down.

"Amanda showed up at the flat last night. Completely uninvited and unannounced. Just waltzed in and started searching drawers for anything she'd left behind."

Claudia's eyes widened slightly. "While Allegra was there?"

"Yes, exactly. I've had the conversation with Amanda. Made it very clear we're not doing that again, but it's like she doesn't want to take no for an answer. And last night, of all nights…it really could have thrown a spanner in the works."

"And did it…throw a spanner?"

Blythe hesitated. "Thankfully not…despite the fact Allegra doesn't feel like she's mature enough, she handled it brilliantly. I was the one put out by it." Her voice tightened on the last words.

"Well, you would be. It was a total invasion of your privacy."

"Right?" Blythe said, standing up again to pace. "I know she's my boss, but honestly, I'm starting to get a little frustrated with all the personal ways in which she punishes me."

Claudia frowned. "She's punishing you?"

"Little things. Being here for a start. This was punishment for wanting more from her. She pushed me out of the way. Sent me here to get me out of London—out of her orbit. Then when she missed me and wanted me back, she…well, she made it clear."

"And now she's punishing you again?"

"I've been informed this will now be a permanent move. I won't be returning to the London office as promised."

Claudia's expression darkened. "That's not acceptable."

"I know," Blythe said quietly. "But honestly, part of me wonders if staying here isn't the better option anyway."

"Surely you have grounds to go to HR?"

Blythe nodded slowly. "Probably…but equally it's a 'she said-she said' situation, isn't it? And I don't want to get her into trouble." She glanced around the room. "Woodington isn't the worst place to be…"

"Not now there's a certain young footballer keeping you happy."

Blythe's expression softened despite everything. "It has its perks, don't you think?" Blythe laughed. The door opened and Ros came in carrying a tray, files tucked under her arm. Blythe moved quickly, taking the tray. "You could have just asked for help."

"And ruin my reputation for being superwoman around here? Never." Ros grinned. "Coffee for you both, tea for me. You can be mother," she said to Blythe, indicating the two pots and the empty cups that needed pouring into.

"Right. Now we have the site agreed upon, architects' drawings are…" The question was left open-ended for an answer.

Claudia took the mug pushed towards her. "Arriving tomorrow with the adaptations requested. We have a meeting with Gabby to discuss how the complex might look with the blueprints they have for the stadium design they'd prefer."

"Good." Her phone buzzed in her pocket. "So, we're all set. Any issues to deal with?"

Ros handed out files, each of them filled with the information they'd already had compiled. "You have a set of questions from various departments regarding their input, but honestly most are just fishing."

Blythe rolled her eyes. "Of course they are."

Blythe flipped through and stopped at one. "Décor? We don't even have a spade in the ground and they're already wanting to know which mattress we will require?" She shook her head in disbelief.

Claudia smiled. "They do like to be in the know as soon as… I'll email them and get the ball rolling. It feels like a long way away, but with one hundred and twenty potential rooms to furnish, it won't hurt to get a head start on it."

"I can handle the initial correspondence if you'd like," Ros offered.

"Of course." Blythe's phone buzzed again. "Excuse me a moment." She pulled it free and glanced quickly. Her expression shifted—first, concern, then something softer. "I'll just be…" She pointed to the hall. "Two minutes."

"Of course." Claudia smiled knowingly. "Take your time."

In the hallway, Blythe pressed Call.

"Hi," Allegra's bright voice said into her ear. "Can you talk?"

Blythe smiled. "I'm calling you."

Allegra's laugh gave her a buzz. "Oh, yeah, of course. Anyway…just wanted to know if you would like to go out with me tonight to celebrate?"

"What are we celebrating?"

"I'm back on the treadmill, running. I have a goal now for my return."

"Wow, that's awesome, sweetheart. Of course I want to celebrate. Let me organise something."

"You're sweet. I've already booked a table, though, at Joie. I also invited some friends. I thought…well, I hoped you'd be okay with meeting them."

"I'd really like that," Blythe said honestly. "I have to get back to my meeting, but I'll pick you up, around seven?"

"That would be perfect… Oh, and Blythe?"

"Yes, Allegra?"

"Make sure you're ready to handle me. I plan to *really* celebrate when we get back to your place. I haven't forgotten about that toy you promised."

"Ah, I see, well…I'd best top up on some caffeine." She chuckled. "I'll see you later, darling."

"Bye, babes."

The call disconnected.

SEVENTY-SEVEN

The Uber pulled up and Blythe noted Allegra already waiting on the kerb with two other people, both of whom Blythe recognised.

In an instant, Sammy-Jo opened the passenger seat and jumped in. Blythe shifted along the back seat and pressed herself up against the door as Allegra, and then Daisy, piled into the back with her. Allegra's thigh pressed warmly against Blythe's.

"Hey, babe." Allegra smiled. "Thanks for organising the ride."

"My pleasure." Blythe grinned, her hand landing easily on Allegra's thigh, the skin-tight jeans warm against her palm. Allegra didn't pull away. If anything, she leant into the touch. "Sammy-Jo and Daisy, right?"

"Yes." Daisy leant forwards to wave at Blythe. "Hope we're not crashing your style, just seemed to make more sense if we're all going to the same place."

Blythe nodded. "It's all good." She meant it. Meeting Allegra's friends felt important—a sign this was real.

Sammy-Jo twisted in her seat to look over her shoulder and into the back, straight at Blythe. "Don't worry, we're not coming back with you."

Allegra's cheeks flushed and Daisy laughed. "SJ!"

Blythe chuckled, squeezing Allegra's thigh. "To be fair, SJ, you weren't invited." She added a wink and smiled even wider when SJ blushed and turned back to face forwards.

"Touché," SJ said without looking back again, but Blythe could see the grin on her face in the window's reflection.

Allegra leant towards Blythe, letting her head rest almost on her shoulder. Blythe turned and kissed her head. "Hi."

"Hey." Allegra's hand found Blythe's, fingers threading together.

Arriving at the restaurant, they walked in to find half the team already there, sitting around three large tables. The noise level was already high, laughter and conversation filling the space.

"Here she is!" Jess shouted.

Allegra grinned, her hand still firmly in Blythe's. A loud whooping went up as people stood up, wanting to greet Allegra properly. Blythe stepped back slightly, giving Allegra space but staying close by. "'Bout time you were up and running again." Ladonya winked.

"Literally." Allegra laughed, accepting a hug.

Several eyes curiously checked out Blythe, assessing but welcoming.

"Everyone, this is Blythe." Allegra beamed as she turned back and reached for Blythe's hand again, squeezing it reassuringly. "I should have made them all wear name badges."

Blythe laughed. "I'm sure I'll catch on as the night progresses." She glanced towards some empty chairs. "Shall we take our seats?"

Allegra nodded, guiding them to side-by-side chairs. The moment they were settled, drinks ordered, and menus in hand, a slim Asian girl leant across a smaller redhead and said to Blythe, "So, I'm Jas and this is Kayla."

"Hi, great to meet you," Blythe responded. She was already trying to commit names to faces.

"We both play on the team with Allegra," Jas continued. "She's like our mentor, really. We both look up to her. And Nora, obviously." She glanced across at the woman Blythe knew to be Gabby's wife. No sign of Gabby, though, she noticed.

Allegra's cheeks pinked slightly. "They're being generous."

"And you're being humble." Blythe smiled and leant closer, her voice dropping low. "And it's really attractive."

"Oh, and what does that mean?" Allegra said, coyly twirling her hair as she stared down at Blythe's lips.

"It means that later…you'll get what you asked for…but in the meantime, I might kiss you in public."

"Uh huh, that sounds delightful." Allegra grinned, lost in the moment of just them. The restaurant noise faded. Nothing else mattered.

A commotion broke the magic, the sound of something clicking and flashing, as a man's voice broke through the moment. "Allegra, give her a kiss, darling."

The entire table went silent, then erupted. It was Nora and Sammy-Jo who reacted first, jumping up from their chairs and blocking the view as they pushed and jostled two men backwards. "Get out!" Nora's voice was sharp, commanding.

The one with the camera held it up in the air, above SJ's head, still snapping away. Sammy-Jo snatched at the lens. Getting a hand on it, she yanked and almost knocked it out of his hand. "Delete them. Now," she demanded.

"Hey, watch it. That costs more than you earn in a week," he sneered.

Allegra's hand found Blythe's under the table, gripping tight. Blythe could feel her trembling—not with fear, but rage. Around them, chairs scraped as more teammates stood, forming a wall.

Staff moved in fast, escorting them out before the manager came rushing over. "I am so sorry. Please, let me get some drinks as an apology. We really do not allow such behaviour at Joie." His eyes darted nervously between Allegra and the door where the men had been removed.

"It's fine. Thank you," Allegra said. But her jaw tightening said she was anything but fine. Her breathing was shallow but controlled, holding herself together by a thread.

"You don't have to be brave," Blythe whispered. "Do you need a moment?"

Allegra's eyes were bright with unshed tears. "Maybe," Allegra said quietly.

Blythe's chair scraped back. She reached for Allegra's hand. "Come on."

Sammy-Jo caught Blythe's eye and nodded—*go, we've got this*. Allowing herself to be pulled to her feet, Allegra followed Blythe through to the ladies' room. The door swung shut behind them, muffling the restaurant noise. Suddenly it was quiet.

Allegra spun around in her arms, staring intently. "Fuck me like you don't even like me?"

Blythe's breath caught. Heat flared low in her belly, pooling between her thighs. "Is that what you want?" Her voice had dropped, rougher now.

"A little..." Allegra's arms came up and over Blythe's shoulders, pulling her closer. Her fingertips played lightly at the back of Blythe's neck. "Bite me. Mark me. Tease me until I'm begging..." Her lips brushed Blythe's ear. "Fuck me so hard I forget my own name—make me feel you for days after. I want bruises. I want to remember exactly how you made me come undone."

Blythe's pupils dilated. Her grip on Allegra's waist tightened. "You're a surprise every day, Allegra Mann." She leant in and kissed her softly—a promise of what was to come. "Now, let's go eat. You're going to need your energy."

SEVENTY-EIGHT

She wore the strap-on like it was made for her, confidence oozing from every pore as her hands pulled and pushed Allegra's body into position.

"That's it," Blythe murmured, her voice low and commanding. "Just like that."

Naked, pliable, her lover let go of all fight for control and let herself be moved and moulded, her body reacting to every touch. Every nerve ending was on fire as Blythe's mouth covered every inch of her—teeth marking, mouth sucking and bruising, fingers squeezing around her biceps, wrists, ankles.

Allegra gasped as Blythe's teeth sank into the sensitive skin of her inner thigh, hard enough to leave a mark. "Fuck—"

"Language," Blythe teased, her breath hot against the fresh bite. She soothed it with her tongue before moving higher.

And not once had Blythe touched her where she *needed it most*.

Allegra's hips bucked involuntarily, seeking friction that wasn't coming. Her hands fisted in the sheets, knuckles white.

"Please…" Allegra moaned as her clit throbbed, needy and wanting attention. "Blythe, please—"

"Please, what?" Blythe's hands gripped Allegra's thighs, spreading them wider, holding her open. "Tell me exactly what you want."

"Touch me," Allegra breathed, her voice breaking. "I need—God, I need you inside me."

Blythe's eyes darkened. She dragged her thumb torturously slowly up Allegra's inner thigh, stopping just short. "You said you wanted to beg." Her lips curved into a wicked smile. "So beg properly."

Allegra whimpered, her pride warring with her desperation. "Please, Blythe. Please fuck me. I need to feel you. I need it rough. I need—" Her words dissolved into a moan as Blythe's fingers finally—finally—brushed against her clit, feather-light and nowhere near what she needed.

"Good girl," Blythe whispered, her voice dripping with satisfaction. "Now let's see how loud I can make you scream."

Blythe positioned herself between Allegra's thighs, the head of the strap-on pressing against her, not entering, just there—a promise and a torment all at once.

"Look at me," Blythe commanded.

Allegra's eyes snapped open, hazy with need, locking onto Blythe's. The intensity in that gaze made Blythe's breath hitch. She reached for the lube, applying it to the phallus without taking her eyes from Allegra.

"I want to see your face when I make you come undone." Blythe's hand wrapped around Allegra's throat, not squeezing, just holding—possessive, grounding. "You're mine tonight. Understood?"

"Yes," Allegra gasped. "Yours."

In one smooth, deliberate thrust, Blythe filled her completely.

Allegra cried out, her back arching off the bed, hands scrambling for purchase on Blythe's shoulders. The stretch, the fullness—it was everything and not enough all at once.

"Fuck, you feel incredible," Blythe groaned, holding still, letting Allegra adjust. Her thumb traced Allegra's jaw tenderly, a stark contrast to the bruising grip on her hip earlier. "Okay?"

"More," Allegra panted. "Please, more—don't hold back."

Blythe's restraint snapped. She pulled out almost completely before slamming back in, setting a punishing rhythm that had Allegra gasping with every thrust. The sound of skin against skin filled the room, punctuated by Allegra's increasingly desperate moans.

"That's it," Blythe praised, her voice rough. "Let me hear you. Let the entire building know who's fucking you this good."

Allegra's nails raked down Blythe's back, leaving red trails in their wake. "Harder—God, harder—"

Blythe shifted the angle, hitting deeper, and Allegra cried out with pleasure. Blythe's hand slid between their bodies, fingers finding Allegra's clit and circling with practised precision.

"Oh, fuck—Blythe, I'm—" Allegra couldn't finish the sentence, couldn't think, could only feel.

"Not yet," Blythe ordered, slowing her pace torturously. "You don't come until I say you can."

Allegra whimpered, her body trembling on the edge. "Please—I can't—"

"Yes, you can." Blythe's lips found her ear. "You're going to hold it for me, because you're so good at doing what you're told, when you want to be." She punctuated the words with a particularly deep thrust that had Allegra seeing stars.

Tears of frustration and overwhelming pleasure pricked at Allegra's eyes. Every muscle in her body was taut, straining, desperate for release.

"Look at you, so beautiful like this, so desperate." She kissed away a tear that had escaped. "Now, Allegra. Come for me now."

Permission granted, Allegra shattered. Her orgasm ripped through her with such force she couldn't even scream, her mouth open in a silent cry as her body convulsed. Wave after wave crashed over her, Blythe fucking her through it, drawing it out until Allegra was boneless and gasping.

"That's my girl," Blythe murmured, slowing to gentle movements, easing her down. "So perfect."

Allegra's chest heaved, her skin flushed and damp with sweat. Blythe carefully withdrew, immediately gathering her close, pressing kisses to her temple, her cheek, her lips.

"You okay?" Blythe asked softly, her hand stroking Allegra's hair.

Allegra nodded weakly, a blissed-out smile on her face. "I forgot my name," she whispered.

Blythe laughed, the sound warm and affectionate. "Mission accomplished then."

SEVENTY-NINE

She woke still locked in the embrace she'd been in when she'd fallen asleep, Blythe's thigh was between her legs, one arm under her neck, the other slung around her waist, palm pressed against her backside. Even that gentle pressure sent a pleasant throb through her.

She ached, deliciously, her body alerting to every sensitive area with each breath she took. The bite marks on her thighs, the bruises on her hips—evidence of how thoroughly Blythe had claimed her. She smiled as she remembered the way it had felt to have Blythe inside her, hands and mouth free to pleasure her simultaneously.

The memory alone made heat pool low in her belly again. She could still feel the ghost of Blythe's teeth on her neck, and the delicious ache where fingers had gripped too tightly.

She shifted slightly, testing her body's response, and bit back a small moan. Blythe's arm tightened around her waist instinctively, even in sleep—protectively, possessively.

"Too early," Blythe mumbled and pressed her face into Allegra's neck.

"To get up...yes," Allegra replied. "I wasn't planning on that...not when my clit is still throbbing for you."

Blythe groaned. "You cannot possibly still be horny..." She smiled against her skin. Her hand slid from Allegra's backside to her hip, steadying her.

"Try me." Allegra laughed and moved her hips, pressing herself against the strong thigh—slick, warm, wet.

Blythe's breath hitched, suddenly more awake.

"Fuck, you're soaked." Her thigh flexed, giving Allegra more pressure to grind against.

Allegra's movements found a rhythm. "Don't move. Let me...just like..." Her words dissolved into a breathy moan as she found the perfect angle.

"You're insatiable." Blythe's voice was thick with arousal and affection. Her hand gripped Allegra's hip tighter, guiding her movements. "That's it, sweetheart. Use me. Take what you need."

They stared at each other. Blythe enjoying the way Allegra's eyes dilated, closed, and opened again. The intimacy of it, the trust—Allegra completely unguarded in her pleasure.

"So hot," Blythe whispered.

Allegra's hips pulsed, her breaths faster, short whimpers escaping as she got close.

"Blythe—oh, God, Blythe—"

"That's it...come on me." Blythe's free hand cupped Allegra's face, thumb brushing her cheek. "I've got you."

Fingers clenched and dug into Blythe's skin, her face scrunched, hips jerking—it was all just beautiful. Allegra came with a broken cry, her whole body tensing before the tremors took over. Blythe held her through it, murmuring soft praise, feeling the wetness spread across her thigh as Allegra shuddered and gasped.

"That's my girl," Blythe whispered against her temple. "So beautiful when you let go."

Allegra's movements slowed, became languid, drawing out every last aftershock until she was too sensitive to continue. When the last tremor faded, Allegra collapsed against Blythe's chest, boneless and panting.

"Holy hell," she breathed, her heart hammering against Blythe's.

Blythe wrapped both arms around her, pressing a kiss to her damp forehead. "Good morning to you too."

Allegra laughed weakly, the sound muffled against Blythe's skin. "That was…fuck."

"Eloquent," Blythe teased, her fingers tracing lazy patterns up and down Allegra's spine.

"You've broken my brain," Allegra mumbled.

Blythe's hand drifted lower, grazing over the marks she'd left the night before. "Still tender?"

"Everywhere," Allegra admitted, not moving. "In the best possible way."

Blythe tilted Allegra's chin up, searching her face. "No regrets?"

Allegra's eyes were soft, sated, utterly content. "Not a single one." She pressed a slow kiss to Blythe's lips. "Though I might need to live here permanently if you keep fucking me like that."

"I can work with that arrangement," Blythe murmured against her mouth.

They lay tangled together, the morning light filtering through the curtains, neither in any hurry to move. Blythe's hand continued its soothing path along Allegra's back while Allegra's fingers played absently with the chain around Blythe's neck.

"What time is it?" Allegra finally asked.

Blythe glanced at the clock on the nightstand. "Just gone seven."

"We should probably get up eventually."

"Probably," Blythe agreed, making no move to do so.

Allegra propped herself up on one elbow, looking down at Blythe with a satisfied grin. "You know what's funny?"

"What?"

"Last night I was so angry about those photographers. Felt like everything was ruined." Her expression softened. "But you made me forget all of that. Made me feel…safe. Wanted. Seen."

Blythe's chest tightened with emotion. She tucked a strand of hair behind Allegra's ear. "You are all of those things. Always."

"Even when I'm being demanding and insatiable?"

"Especially then." Blythe laughed. "Though you're going to have to let me feed you at some point. You need to keep your strength up if you're planning on more of this."

Allegra's stomach chose that moment to growl and they both dissolved into laughter.

"Okay, fine," Allegra conceded. "Shower. Then maybe some breakfast."

"Together?" Blythe raised an eyebrow.

"Obviously." Allegra grinned wickedly. "Though that might delay breakfast even further."

"Worth it," Blythe said, already pulling her in for another kiss.

Eighty

Friday mornings on a weekend before a match meant a presser with the manager and a player speaking to journalists regarding the upcoming game. Today was no different. Katrine sat at the counter, a microphone in front of her, surrounded by sponsors' logos and perfectly positioned advertising paraphernalia.

To her left was Satty Basra, star striker and media trained to the nth degree.

They were answering questions, starting with the BBC and local radio.

Five minutes in the door opened. Gabby Dean strolled in. She looked immaculate—blonde hair styled perfectly, make-up on point, tailored suit. The room fell silent, every journalist looking up.

"Sorry to barge in," she said to the journalists, smiling, "but I have something to say, and I need to make sure I catch you all." Katrine and Satty shared an 'I've no idea' look between them, but both sat back, giving Gabby the floor.

Gabby stood in the space between her team's manager and their star player. The power move was deliberate—she was literally standing between them and the press.

"Thank you, Katrine, Satty…I won't take long." She smiled at them before turning to face the room. "I'm going to say this once," she began, "this is a football club. You are invited here and accredited members of the press in order to report on the games, the team, and any other sporting matter concerning Bath Street Harriers. If I so much as see one more comment on how my players look, dress, or date, I will revoke access to every corner of the club. Am I clear?" She stared at them all before landing her gaze on the culprits. Silence. A few journalists shifted uncomfortably in their seats. "You will not harass my players or any other member of my staff at the gates, in here, and especially not in the middle of a restaurant when they are trying to have a nice time. If you do, I will make it my personal mission to ensure you never work in this town again, and if you really piss me off, I'll make sure you never work again—full stop." She let the words hang in the air, her expression unwavering. Then she smiled—sharp, dangerous. "Now, I believe you have questions about Sunday's match?"

One hand raised timidly at the back of the room.

Gabby's smile was icy. "Good. Carry on." She turned on her heel and left as abruptly as she'd arrived, the door closing with a decisive click behind her.

All eyes turned to the two men at the back of the room.

"So…shall we continue?" Katrine said.

"Holy fuck balls," Sammy-Jo laughed as she stared out across the pitch.

"I know." Satty chuckled. "You should have seen her, she was magnificent."

"Who was?" Nora asked as she sidled up to the pair. "How did the press thing go?"

Satty nudged her. "Like you didn't know."

Nora frowned. "Know what?"

"Really? She didn't tell you she was doing it?"

"You're going to have to be more specific about who *she* is and *what* she was doing." Nora chuckled.

"In the middle of the presser, Gabby walked in and tore the journos a new one. She threatened to remove their accreditation and access to the club if they continued to harass her players."

"Sounds like my wife." Nora grinned. "She was pretty angry when I got home last night and told her about those idiots."

"Well, looks like she decided enough was enough," SJ piped up. "And good for her. I like that she has our backs on this. Leggy gets way too much of this crap."

"Speaking of…look what the cat has dragged in." Satty smiled as Allegra trotted over, looking every inch the woman who didn't get enough sleep. Her hair was still damp from the shower, cheeks flushed. "You know, you're not supposed to be staying up all night when you're in training," Satty scolded gently.

Allegra yawned. "I know, it was a one-off." But the satisfied smile tugging at her lips suggested she didn't regret it one bit.

They all laughed. "Yeah, right," Sammy-Jo poked at her. "Honeymoon phase!"

Allegra's cheeks pinked, but she didn't deny it. "Shut it," Allegra poked back. "Why you all standing around anyway?"

"Just discussing Gabby's bitch slap at the journos," Satty informed her. When Allegra frowned, confusion written all over her face, Satty added, "She basically tore into them all this morning and threatened their jobs if they didn't stop harassing you."

"What? Really?"

The three of them nodded at her.

Allegra's throat tightened. Gabby had done that for her—for all of them. "Apparently, my wife is magnificent—which I already knew, of course." Nora grinned. "And I'm going to pop up to her office and tell her."

"Give her a kiss from us too," SJ called after her.

Nora laughed. "I'll give her my own, thanks."

Allegra watched her go, something warm settling in her chest. This team, this club—they had her back.

At two-thirty in the afternoon, Blythe stretched her neck from side to side. Claudia sat opposite her, Ros to her right, just like the previous day, only now they had nothing much else to do other than more paperwork, and none of it had a deadline beating at the door. The morning's intensity had faded into a comfortable lull.

"You know what?" she said, putting the lid back on her pen. "I think we should all have the rest of the day off."

"I'm not saying no to that offer," Ros said, instantly getting to her feet and packing up in case Blythe changed her mind.

Blythe smiled and watched. Ros was headed for the door in record time.

"Have a good weekend," she said as Ros gave a quick wave and was gone. Blythe turned her attention to Claudia, who was smiling at her. "What?"

"Nothing…just noticing you look a little tired, and yet, you're not unhappy about it." She chuckled. "I love those days."

Blythe's cheeks warmed slightly. "Those days?" she asked, but couldn't hide the smirk.

Claudia nodded. "Mm hm, when they've kept you up all night with that insistent—"

"Claudia!" Blythe protested, though she was laughing. "That obvious, huh?"

"Only to the trained eye." Claudia winked. She stood, gathering her things. "Enjoy your weekend, Blythe. And give Allegra my congratulations on the treadmill progress."

"Go on, get out of here. I'm sure you have plans you can make."

"I do…" Claudia smiled. "I just need to inform my wife of them." She winked again as she pulled her bag over her shoulder and headed for the door. "See you on Monday."

And with that, Blythe was alone in the office with nothing more than her thoughts, and those led to only one place.

The estate agent's office in town was quiet when Blythe pushed open the door and stepped inside. A woman at the back looked up and smiled.

"Hi, can I help?"

Blythe exhaled. This was real. She was doing this. "Yes, I'd like some information on available properties to buy."

"Perfect, take a seat." She stood and held out a hand. "Grace Hart. Are you looking to move, or increase a portfolio?"

Blythe shook it. "Blythe Daniels. I guess both. I have a flat in London that I'd like to put on the rental market and make an income that will pay the mortgage on any property I buy here to live in."

Grace's eyes lit up. "Excellent. Let me get some details and we can look at what's available in your price range. Do you have a particular area in mind?"

"I'm looking for something with at least two bedrooms, ideally three. A garden would be nice, and in or around Woodington."

Grace pulled out a folder and opened her laptop. "And when are you looking to move?"

"As soon as possible," Blythe said. The words felt right. Permanent. This was home now.

Eighty-One

Sadie placed the soda and lime in front of Allegra and waved away the offer of a card to pay for it. "On the house for our star player." Sadie winked.

"Thank you." Allegra smiled and took hold of the cold glass, twisting it in her fingers. Nervous energy of the good kind filled her. She couldn't wait to see Blythe. She looked at the time on her phone again and glanced towards the door, but still no sign of her. Allegra smiled to herself, recognising she was early, as usual.

A Friday night out wouldn't be the option once she was back, fully fit and raring to go, but for now, she was happy to meet Blythe in the bar for a couple of drinks before dinner.

The door opened and Allegra's head snapped up. Not Blythe. She took a sip of her drink and tried to relax.

It hadn't gone unnoticed that the moment she'd just let herself enjoy and feel it, her excitement around Blythe had built rapidly. She'd never felt this way before, grounded and exhilarated all at once—sensibly, healthily, not chaotic or toxic, or her usual go-to where relationships were concerned—unbothered.

She'd spent years chasing intensity and mistaking chaos for passion. This was something entirely different. Something real. Something worth keeping.

Blythe was patient, soft, calm, and still able to make her heart beat faster and her clit throb constantly.

She'd never wanted someone this much—in every way that mattered. It terrified her a little, how much she wanted this to work. How much she wanted Blythe.

She was so lost in her thoughts, she didn't hear the door open, or the soft-footed approach. It wasn't until Blythe's perfume wafted, and the faint touch of her palm landed on her shoulder, that Allegra turned and came face to face with her lover.

"Hey." Blythe grinned, leaning in to kiss her. Their mouths met, eyes still open and connected—intimately and deliberately—a hello that said more than words. "You look great."

Allegra breathed her in. "Thanks. I had the time to get—"

Blythe stopped her from making up a reason why she looked good. "You look great," she repeated. "So, how's your day been?"

Blythe pulled a stool free and slid onto it, keeping her knees as close to Allegra as she could get, her hands free to reach out and touch.

Almost magnetic.

Allegra's hand found Blythe's knee, mirroring the need for contact.

"Actually, really good." Allegra grinned as she waved towards the other person working behind the bar—a new girl she didn't know yet. "What are you having?" Allegra asked Blythe.

"White wine, house is fine," she responded to the barkeep. "Tell me about your day," she said, returning her attention to Allegra. Blythe's eyes were warm, genuinely interested, like Allegra's day actually mattered to her.

"Well, firstly...the knee is holding up really well with the treadmill and weights," Allegra said, pausing to enjoy the way Blythe smiled at that news. "And then, I'm not sure why...but Gabby blasted the media."

"She did?" Blythe's eyebrows rose slightly. She hadn't expected Gabby to move so fast. "How so?"

"Apparently, she interrupted this morning's press conference and tore the journos a new one. Satty said she told them if there was any repeat of last night, or any further harassment of her players, then she'd revoke all access to the club for their outlet and make sure they never worked again."

"Wow, that is awesome." Blythe squeezed Allegra's knee. "She's protecting her own. That's what good leadership looks like."

"She is magnificent," Allegra said, genuine admiration in her voice. Allegra took Blythe's hand. "What about you? How was your day?"

"Not as exciting as yours." She laughed. "Actually, it was kind of slow. This project we're working on…it requires patience, which I find frustrating at times. So, I gave my team the afternoon off, and…" She took a deep breath. "I signed up with the estate agents in town."

Allegra's eyes widened. "You're moving here?"

Blythe nodded. "I think so, yes. It makes sense. The London office has always been the pinnacle of my career so far, and sure, I had planned to return once things settled, but now…" She reached up and tucked a strand of hair behind Allegra's ear. "Now I have a reason to stay. And if I'm honest, I don't think things with Amanda will ever mean an easy life in London. Here, I'm in charge of my life, and the project is—"

Allegra frowned. "What *is* the project? You never talk about it, and actually, I don't really know what you do."

"I'm head of expansion strategy for the Olsen Group. We…build hotels."

"That's awesome. So, you're high up in the company?"

Blythe shrugged. "High enough, for now."

Allegra grinned. "Ambitious for more?"

"Maybe one day. Right now, I feel like I'm where I am meant to be…with who I'm meant to be with."

"Keep talking like that and you'll be getting a whole lot of what you're meant to get…later." Allegra winked.

"Is that so?" Blythe teased and leant in. "I want to kiss you."

"I'm not stopping you," Allegra whispered, but then she held her palm out. Her mind was racing, pieces clicking into place. "Wait, so you're building a hotel here? In Woodington?"

"Yes."

"And Gabby is involved?"

"Yes, but I'm not able to say any more…yet." Blythe smiled. "But when I am…you'll be the first person I'll want to tell. Right now, though, I'm going to kiss you." She didn't wait for permission this time. Her hand cupped Allegra's face as she leant in, capturing her lips in a kiss that was both a promise and a claim.

Eighty-Two

Blythe woke up to two things that made her smile. There was the naked body beside her—prone, relaxed, worn out, and still sleeping. Blonde hair fanned the pillow and half of Allegra's face, her mouth slightly agape, and just the softest sound of snoring.

Blythe found this unguarded version of Allegra endearing. "And I'm the older one," Blythe murmured to herself with a chuckle as she pulled the sheet up and covered Allegra from the morning chill. It was almost November and she'd put the heating on, but probably still needed to adjust the timings.

She lingered for a moment, just watching her sleep, feeling something settle in her chest.

Home. This *was* home, wasn't it?

The second thing to make her smile was an email from Grace with a list of properties Blythe might like to take a look at. She scrolled through them, most forgettable, until—

One stood out: a white-painted townhouse on three floors with a small, gated drive to the front and a largish garden at the back. It had a hot tub and a patio built for entertaining—something Blythe wanted to do if she moved here. She could already picture it, Allegra laughing with friends on the patio, Blythe's hand on her back. She'd already made a few acquaintances, some of which she'd like to make friendships with. Claudia, for one.

She messaged Grace about an appointment. Within minutes, a response came through. She could see it today at two. Blythe smiled. Things were moving fast, and that was fine by her.

Shifting from under the covers, Blythe got up and padded across the carpet to the back of the door where her dressing gown hung. She pulled it on over her naked body and tied it loosely before exiting the bedroom as quietly as she could.

In the kitchen, she set about breakfast. Two bowls, two spoons, two mugs and one tray. The set-up gave her a warm fuzzy feeling inside. This was what she wanted in her life. Domestic. Simple. Real.

From the fridge she took a large tub of Greek yoghurt and dropped two large spoonfuls into each bowl, then she topped it off with handfuls of mixed berries: raspberries, blueberries, and blackberries. She cut several strawberries into quarters and scattered them between the dishes, then drizzled a healthy amount of honey and a sprinkling of pistachios. The bowls looked almost too pretty to eat. Almost.

She made two mugs of tea and balanced both mugs on the tray alongside the bowls, then made her way back to the bedroom. Allegra stirred, reaching for the warmth Blythe had left behind.

"Babe?" she mumbled, before slowly rolling over onto her back. Her small perky breasts and hardened nipples were just visible as the sheet slid away. Blythe's breath hitched. Even half-asleep, Allegra was stunning.

"I'm here." Blythe smiled down at her, placing the tray on the end of the bed. She slid her dressing gown off and, with one knee at a time, she carefully climbed back onto the bed, lowering to take a nipple between her lips. "Good morning."

Allegra's back arched slightly, a soft moan escaping her lips. "Mm, that's a nice way to wake up." Allegra smiled, her hand threading through Blythe's hair. She hissed when Blythe's teeth bit gently. "Tease," she breathed, but there was no complaint in her tone. "You already in the mood?"

Blythe raised her head. "I'm always in the mood for you, sweetheart." Her hand drifted down Allegra's body, fingers tracing the curve of her ribs, her waist, lower still.

"Good," Allegra sighed, relaxing into the touch, her legs parting in invitation to go further. Blythe chuckled against her skin, but took the offer and slipped her hand between warm thighs.

She kissed a path down Allegra's torso, nipping at the soft skin around her hips before crossing the line into fine hair and the scent that drove her wild. Blythe groaned, unable to help herself. This was her favourite place—wedged between Allegra's thighs, tasting her, making her fall apart.

"Oh, fuck, yes," Allegra cried at the first touch of Blythe's tongue sweeping between her folds and her clit. Blythe teased and tested. The angle was new, with short licks and gentle sucks until Allegra's fingers in her hair tightened and her hips pushed upwards and rocked, chasing the friction, the pleasure.

"Don't stop, don't stop—" Allegra's words disappeared into a silent cry as her throat constricted and she focused on the pleasure, falling over the edge when Blythe's fingers slid inside and found that sweet spot.

Her body tensed, trembled, then released in waves. Blythe held her through it, her mouth and fingers working in perfect rhythm, drawing out every last aftershock.

When Allegra finally stilled, Blythe carefully withdrew and pressed soft kisses to her inner thighs before making her way back up.

Blythe grinned. "I made breakfast."

Allegra kissed her quickly, tasting herself on Blythe's lips. "I think you've just eaten."

"Best breakfast I've ever had," Blythe murmured, stealing another kiss before reluctantly pulling away and lifting the tray towards them. "Do you have any plans for today?"

"No, nothing important," Allegra said, taking the mug of tea that had somehow survived on the tray despite the way her body had reacted to Blythe's ministrations moments earlier. "Why? What did you have in mind?"

Eighty-Three

"Are you really thinking about buying it?" Allegra said as she looked up at the house.

"Do you not like it?" Blythe asked as they waited for Grace to arrive with the keys.

"I love it. I just... It's pricey. Gabby and Nora live around the corner."

Blythe moved closer. "Grace assures me it's very competitively valued for this area, although I am sure there is some room to haggle." Blythe's smile was knowing. She'd negotiated far bigger deals than this. She gripped Allegra's lapels and pulled her closer. "Lots of room to enjoy you in." Allegra's cheeks flushed, but she didn't pull away. She kissed her. "Oh, and did I mention...there's a hot tub?"

"You're really selling this, aren't you?" Allegra laughed, but she was already imagining it.

"I just think...if I'm going to live here, settle down and...make a life, hopefully with you in it, then I want to be somewhere that fits the lifestyle I intend to enjoy."

Allegra's smile wasn't quite so sparkling as she looked away from Blythe. Blythe felt it immediately—the shift, the worry.

"What's wrong?" Blythe asked, sensing the change. One finger under Allegra's chin, she pulled her lover's eyes back to her own, gently but firmly, refusing to let Allegra hide. "Allegra?"

"It's just…I'm not sure this is a lifestyle I can afford."

"I'm not asking you to."

"But you will eventually, won't you? That's how these things work."

Blythe nodded. "Yes, I suppose so."

"Okay, but financially…I'm not equal, and I doubt I ever will be. Women footballers are nowhere near being paid what the men are. I'm twenty-eight, my next contract might be worth three years, and then who knows. I make more money modelling, and I hate that."

"Right now…I'm just looking at a house. No decisions have been made, and they won't be without us both having a long conversation, but ultimately, if I can afford something like this…and I want to share it with you at some point…I don't see the problem." She smiled genuinely. "Does Nora have the same finances as Gabby?"

"No," Allegra acknowledged.

"There you go…and they're married, and living together in a house probably nicer than this."

"I don't even own my flat," Allegra said deflated. Her voice was small, almost ashamed. "Getting a mortgage when you can only guarantee two years of work… It's difficult."

"I can imagine it is." Blythe's hand found hers, squeezing gently. The figure of Grace walking along the road towards them caught Blythe's attention. "We'll figure it out. Together."

"Hi, sorry I'm late," Grace said to Blythe before turning to Allegra. "Hello."

"Hi." Allegra smiled politely, though she felt a little out of place.

"Ready to go in? It's such a lovely area, isn't it?" Grace was saying as she fiddled with the gate lock and opened it for them all. Grace's enthusiasm was infectious, professional. "As you can see, there is a lovely space for at least two cars. Electric gates too." She ushered them towards the white-painted townhouse, its windows gleaming in the afternoon light. The house looked even more impressive in person than in the photos.

Blythe glanced at Allegra, gauging her reaction. She squeezed her hand briefly—a silent reassurance.

The bar was quiet when Blythe and Allegra walked in. Blythe pointed at a free booth. "Grab that and I'll get us some drinks. Soda and lime?"

"Please." Allegra smiled. She walked away, fingers slowly slipping from her grasp. She felt unsettled in herself. The house viewing had stirred something in her. Fear? Or maybe the weight of wanting something so badly it terrified her.

Sitting down, she faced the bar and watched as Blythe chatted easily to Sadie. Blythe was the best thing that had ever happened to her, and yet, she felt the urge to just get up, walk out, and get as far away as she could. It was sabotage—the familiar pattern. Push away before you could be pushed.

"Stop it," she told herself. "You're not doing that. Not this time. Not with her. Whatever this is—" Her thoughts cut off as Blythe turned her way, carrying two glasses and smiling as she all but danced across the floor to the music playing gently in the background. Allegra's chest tightened. God, she loved her. The realisation hit like a punch.

The look on her face must have changed, because Blythe stopped in her tracks and stared at her. The fun dance became a slow walk.

"Everything okay?" she asked as she slid into the seat opposite and pushed a glass towards her.

Allegra considered it. Understanding the silence was making it worse, she blurted, "Yes, all good."

But Blythe wasn't buying it. She knew Allegra too well by now—knew when she was running.

"Do you want to try that again? You can take a moment."

Allegra felt tears in her eyes, her throat was tight, chest hammering. She was terrified. Not of Blythe, but of how much she wanted this. She nodded and took a deep shuddering breath. The words came slowly, painfully.

"I just think…I'm overwhelmed."

Blythe's expression softened. She'd been waiting for this—for Allegra to let her in. "Thank you for being honest," Blythe said and reached out for her hand. "There's no rush here, Allegra. Life is moving me forwards, onto a new path that I'm hopeful you will continue to walk beside me on, but I'm not pushing for you to step off of your path and onto mine." She squeezed Allegra's hand gently. "When we are ready, that's when we build something new together. A third path. Does that make sense?"

"It's just…terrifying."

"Can you explain what is terrifying?" Blythe asked softly, her thumb rubbing soothing circles.

"You," Allegra said with more force than she'd intended.

"In what way?" Blythe continued to probe—not defensive, not ego-led and hurt, just curious.

Allegra rubbed her face. "It's going to sound ridiculous."

"I think I can handle ridiculous." Blythe grinned, "Afterall, I did come to your game wearing your shirt hoping you'd see how much I liked you."

Allegra laughed. "Okay, fair point, but…can we have this conversation…not here?"

"Yes. It's on hold." Blythe picked up her drink. "So, are we going to the game tomorrow?"

Eighty-Four

Blythe walked inside of Allegra's flat for the first time. It was in a nice area, expensive. There was a gym and coffee shop inside the building, but it felt cold. She hadn't been living here for weeks and hadn't been back to switch the heating on. It felt abandoned, like a place she'd already left behind.

"Sorry," Allegra said, rubbing her palms up and down her own arms. "It won't take long to warm up."

Blythe noticed the sparse furnishings and the lack of personal touches, concluding this didn't feel like home to Allegra either. "It's fine," Blythe said, "although we can just go to mine if you prefer?"

Allegra spun around. "No...I mean, later, but...I brought you here for a reason."

"Okay." Blythe's eyebrow rose slightly. She was intrigued. Blythe studied the room a little more and the small two-seater sofa. "May I?"

"Of course. Make yourself...at home." Allegra shrugged. The irony wasn't lost on her, inviting Blythe to feel at home in a place that had never felt like home to Allegra herself. "This is it..." she said, looking around herself. "This is where I live...and nothing in here belongs to me other than clothes and those." She pointed at a group of awards and photos. Her eyes scanned the walls. "I don't even own the pictures."

Blythe remained quiet.

"I moved in here when I met John. The club put me in a little flat share with some of the girls when I signed for the Harriers, then I lived with Sammy-Jo for a while. After John and I hit it off, and when SJ met Daisy, we moved here—fully furnished," she said without any emotion.

"When John left, he paid the rest of the contract, but in three months, I won't be able to pay the rent to stay here." Her voice cracked slightly on the last words. She shook her head and laughed ironically. "We didn't need to live here, but John was adamant it fit 'our brand'. He earned more of course. And I guess…" She paused before admitting, "In all honesty, I had him wrapped around my little finger. I liked that he made my life easy."

Blythe sat forwards, wanting to reach out, but holding back. The last thing she wanted to do was interrupt Allegra opening up.

"I spent all my money on clothes, make-up, and things I didn't really need, but they made me happy, and it was easy because John encouraged it." She looked up at Blythe. "But I don't want that with you. I don't want you having to look after me because I'm not adult enough to do it myself."

"That's not what this is," Blythe said gently. "This isn't about looking after you. It's about building a life together where we both contribute."

"There's something else…"

"Go on."

"The thing is," Allegra said, wringing her hands as she composed herself, "I know we've only known each other a short while, but…it's just that…I realised something when you were dancing across the floor with that silly grin on your face."

Blythe chuckled. "Fair," she said. "What did it make you realise?"

Allegra took a breath. The words felt enormous, terrifying, true. She stopped moving. Her eyes met Blythe's and stayed there as she said, "That I'm…falling in love with you."

Blythe's breath caught and she reached out for Allegra's hand. "And that terrifies you?" Blythe asked gently. There was no judgement in her voice, only understanding.

Allegra nodded. "It doesn't, you?"

Blythe smiled—soft, certain. "No. It just makes me want to love you more."

Allegra's eyes widened, glistening slightly. "Oh…well, that's good then." She was trying for lightness, but her voice trembled slightly.

Tugging her hand, Blythe pulled Allegra onto the couch beside her. "So…did you just, in a roundabout way, tell me you might love me?"

Allegra's cheeks flushed deeply. "I think I did." Allegra scrunched up her face. "I told you it was ridiculous." She laughed before the seriousness of it all caught up with her. "Is that…okay?"

Blythe cupped her face, wiping away a tear Allegra hadn't realised had fallen. "I think it's more than okay…and I think it's reciprocated." She leant in and kissed Allegra slowly, deeply. "I'm definitely falling."

"Yeah?" Allegra whispered against Blythe's lips.

Blythe's lips curved into a smile against hers. "Mm hm… Want me to show you?"

"In a minute—it's too cold to get naked." Allegra's hands were already moving, one threading through Blythe's hair, the other gripping her shoulder, pulling her closer. Heat built between them despite the chill in the flat.

Blythe shifted, pressing Allegra back against the couch cushions. Her thigh slipped between Allegra's legs and she felt the immediate response, Allegra's breath hitching, her body arching into the contact.

"Who said we have to get naked?" Blythe murmured against her ear, her hand slipping under Allegra's jumper, fingers splayed across her ribs. "There are plenty of ways to warm up first."

Eighty-Five

It was Saturday evening, and Sammy-Jo lounged on her couch with Daisy, watching Allegra across the room in the armchair.

She'd been seeing a new side to her friend recently. Not just the tough, no-nonsense friend of old, but someone new, someone more thoughtful—dare she say it— vulnerable.

It suited her, the softness. Made her more real somehow.

When SJ had been getting together with Daisy, Allegra was her wingman, the woman who told Daisy in no uncertain terms not to hurt SJ, and SJ loved her for it. It was nice to have someone who had your back, which was how she was feeling now. Daisy had told her to let it be, that Allegra would speak when she was ready, but that wasn't really their style, was it? SJ had never been good at patience.

She preferred directness.

"Oi, Princess, what are you moping about?" she finally said with half a smile on her face.

There was a beat of silence before Allegra's lips twitched. "Sammy-Jo!" Daisy hissed, and punched her arm hard enough to feel it.

Allegra looked up and returned the smile. "I think you'll find I'm a *fucking queen*."

Damn right you are, SJ thought as she laughed and sat up. "Sorry, your highness." She mocked a bow. "I was just inquiring as to your well-being."

Daisy rolled her eyes but was smiling too.

Allegra sighed but properly turned her attention to them both. She leant her elbows on her knees, clasping her hands together. It was a nervous habit SJ recognised immediately.

"Actually, I do need to tell you both something."

"Oooh, all ears, fire away." SJ continued to keep it light, but she could sense this was going to be something deep. Daisy did too, and sat up, poking SJ to be quiet.

"The thing is…I've been spending a lot of time with Blythe and—"

"You're in love and going to move in with her?" SJ blurted.

"No…well, maybe partly that, but no, I'm not planning to move in with her."

"Oh, but you are in love?" SJ continued to probe.

Allegra paused, unable to stop the smile that crept across her face. It was answer enough.

"Oh, she is." SJ patted Daisy's knee. "This is wild."

Daisy beamed at Allegra, genuine happiness radiating from her.

"I admit that I am falling in love, yes," Allegra continued. "And while that is exciting and terrifying all at once, I am not running from it."

"This is great news, Leggy," Daisy said.

Allegra nodded. "It is…and I feel like I've learned a lot about *me* in the last few months and…well, it's time I stopped messing around and treating my life like it's just a big playground. I need to be honest, with myself, and you," she said more quietly.

"You can tell us anything," Daisy offered. She looked at SJ with a: *Do not say a word!* look on her face.

"Thanks." Allegra raised her hands as though in prayer before lowering them again and saying, "I'm skint. I'm about to be evicted from the flat." The words tumbled out, each one a small admission of failure. "I have nothing but clothes and awards to my name, and I feel like it's time I started acting like the adult I want to be, and that means…asking for help."

For once, SJ didn't joke around.

"Whatever you need, just say it and I'll get it."

Allegra smiled at her friend—her best friend. "I was hoping that maybe...I could move back in properly. For a while, until—"

"You're ready to live with Blythe?" SJ asked.

"Maybe. I don't know yet. I'm learning that I don't need to know the answers to everything right now. I'm falling in love with her, and I see a future with her, but I don't want another *John* relationship where she takes care of me and I'm just a trophy on her arm." She laughed. "Not that she'd ever let me be that, but you know what I mean? I just want to be the adult she deserves before I put myself into her life permanently."

Daisy's eyes glistened as she looked at Allegra across the room. "You're already that person," she whispered. "You're just learning to believe it."

"Our home is your home, for as long as you need," SJ said. "And if you need money—"

Allegra laughed. "I'm not *skint*, skint, but I've been living pay cheque to pay cheque. When I was with John, it was fine, he paid the credit card bills, but now...it's all on me and...I guess sometimes, I've still been frivolous with shopping, trying to make myself happy with a new dress, or shoes I don't need."

"We've all done that," Daisy confirmed.

"I haven't," SJ said, "but I did have a rash few months of drinking, so...we all do stupid things, right?"

Allegra smiled. It felt good being seen, being supported without judgement.

"When do you want to move in officially? I mean, we still need to shift all your stuff and clean the flat so you can move out," Daisy asked, ever the sensible one.

"It's international break next week. Most of us will have nothing to do all weekend." SJ shrugged. "I reckon they'd all be up for helping...if you wanted them to."

Allegra's throat tightened. The team rallying around her—it meant everything. "I'd like that," Allegra answered.

Daisy raised her mug of tea. "To new eras and owning our shit."

They clinked their mugs together, a small but significant gesture of friendship and found family.

Eighty-Six

Allegra stood perfectly still as hands fussed around her—a make-up artist dabbing at her cheekbones with a brush, a stylist adjusting the drape of fabric across her shoulder, an assistant smoothing down a strand of hair that had dared to move out of place.

"Chin up slightly," the photographer barked from behind his camera. "No, too much. There. Hold it."

She held it. Held the smile that didn't reach her eyes. Held the pose that made her shoulders ache. Held the breath she wasn't supposed to be taking.

The studio was chaos masquerading as control. Racks of clothes lined the walls, lighting rigs cast harsh shadows, and at least a dozen people moved around her in a coordinated dance she'd learned to tolerate but never enjoy.

"We need more energy, Allegra," the photographer called out. "You're supposed to be selling luxury watches, not attending a funeral."

A few people laughed nervously. Allegra forced her smile wider, though it felt brittle.

Another make-up touch-up. Another adjustment to the fabric. Someone's fingers brushed against her ribs as they repositioned the material and she had to resist the urge to flinch. She wasn't used to being handled like a mannequin anymore—not since Blythe. Not since someone had touched her with intention and care, rather than professional necessity.

"Move your left foot forward. Rotate your hips. Tilt your head to the right. No, your right. Yes, there."

Click. Click. Click.

The photographer was relentless, firing off shots like he was trying to capture lightning in a bottle. Allegra had done this dozens of times—the endless repositioning, the constant corrections, the dehumanising efficiency of it all.

But this time felt different. This time, she was acutely aware of how much she hated it. How the money—substantial as it was—came at the cost of her autonomy, her comfort, her time.

Time she could be spending with Blythe.

"Perfect! We've got it," the photographer finally announced after what felt like hours but was probably only forty-five minutes. "Great work, Allegra. You're a pro."

She didn't feel like a pro. She felt like a shell.

The hands descended again, removing the watch, adjusting her back into street clothes, and wiping away the carefully applied make-up. Within minutes, she was herself again, though it never quite felt like a smooth transition. It always felt like stepping back into her own skin after someone else had borrowed it.

She checked her phone as she gathered her things. A text from Blythe: *All packed. Meet you at the flat? I'll order dinner.*

Allegra smiled—a real one this time. She typed back: On my way. Can't wait to see you.

The money from today's shoot would help. It would pad her savings, give her more breathing room, more independence. She could tell herself that was why she did it. And it was true.

But as she headed towards the tube station, she couldn't shake the feeling she'd spent the last few hours being someone else, and now she just wanted to get back to being herself—the version of herself that existed when Blythe was looking at her like she was the most beautiful thing in the world, not because she was being paid to be, but because she simply was.

Eighty-Seven

Blythe taped up the final box with deliberate precision, the sound of the tape gun sharp in the quiet of the flat. It was nearly empty now. The walls bore the ghost marks of where pictures had hung and where furniture had sat for years. It looked smaller somehow, diminished.

She'd lived here for eight years. Eight years of climbing the corporate ladder, of late nights at the office, of coming home to silence and a glass of wine. Eight years of thinking this was success—that this was enough.

The removals team would arrive tomorrow morning. Everything was going into storage except for a few essentials she'd pack into her car later.

The flat was on the market, and she'd already had three offers. It made sense to empty it now and get a tenant in. Even though it would be weeks before the townhouse was completed and finally hers, she wasn't homeless.

She picked up the box and carried it to the hallway, stacking it with the others. Her phone buzzed. Another text.

Allegra: On my way.

Blythe smiled. Allegra was heading straight from her shoot to the flat. They'd spend the evening together here before driving back to Woodington.

She was proud of Allegra for taking the job, knowing it was not something she really enjoyed, but she'd made a plan to change her financial situation and decided modelling was a simple enough way to earn a lot of money in a short period of time.

Blythe packed some more while she waited, methodically moving through the flat. She'd been surprised with just how much stuff she had compared to packing up Allegra's flat, but it still hadn't taken her long.

She'd spent the morning at the office making it very clear to Amanda that things were different now.

"I will go to HR if I need to," Blythe had said.

Amanda had sneered, "For what?"

"I still have our text messages. If you continue to punish my career over this, I promise you, I will make a stand."

This time Amanda remained quiet as Blythe turned and left the office.

She'd just finished stacking the last box when the intercom buzzed, and she smiled at the image on the small screen.

"Come on up," Blythe said, pressing the button that would open the door. "8th floor. Number 348."

She quickly glanced in the bathroom mirror and fiddled with her hair. She looked alright, she thought, casual, in jeans and a sweater befitting the end of November.

The gentle knock on the door made her smile.

Allegra stepped inside, still in her street clothes, but with that particular exhaustion that came from being looked at all day. Her make-up was fresh, but her eyes were tired. There was a tension in her shoulders Blythe recognised immediately.

"Hey," Blythe said softly, moving towards her. "How was it?"

Allegra dropped her bag by the door and walked straight into Blythe's arms. "Tedious," she murmured against her shoulder. "But lucrative."

Blythe held her, feeling the weight of the day settle against her. "You did good."

"I hated every second of it," Allegra said, pulling back just enough to look at her. "But the money…"

"Is yours," Blythe finished. "You earned it. You should be proud."

Allegra glanced around the flat—at the stacked boxes, the bare walls, the emptiness of it all. "This is surreal," she said quietly. "Eight years of your life, packed into boxes."

"Eight years of a life I'm leaving behind," Blythe corrected gently. She took Allegra's hand and led her inside for the first and last time.

They moved through the flat together, Blythe narrating the ghosts of her past—the kitchen where she'd microwaved countless ready meals and the bedroom where she'd slept alone, dreaming of something she couldn't quite name.

"No bed," Allegra said with a hint of mischief. "Shame."

"Is it?" Blythe matched her. "I don't think we need a bed, do we?" An idea formed—bold, a little reckless, entirely them.

"I guess not…but where?" Allegra looked around and laughed when Blythe grabbed her by the hand and pulled her into the lounge.

"I do have this," Blythe said as they reached the living room, gesturing to the floor-to-ceiling windows that overlooked London. "It's where I spent most evenings, watching the city, feeling very important and very alone."

Allegra looked out at the sprawl of London—the lights beginning to twinkle as evening fell, the endless grid of buildings and lives happening without her. "It's beautiful," she said.

"It is," Blythe agreed. "But it was never home."

She felt Allegra turn to look at her, and when their eyes met, something shifted. The air between them changed—charged, intentional.

"No?" Allegra asked softly.

"No," Blythe confirmed. She reached out and cupped Allegra's face, her thumb brushing across her cheekbone. "Home is wherever you are."

Allegra leant in and their kiss was slow, deliberate—a claiming of this space before they left it behind forever.

When they broke apart, Allegra was smiling. "That was very romantic."

"I have my moments," Blythe murmured. She glanced at the window, at the city beyond, and then back at Allegra. "Come here."

She guided Allegra towards the window, pressing her gently against the cool glass. The city sprawled beneath them, oblivious. No one could see in—the angle was wrong, the height too great—but the illusion of exposure, of being watched, made Allegra's breath quicken.

"What are you—" Allegra started, but Blythe silenced her with a kiss.

This one was different—deeper, hungrier. Blythe's hands found the hem of Allegra's top and pulled it over her head in one smooth motion. Cool air hit Allegra's skin and she gasped against Blythe's mouth.

"I want to make love to you here," Blythe whispered. "One time in this flat. One time before I leave this life behind completely."

Allegra's eyes widened, but she didn't pull away. Instead, she reached for Blythe's jumper and tugged it upwards. "Yes," she breathed.

They undressed each other quickly, urgently, until they were both naked.

Blythe pressed Allegra against the glass, feeling her shiver. Her hands found Allegra's waist, and she turned her, guiding her into position—face pressed against the cool pane, feet gently eased apart.

"I want you like this," Blythe murmured against her ear. "Right here. Against this window."

Allegra's breath hitched as Blythe pushed up against her back, skin to skin now. One hand roamed down her torso, over her hips, tugging gently until Allegra arched slightly, pushing her backside into Blythe to create a space between her body and the window. Blythe's free hand snaked around, fingers finding Allegra's clit, and she began a slow, deliberate rhythm.

Allegra's nipples hardened against the cold glass, her body responding even more to Blythe's touch, hips undulating, seeking more pressure against her throbbing clit, riding her lover's fingers against her.

"God, you're so sexy when you just let go," Blythe whispered in her ear, her breath hot against Allegra's skin. "When you stop thinking and just feel."

Allegra's head turned slightly, her cheek still pressed against the glass. "More," she gasped.

Blythe's free hand moved up against the glass, cupping her breast, fingers finding her nipple and rolling it gently. She increased the pace of her other hand, feeling Allegra's body tense and respond.

"That's it," Blythe urged. "Come for me. Right here against this window. Show me how much you want this."

Allegra's breathing became ragged, her movements more urgent. The glass fogged with her breath, the city disappearing behind condensation until there was nothing but the two of them.

"God, I love you," Allegra cried out, her body tensing as she climbed towards release.

"Come for me," Blythe repeated, increasing the pressure. "Come for me, and then I'm going to marry you one day."

Allegra's eyes flew open for just a moment before pleasure overtook her. She came with a cry that was half laugh, half sob, her entire body shaking against the glass.

Blythe held her through it, her hand continuing its rhythm until Allegra stilled, boneless and gasping.

When they finally pulled apart and Allegra turned around, she was laughing—breathless, flushed, absolutely radiant.

"Did you just propose to me against a window?" she asked, her voice still shaky.

Blythe grinned. "I mean, not officially. But consider it a preview of things to come."

"A preview," Allegra repeated, shaking her head in wonder. "You're insane."

"Maybe," Blythe said, pulling her close again.

Eighty-Eight

Snow covered the ground, but it would melt away fast. This wasn't going to be a winter like last year, but it was cold and a time for knitwear. Colourful hats and scarves made it feel brighter than the grim grey sky would suggest it should be.

Blythe wandered through town, stopping to browse in each shop that drew her attention. She loved Christmas, but it had become a quieter time for her over the years.

If she was being honest with herself, she'd been lonely. Her parents were gone. She had siblings, but they all had their own lives and families, and were scattered around the country.

Blythe had always put her career first, opting to stay in London and finish off a project rather than take the time off to enjoy the festivities. But not this year.

Now she had a real reason to close her laptop and switch on the 'out of office' message. She had Allegra.

Their relationship was already the most precious gift she could give or receive, and yet, here she was, staring into jewellery shop windows wondering if... Was it too soon? Just four short months of knowing someone, barely three of being in a relationship with them, but everything told her it felt right. Everything said, 'This is the one.'

The certainty of it was almost frightening, and hadn't she already somewhat proposed?

She smiled at her own reflection, noticing how much happier she looked nowadays. That spring in her step was back, all because of Allegra Mann being in her life, her bed, and her heart. She'd never felt this way before—this grounded, this alive.

"What are you doing?" It was a voice she recognised instantly. She glanced to the right of her reflection and noticed Sammy-Jo grinning at her. "Are you thinking what I think you're thinking?"

Blythe's heart skipped. Had she been that obvious? "I'm not sure." Blythe returned the grin. "What did you think I was doing?" She turned to actually face SJ, seeing rosy cheeks from the cold air, and all that hair flaring out from her hat. Blythe raised a brow and waited for the answer.

"Making an honest woman out of her. I mean, someone has to take one for the team."

"*Someone* has to?" Blythe raised an eyebrow and laughed, as if marrying Allegra would be such a hardship. It wouldn't be. She knew it would be the easiest decision she'd ever make. Suddenly, the ring in the jeweller's window felt less like a question and more like an inevitability.

SJ shrugged. "She's a pain in my arse, but I get that for you, she's a dream."

"She is, and maybe one day, when I think she might say yes, I'll take one for the team." Blythe winked.

"What makes you think she wouldn't say yes?"

"Her pride mostly," Blythe answered honestly. "She's still determined to prove she's a grown-up capable of doing life on her own, and I respect that." They turned and walked on to the next store and the big Christmas-designed window. "I'm hoping that by the time everything has gone through, and I can move into my new house, she might want to join me, but if she's happy with you for a little longer, I can manage that."

"She's always welcome at ours, but I will encourage her to move out, whether into your place or her own," SJ answered. "It will do her good."

"Maybe." Blythe swapped all her bags into one hand, linked arms with SJ, and continued walking towards the coffee shop. "But we won't push her too quickly. Let her get there in her own time."

SJ nodded, appreciating Blythe's patience. The coffee shop windows were steamed up, and as they pushed the door open, the sound of overexcited chatter erupted, mixed with the Christmas carol playing on the speaker. Warmth enveloped them—both from the heating and from the atmosphere.

"There they are," SJ said, pointing to a table in the corner. Allegra and Daisy were deep in conversation, oversized mugs of hot chocolate in their hands. Blythe's heart lifted at the sight of Allegra, flushed and happy. "I'll get us a fresh round in."

When Blythe was no more than three feet away, Allegra turned, almost as though she sensed her presence rather than saw her. Her face lit up instantly and broke into a smile—*that* smile—the one that was just for Blythe.

"Hey, babe." Allegra shifted along the seat and made room for Blythe to squeeze in beside her and a woman trying to control two unruly, overstimulated toddlers.

"Hey, you." Blythe smiled. There were still moments when it was difficult to pull her eyes away from looking at Allegra, but she managed it. Barely. "Hi, Daisy. SJ is getting another round of hot chocolate in."

"Excellent. I still haven't thawed out. All that snow last year and it feels colder this year," Daisy said.

"Speaking of which, I am aware that it's yours and SJ's one-year anniversary in a couple of days. I'll get out of your hair." Allegra smiled and winked all at once. There was genuine affection in the gesture, no awkwardness.

"You don't have to do that." Daisy giggled, her rosy cheeks reddening at the thought of how they might celebrate.

"I do." Allegra laughed, turning to Blythe. "I thought…I'd stay with you over Christmas, if that's okay?"

"I would love that," Blythe whispered.

"Me too," Allegra whispered back, leaning in closer, their foreheads almost touching, a moment meant just for them.

"Oh, get a room, you two," SJ said, appearing out of nowhere with a large tray and four of the oversized mugs, but she was grinning, not complaining.

"Don't worry, we will." Allegra laughed, taking one of the mugs for herself. "I was just telling Daisy, I'm going to spend Christmas with Blythe at her place, so you two can enjoy your anniversary."

With the tray now on the table, SJ rubbed her hands together. "Fantastic, back to christening every room again."

Daisy rolled her eyes. "We will be at Mum's most of the time. The twins are very eager to see what you've come up with for this year's present."

Her younger sisters had instantly taken a shine to Sammy-Jo the previous Christmas when she'd been the impromptu guest, and Daisy's gift to herself. SJ had charmed them with terrible jokes and endless patience.

"Will never beat last year's last-minute shop at Mrs Patel's," SJ said. "Anyway, I thought you were doing that?"

"No," Daisy said seriously. "You can buy your own gifts, and if I approve, you can add my name to it."

Sammy-Jo's eyes widened. Panic flickered across her face. It was Christmas Eve. "But I…"

Daisy burst out laughing. "As if I'd leave you to organise something as monumental as Christmas gifts for the twins." She reached over and squeezed SJ's hand. "I've got this. You just focus on us."

"Did you get everything you wanted?" Allegra asked, pointing to the shopping bags Blythe had at her feet.

Blythe caught Sammy-Jo smiling at her but ignored it, though she could feel the knowing look burning into the side of her face. "I think so, yes, although, we will need to get food in for tomorrow."

"And decorations," Allegra said. "Can we get a tree?" There was hope in her voice.

"I guess so," Blythe acquiesced. "I hadn't thought about it, but…yes, if you're going to be there now, and we're going to have our first Christmas together, then we should make it special." Blythe looked at Allegra, really looked at her, and felt something settle in her chest.

Eighty-Nine

"It looks a little pitiful," Allegra said, looking at the tree in the corner of the small living room.

Blythe tilted her head at it. "Well, there weren't that many choices being Christmas Eve and needing one that would fit." She moved a piece of tinsel, adjusting it with care, as if the small, scraggly tree deserved tenderness. "I think it's perfect."

"Really?"

Allegra didn't look convinced.

"Yes, I think it's perfect." Blythe smiled and turned towards Allegra, taking hold of her jumper—the Christmas one they'd bought each other—and pulled her close enough to kiss her. "I think *you're* perfect. *We* are perfect." Her hand slipped under Allegra's jumper, fingers finding warm skin. The kiss she delivered finished the sentence, slow and firm, a statement of its own. When they pulled apart, Allegra's eyes were still closed, a small smile playing on her lips.

"I think this might be my favourite Christmas ever," Allegra said dreamily.

"That's going to be every Christmas from now on," Blythe promised. This time when she kissed her, it deepened with an urgency. She felt Allegra reach for the button on her trousers, opening it with ease and sliding her hand beneath the band. Blythe grabbed it, stopped the movement, and stared deeply into her eyes—a moment of intention, of choice. "I want to make love, not a quick fuck."

"Okay." Allegra smiled, her breath catching a little. She understood. This was different. This mattered. She stepped back and raised the hem of her jumper, lifting it up over her head and off. Her skin flushed in the soft light of the living room. "Bedroom?"

Blythe nodded and reached out to take the hand Allegra held out, following as Allegra walked backwards towards the room with the bed.

The bedroom was dim, lit only by the soft glow of fairy lights strung along the headboard. Blythe had thought of everything.

Allegra stood at the foot of the bed, bare from the waist up, her chest rising and falling with anticipation. Blythe closed the door behind them, the soft click sealing them away from the rest of the world.

"Come here," Blythe whispered, her voice low and intentional. She was already pulling her own jumper over her head, revealing the soft curve of her breasts and the defined lines of her shoulders. Allegra's breath hitched at the sight.

Blythe moved towards her, slowly undressing, deliberately, giving Allegra time to see her, to want her. When they met, it wasn't rushed. Blythe's hands found Allegra's waist, fingers splayed across warm skin, and she pulled her close until their bodies aligned, chest to chest, heartbeat to heartbeat.

"I love you," Blythe murmured against Allegra's neck, lips finding that sensitive spot just below her ear. Allegra's head tilted back, exposing more of her throat, and Blythe took her time, kissing slowly down the column of her neck, tasting skin, feeling the pulse of Allegra's racing heart beneath her lips.

Allegra's hands moved to Blythe's back, fingers tracing the curve of her spine, pulling her impossibly closer. "I love you, too," she breathed, her voice trembling with emotion and desire.

Blythe guided her backwards until the back of Allegra's legs met the bed. She pulled back just enough to look at her—really look at her—before gently lowering her onto the mattress. Blythe followed, settling between Allegra's thighs, her weight supported on her forearms.

"Slow," Blythe promised, and kissed her again. Deep. Thorough. A kiss that spoke of devotion, of forever, of all the Christmases yet to come.

Allegra's hands roamed across Blythe's shoulders, then her back, committing every muscle to memory. There was no urgency now, just the slow burn of desire building between them. Blythe's mouth moved lower, tracing a path down Allegra's collarbone, across the swell of her breast. She took her time, her lips and tongue worshipping every inch.

Allegra's breathing deepened, her fingers threading through Blythe's hair, guiding but never demanding. "Please," she whispered, though she wasn't entirely sure what she was asking for.

Blythe understood anyway. She always did. Her hand drifted down Allegra's body, fingers trailing across her ribs, her waist, lower still, until she reached the waistband of Allegra's trousers. She paused, looking up at Allegra for permission. The nod was all she needed.

Blythe undid the button and zip with deliberate slowness, peeling the fabric away inch by inch, revealing more of Allegra to her. She kissed every newly exposed stretch of skin—her hip, her thigh, the inside of her knee. Allegra trembled beneath her touch, her body responding to every caress.

When Allegra was finally bare before her, Blythe took a moment to simply look. To appreciate. To acknowledge the trust and vulnerability being offered to her.

"You're beautiful," Blythe whispered, and meant it with every fibre of her being.

Allegra met her gaze, steady and sure. "Come back up," she murmured, reaching for Blythe.

Blythe obliged, settling back over her, skin to skin now. Their foreheads touched, breaths mingling, as Blythe's hand found its way between Allegra's thighs. She moved with intention, with care, her fingers finding Allegra's centre and beginning a slow, deliberate rhythm.

Allegra's hips rocked gently against her hand, meeting each stroke. Her mouth found Blythe's neck, lips and teeth leaving marks—not aggressively, but making tender claims of her own. "God, I love this," Allegra whispered against her skin.

"I know," Blythe replied, increasing the pressure slightly, feeling Allegra's body respond. There was confidence in her tone, a knowing.

The pleasure built slowly—a wave rather than a crash. Allegra's breathing became ragged, her movements more urgent, but Blythe maintained her pace—steady, purposeful, intimate. She wanted Allegra to feel every second of this, to know this was different. This was love.

When Allegra finally reached her peak, it was with a soft cry, her body tensing and then releasing in a delicious rhythm. Blythe whispered endearments against her skin, her hand continuing its gentle movement until Allegra finally stilled and Blythe pulled her fingers away.

They stayed like that for a long moment, tangled together, breathing in sync. Blythe's hand rested on Allegra's stomach, feeling the gradual slowing of her heartbeat.

"That was…" Allegra started, but seemed to lack the words to finish the sentiment.

"Yeah," Blythe agreed softly, pressing a kiss to her forehead, "it was."

Blythe moved to her side, pulling Allegra with her, their bodies still intertwined. Allegra's head rested on Blythe's chest, her ear over Blythe's heart. They lay in the quiet of the bedroom, the fairy lights casting soft shadows across their skin.

"I can't wait to wake up Christmas morning in your arms," Allegra said, moving until she was able to roll on top of Blythe.

"Chances are…you'll be the best gift ever," Blythe said, reaching for and holding out a small box for Allegra to take.

Allegra gasped. "Are you… Is that…" She pulled back a little as Blythe smiled at her. "Are you?"

"I am," Blythe answered. "I know it's ridiculously too soon. And I know we don't even live together yet, and we've not met each other's parents, and all the reasons why I shouldn't do this, and yet, none of them are enough to stop me."

Allegra laughed nervously as Blythe opened the box and she saw the diamond sparkle.

"We don't have to get married right away, but my intention is to do so…at some point, and so, Allegra Persephone Mann, will you consider becoming my wife and wear my ring until such time as we want to make it more permanent?"

"You have such a way with words. I see now how you persuaded Gabby to build the hotel."

Blythe grinned. "What can I say? I get what I want." She took the ring from the box and reached for Allegra's hand.

"Chances are, you'll get it now too," Allegra said. "Yes, I'll marry you."

The End

About the Author

If you've enjoyed this book, I'd be incredibly grateful if you'd take a moment to leave a review. With the recent algorithm changes on Amazon and across the social platforms authors rely on to share their work, every single review has become more important than ever. A few words from you can make a tremendous difference in helping readers discover this story—and every story you love. Thank you for supporting authors by taking the time to share your thoughts.

www.itsclastevofficial.co.uk/books

You can find out more about Claire on her website at www.itsclastevofficial.co.uk and on most social platforms—including Patreon, TikTok, YouTube, and Facebook—using variations of *ItsClaStev*.

Other Books By Claire Highton-Stevenson

Out: A Cam Thomas Story
  Next: A Cam Thomas Story
  Escape and Freedom
  The Doll Maker
  The Promise
  Yes: A Cam Thomas Story

Forget it
In Dyer Need
Grave Decisions
Leaving Bree
In Dyer Circumstances
Model Behaviour
It's a date
What Happened in Vegas
Loves witness
Life: A Cam Thomas Story
Blinded by Love
Cast away her fears
The Goddess and the Doctors
Stranger on the shore
Blisters and Beer
Keep her safe
The Consciousness
Letting go
Heal their hearts
Scarlett Fever
Scarlett
Goddess of the moon
Euphoria
Last Chance
You're Still the One
Take a Chance
Leila & Camille: The Full Story
The Last to Know
Catching Carrie
Je T'aime. Actually
Chances Are…

Printed in Dunstable, United Kingdom